KITTY PECK AND THE CHILD OF ILL-FORTUNE

Kate Griffin was born within the sound of Bow bells, making her a true-born cockney. She has worked as an assistant to an antiques dealer, a journalist for local newspapers and now works for The Society for the Protection of Ancient Buildings.

Kitty Peck and the Music Hall Murders, Kate's first book, won the *Stylist*/Faber crime writing competition. It was shortlisted for the 2014 CWA Endeavour Historical Dagger. Kate's maternal family lived in Victorian Limehouse and Kitty's world is based on stories told by her grandmother. Kate lives in St Albans.

Praise for *Kitty Peck and the Music Hall Murders*:

'Terrific debut novel . . . Victorian London has never been better illustrated . . . if this standard keeps up, we have a major new talent on our hands.' *Sunday Express*

'Occasionally a new writer bursts onto the scene with almost explosive force . . . [Griffin's] hugely entertaining debut, set in the squalor, filth and depravity of Victorian Limehouse is all things to all readers – almost gothic in its intensity, but full of shades of dark and light, combining the macabre and wit of the music halls with a rattling action yarn which will appeal to historical readers, crime readers and people who just like a really well written adventure story . . . the book is an

absolutely first class read and I shall be surprised if there's a better debut this year.' *Crime Review*

'Kitty's narrative voice . . . is sharply memorable and deserves to be heard in a further adventure.' *Sunday Times*

Kitty Peck and the Child of Ill-fortune

KATE GRIFFIN

FABER & FABER

First published in 2015
by Faber & Faber Limited
Bloomsbury House,
74–77 Great Russell Street
London WC1B 3DA

Printed and bound by CPI Group (UK) Ltd, Croydon CR0 4YY

A CIP record for this book
is available from the British Library

ISBN 978–0–571–31085–2

2 4 6 8 10 9 7 5 3 1

For Stephen

Prologue

Black eyes glinted up at me. Bleedin' thing was poking its nose out from under the hem of my dress, bold as a bishop come Christmas. I stamped my foot, pulled the fabric sharp to the side and watched the mouse dart over the rug, skittering across the polished boards to a hole in the skirting. The Palace was running alive. I lay awake most nights listening to them scratching in the walls. I wondered Lady Ginger had stood for it, considering the way she dealt with most things.

Traps, that's what we needed, or a cat – a big hungry one.

I shifted in the chair so I couldn't see the hole and ran my finger down the page again, memorising the names and the numbers, repeating them over in my head until they was locked into place. I'd be ready for the Beetle tomorrow – it unnerved him and I enjoyed it.

From that first meeting with her lawyer, Marcus Telferman, almost three weeks ago now, one thing, at least, was clear: Lady Ginger, my grandmother, had left me an estate that went a lot further than a mouse nest and three bob scrag halls on the edge of the City.

I knew she was a Baron – we all did – but I hadn't understood what that meant until I began to go through her papers. Put together they told a ripe story. Names, buildings, trades, ships, goods, men, women, even little children for Christ's sake – all bonded to her and none of it the sort of thing you'd jaw over with a vicar, let alone a rozzer.

Elsewhere in the City, other Barons ran their own territories. From what I could make out, sometimes that was a distinct area bounded by landmarks or streets, other times it wasn't so easy to catch. I got the impression from reading some of the documents Telferman gave me that the Barons themselves – the criminal lords of London – watched each other like yellow-eyed gulls at Billingsgate wharf.

In the main, Lady Ginger's patch ran from east to west along the river taking in the docks and some other choice spots hemmed up to Mile End. It was called Paradise and she'd ruled it like Queen Victoria ruled the Empire.

And now she'd left it all in my hands.

I still didn't know with a clarity how I felt about that. In the day, part of me saw it as a way to make changes; to sweep out the dirt and make things clean as far as I could. But, I'll admit it, in the dark, when I was awake and listening to them mice, part of me was scared.

If Lucca wondered what I was looking at on the page in front of me, he never let on.

He was curled in the crook of the couch, engrossed in a book in his lap. I couldn't see what it was on account of the padded scroll of the arm, but I could tell he was in deep. He leaned forward and strands of dark hair fell across his face. As I watched, he pushed it back behind his ears so I could see his fine Roman nose, the angle of his cheeks and the fringe of his lashes.

He would have been a looker.

If a girl didn't know different she'd make a play for him – until she saw the scars that melted the right side of his face, pulling his lips and nose out of line and sealing his eye into a crimson knot of puckered flesh. Then again, what girls thought of him didn't much matter to Lucca Fratelli.

I slipped the page of columns and figures back into place. It was raining again. I could hear the drops spatter against the panes. We were quiet together in the first-floor room I'd set up as a parlour. Apart from the mice it was clean and warm. I was sitting across from Lucca on a low-backed chair drawn up to the fire.

As I sorted the papers a small cream-coloured square fell to the rug. It was the gilt-edged card I'd found waiting for me here at The Palace the day Lady Ginger disappeared leaving her filthy house and all of Paradise in my hands. I reached down and ran a fingertip over the letters. The address, 17 rue des Carmélites, was slightly raised. I flipped it over and read my grandmother's looping script.

Full Recompense

All that time she'd allowed me to think my brother was her prisoner – or worse, that he was a corpse wrapped in oilcloth and weighted down in the river. She'd bobbed gobbets of information in front of me like she was teasing a kitten with tidbits of bacon rind. She had me dancing for her all right. The worst of it was I reckoned she'd enjoyed it, been entertained by it, you might say. I'd been hauled up into place every night in that pretty glittering cage and I sang and I twirled seventy foot over the heads of the punters – and then I reported back to her on what I'd seen below, thinking what she wanted was a clear pair of eyes taking it all in for her benefit. The thieving, the whoring, the gambling, the gentlemen trippers who treated Limehouse like a zoological garden – I told her everything.

But as it turned out, that was only the half. She was testing me like she'd tested Joey, to see if I had the mettle to take her place. I brought back the last time I saw her in the churchyard at Ma's grave. Eyes like jet buttons sewn on a chalk-white face, sticky black lips opening:

He was weak, Kitty. And you are strong.

I turned the card again and looked at the address, wincing as the sharp edge sliced the ball of my thumb. I heard her fluting, oddly girlish voice again.

I will return your brother to you in due course but whether you will accept him . . . ah, that is a different matter. You will find him much altered.

Altered? I knew she'd cut off his finger. She'd given it to me in a box ribboned up like a birthday gift. What else had the old cow done to him?

He was always so proud of his looks. What if . . .?

As if he'd caught my mind, Lucca glanced up from his book and smiled. I looked down and shuffled the papers in my lap. Don't take it wrong – I loved Lucca. He'd saved my life and since Joey had . . . disappeared, he'd been the closest thing I had to a brother. Lucca knew everything about me and, these days, I knew everything about him.

Tell truth, it didn't matter one jot to me who Lucca cared for. It was his business and anyways there's plenty in the halls what don't live regular. Who am I to tell a person who they can lie down with when the only man I've taken to my bed turned out to be . . .

I shook my head, forcing that bastard into the furthest darkest space in my mind, taking care to shut and lock the door. He didn't deserve my thoughts. A couple of pins came loose and my hair sprang free from the plaited coil at my neck. I leaned forward to scoop them up from the rug where they'd fallen. When I sat back Lucca grinned wider and held up his book, the page opened out so I could see it clear.

I was wrong. He hadn't been reading, he'd been drawing – as usual. The girl on the page was me, my head tilted as I read the card. I recognised my pointed chin and the scribble of curls around my face that had escaped from the coil even before I shook the pins free. He'd caught me in a few deft lines.

In the drawing I looked sad.

I smiled, leaned across and offered him the card. As he took it from my hand I noticed the gilt edges were newly stained with blood.

Chapter One

The Beetle didn't answer. Sunlight pooled in the cups of his half-moon spectacles as he sniffed and shifted his head so I couldn't see direct into his eyes.

I repeated the question. 'I think I've got a right to know, Mr Telferman, don't you?' He looked down and started to leaf through some papers piled up on the desk. He licked his thumb and drew out a sheet from the centre of the stack.

'I need you to sign this, Miss Peck.' He stared at me now. 'You are quite sure you wish to retain that name?'

I nodded as he pushed the page across the desk. 'It is a matter of some urgency. You will find a pen in the drawer to your left.' He sniffed again, hunched his narrow shoulders and drummed his dirty nails on the wood.

The Beetle was a good name for Marcus Telferman – he was a man of dust and shadows. The first time I'd come across him was at Ma's funeral when me and Joey had thought he was at the wrong graveside. In his shiny black coat and tall hat with the trailing ends of a crêpe band flapping about his head he'd put my brother in mind of an insect.

I'd met him five times now, and the more I saw the more I was inclined to agree. Every time I thought I could slip away from Paradise there came another summons to Pearl Street and more urgent business – documents, transfers, contracts – waiting on his desk for my name. I swear it was like he lived with the mice in the skirting at The Palace. When his little twitching horns caught the faintest rustle of me packing a bag he'd find something for me to do.

The clock on the stone mantlepiece behind the desk made a sharp clicking noise before it gathered itself together and chimed the hour. The Beetle fished into the top pocket of his waistcoat and drew out a fob watch. He flicked open the golden case and brought the dial close to his eyes, then he placed it on the desk to his right.

'Three already. Come, Miss Peck, I have other appointments. Your signature, please.'

He didn't talk London natural. His clipped accent and the stiffness of his speech marked him out as an incomer – like the half of us in Limehouse. Lucca said he was almost definitely a 'son of Abraham' and I reckoned he was right on that score. He didn't look like a man who enjoyed a pork chop with his greens. Then again, he didn't look like a man who enjoyed anything much.

'Like I said, Mr Telferman,' I started up again, 'I think I've got a right to know where she is. She's my own grandmother, she told me that herself. It's all very well her handing Paradise and everything in it over to me, but I need to know more. Not about the legal stuff – I want to know about her and about my mother. Then there's our father – surely Lady Ginger can tell me something about him. She must know who he was. I want to know about . . .'

About me and Joey and who we really are, I thought, though I didn't say it. So many questions I still needed answers to.

The Beetle removed his specs. He placed them carefully

7

on top of the papers and leaned forward, steepling his long bony fingers. An oily lick of thin grey hair fell across his face and he pushed it back and upward so that it rose above his head and sat there in a greasy roll. It was distracting the way it stayed put. As he spoke I kept looking at it.

'Lady Ginger was most specific, we both know this to be correct, do we not? I am bound by her wishes. I can tell you nothing more than she wishes to divulge. If she wants to contact you it will be through me and only through me. By the same token, if you need to . . . consult her, then I am to be your conduit.'

'My what? That some fancy legal term?'

He shook his head and pursed his lips. The greasy roll stayed exactly where it was. When he spoke he sounded disappointed, like he was talking to a child in a schoolroom who couldn't do a simple sum. 'I am your means of communication. Your go-between. I am not at liberty to discuss the issue further. Now the paper, if you please.'

I leaned back in the chair and folded my arms. 'And what if I don't sign it?'

'This is most tiresome. You are not a child any more, Katharine.' I noted he used the name she'd given me. 'People depend on you now. You have responsibilities – as I explained so very carefully that first day.'

That was nearly three weeks ago. When me and Lucca came out of Lady Ginger's empty room at The Palace and went downstairs, Marcus Telferman, face long and grey as an old man's nightshirt, had been waiting in the hallway, just as she'd written. I caught the smallest twitch of his lips as he took me in. There was a pile of boxes at his feet and a sheaf of papers under his arm. He nodded, but he didn't say a word as he held out a page covered in handwritten lines packed so close together the sheet looked black. I noted there was a space at the bottom for my signature.

'What will you do?' Lucca repeated the question he'd asked upstairs when I read my grandmother's letter. I stared at the paper in the lawyer's hand and ran her message through my mind.

Telferman knows my wishes and will be ready to act for you should you decide to accept my terms. The document of transfer must be signed within the day or this offer will be rescinded.

The paper in front me was the 'document of transfer'. If I signed, The Palace and everything, *everything*, of my grand-mother's would become mine.

Of an instant the hallway went dark. The room blurred to a shadow except that narrow white space at the foot of the page. Just for a moment back then I thought of running to the door and out into the light.

Now I stared out of the Beetle's grimy window. The sunshine showed up the cloudy smears on the panes. He lived in a grand house – Lady Ginger must have paid him well – but he didn't go much on cleaning so far as I could tell. Four storeys high it was, every room filled with books and papers, statues, bits of stone (I couldn't for the life of me think why you'd want to display a lump of old brown rock on your mantle) and creatures – most of them dead. There was a fox in a glass case in front of the window giving me the eye.

Over the street a ragged woman with a baby on her hip stopped a passer-by. Mumping him for pennies, I supposed.

I watched her spit at his back after he shook his head and moved on.

Was that how they all felt about me, I wondered? All the men and women in Paradise who looked to me for their bread and bacon. The people who worked for me now – the ones who knew it, leastways – did they spit at my back when I left a room? The woman pulled her shawl around the baby and pushed on. She limped badly. God knows what would become of them both eventually. For most of them on the streets it was hard enough just feeding yourself without bumping a child about too.

Perhaps I could find her a place in one of my establishments? At least she and the kid would have a roof over their heads.

My establishments.

I caught myself thinking it and shuddered. See, it wasn't just the music halls that Lady Ginger ran. No, her world ran deeper than me and Lucca had ever imagined – and we'd imagined quite a lot. The Gaudy, The Comet and The Carnival were what you might call front of house. The rest of it . . . well, tell truth, I still wasn't entirely sure how much more there was to know. The Beetle enjoyed ladling out his little bits of information like a clergy at a soup stand.

When the pair of us had gone through the boxes of papers that first day I couldn't keep track of it all. Not just here in Limehouse, mind, but across the City. You name it, however low you want to go, and she was in it right up to them blood-clot rubies hanging off her ears. Flesh houses catering to every appetite, opium pits, gambling rings, dog fights, cock fights, even rat fights in the meanest quarters.

From the books she appeared to have a dozen customs men tied to every finger. And there was respectable stuff, too – ships, warehouses, stocks, bonds, even a bit of a bank.

'Miss Peck!' The Beetle's clipped voice was sharp. 'Time is money. Your signature.'

I stared at the paper on the desk.

'What's this when it's at home?' I turned it over and scanned to the end where there was evidently a place for my name. I looked up. 'I'm not signing nothing I can't read. I might be new to this malarkey, but I'm not that green – and you know it.'

It was true. From the first I wouldn't put my name to anything I hadn't read and understood, right to the smallest line. If it was Latin – and of occasion it was – I got Lucca to help out. I trusted the Beetle, but I didn't much like him, and if I was going to be running Paradise I needed to know exactly what was in it.

'What language is this?' Tell truth, I thought I knew, but I wanted the confirmation.

The Beetle picked up his fob watch and snapped the case shut. Then he reached for his specs and balanced them on the end of his long nose. He stared at me across the desk.

'Well?' I asked.

He didn't blink, just kept staring at me, that roll of hair still perched on his head like a starched napkin in a cookshop.

'French.'

I felt a little ball of excitement tumble in the pit of my stomach. I thought I knew where this was going. Under my bodice I became suddenly aware of Joey's ring and his Christopher. When I'd thought he was lost, I'd hung them on a chain about my neck and clung to them for luck every time I went up in the cage. I didn't want to give the Beetle the satisfaction of knowing how much the thought of seeing my brother again meant to me. Partly because I didn't want to show a weakness and partly because I was tired of being treated like a child.

'And?' Despite the flutter in my chest my voice came out crisp. I was pleased about that.

I didn't take my eyes off his. We glared across the table at each other like a couple of sparring cats. The Beetle broke first. He glanced down and started to gather the papers together, shuffling them neatly so that the jagged edges of the pile smoothed out.

'It is a document pertaining to a house in Paris. Once you have signed it, Miss Peck, you will be the owner of that property. The Lady set this in motion some days before she . . . went away. The papers arrived yesterday.'

I stood up. 'And?'

He sighed. 'You really are most exasperating. Will I always have to spell everything out to you? Truly, I am beginning to wonder if The Lady made the right decision.'

'That right? Well, truly, I'm beginning to wonder if that French house on the paper there happens to be number 17 rue des Carmélites, where – according to my grandmother – I'll find my brother.'

He raised an eyebrow and shrugged. 'As you know, The Lady had many interests. Property is another strand of her . . . portfolio, that is to say, *your* portfolio.'

I started to laugh.

'I fail to see anything amusing, Miss Peck. It is merely a

foreign business transaction, the first of many you will be required to undertake during our association. Now please . . .' He waved at the document. '*Tempus fugit.*'

'Time flies, does it?' I grinned down at him. 'The funny thing is, I'm planning on making a trip to Paris. Me and Lucca, we're going over together.' I saw the look on the Beetle's face. 'Oh, don't worry. I'm not reckoning on staying. I just want to see my brother again. I want to make quite sure he's . . .'

Alive was what I meant. But this paper finally proved it, didn't it? I really was going to be my brother's keeper. I ran my finger down the first page looking for the familiar words in all that foreign and then flipped it over. I was right – third paragraph down, the address I knew I'd see.

I looked up to find that the Beetle was watching me close. Of a sudden he seemed interested. I cocked my head to one side. 'I might collect his rent while I'm over there. Joey owes me.' That last was true enough.

'You may do as you wish . . .' He sighed and flicked at a stain on his cuff, but then he looked up sharp. The sun caught his specs again, making them shine like the coins they put over the eyes of a corpse. His mouth twitched, '. . . as long as you are here in London during the first week of May. The Barons, Miss Peck. I trust you have not forgotten?'

I shuddered for the second time that afternoon. Of course I hadn't forgotten. Now the Beetle smiled. 'Your signature, please, the pen is . . .'

'I know, in the drawer to the left.'

I took the handle and pulled. There was a pen there, just as he said, and a long pale envelope addressed in a familiar hand to Katharine Redmayne.

The Beetle sniffed. 'If you had had the courtesy to allow me to finish, Katharine, I was going to say that the pen is resting on a letter from your grandmother.'

Chapter Two

The wind caught the sheet and almost whipped it out of my hand and over the rail. I turned around so that the white cliffs were behind me. For all that I'd spent my life on the banks of the Thames, I'd never been so far out on water before.

I'd been on a coal barge to Rotherhithe once when I thought I was sweet on a lad called Freddie Coates whose dad owned a couple of carriers at the basin. I made up an errand and asked him to take me over the river just so we could get friendly. Trouble was, Freddie got a bit too friendly, if you get my meaning. Joey went round to have a little chat with him when he saw the black print of his hand on the back of my skirt.

Freddie didn't talk to me after that, but he didn't talk much on the barge neither, so I wasn't too put out. And there was another time when Nanny Peck took me and Joey out in a tuppenny row boat on the lake at Victoria Park. We were only small so she took charge of the oars, but the old girl hadn't got a clue. We just went round and round on the same patch of water. All the while Nanny Peck was puffing like a deal porter and looking likely to burst a vessel. I remember us laughing so hard we almost toppled the boat.

I wondered if we'd ever laugh like that together again.

Lucca grinned at me. 'What do you think, Fannella? How do you like the sea?'

'I don't feel noxious, if that's what you're asking.' I kept a tight hold of the letter, stood on tiptoe and leaned over the side to watch the bottle-green waves shatter into foam against the side of the boat. Another gust caught the brim of my new hat and I had to slam my hand down on the crown to keep it from flying away. I took a deep breath and looked back at Lucca.

Fannella was his name for me. In his natural speech it meant little bird. It was appropriate seeing as how that's what I'd been. Night after night swinging and trilling in that cage seventy foot up over the punters' heads, caught in my grand-mother's trap.

I first met Lucca at The Gaudy. He was – and still is – the finest set painter working the halls. He was wasted in Paradise, I've told him that often enough even though I wouldn't want him to go. All the same, he had a rare talent and he was clever with it. Michelangelo, Leonardo, Raphael, Titian – all them old-time painter boys from his country – he worshipped them. He talked about them like they was liv-ing down his street. I reckon I knew more than most about art and that was entirely down to spending so much time listening to Lucca. To speak frank, of occasion, I wished he'd show a bit of interest in something more lively, but Lucca was Lucca. And I wouldn't change him.

The first time we spoke proper was a couple of years back. I was a general help at The Gaudy then and on that particular night I was slopping out the gallery and singing a song to keep my mind off what I was dealing with. Lucca was working on the stage.

When I finished he came down to the front and clapped. I was surprised, tell truth. Of a general rule he kept himself apart. We Gaudy girls reckoned it was because he didn't want anyone's pity. In the halls we all knew how vicious the lime-light could be. Back then we – that's to say me and my friend Peggy – assumed the angry crimped flesh that ran from his hairline down into his collar on the right side of his face was the result of an accident with the flares. We were wrong.

As it happens, we were both wrong about a lot of things when it came to Lucca. God love her, Peggy still thinks we might be a couple.

He steadied himself as the boat rocked. 'Well, Fannella, you didn't answer my question?'

I breathed out.

'Actually, I like it very much – the feeling of it. And the air here, it tastes . . . clean. Like it's doing you good to swallow it down. How long will it take, do you think?'

He shrugged. 'Not so long. These small boats are fast and the weather is clear. On a fine day you can see France from the cliffs back there.'

A pair of smartly dressed passengers came to stand at the rail just behind him. Lucca pulled his hat lower and fiddled with his scarf and the collar of his coat so that the scarred side of his face was masked from view. I supposed there'd never come a day when he wasn't conscious of his looks.

'So, the letter?' He nodded at the paper in my hand. 'Will you tell him?'

'That I'm his landlady?'

Lucca narrowed his good eye. 'I mean the other.'

I looked down at the paper again and flattened it out over the rail, careful to pin it down. Lady Ginger's elegant, looping hand was as familiar to me now as my own.

Katharine,

Today you have signed the final deeds of exchange to a property in Paris inhabited by your brother, Joseph. I have no doubt that you will wish to visit him there at the earliest opportunity. Indeed, Telferman informs me that you have already attempted to make plans to this end. I trust that you will not waste time on this reunion. I do not need to remind you of your responsibilities.

While I cannot forbid such a journey, I feel I must warn you that your brother's world is one of complication. He is not the man you lost. Do not speak of your brother or his place of residence to anyone except your most trusted colleagues. Even then, think carefully about those you confide in.

I leave it to you to decide whether or not you inform him of the nature of his tenancy. Joseph Peck believes that I am his sole benefactor in this.

There is one thing you must communicate to him as a matter of some importance. He can never return to London. Tell him that Bartholomew waits.

That was it. No date, no address, just her signature scrawled across the bottom and another line added as an afterthought.

Telferman also informs me that you show promise.

'How can I tell him he can never come back? He's my brother.'

Lucca fussed at the trailing ends of his scarf. 'The Barons, Kitty. Joseph made some powerful enemies among men who—'

'That was a lie! Joey didn't do it.' I cut in sharp, but I knew Lucca was right.

He didn't like to speak about the fire that had melted half his face away. Lucca was supposed to have died that night along with the rest of them – not one over eighteen years of age. Every Baron believed that my brother, Joseph Peck, had started the blaze in which the pick of the boys from their houses of singular entertainment had perished and they wanted revenge. Lady Ginger had spirited Joey away to Paris to protect him.

But now I could make it right. I caught Lucca's arm.

'Listen, I can explain what happened. I'll tell them Joey was there to stop the fire. I'm in a position now to make it right again. *I'm* a Baron, aren't I?'

I spoke too loud. A donkey-faced woman in a fine fur-edged cape standing just along the deck from Lucca tutted, nudged the arm of the gent with her, presumably her husband, and whispered something into his ear behind her gloved hand. They both turned to look at us.

Her eyes raked my outfit from the tip of the feather bobbing above my bonnet to the toes of my boots. I could see she was pricing up every bit of clobber to put a value on me. The gent did the same, but whereas his missus found me wanting, he clearly liked what he saw.

Neddy must have dialled that because her voice clipped up. 'Come along, Rufus. The salon is reserved for First Class travellers. It is so difficult to avoid unfortunate encounters on these compact vessels.'

She released his arm and trotted briskly up the deck. The gent stared at me for a moment, then he smiled and tapped the side of his nose. 'The Limehouse Linnet – I'd know you anywhere. I saw you perform in your cage three times.' He spoke quietly so that his wife shouldn't hear.

'Rufus!' The voice was shrill. He tipped his hat to me and turned to follow her.

'Unfortunate encounters!' Lucca snorted. 'If only she knew.'

'Knew that I could likely buy her husband and everything he owns and still have small change for twenty acres up west, or knew that I'm one of the twelve most dangerous people in London? Take your pick.'

I watched as the man who'd spoken to me held open the half-glazed door to the salon for his lard-faced wife. He stared back at us and nodded once as he followed after her.

The *Prince Leopold* rose and fell on the waves and I planted my boots wider to keep straight. 'You didn't answer me, Lucca.'

He shrugged and pulled at the fingertips of his new green Spanish leather gloves. I'd given them to him this morning at Victoria, just before we got on the boat train, in the way of a thank-you for coming with me. He likes a bit of fancy gear, does Lucca – I knew they'd be right up his alley, in a manner of speaking.

Nanny Peck held that you should never give a pair of gloves as a gift or a love token. 'Handing away the feelings – that's what you'd be doing.' I heard her voice in my head clear as Old Peter's cornet when I chose them in Zedelman's on Burdett Road. I wasn't one for superstition so I ignored her. I bought a neat leather travelling trunk, too – that's why I'd gone there – and when I put the coins on the counter the proprietor looked at me narrow through his rambling eyebrows and bit down hard on one of the sovereigns to test it for a dimmick.

At the time I wished he'd crack a tooth, but I suppose he had every right to wonder how a girl like me came to have a purse full. He didn't look the entertainable sort so he wouldn't have known me from the halls, not like the gent in the salon. But he would soon. They all would.

I tightened my grip on the rail. The low spring sun was sparking on the water and beneath the soles of my boots I could feel the thrum of the engine through the deck boards. It was a good day for a crossing.

'I'm still waiting. Who am I?' I turned to Lucca and pushed a stray blonde coil loosened by the wind out of my eyes.

'What do you want me to say, Fannella? We have gone over this a thousand times. You are your own woman. You do not have to do things as she did. Paradise is yours now and you will run it your own way – a better way.'

'That's all very well but we both know, however I shine it up, that it's a dirty place. Everything I have now is . . . tainted.'

He was quiet for a moment, his good brown eye unblinking. 'I watched you sign the paper. You made a choice that day.'

'But was it the right one? I might have high ideas about setting things right, cleaning things out and making things fair and decent – but what if that's just unicorn shit . . .'

Lucca winced and glanced around to make sure no one heard me. He could be quite high-minded of occasion. Usually it made me laugh, but today it didn't. I think I was tight wound about the prospect of seeing Joey and I took it out on the next best thing.

The edge in my voice sharpened. 'You know what I mean, Lucca. How can I give the girls who work in Lady Ginger's dab-houses a better life? I can't just close up and turn them out on the streets, can I? And maybe you think I should have a nice little chat with the rozzers about what goes on at East India when my customs boys aren't looking too closely? Then there's her opium doss-houses – nine of them off Narrow Street as far I can make out, although Telferman's tight as a wren's arse on that score . . .' Lucca looked pained again, but I carried on, 'and there's her toolers working up west – tidy little business that is, given as how she owns all the jerry-shops out east – her bit fakers, a dainty line in blackmail – Telferman's got a safe laid flat in his office so cram full of letters from notables that he has to sit on it to make it close – her collection boys, her—'

Lucca raised his hand. 'They are not *hers* any more, they are yours. And you will find a way to make it better. I know you will. It is not in your nature to be cruel. Think of it as a business, Kitty.' His puckered mouth gathered into a sort of smile. 'The wealth and reputation of every great man in London is built on the backs of others. In their comfortable clubs, their grand houses, their gilded restaurants and their panelled offices they are still in the business of buying and selling lives. You are the same now, I think?'

'I'm not!' I couldn't think of anything else to say. I glared up at him and felt my cheeks flush up with anger as he began to smile.

'Oh, I think you are, Fannella – but there is an important

22

difference. Remember The Lady saw herself as a mother?'

Now, maternal is a word you could never bring to mind when thinking of my grandmother – and that was another word I had problems with as well – but she harped on about family like all of us in Paradise was tucked up in a cot together and she was warming our milk and singing us a lullaby.

'What are the things children want most from a mother?' Lucca ducked his head as a shower of sea spray came over the rail and spattered around us.

I thought about Ma.

'Love . . . and protection?'

Lucca nodded. 'And . . .? Think about when you and Joey were small. How did she treat you?'

Tell truth, it was still painful to think about Ma. Every time I tried to bring her to mind I felt an ache behind my eyes. Nanny Peck was easy to picture, bustling about in her stiff black dress with her plaid shawl pinned tight at her neck. Round as a winter robin she was and twice as cocky. Looking back, it's easy to see that her and Ma had as much in the way of family ties as me and Princess Alexandra, but if you don't suspect anything you don't go poking around for it.

Ma was skinny as a sighthound and fair like me and Joey, only in her it was fragile, like you could pick her up, drop her down and she'd splinter into tiny little pieces. Nanny Peck called her a beauty and she was, I suppose. But doesn't every child think that of its mother?

She had a lovely clear singing voice, I remember that, and when she laughed it was like the sun coming out from behind a cloud. But there were dark days too when Nanny Peck took me and Joey out and away from our neat three-room lodgings off Church Row, and away from Ma. When we came home she'd be all smiles and stories again. I only realised that when they were both gone.

One time, when we got back, Ma had set the table for a feast. There was a white napkin, candles, boiled potatoes and a cold ham sitting on a dish. And when we'd had our fill of that and our fingers were all greasy from the meat, she'd gone to the cupboard in the wall by the fire and brought out a small round russet-coloured thing.

I took it for an apple until she put it on a saucer and cut it in two. Then, for a moment, I thought it was a jewel box on account of all the little rubies that spilled out. Ma handed one half to Joey and said it was a pomegranate – God knows how she came by one of them in Limehouse – and that he should try it.

I watched him bite into it and chew the meat off the pips before spitting them out. It was obviously good eating. Next thing he crammed the pomegranate against his lips and began to suck loudly. I laughed as all the red juice streaked down his chin and over his hands. He licked the sticky sweetness off them.

Then it was my turn. I reached out for the other half, but Joey snatched it up and wouldn't let me have it.

'It's mine. She gave it me,' he said. But Ma stood there with her hands on her hips and gave him daggers. 'What do I always tell you, Joseph?'

Joey looked at the half pomegranate in his hand and twisted it about so that all the pips glistened in the candlelight, and then, reluctantly, he put it back on the saucer. I grabbed it.

'What's the word?' Ma asked again.

Joey mumbled something and fiddled with the ends of the napkin.

'I can't hear you, Joseph.'

'Share. We must always share, that's what you say, Ma.'

Of course! That was how she treated us. It's what children want from a mother. I turned to Lucca.

'Fairness – that's it, isn't it?'

He nodded. 'I know you, Kitty. You cannot abide injustice. No matter what comes – and I think it will be . . .' he paused, looked down and stretched his fingers wide like he was searching for the right word there in his green leather palms, '. . . complicated, you will always be fair and you will always be loyal to those who are loyal to you. People will grow to respect you and perhaps even to love you for that.'

Complicated – that's what The Lady said about Joey too, wasn't it? What a family we'd turned out to be. I reached out to brush a hair from Lucca's shoulder.

'It's not going to be easy, is it? It's not like I've inherited a nice little fish business up Billingsgate or a fancy draper's store. I've got more than market porters and shop girls working for me. I don't know how they're going to take to being told what to do by a twist who was slopping out the gallery at The Gaudy not three months back. Look at Fitzy, Lady Ginger's right fist. According to Peggy he's been chewing up the cushions in his parlour. Not that it's going to be his for much longer.'

'Exactly! The cage, Fannella, remember the cage.'

I snorted. 'I'm not likely to forget that, am I?'

Lucca tilted his head to one side so that his thick dark

hair flopped forward to cover the scarred half of his face. He smiled and I was minded over again that he really must have been quite the dazzler – before my brother saved him from that fire.

'I mean you have shown yourself to be fearless. There are not many who could have performed as you did, night after night. You have . . . *coglioni*.'

'I've got what?'

Lucca arched his brow. 'It is not a word I care to translate. I mean you are brave, bold. People will know that of you. It was part of her test, was it not?'

'Part of her trap, you mean.'

He shook his head. 'She knew what she was doing. The Lady rarely made mistakes.'

'She was wrong about Joey.' My hand moved to my neck. Under the thick stuff of the coat and the high collar of my dress I could feel the bump of my brother's ring and his Christopher.

'No – I believe she was temporarily blinded by his sex. It is the order of things, is it not, for a man to inherit the family estate? The Lady did not follow the usual rules, but in that one case she was a traditionalist. Then she saw you and recognised—'

'Are you saying I'm like her?' I bristled up like a fighting cock. 'Because let me tell you, Lucca Fratelli, I am nothing like Lady Ginger. For all that she's my blood, there's nothing about me that comes from her. She's as much like me as old Tan Seng back at The Palace. Actually that's a lie, because at least he's got a kind heart.'

Lucca raised his hands. 'I meant your spirit, Kitty. She

must have seen something in you, some . . . *riflesso*, reflection, that showed her that you were the one.'

'Reflection! I don't even look like her. When I stare at myself in the mirror I can't see a smudge of her there, no matter how deep I look. And don't think I haven't tried because it . . . it . . . Tell truth, it worries me that me and her are—'

I broke off. 'Why are you grinning?'

'Because in a way you have just answered your own question. *That* is exactly how you must remake Paradise, Fannella. In your own image.'

The *Prince Leopold* lurched as a wave crashed against the side. I reached for the handrail to keep upright, but as I did so Lady Ginger's letter was snatched from my fingers by a gust of wind. For a moment it flattened itself against the side of the boat a couple of foot below us. Lucca knelt and reached down to try to get it back, but another wave came up and swept it free. I watched it unfurl in the frothy wake of the steamer. For a moment or two it was near enough for me to see the ink slide off the page.

'I'm sorry, I couldn't catch it.' Water dripped from the brim of Lucca's hat where he'd been caught by the swell. He stood and leaned out over the rail to track the paper bobbing about in the choppy water.

'Don't worry. It's all in here, every word.' I tapped the side of my bonnet. 'Telferman tells me I have a gift for memorising things. I can quote whole documents back to him after just one read through. I think it unnerves him.'

Now Lucca snorted. '*You* unnerve him, Kitty. I don't think you realise that you are . . . *eccezionale* – remarkable.'

I smiled and reached for his hand. 'Well, this is a day for

compliments, isn't it? First I'm kind and fair, then I'm brave and loyal and now I'm remarkable with it. Thank you very much, kind sir.' I dipped him a mock curtsey and pulled his hand. 'Come on. Get the tickets out just in case and follow me.'

'Where?'

'I think we'll go and find ourselves a cosy seat in the First Class salon – right next to that woman we saw earlier. I'm going to show her my coglionis.'

Chapter Three

'It's on the map. Look – rue du Colombieris there and rue des Carmélites should be the third turning on the left.'

I turned the map around again. The print was small, but I could see the place I was looking for. The trouble was it only seemed to exist on paper. There was no third turning in the narrow passage ahead.

'Let me see.' Lucca took the flimsy sheet from my hands and held it out in front of him. He frowned as he looked from the paper to the gloomy alley. 'It can't be right.'

'The man in the kiosk didn't look right to me. That black thing under his nose wasn't normal for a start. It was so rigid with wax that it didn't move when he talked. I reckon he has to chip it off at night. I think you were done back there at the station, Lucca. I thought you said you could speak their lingo?'

'I said I can speak a little French, Kitty. It is a Latin language, like Italian – not so hard for me, *si*? I know enough to make myself understood.'

'Old rat lip understood all right. He took us for a pair of daisies and sold you a fake map. I said we should have taken a hack or whatever they have here.'

My voice scratched like a wire brush. I was in a coil about seeing Joey, and Lucca was still getting the benefit of it.

It was almost dark now. Lamps glowed behind the tall

shuttered windows of the flaking stone buildings around us. If rue des Carmélites was nearby it wasn't in what you'd call the finest part of town.

I was disappointed. I wanted Joey to be . . . Tell truth, I don't know what I wanted him to be, exactly, but I think I was hoping for more than a back alley that reeked of cat piss.

I imagined I might find it exotic to be in Paris. I thought I might feel the difference of it through the soles of my boots from the moment we stepped into the street. Look at you, Kitty Peck, I thought to myself as we walked down the platform at the Gare du Nord, a porter following up with our gear, you're a long way from Limehouse now, girl.

But the fact of the matter was that apart from the way everyone spoke – and a certain manner of dress I'd noticed in some of the women . . . and a couple of the men, come to that – the streets we'd been walking for the last hour or so looked curiously familiar. When it comes to it, I suppose one city is much like another, but I'd swear there were corners up Spitalfields way that were the double of the quarter we'd just gone through. Even the sound and the smell of the place was the same – carriages on cobbles and horse shit. Mind you, it was colder than London, which came as a surprise seeing as how France was continental.

I shivered and stamped my feet. I wasn't sure what I was going to say to Joey when I found him, but it was, after all, why I was here. I certainly didn't want to spend the rest of the night searching for his house. *My house*, I corrected myself. I wasn't sure what I was going to say to him about that neither.

'Perhaps the scale is wrong. Wait there.' Lucca folded the map into a square and walked a little way up the cobbled passage. I watched as he craned to check the names painted on the walls just above head height. Soon it would be too dark to see them.

'What about the trunk?' I called after him. 'We won't be able to collect it after nine. That's what they told you, isn't it?'

Right on cue a church bell somewhere off to the right began to sound the hour. After eight metallic strikes the echo faded gradually off the stone walls. It was the only sound. This part of the city wasn't just shabby, it was deserted.

'Lucca, we'll have to go back to the station for it and find a hotel for the night. We'll buy a new map tomorrow.' My voice was tight as a docker's bowline. Looking back, I think I was close to tears.

'I'll go just a little further.' I watched him disappear into the shadows and kicked at some loose stones. This couldn't be the right place.

A door opened halfway along the passage and a tall woman stepped out. She looked left and right, glanced up at the crack of starry sky overhead and patted the ivory handle of the ruffled black umbrella hooked over her arm. As she came towards me I noticed her clothes were far better than you'd expect of someone living on these streets. Sleek fur trimmings sheened at the neck and hem of a velvet cape worn over a heavily beaded skirt. I could hear it rustle and crackle as she came towards me.

The woman's dark hair was piled high on the top of her head, curled and pinned in a way I couldn't begin to emulate, and her face was so artfully painted that anyone who hadn't worked the halls would have taken her for a natural.

So, I thought to myself as she drew level and I found

myself admiring the way her boot-black lashes curled up-wards, it's true what they say about French women after all. She must have seen me gawping because a couple of seconds after she'd passed by I heard her stop and rustle some more.

A gloved hand that smelt of fresh-cut violets touched my right cheek.

'*Josette! Est-ce que vous?*'

I whipped about.

The woman stared at me confused. Her darting black eyes took in every angle of my face and then she looked down at my dusty travelling coat and at the tips of my new boots poking out from underneath. Shiny brown leather, they were, like a pair of fresh hatched conkers. This morning when I buttoned them up I thought them very fine indeed, but now they were giving me the gyp. I couldn't wait to tear them off and toast my bare feet in front of a fire.

She frowned and shook her head.

'*Pardon, mademoiselle. Je suis désolée, je me suis trompée.*'

I didn't understand a word of that, but all the same I reckoned she was apologising for something. She nodded her head and the glittering black jewels dangling from her ears fell forward over the fur of her collar. She turned away and carried on up the street.

'Wait, please!' She didn't look back so I called after her. 'Why did you . . .?'

'You may be right, Fannella. I went to the end and there's nothing. The map's useless.'

I turned to see Lucca folding the tissue roughly before forcing it into a pocket of his coat. He glanced at the woman who was a dozen yards away now.

'You called out to her?'

I nodded. 'I think she mistook me for someone. We could ask her for directions?'

Lucca sprinted to catch the woman, who had almost reached the corner. I followed and heard him gabble a string of words. The woman halted and looked back. Lucca pulled the map from his pocket and flapped the creased paper open. I noticed again how the woman stared at me, like she'd lost something in my face and was searching for it.

'*Nous sommes ici, madame?*' Lucca took a couple of steps closer, holding the map out so that she could see it clearly too. '*Ici?*' He pointed at the sheet and looked direct at her. Then he paused. For a moment he froze like one of them old marble statues he was so fond of drawing at the Victoria and Albert. Of a sudden he rattled off something in French and the woman shook her head so violent that a couple of hair pins came loose and chinked down on the cobbles. She raised her hand to cover her mouth and backed away.

I was so used to Lucca's face that most of the time I forgot about the scars. You couldn't blame her, I supposed, for taking fright like that, but all the same I felt for him. Usually he took it quite personal, but this time I was amazed to see him go after her. He caught her arm and carried on in French, speaking so soft that I couldn't hear the words distinctively, just make out the fact that he sounded . . . concerned, like *he* was trying to comfort her, not the other way round.

At first she tried to pull away, but he kept on speaking. He minded me of one of the Fore Street dray lads calming a skittish mare. When he stopped we all stood there in silence. I noticed that the woman had flushed up like a rose and

33

that she was breathing fast under that fancy cape. Surely she could tell we didn't mean her any harm? And as for Lucca's face . . . well, you get used to that soon enough. The polite thing is not to stare.

And tell truth she didn't. Instead, she kept glancing at me through them thick black lashes, sidling her eyes away if I caught her. I didn't have a clue what Lucca had said, but it must have done the trick because after a minute she took the map from his hand and started to speak very quickly and very quietly.

She flattened the map against the wall behind her and pointed. Lucca leaned forward and nodded. Then the two of them were off again, rabbiting away like a couple of schoolgirls.

I couldn't hold it any longer. 'What's she saying?'

Lucca didn't look at me. 'In a moment, wait please.'

'Does she know where rue des Carmélites is?' I tried again, moving closer. I was beginning to feel like a teetotal at a gin palace. The woman clammed up. Lucca leaned forward and whispered something to her and her expression changed. Handing him the map, she reached out to touch my face. The smell of violets, expensive ones at that, came strong again.

'*Oui, je vois, il est vrai.*' She murmured. '*Jolie fille.*'

Without another word, she turned her back on us both and walked on down the street. The beads on her skirt made a brittle scratching sound as they brushed the surface of the cobbles. Just before turning the corner she raised her left hand in a sort of salute before disappearing.

I waited until her footsteps faded to nothing before turning to Lucca.

'Well? What was all that about, then? You two were having a nice tête-à-tête, weren't you? See, I know the French for getting on like a house on fire, all right.' I stopped myself. Under usual circumstances I would have thought it through proper and chosen my words more careful. But if Lucca noticed he didn't let on, in fact he began to smile, and that riled me.

'Anyway, I wouldn't have thought she was your type!' I said, pointedly.

Now he laughed out loud.

'It's not bleedin' funny to me, Lucca. Did she tell you anything? The map for a start – what did she say about that? She showed you something, didn't she?'

He nodded. 'I know exactly where rue des Carmélites is now.' His face softened and he looked at me, almost sadly I thought, like a crow giving bad news to an invalid. He took my hand and squeezed it. 'And now I know exactly what we will find there. Come, Fannella, it is this way.'

We started back towards the narrow passage where we'd already been. I pulled on his arm, confused.

'But that can't be right. We've already tried up there. What did she tell you?'

'Quite a lot, actually, Fannella . . .' Lucca paused. 'By the way, she was a *he*.'

Lucca stepped back and stared up at the tall narrow house. It must have been six storeys at least and as far as I could tell in the dark there was another row of windows set along the roof.

'She said it was here – a side passage leading to a courtyard, but there's nothing.' He rubbed his hands together, but not because he was cold. Fiddling with his fingers was something he did when he was thinking. If it wasn't for the new green gloves he'd be picking at his nails.

I looked up too. The woman had told him to look for a passage after the fifteenth house along the left-hand side of rue du Colombier. We'd counted it out and that was where we were now, but there wasn't a passage like she said.

She? I wouldn't have known her for a man. Lucca said he could tell as soon as he got a clear view of her face, but apart from her height, which I put down to her being foreign, there was nothing to make me think that under all that fancy rig she was so very different to me.

Something twisted about in my belly. Lucca and I hadn't talked much about Joey, not since he told me about the fire and why my brother was there that night.

I'm not green as Albert's Ointment. I knew what he was telling me all right, but I didn't dress it up in my mind and have a good long look. It felt like prying – like that time I found Lucca's drawing of Joey standing there without a stitch on his back, or his front come to it. No, Joey was my brother and whatever he was doing here in Paris that was his business. I just wanted to make sure he was alive as I'd been promised.

And that he was . . . content.

I scanned the shuttered windows. There wasn't a single chink of light showing. That was odd, I thought, because all the other houses around us were clearly occupied whereas this one was lifeless. As I looked I realised that wasn't entirely true. The shutters had been painted quite recently, a shade of red was it? It was hard to tell in the dark. And the double doors to the left weren't flaked and battered like the other entrances along the passage. Someone cared about appearances here, they'd even painted a trail of leaves across the top and down one side of the door. It was clever work to trick the eye, like one of Lucca's scenery flats for The Gaudy.

That tipped something. I frowned and peered at the building again. Of course! Now I saw it clear. I tugged at Lucca's sleeve. 'Come and see this.'

I crossed the passage and stood on tiptoe to work my fingers between the painted slats of a shutter covering one of the two windows at street level. It was a narrow gap, but just as I expected I felt flat stonework underneath, nothing more.

'It's not a house.' I turned to Lucca. 'It's painted to look like one, but there's nothing behind these shutters – that's why there's no light. Most people passing by wouldn't give it a second glance, but that's not a proper house. It's a shell.'

Lucca pushed up the brim of his hat to get a better view and nodded slowly. 'Si – and it is good work, but when you know, it is obvious. It is *una facciata* – a facade.'

'So what's behind it? And how do we get there?' I went to the doors. There was no knocker or bell, not even a handle. I smoothed my hand over the painted wood considering whether or not to beat my fist on the panels and call out.

There was a scratching noise from the other side. It came from low down and I knelt to listen. Lucca bent next to me. The noise came again and as we crouched there on the cobbles half of the door swung silently inward.

'*Allez!*' A small grey cat slipped between us and into the passage. For a moment it paused and stared back, affronted by the fact that we'd blocked its path, and then it pressed itself against the wall opposite and disappeared into the shadows.

'*Qu'avons-nous ici?*'

The quavering voice came again. I looked up to see a spindly elderly man holding the door open. Beyond him I could just see a hallway lit by a single fat candle in a glass lamp box suspended from an arched ceiling. I nudged Lucca and we both straightened up. The man, who was wearing clothes at least fifty years behind the fashion, all frothy with dainty lace and twinkling buttons, wrinkled his nose. '*Qu'est-ce que vous voulez?*'

Lucca began to speak very rapidly. The old man seemed to find it hard to stop staring at his face, mesmerised he was, like one of the punters Swami Jonah takes up on stage for his mental act. The old boy even shifted to let more light spill out from the hall behind. I saw the way his lips twitched as he took in the scars.

If Lucca was insulted he didn't let it stop him. He carried on jawing away and then he drew out the map and pointed at the place where rue des Carmélites should be. The place where, by my reckoning, we were standing right now.

'*Nous recherchons rue des Carmélites.*'

The old man's face took on a guarded expression.

I'd seen that look before at The Lamb when a stranger dropped by of an evening to ask if anyone knew where he might find his 'good friend' Dutch Max. Now, we all knew that meant he was after spirits siphoned off the docks to trade, but how could you tell if he was honest or a nark? A mistake like that could land you in trouble with the customs boys, and I could tell old spindleshanks was thinking something along those lines as Lucca finished up.

'Joseph. Joseph Peck. *Est-il ici?*'

The name seemed to freeze the air.

'*Non.*'

The old gent span around sharp and tried to close the door, but Lucca wedged it open with his foot.

'*S'il vous plaît, monsieur. C'est sa sœur.*' He pulled me into the light. I couldn't follow the chat, but I recognised the words for 'please' and I saw the way the old man started.

'*Mon Dieu!*' He delved into a pocket and produced a 'kerchief fringed with more delicate lace. I caught the powerful waft of sweet cologne as he flapped it open and dabbed at his temples. His watery eyes flicked over my face and then moved on to take in the rest of me. I was reminded of the woman we'd met a few minutes back. When he'd satisfied his curiosity he raised an eyebrow to Lucca and held the half door open wider, motioning for us to come through.

'*Suivez-moi. Je vais vous prendre à lui.*'

'What did he just say?'

Lucca took my hand. We followed the old man down a short dingy hallway that kinked right and suddenly opened into a street flanked by a garden on one side and a single fine broad house on the other. I looked up behind us and saw that, just as I thought, rue du Colombier was screened off from rue des Carmélites by nothing more than a thick wall painted and tricked up on the outside to resemble the front of a house. I say 'rue', but it was more like a courtyard. Light from many windows pooled on the golden flagstones spread out before us and I could hear music and laughter coming from inside.

Lucca's grip tightened. '"I will take you to him." That's what he just said, Fannella.'

Chapter Four

There was a sort of triangle made of stone set over the wide double doors and some curling words I couldn't make out carved into a roundel at the centre. I nudged Lucca.

'What's it mean up there? It's Latin, right?'

He took off his hat, pushed his hair back from his left eye and looked up. His lips moved as he mouthed the script to himself. 'It is Italian, not Latin. They are words from Dante, from *L'Inferno* – hell.' He frowned, confused, but immediately I saw it for what it was – another of The Lady's tricks.

I stared up at the fancy writing. There was a small dead bird lodged in the corner of the stonework, its tufted head lolled over the edge. Nanny Peck always said birds were messengers – it was another one of her superstitions. Depending on the type, they brought good news or bad news. Robins and song thrushes, they always had something pleasant to tell you, whereas birds with black feathers, they wasn't so welcome.

She never mentioned dead birds.

I shivered and gathered up my skirts to climb the steps.

'Well, that sounds about right. I get Paradise and my brother gets the other place.'

I meant it to come out light, but it sounded tart like I was sucking a lemon moon. Now I was here standing on his doorstep, it was real. Everything around me showed up unnaturally sharp. In the halls, when they get the limelight going, anyone watching from the slips sees the truth of it all – cracked white faces, sweat trickling between shoulder blades, shiny dolly pins keeping the hair pieces up top, holes in the costumes where moths have had a bellyful. Out front you don't see any of that, just the general glow, but from the side the lights are cruel – taking your eyes direct to the smallest fault.

It was like that now. I could see the knots beneath the green paint in the wooden door and every scratch and blemish on the polished knocker – a woman's head with a garland hanging from her ears. There was a dent in the tip of her brass nose.

Lucca held my arm. 'No, they are words of hope, listen: *"Do not be afraid; our fate cannot be taken from us; it is a gift."'*

I was about to ask what that meant when the skinny gent barked something over his shoulder. Lucca let go and followed me into a broad candlelit hallway.

The first thing that hit me was the smell. Despite the season, scores of drooping fat-headed roses, mostly dirty pink, sat in gaudy vases arranged on bow-fronted chests lined up in pairs along the hallway. Each vase was positioned in front of a mirror reflecting endless avenues of unravelling blooms. It should have been beautiful, but it was overwhelming. I felt my heart starting up under my bodice as I breathed in the sticky sweetness. The mirrors should have made the space seem bigger, but clouded with billows of flesh-coloured petals the effect was quite the opposite.

Once, when I was no more than five or six, me and Joey had paid a penny each to a showman who'd set up a spiegeltent in the yard of The Mermaid, off Cock Hill. It was a poor affair – you could still see daylight through the holes in the roof – but I remember most clearly that I didn't like what the mirrors did to you, stretching out your limbs so that one minute your head was wavering up near the ceiling, your neck pulled out from your body like a sea captain's telescope, and the next you'd be squat and ugly as a goblin from one of Nanny Peck's stories.

The worst thing was Joey. When I looked up at my brother in the mirrors it wasn't him any more. There was someone else looking back at me, someone with mole eyes, a gaping mouth as wide as the glass and hands the size of hams. I'd started to cry and Joey had to bundle me out of there before we'd done the round. And we didn't get our pennies back.

Something of that feeling came back to me now.

The old man motioned for us to wait just inside the doorway and he went to a room on the right. As he opened the door, the sound of music we'd heard from outside – someone playing a piano – came more clearly. I could hear voices too, male and female. There was a regular little soirée going on behind the door. As we stood there, the rich scent of good tobacco wafted into the hallway, winding itself into the heavy rose.

A minute later the Monseigneur – I found out later that was what the scented skinny old gent was called – stepped out and led me and Lucca up a set of marble stairs. On the way we passed a woman coming down. She was dressed in a close-fitted red velvet evening dress, with a train caught up in a loop at the side. She hid half her face with a feathered fan, but even I could tell she was hiding a chin like a butcher's mallet.

'*Attendez ici.*' The old boy pattered along the first landing, pushed open a door and ushered us into the room beyond. He nodded to Lucca and disappeared, leaving us staring at each other. A log that smelt of sweet apple wood spat in the hearth, a single gas lamp glowed on a cloth-covered side table and candles burned in a couple of wall sconces.

Lucca took my hand.

'Fannella, I think you should know . . . this house . . .'

I squeezed his fingers. 'I reckon I know what you're about to say. Tell truth, I think I run a couple of these establishments back home. Telferman's a bit chary on details, but there's a place up Stepney way that does good business, according to the books. It's called The Cloister.' I paused as a thought struck. 'Carmelites – they're nuns too, aren't they? And I reckon I'm the mother superior?'

Lucca shook his head and twisted the brim of his hat. His face was solemn. He had that look of an owl – well, half of one – that comes on him when he's worried. 'It's been a long time. He will be surprised. He doesn't expect you.' He glanced around at the room. 'And this . . . He will be . . .'

'He will be my brother, Lucca. Nothing changes that.' Even as I said it I found myself wondering. I was good at closing doors in my head, making sure that things I didn't want to dwell on stayed locked away. Like I said, ever since I'd learned the truth about Joey I hadn't liked to take it out and turn it in the light. There were things in his past I didn't want to give a picture to in my head, not because I was ashamed of him, but because it felt like trespassing – like rummaging around somewhere I had no right to be.

I busied myself with the buttons on my travel coat and

43

then I fiddled about with the pins securing my hat. It seemed to be caught so I left it.

The room was done up finer than any I'd seen before. It put me in mind of Fitzy's dainty office at The Gaudy, only the person who lived here had better taste – and more money.

I went to the sofa, sat down – perched is more like it – and patted the seat next to me. It was a low couch affair with rolled gilt ends and so many embroidered bolsters I couldn't get a purchase. There were paintings on the walls – some I didn't care to look at too closely – a barrowload of scented flowers, lilies this time, arranged in porcelain basins set around the corners and patterned rugs of the Oriental type layered over each other so it was like walking on a mattress.

I peeled off my gloves. 'He'll be here in a moment – and I've no doubt that when he comes he'll know who's waiting for him. Dapper Dennis couldn't wait to be off with the news, could he?' As I rolled the gloves in my lap I noticed that my hands were trembling.

At first we tried to carry on talking while we waited like this was some everyday social call. Lucca did most of the chat – looking back I think he was trying to distract me. He told me how the smell of lilies always reminded him of his village back home. At Easter, he said, the men took turns to carry a life-sized statue of the Virgin Mary out from the church and around to the three springs on the outskirts that supplied all their water. The statue was decorated with armfuls of lilies and the women and children followed behind with more flowers which they threw over the heads of the men and in front of the statue as it bumped along the pathways and up the hillsides. When I said it didn't sound like something we'd do in Limehouse Lucca smiled sadly and agreed. He went quiet for a bit and then he started up again, talking about the wallpaper. Chinese hand-painted, he reckoned.

I didn't have an opinion on where it came from, but I remarked that I didn't much like the yellow.

I didn't say anything else after that. I couldn't. My mouth was suddenly dry as a sparrow's dust bath. My fingers went to the Christopher and the ring at my neck. Every time I heard the boards creak beyond the door I tightened my grip. I tried to bring Joey's face to mind. The handsome laughing brother who brought me ribbons and trinkets. The golden lad who held court at The Lamb. The boy who could winkle a smile out of Ma on the bleakest days.

But the pictures kept dissolving and breaking apart.

For two years I'd thought Joey was dead. And in a way he was – the brother I thought I knew was gone. I wasn't sure who was coming through that door. Truly, until that moment, I hadn't allowed myself to really think about what this meeting might bring.

There was a murmur of conversation outside and I felt my stomach fold upon itself as I recognised a voice.

'*Je vais traiter plus tard, Monseigneur.*' The old man opened the door and bowed as someone dressed in a long dark blue dressing gown stepped into the room.

'Joey!'

I leapt up, scattering cushions to the floor, and ran to him.

He didn't come to meet me. In fact, when I reached out to take him in my arms he stepped back. I felt something hard forming in my throat. I had to keep swallowing to keep myself breathing.

'It's me – Kitty. Don't you recognise me?'

My brother didn't answer, he just stared at me and then he looked across at Lucca, who was standing now, turning the brim of his hat around and around. Lucca tilted his head. 'Joseph.'

I wiped the back of my hand across my eyes, as the smoke from the fire was irritating, and then, confused, I held out my hand in a sort of formal greeting. It was still shaking and I tried to steady it.

'Joey?'

A part of me watched myself from somewhere high above and wondered what on earth I was thinking. Jesus! The brother I'd mourned until my eyelids were scalded by the salt of my tears was standing right there in front of me and I was offering him my hand like a simpering charity type. Then again, what was *he* thinking? When he didn't take my hand I pulled it back and hid it behind me. I felt a wetness on my cheeks as the tears I didn't expect brimmed over. I looked down quickly so he couldn't see.

'Your hand! The fingers – they're all there?' I blurted the words out before I could stop myself. It was a ridiculous thing to notice at such a time, but all the same, Lady Ginger had lied to me about that too. She hadn't cut off his ring finger after all. It was there on the end of his hand.

If Joey wondered what I was on about he didn't let on. Instead he walked past me into the room and stood in front of the fire with his back to us both.

'I thought I made it clear to you.' His voice was crisp.

'That you were dead? Oh yes – that was very clear.' I wiped the tears off my face and went to stand close behind him, so

46

close I could smell the floral cologne on his skin. I was beginning to feel the flarings of something different now.

'I wasn't talking to you.' Joey didn't turn to look at me. 'I was talking to Mr Fratelli, who should not have brought you here.' That came out much more cultured than anything he'd said in Limehouse. My brother spoke like a toff.

I glanced at Lucca, who was still fiddling with the hat like an infant with a comfort rag.

'I didn't, Joseph. I didn't even know where you were.'

'Then what is this? Why are you here?'

Joey span about now. In the firelight his face looked old, much older than his twenty years. Lucca shook his head. The hat dropped to his feet as he spread his hands wide. 'I should go. I should not be here now. This is not my story. Fannella – you must tell him. I will send word when I have found a room.'

'No!' Of a sudden I had a clarity. I was standing in a room in Paris with the two people who meant more to me than anyone else in the world, only one of them, my actual brother, was acting like we'd never met. I didn't understand what was going on, but one thing I knew for certain was that I didn't want Lucca to leave.

'Stay, Lucca. I haven't got any secrets to hide from you.' I glared at Joey and I must admit I was quite gratified when his eyes slipped away first.

I took a deep breath.

'He didn't bring me here. I got this address from Lady Ginger. I think we need to talk family business, don't you?'

Joey didn't say much as I rattled on. He sat very still in a high-backed chair to the left of the fire and listened. Occasionally, he glanced at Lucca who was next to me on the sofa, leaning forward with his head bowed so that his hair covered his face. His hands were never still – all the time I talked I was aware of Lucca picking at his nails and worrying at scraps of skin.

I told Joey almost everything that evening. I told him about the cage and about the girls who'd gone missing from the halls. There were some things I left out – the kind of things a brother wouldn't want to hear of his little sister, even when he barely seemed to know her – but I tried to tell him enough to make him understand what I'd done for him, right down to how I, Lucca that is, had dealt with the bastard who had corrupted those boys and murdered them – the man responsible for the fire. That made Joey sit up.

'You killed him?'

Lucca nodded. '*Sì*. I did not work alone, but yes, the shot was mine.'

He raised his head now and stared directly at Joey.

'It was an execution.' Lucca's voice was oddly flat.

Joey nodded curtly, just the once.

Now, there was a world of story in that little sentence of Lucca's. Justice, I called it – and God forgive me, I didn't feel guilty. I didn't delve too deeply into what Lucca called it. Whatever it was, we could sleep at night.

Of course, there was the final kick to my story, the one that had brought me to him. When I told him about Lady Ginger and about me and Paradise, his face went stiff like a mask. He turned away and stared into the fire. The room was completely silent except for the crackling of the logs. There was something I had to know.

'When . . . when did you find out she was our grandmother, Joey? You were working for her for a long time before you . . . went.'

He didn't answer. Instead he stood and lifted an iron to poke the grate. A shower of sparks burst from the logs and leapt into the throat of the chimney. Despite the fire, the atmosphere in the room was as cold as a workhouse itch ward.

When he spoke he didn't look at me.

'It was Nanny Peck,' he paused. 'Just before she died I . . . *found* some papers in her purse – chits signed Elizabeth Redmayne. I thought it might be something to do with our father and his family, some payment to keep us quiet, and I was angry with the old girl for keeping him from us so I confronted her.'

I stared at my brother's back. I thought I'd known him through and through, but the person standing in front of me now was as foreign as skinny old Frenchie with the scent and the lace.

'You went through her purse! You know she would have given us anything. I didn't have you down as a thief, Joey, whatever else you—' I buttoned it before I said something wrong. I looked down and plucked at a fraying loop of brocade detaching itself from the upholstery of the couch.

'You don't have to tell me that, little sister. Don't you think I knew how low it was to steal from my own grandmother?' He rolled his shoulders and muttered something under his breath.

'At the time I was in a deal of trouble. I couldn't tell—' He stopped and shifted a small china ornament on the marble fire surround an inch to the right.

'I didn't know what to do – you don't need to know the details, but please believe that I meant to pay her back. Then, when I found the notes in her purse I thought I could use them. I was harsh. I made her cry and I bitterly regret that because she was kind and good – the closest thing we'll ever have to a grandmother. When I forced her she told me about The Lady and our . . . *connection* and so I went to The Palace to see her. That's when it all began.' He turned round and smiled – it was the first time I'd seen him do that since we'd arrived – only it was a sour look.

'I thought she liked me. Everyone did – back then.'

He rested the iron on one of the fire dogs and crossed to the table beneath the uncurtained window overlooking the courtyard. Moonlight caught his cropped fair hair, turning it silver for a moment. He reached for the neck of a bottle standing in a bucket of ice and poured out three glasses of something that frothed and spilled over the rim.

'Have you tried champagne, Kitty?' He offered me a brimming glass. 'I know Lucca has, but what about you? After all, you can afford it now.'

The edge in his voice cut me.

I reached to take the champagne and tried to brush the skin of his fingers to reassure myself that he was real. There'd been no physical contact between us so far, no brotherly embrace for the little sister he'd allowed to believe him dead.

Back in London when I made my plans about coming over to Paris I'd run through several little scenes in my head and all of them had ended up with him folding me in his arms and swinging me round and round so that my skirts and my hair tangled about us. And then, when we were both so dizzy that we couldn't stand up any more, we collapsed in a heap and sprawled on the floor laughing at the ceiling.

That was what used to happen anyway. But we were both kids then, not the strangers who stared at each other now. I looked up at him.

In two years Joey's face had become leaner, the angles more defined. His eyebrows were darkened and shaped – he plucked them into submission I guessed, like Mrs Conway – so that they framed his long heavy-lidded eyes. It was the look in those blue eyes that had changed most. Once they had a sparkle that could charm a profanity from a Methodist, but now they were hard.

And there was something else there too, something elusive and contained, like he was hiding someone else deep inside and was frightened they might show their face. I thought I knew who that was. Tell truth, I was glad about the dressing gown.

As I brushed his fingers I felt the fine hairs stand up on the back of my hand and at the nape of my neck. Of an instant I knew he'd felt it too. He was looking at me now as if he was taking me in for the first time. His eyes darkened as the pupils bloomed. He reminded me of her in that moment, just a flash of the old cow – brilliant black beads in a gaunt pale face. I think it was only then that I really knew it was true.

I took a deep breath. 'I can afford a lot of things now, Joseph Peck, but if you want to know the truth, I'd have given everything to find you again. Lady Ginger – our grand-mother – knew it and that's why she used me and nearly got me killed. You're the reason I've got Paradise.'

Something flickered across his face. I couldn't tell if it was anger or pain or something in between. He closed his eyes and a muscle worked in his jaw. I stroked his wrist and spoke softly. 'Look at us both. What would Ma think of us circling each other like a couple of strays? I'll happily take a glass with you, Joey. This should be a celebration, not a wake. We're both alive, aren't we?'

He blinked and the tears spilled onto his cheeks, leaving a glittering trail over his sharp high cheekbones.

'Kitty.' My name sounded like it was caught halfway down his throat.

The glass dropped to the floor and the contents fizzled into a rug. He knelt in front of me, clasping my shoulders in his hands. He rested his forehead on mine, looked into my eyes and smiled at me, properly, his handsome face falling easily into the lines and dimples I recognised.

'Forgive me. Please forgive me. I thought it was better, safer, if you believed I was dead. Then when you came here today . . . it was a shock. I . . . I was angry and I was afraid that you . . .' He broke off and closed his eyes. 'There are things about me that I didn't want you to know, little sister . . . I am sorry, so sorry . . .'

The door clicked softly as Lucca left the room. I took my brother's face between my hands and smiled. I could feel the tears streaming down my own face again.

'It doesn't matter, Joey, nothing matters. We're both safe now.'

He kissed my forehead and I felt him rock in my arms. At first I thought he was weeping, but then I realised he was laughing.

Chapter Five

For a long time I'd buried my brother. Then, when The Lady told me he was alive I didn't allow myself to believe it – not entirely. And now, even though he was sitting at my feet leaning back against the couch and smiling up at me I couldn't quite believe he was real. I had to keep touching his head, stroking his cropped hair, to reassure myself he was there.

Once he melted back into the brother I knew, we talked until the sky outside that elegant room in rue des Carmélites was swimming with shoals of salmon. Mostly we talked about Ma and Nanny Peck – the good days when we was small. It was like we were finding our way to each other again. I told him I felt like that girl who followed a trail of crumbs to track her brother through the forest. He laughed and said there was a witch in that story too, and then he asked me about Mrs Conway and Fitzy.

See, Joey was nimble that night. We didn't talk much about Lady Ginger – he kept veering off the subject, taking the conversation back to Nanny Peck's stories or the characters at the halls. There was so much I meant to ask him – about Ma, about Nanny Peck, about our father – about our grandfather too, for that matter – but he always wound the conversation back to something designed to make me do the telling.

Looking back, I reckon I learned more from what he didn't

say than what he did. I tried to broach the subject of his living in Paris – more exactly the way of it, if you follow me – and I tried to make it very clear that it didn't trouble me a sparrow's fart how he chose to spend his days – or his nights. But he didn't open out.

When it was fully light outside he called the Monseigneur back into the room and the two of them had a conversation in pattering French. The old gent skiddled off into the hallway and ten minutes later I heard a hand-bell ringing from the hall below.

'Your carriage has arrived.' Joey held out a hand to raise me from the couch. 'It will take you, both of you, to Le Meurice – it's a hotel, one of the best in Paris. I'm sure Lucca will approve.'

'Can't we stay here with you?' Confused, I took his hand and stood up. I realised I was almost looking him straight in the eye. I'd grown three or four inches since I last saw my brother.

He didn't answer. Instead he smiled, wrapped his arms around me and hugged me so tight against him I could taste the flowers on his skin. Joey stroked my hair and I felt his heart beating beneath the blue robe.

'I will call on you later today and I will show you Paris. You don't know how much I've missed you, little sister.'

Them four days went fast, too fast.

I fell in love with Paris and I fell in love all over again with Joey. I was proud to be escorted by my brother, the dashing young Englishman who, in perfect French, had the knack of charming everyone we met, from the most dismal droop-tached waiter to a goat-faced woman at the opera who was introduced to us as the Duchesse de Somewhere or other. I could tell she liked Joey, but when her eyes sidled over me her mouth puckered up like a cat's arse and the bristles growing through the powder on her chin fetched the lamplight.

Lucca joined us for part of the time. Him and Joey was wary at first, civil enough to each other, but oddly formal too. When a touring act came back to Lady Ginger's halls after a country ramble, I'd often note that the hands and the girls treated them with a certain caution. They acted like they were strangers when only six months before they'd all been drinking together down The Lamb six nights out of seven. It was like the travellers had to prove themselves again, demonstrate they hadn't changed or got beyond us.

I reckoned I could feel something of that between Joey and Lucca, so on the afternoon of the second day, when we was all supposed to go to some public garden for a stroll about, I said I had a headache. Lucca was all for cancelling, but I insisted he should go with Joey, just for an hour at least, while I rested.

In the end they were out until dark. I didn't ask what they did, where they went or what they talked about, but after that they were comfortable together and I was glad to see it. That evening Lucca left me and Joey alone. He took himself off somewhere – I saw Joey slip him a card – while we ate in my room.

I think that was my favourite time of all. Just me and Joey sitting at a round table set up by the window. We kept the curtains open so we could look down onto the street. There was a gas lamp fixed to the wall outside lighting up the entrance to the hotel. It was directly below us so we didn't bother with any other light in the room, just a fire.

We had chicken. I remember that because I had to ask Joey what it was. I couldn't recognise the meat under all the sauce. To my way of thinking there's something criminal in smothering good meat, but everything in Paris seemed to come in disguise. Back home, people went wild for the French style, but as far as I could make out it was mainly a complication of the natural.

Anyway, the waiter brought our meal up to the room under a little silver dome. He placed the covered platter at the centre of the table and then he fussed about, tweaking the tablecloth and flapping out our napkins until he was satisfied that we were good enough for what we were about to receive.

Then, with a flourish that wouldn't have disgraced Swami Jonah when he was doing the disappearing dove (I say dove, but the mangy thing was really a pigeon caked in chalk dust), he swept the dome away to reveal a pool of lumpy yellow gravy.

'*Voilà!*'

He stood, expectant like, by the side of the table, the cover held high in his white-gloved hand. I wasn't entirely sure what to do – give him a round of applause or maybe the bird? He was so solemn and impressed with himself that I got the urge to laugh. Once it came on me, I couldn't stop it. I tried to pretend I was coughing into my napkin, but I caught Joey's eye and that was the finish of us.

The steaming liquid in the dish jiggled about as the table

rocked under my elbows. Joey just about managed to draw himself together. He said something to the waiter and pressed a coin into his hand. Then we watched in a most painful silence as the man stalked back to the door, giving every impression, if you'll pardon another of Nanny Peck's observations, that he had a ripe Kerry Pippin stuffed up his fundamental.

Once he was gone, I repeated this to Joey, who remarked in his beautiful toff English that with an arse that tight it was more likely a pineapple. The two of us began to laugh so loud that I'm sure the carriage men lined up on the street outside three storeys down could hear us.

That was a thing about Joey – he wasn't like Lucca who wrinkled his nose whenever I used an expression unfit for a lady. No, my brother had always had a way of talking low, but making the words sound like something Queen Victoria herself might let slip. I remembered then how he held court with his fancy friends at The Lamb, and at that moment I realised how blind I'd been.

That second evening was when we really began to act natural together again – like the past two years hadn't happened. We were just a couple of kids, larking about and teasing each other. After our meal – which, to be fair, tasted better than it looked – we sat there in a comfortable glow and made up stories about the men and women passing in and out of the hotel. It was a game we played when we were small.

The front room of our old lodgings in Church Row looked out over the street. If you closed the shutters up behind you and squeezed into the narrow space before the window you could see down to the corner and into the houses opposite. When Ma was taking a bad turn and Nanny Peck was sitting with her in the back room, me and Joey used to play the story game, sitting sideways on the ledge facing each other with our knees and toes touching.

Now we watched the comings and goings outside Le Meurice; elegant city couples, provincial businessmen fluffed out like bantam cocks, silent spouses walking a lifetime apart, lovers with less than a Rizla between them, and the kept women. Joey said you could always smoke them in Paris – their dress was much finer and better set than anything a husband would pay for. He reckoned he could tell visitors from England too. 'Something about the cut,' he said, and I noticed the way he took in my good blue frock.

It was raining hard and every time a carriage drew up a fat little porter in a long red coat bobbed down the hotel steps to shield the arrivals with an umbrella the size of Nanny Peck's Sunday crinoline. Caught in the lamplight, the raindrops looked like a scattering of crystals as they rolled off the rigid black shell and shattered on the steps.

I knew it was a chance to talk proper, but it felt so good to slip back into the old ways that I didn't want to spoil the magic of it. And I do think that my brother worked a kind of spell over me – the sort that blinds your eyes and binds your tongue. I was the adoring little sister again, hanging off his every word, laughing at his stories and lapping up his attention like an abandoned kitten that couldn't believe its luck to be back in a warm kitchen.

If you was to ask me now exactly what it was we talked about for that second evening at Le Meurice, there's barely a full sentence I can recall – excepting one thing that struck me as odd. We watched a family – mother, father and four little girls all done up like porcelain dolls – tumble out of a coach and scurry up the steps into the dry. Joey asked if I'd ever thought about having children of my own. I laughed and said I needed to find myself a man before I could make him an uncle.

When I cast back, I see them days in Paris through a haze of red and gold; velvet-padded restaurant chairs, gilded mirrors, floating down the river on a pleasure barge done out with crimson banquettes, rose-flecked light alive with gleaming sparks of dust falling through the kaleidoscope windows of a darkened church, a night at the opera that felt like sitting in an open jewel box, the scent of the crowd; all leather, lavender, lemon and a hundred other fine foreign things rolling off them in waves of prosperity.

Oh yes, I soon came to see that plenty of the types my brother mixed with were a good deal cleaner and fancier than the ones he'd left behind in Limehouse. Me and Lucca included.

There was one place, though, that put me in mind of The Gaudy. We took a cab and went on there after the opera on the third night. It was a dance and drink hall, hot with the smell of bodies, tobacco and mecks. I could feel the throb of the music and the stamp of the dancers as we pushed through the crowd. Joey went first holding my hand and Lucca followed behind.

The young men, and most particularly the girls there, were a lot wilder than the ones back home. The dancing had a whirling physical violence to it that threatened, but never quite descended into, a riot. It was infectious. The pulse of it spread from my feet up my legs and into my body. I wanted to

be out on that dance floor, spinning and stamping and shrieking with the rest of them.

I tugged Joey's hand. He turned, grinned and mouthed
some words I couldn't make out. I tapped my ear and shook
my head. He nodded and pointed at a row of booths set along
a wall to the left. I noted the way my brother was just as
comfortable among that set as in the grand dining rooms of
the city. I followed as he moved from table to table, a nod
here, a wink there, a smile, some larky patter in the lingo, a
generous tip to the red-haired girl with a tilted nose and a
gap-toothed grin who brought a jug of some gut-rot green
stuff to our booth. Half an hour in and Lucca was over by
the stage talking to a knot of gents gathered by the music pit.
From their looks I took them for four brothers – they all had
white blond hair, cat-slant eyes and cheekbones you could
slice a ham on.

When Joey took me back to the hotel later that evening,
Lucca didn't come with us, but early next morning he was
back at my door with a guilty smile and a ribbon-covered box
of sweet pastries so beautiful I almost didn't want to spoil
them by biting into them.

Little works of art they were, no wonder he bought them.

⚓

'The dress suits you. I think you are made for the Parisian
style.' Lucca stepped back and nodded. 'It is perfect. Turn to
the left.' The grey watered satin skirt whispered as it moved
with me. The dress was cut narrow and low. Complicated
pleats and folds of material gave the bodice the look of a

close-petalled flower about to open and the skirt was caught up at the back in a parted bell-like shape with a fantail of silver lace trailing out behind.

I stared at myself in the mirror and I hardly recognised the girl looking back. I say girl, but with my hair plaited and looped up top, my waist tightened to a pint glass and other parts of me looking more prominent than felt proper, it was a woman I saw there – for the first time ever. I didn't know how I felt about that.

'Does it look . . . decent, Lucca? I don't want to be taken for a bangtail or whatever they call them over here.' I glanced at the handwritten note on the table.

'You look like a lady. And the maid has done an excellent job with your hair.' He smiled and slipped into his jacket, pulling the sleeves so that the buttons at the cuffs lined up. 'She said it was unusual for a woman to travel without a servant, but was happy to assist when I explained that you were travelling on urgent family business and had to leave London without making arrangements. Also, the coins helped – she didn't ask another question when I counted them out in front her.'

He raised a brow. 'I think they find us to be a most interesting couple. At least our rooms are on separate floors, otherwise we would be a scandal.'

Lucca was done up fine too. Matter of fact, I'd never seen him look so smart. I could tell he was revelling in it – there was a streak of vanity in Lucca Fratelli that hadn't been burned away.

Joey sent the evening clothes to our rooms. Monogrammed boxes padded out with scented tissue had arrived that morning. In both cases the fit was almost perfect, although I'd had to ask the hotel seamstress to adjust the filmy, chiffon-covered straps of the bodice so they didn't gape.

I was going to do it myself. Not having been away before I'd packed for all eventuals, I even had my sewing kit with me. Lucca pulled a face when he saw my things laid out on the brocade cover of the hotel bed and he laughed out loud when I showed him all the clothes hung up by a chamber maid in a mahogany wardrobe half the size of my old room at Mother Maxwell's. I pointed out that as I'd bought a trunk for the trip it seemed a shame not to use it.

I told him about the straps on the evening dress and what I needed to do to make them sit straight, but he said that when you are staying in an establishment as grand as Le Meurice, there are people to take care of that sort of thing. It made me wonder again about his way of living in the days before the fire took his looks, but I didn't say anything. That was the past, and I didn't want it to cast a shadow now I'd found Joey again.

'How do I walk in this rig without taking a tumble?' I moved away from the mirror and felt the waterfall of lace at the back of the dress twist with me. It was heavy and made of many layers, some of them sewn with tiny glittering beads. I couldn't work out how to keep it from winding round my ankles.

Lucca knelt beside me. 'There is a loop here in the under-skirt. May I?'

He burrowed around at my feet. 'Here – take this in your left hand, hook it around your ring finger. When you walk along a hallway let it drop so that the dress flows behind you.

If you go upstairs or if you dance—'

I snorted. 'We've been invited to dinner, not a bleedin' ball, Lucca.'

He glanced up at me. 'Perhaps not tonight, but you will wear this dress again, Kitty, trust me, I know you will. You look like a Botticelli.'

He must have dialled the look on my face because he sighed and followed up on that immediately. 'Sandro Botticelli – a painter of the Renaissance, famous for his beautiful women – angels, goddesses. That's how you look in this dress. Joseph chose well.'

It was our last evening in Paris. We'd spoken about meeting in the early afternoon and later going out to dine, the three of us, so I was surprised when I read the note that arrived with the clothes. I'd got the distinctive impression – mostly by omission – that Joey wanted to keep us away from rue des Carmélites and his life there, but the invitation was clear.

Kitty,

Forgive the formality and brevity of this note. I am afraid I cannot join you early today as planned. There is something I must attend to. To make amends, I write to invite you to dine at my house tonight. We gather at nine.

I have taken the liberty of selecting a gown for you. You will find it in the box labelled 'Maison Cordelle'. I hope you like it, little sister, I chose it most carefully; firstly as a gift and secondly because I want you to shine for my friends. I will send a carriage. I trust Lucca will also join us.

It is time for honesty.

J

I'd read that note a hundred times. *We gather at nine.* I wondered what that meant, exactly. And there was the other line too, *I want you to shine for my friends.* I looked at my blue frock folded neatly at the top of the open trunk. I would have worn it this evening if Joey hadn't sent the dress I was wearing now.

Lucca fussed around my ankles again, smoothing out the train so that it pooled in a shimmering semi-circle behind me. He cleared his throat. 'You understand about tonight, what you will see?' He didn't look up. Instead he busied himself with his cuffs, pulling them down so that just the right amount of white showed at the wrist.

Then he stood, brushed lint from his knees and stared at himself in the long dressing mirror, adjusting the starched collar of his shirt so that it rose higher on his scarred neck. He swept his dark hair forward and nodded at the half-handsome young man reflected back at him.

After a moment he caught my eye in the glass. 'You do know what I mean, Fannella?'

I nodded. '*It is time for honesty*? That's what his note said.'

'But are you ready for it?'

Tell truth, I did wonder about that – when the images came I chased them out of my head. I pulled myself up straight and shifted my shoulders to bring the gauzy straps higher.

'I've seen a lot in the halls, Lucca – and on the streets. I'm not a country parson's chavy, am I? I know right enough what you're on about.'

'To know is one thing, but . . .' He stared hard at me and I couldn't read his expression, not exactly. It might have been concern, but it could just as easily have been a challenge.

The little gilt clock on the mantle struck three notes, it was quarter to nine already.

I tried to smile. 'I'll deal with it.'

Chapter Six

The conversation and laughter died the moment the Monseigneur ushered us into the vaulted candlelit dining room. At the far end of the table someone rose to greet us, but I didn't, immediately, realise who it was.

I knew what I was expecting to see. I knew what that house was, and I knew what my brother was, even though I hadn't put it into words, but the reality of it, perhaps I should say the *unreality* of it, was almost impossible to take in.

The air was heavy with scent and wine. Little points of light sparked off the crystal ware set along the table. They flickered on the walls giving the oddest impression that everything was moving, like we were on water.

A score of blurred faces turned to me and a trickle of sweat ran down my back under the stiff grey satin as Joey walked towards me. His face was artfully and perfectly painted – just enough to emphasise the delicate curve of his lips, the tilt of his heavily lashed eyes and the slant of his cheekbones.

Joseph Peck was a beautiful woman.

Just as Lucca had told me that night when it all came tumbling out, '*He could pass. You might take him for a girl – for a woman.*' I tightened my hold on the feather fan that had arrived with the dress.

Then from nowhere the old cow's voice went off. '*I will return your brother to you . . . in due course. But whether you will accept him, now, that is another matter. You will find him much altered.'* I was back in that churchyard by Ma's grave staring at Lady Ginger's white-painted face – her lips cracking into a sticky black smile.

She knew.

She knew how I'd feel at this moment and she enjoyed the power of knowing it. I heard a snap and something clattered to the floor. I'd gripped the carved ivory handle of the fan so hard I'd cracked it in two.

I wasn't aware of anyone in the room, now, just Joey in his elegant sea-green gown. A thick golden rope of hair was coiled and set high on his head, soft ringlets framed his pointed face, green tear-cut gems trembled from his ears and a treble row of glittering jewels wound about the pale skin of his throat. He was like some mythical creature, a mermaid or a siren – something alien, not my brother.

'You are most welcome.' He said the words softly and smiled. As he came close I could see a vein moving in his neck and a muscle twitching at the corner of his eye. He held his hands out to me – they were trembling. To cover, he clasped them firmly together and repeated my name, but when he spoke his blue eyes slid down away from mine.

I felt my belly boil with anger and something sharp stabbed at my temples. I felt the skin on my neck and face flush up.

You mare, I thought. You monstrous, unnatural, wicked creature, Kitty Peck.

I hated myself.

Of a sudden I realised how difficult this was for *him*, not me. I was so wrapped up in my own concerns I couldn't see what was happening. This wasn't about me, at all.

'Kitty?' The whisper sounded like a plea.

For a second I couldn't answer. I looked down at Joey's tight locked hands and I truly grasped how much this moment meant. He was trusting me with his secret, with his soul. He was honouring me with the truth. In front of his friends, Joseph Peck was making himself utterly vulnerable because I was his sister and because he loved me.

God knows what he thought I might do or how I might react. I thought then, and still think now, that it was the bravest thing I've ever seen anyone do. At that moment my heart nearly burst with pride and love for my brittle, brilliant, beautiful brother.

I didn't say anything, I couldn't, there was something balling in my throat. The tip of my nose prickled and my eyes glassed up. I reached to take Joey's clenched hands in mine and raised them to my mouth. I kissed them gently and then I looked direct at him. There were tears slipping down his cheeks too. They left a silvery train in the fine pearly powder that made his face gleam in the candlelight. I shook my head and reached across to wipe them away.

'No need for these, eh?' I smiled and suddenly caught him up in a fierce hug, burying my face in the scented lace of his neckline.

'You are beautiful, Joseph,' I whispered. 'You always have been and you always will be.'

I felt a huge shudder go through my brother's body. He kissed my right cheek and then my left and then took a step back and held me away from him a little way.

'Thank you.' He couldn't quite say the words aloud, so he

mouthed them and blinked hard as more tears threatened to ruin his makeup. Then he pulled me tight against him and murmured into my ear.

'Josette, that's what my friends call me here.'

I nodded. 'I already know that. It's a pretty name.'

As we stood there locked together I was dimly aware of a great sound crashing around us. It wasn't the end of the world or anything biblically judgemental, it was the sound of whoops and cheers and applause.

I liked Joey's – rather, Josette's – friends.

Upwards of twenty of them were gathered round the table that night, mostly French, but I was introduced to a couple of English lads who were nearly as pretty as my brother, a striking Spaniard who sang for us with such sweet sadness that she (he) would have been an asset to any of my theatrical establishments (the punters always liked a bit of misery, 'specially if it was foreign and came with a good pair of ankles), and a little party from the East.

Two of them were dressed as girls and two of them were dressed as men, but according to Joey, they were all male and all Russian, and they were nearly all dancers from The Moika.

It was the second winter The Ballet Moika had come to Paris. The performers – the male and properly female ones – were, according to Joey, the toast of the city. Half the Imperial court had followed them and the locals had gone wild for '*le style russe*', wrapping their heads in jewelled turbans and paying over the odds for cobble-dusting furs. Apparently there was a particular fashion for emeralds among the noble Russian ladies and now the women of Paris were draping themselves with rivers of stones to keep up with them.

Joey reckoned the hock shops over on rue des Rosiers had never done such trade seeing as every woman of taste was prepared to pawn her grandmother's jewels – and quite possible the old girl along with them – in order to wrap a string of emeralds round her neck.

'They are striking, don't you think?' Joey reached for his glass.

I laughed. 'Emeralds? I've never given it much thought. You don't see many in Limehouse, that's for certain. Do you remember Ma's pearls? She used to let me wear them in Church Row, but they went missing—'

I stopped myself. Ma's pearls had gone missing around the same time as Joey. I likely knew what had happened to them now, but if my brother picked anything up from that it didn't show.

'I didn't mean emeralds, Kitty, I meant my guests – the Russians. They have a certain look to them, don't you think?'

As if he sensed us watching, one of the dancers dressed in men's gear – breeches and a loose white shirt open at the neck – turned to look back down the table towards us. Joey raised his glass.

The lean handsome face was familiar. I was sure I knew him.

Of course! He was one of the cheekbones who'd been chatting to Lucca at the dance hall the night previous. Now I looked proper, I realised that they all – all the Russians that is – had luminous pale hair and slanting pale eyes set into wide angular faces. They were striking, I couldn't deny it, that was surely the right word for them all, but there was something fierce about them too.

The man stood and raised his own glass in reply to Joey. Then he raised it to me, smiled and winked. He was tall and muscular – his gesture had a sweeping grace.

'Ilya. He is one of The Moika's principal dancers.' Joey nodded his head in reply and took a sip from his glass. 'On stage he jumps so high that sometimes you hold your breath watching, wondering when or even if he will come down again. I met him last winter during their first season in Paris and he introduced me to his friends. Akady is to his left, in the blue gown, Stefan to his right, in red, and directly opposite Akady, our friend Lucca is talking to Misha, who is the leader of the orchestra, not a dancer. He is a very clever man, a linguist – Misha is also The Moika's fixer in chief.'

'I wondered who that was. He doesn't look like a dancer.' I smiled. 'Lucca's hardly said a word to me all night.'

Joey looked down the table to the midpoint where Lucca was engaged in deep conversation with a broad-shouldered man whose hair was so fair it was almost white in the candlelight. Lucca was sitting with his back to me, elbow on the table, resting the scarred half of his face in his hand. I knew he was trying to cover the worst of it, but it didn't seem to matter to the intense young man with him. I remembered that Giacomo, Lucca's great love, had been a musician too.

'I . . . introduced them on the second day you were here, when you had a headache – or said you did.' Joey adjusted one of his dangling earrings which had got twisted up in a ringlet. 'You were right. There were things Lucca and I needed to say.

It was clever of you.' He paused. 'You know, he told me a lot more about you, that afternoon – what you'd done, how you really saved those girls.'

He smoothed a wrinkle in the starched white tablecloth, the gemstone bracelet at his wrist glittered in the candlelight. 'She chose well.' The words were almost a whisper.

I covered his hand with mine. 'From what I heard, I don't think she had much choice.'

He shook his head. 'Our grandmother knew exactly what she was doing. She always does.'

There was a shriek as a log burning in the depths of a huge marble fireplace halfway down the room spat out a shower of golden sparks. A man who was sitting with his back to the hearth erupted from the table and made a great show of flapping out the trailing skirts of his lacy dress. When he was satisfied he wasn't incendiary, he stood to one side and fanned himself most energetically as the Monseigneur moved his chair to a safer place.

I wondered if the old boy had come with the house, and if so I wondered what I was paying him. I watched as he ushered flustered Fanny back to a seat and discreetly arranged her skirts so they were folded away from any possibility of ig-nition. He was almost like part of the furniture. Perhaps he'd been in Lady Ginger's employ here long before Joey came? The thought came to me then that he still might be. Perhaps the old cow had set a spy on my brother? I wouldn't put it past her.

'Do you know where she's gone?' It was the question I asked the Beetle every time he scratched up another legal piece for me to sign.

Joey shook his head. 'I didn't even know she had gone until you came. I do know this – she had another place. My guess is that it was somewhere far away from Limehouse and Salmon Lane. She went there once when she was taken with the winter sickness and didn't want people to know how frail she was. If the Barons . . .' He paused and his fingers tightened round the stem of his glass. 'She came through and she came back, but she never told me where she'd been. Lady Ginger doesn't like to show weakness and she never makes mistakes.'

He turned to look at me directly. His blue eyes darkened and his mouth twitched into a sort of smile. 'And I don't think you will either, Kitty.'

Mistakes?

For a moment another face swam into my head. James Verdin looked at me in just the way he'd done when he sat at the end of my bed after that first time, after that only time. Of a sudden I felt my cheeks burn up.

'So, you're running an establishment here?' The question tumbled out of my mouth before I'd had time to phrase it more elegantly. Fact was, I didn't want James in my thoughts and I said the first thing that came into my mind to replace him.

Joey was silent. He frowned and turned the glass about in his hand so that the cuts in the crystal caught the light. I cursed myself.

'I like to think of it as a refuge.'

He looked down the table. Someone was playing a piano now in the next room and a couple of Joey's friends rose from their places, wrapped their arms around each other's tightly corseted waists and drifted off in the direction of the sound.

The Monseigneur appeared with another bottle of champagne and began to fill glasses lined up on a tray set to the side of the door. The room was filled with the murmur of conversation punctuated by laughter. You'd have taken it for a society feast – if you didn't look too close at some of the ladies present.

Joey took a sip and placed the glass carefully back on the table, moving it a little to cover a stain on the cloth. 'The world isn't kind to people like us, Kitty. My friends come here because they know they will be safe and for a short time they will feel . . . ordinary. Do you . . . *can* you understand that?'

I looked down at my hands in my lap as he continued. 'I was blinded by her, you know – our grandmother. When she told me about Paradise and all the doors that were going to be opened it was as if a kind of madness descended on me. It was the same at first with—' He broke off and filled my glass to the brim.

'I . . . I've done a lot of things I'm not proud of, Kitty, but I am proud of this.' He gestured at the room and the easy, comfortable people settled around us. 'It's one thing I am not ashamed of.'

I knew then that I would never tell him who really owned 17 rue des Carmélites. Better that he thought The Lady had allowed him, *trusted* him, to prove himself here without any strings attached.

'It's a fine place, Joey. You should be proud.' I raised my glass as a toast, and champagne fizzled over my fingers. Tell truth, I didn't like the stuff much. It didn't taste clean like gin and it gave me a roaring head.

'To you and to your friends, J . . . Josette. I'm glad you've introduced me to them.'

'Are you?' He sounded oddly eager and there was something else there.

I nodded. 'This is your home now. They're your family too, aren't they?'

He reached for my hand and squeezed it. 'Yes . . . yes, I suppose they are.' He looked down the table at the people still lingering in the room. His perfectly arched brows knitted together for a moment as he ran a thumbnail over his full lower lip. I recognised the gesture – when we were kids and played at cards together I always knew if he was about to take a risk. He was turning a question in his mind.

'Actually, there's someone else I want you to meet, Kitty. He's been waiting upstairs.'

Chapter Seven

Joey knocked twice on the door and pushed it open. He stood to one side and let me go in first. The room beyond was in darkness apart from a small fire burning in the grate. I could smell apple wood again, laced with a rich leathery scent, and I could hear the soft ticking of a clock.

I was confused, the room appeared to be empty. Joey followed me in and closed the door behind us.

'David?'

I wondered who he was speaking to, but then a tall figure rose from a chair set in shadow by the window. As he stood, the man put a tumbler down on the small table next to the chair.

'Will you tend to the lamps, Josette, a little more light?' The voice was low and I recognised a Scottish burr. Joey took a taper from a spill pot in the hearth and crossed the room to light a pair of oil lamps set either end of a long low table pushed up against the wall. The flickering light showed up a painting of a woman in a black evening gown. She was in profile, one hand clutching a string of beads to her chest, the other raised to her forehead. I was minded of Mrs Conway striking one of her tragical attitudes and the guilty thought came to me that it was very likely the old girl would look something similar after we'd had the little chat I'd been putting off.

Joey blew out the taper. 'Kitty, this is my friend David – David Lennox.'

There was a rustling noise as the man closed the curtains. He turned to look at us.

'There, that's better. I can see you both now.'

More to the point, I could see him.

Truly, David Lennox was the most handsome man I'd ever set eyes on. He was almost a head taller than Joey, well put together, but lean with it. His skin was dark, not as black as some of the sailors who put in at the docks – in the soft glow of the lamps it had a smooth russet quality like a roasting chestnut. He had a broad forehead and close-cut dark, wiry hair. It was his eyes I remember most from that first meeting, they were an odd shade of green, like broken bottle glass that's been turned against the stones in the river. Set against his skin they didn't look right, only they didn't look wrong neither.

He smiled and his wide full lips revealed perfect even teeth. I thought he looked like a prince from one of them Arabian tales Ma used to tell us.

'It's true then. You two are almost identical.'

I glanced uncertainly at Joey. I hadn't really thought too deep about it, but in the dim light of the room, now I looked, I could recognise the line of my own features in his. Was that how others saw me?

David stepped forward and bowed. He took my hand and raised it to his mouth. 'Forgive the darkness. I find it easier to think when I stare into a fire.' There was a relaxed warmth to the tone of his voice.

'And it's safer.' Joey went over to the window and adjusted the curtains to make sure they covered the glass completely.

He turned. 'You're sure you weren't followed?'

David shook his head. 'No, I was careful. Anton took my hat and cloak and left The Chapeau Rouge immediately after I went off stage. I waited for half an hour and then I left from the back of the theatre. If anyone had followed I would have known.'

Joey frowned. 'Anton took a risk?'

'Yes, I am grateful to him. But I'm certain that if he was followed they would realise it wasn't me soon enough. He was going on to The Lapin d'Or, so once inside—'

Joey interrupted. 'Kitty, sit down please. There's something we . . . David must ask of you.' He gestured to a chair by the fire, but I didn't move. The pair of them were talking over my head. They were deadly serious about something and it didn't sound like a stroll in the park.

'What's going on?' I planted my hands on my waist and waited. 'Well?'

'So, you want me to take this baby back to London?'

David nodded and leaned forward. He was sitting on the opposite side of the hearth from me, half in shadow. He took a pull on a long dark cigarette. 'You're leaving tomorrow, that's right, isn't it?'

I looked up at Joey standing behind my chair. 'I don't think it's going to be as easy as you two suppose. The kid'll need travel papers for one thing. And what the bleedin' hell are they going to say back home when me and Lucca turn up with a Moses basket?'

'You'll think of something, Kitty. Say you're looking after him for a friend.' Joey put his hand on my shoulder. 'It won't be far from the truth.'

'And what is the truth? I think I've a right to know a bit more before I agree to anything. It's not like taking a stray dog back with me, is it?' I pushed at the ringlets that were springing free from the elaborate coil the hotel maid had pinned to my head. It was beginning to pull at my temples. I longed to tear it all apart and shake my hair free.

'There *is* more, isn't there? You two are keeping something from me. For one thing, whose baby is it?'

I saw a look pass between the pair of them. 'It's complicated—' Joey began, but David cut in.

'He's mine. The boy is mine and his name is Robbie after my father.'

'But I thought you were . . .' I bit my lip, unsure what to say next. Tell truth, I thought he was one of Joey's mates, only not tricked out on this occasion.

David smiled and shook his head. 'No, I'm not . . . what you think, Kitty. I've known your brother since he came to Paris two years ago. Our circles crossed. I make my living as a performer – a ballad singer. I came here from Glasgow in '76 and the city has been good to me . . . until now. Joey and I have many friends in common – in the halls, in the theatres—'

'In the ballet.' Joey cut in sharp there. I saw another old-fashioned look pass between them.

David threw the cigarette into the fire and took my hands in his. 'It's the old story. I . . . got a girl into trouble. It wasn't supposed to happen, but we weren't careful. She can't keep the child.'

79

'Why not?' I was indignant. 'There's plenty of girls back home in that position and they get by. Are you telling me they keep their morals knotted up so high in Paris that a working girl's never had a misfortune?'

David stared hard at me. I blinked and looked down. His eyes were the most unusual shade against his dark skin. Sitting so close, I realised that the deep leather scent in the room was his cologne.

'It's not that, there are thousands of infants in Paris without benefit of a father.' His Scottish accent came more distinct now. I could smell the faint sweetness of brandy on his breath as he continued. 'I didn't realise until just before Robbie was born who his grandparents were. They are an old family – a . . . powerful family who wouldn't want the dark-skinned son of a singer from the halls among them. And now they . . .'

'They are searching for him.' Joey finished the sentence off, but I could tell there was a lot tucked in behind those words.

'That's why we need to get Robbie away.' Behind me Joey moved closer to the hearth. I watched him twist about a china figure perched on the edge of the marble mantle. It was a shepherd boy with a lamb curled close to his heels. I realised with a jolt that it was Nanny Peck's fortune piece, the one she always rubbed for 'the luck of it'. He'd taken that as well.

Joey shifted the ornament a fraction to the right, running the pad of his thumb across the boy's pottery rump. 'When you arrived this week, Kitty, I saw that there was somewhere he could go. We've all been trying to shield him. Our people are close, but it's getting more difficult. This will confuse them – no one would think of looking in London. Not if we are careful and move quickly.'

'What about his mother, what's she got to say about this?'

David answered me. 'She wants him to be safe.' He stared into the flames. I noticed he wore a signet ring on his little finger like the one I still wore on a chain round my neck – Joey's ring. I meant to give it back to him. I felt it cold against my skin under the ruffled neckline of my dress as he continued.

'It's hard, but it will be for the best. We can't risk the family tracing him. That's why I came here alone tonight. The less you know the better. It will be safer that way. I wouldn't want to cause you any harm.' He tightened his grip on my hands and I found myself thinking that despite everything, whoever she was, little Robbie's mother was a lucky girl.

'He's almost seven months old and as bonny a bairn as you could wish for. What do you say?' David's voice was thick like he was trying to swallow down a lump of gristle and there were tears now in his wide green eyes.

I had to look away again. I wanted to help him, but the thought of taking a baby back to Paradise was ridiculous. I didn't know the first thing about looking after a kid.

He squeezed my hands. 'Kitty?'

I cast around for a reply.

'Listen, surely Robbie's mother . . .?' I began. 'Surely the two of you could go off somewhere. I don't see how taking him back to London with me is going to make things right? When all's said and done, the best thing is for a child to be with its mother.'

'That's impossible.' David's voice was almost a whisper.

'There are things I cannot tell you. I wish I could, but if you were to know any more it could be dangerous, for you as well as for the child. You must take my word on that. You are my only hope.'

I caught at something there, '*my*'?

'You two still together? You and his mother, I mean?'

He glanced up at Joey. My brother shook his head.

David cleared his throat. 'We are not.' He paused and made a sound that was almost a laugh. 'And I was sore glaikit to think we ever could be. No, Robbie is my responsibility entirely. The family will never acknowledge him, or me.' He slumped and dipped his head. A warm tear splashed onto the back of my hand caught in his. I noticed how his close-cropped black hair spiralled at the crown of his head and I got the urge to stroke it.

'But we are agreed on one thing. If anything were to happen to our boy . . .' he faltered. 'Will you help us, Kitty? It would mean the world.' He didn't look up.

I could feel something pricking away at me somewhere deep inside, something like a warning I suppose. Nanny Peck would have said that her marrow was calling from her bones. I closed my eyes. I'll say whatever comes into my head, I thought.

David was still holding on tight. I'll admit I liked the feeling of it – my hands were cupped entirely in his like a couple of wrens in a nest. Another warm wet drop fell onto my skin. He smoothed it away gently with the ball of his thumb and carried on stroking.

'All right. I'll take him with me. I don't know what they'll think back in Limehouse, but I'll deal with it.'

I didn't even know I'd said it out loud.

The room went still for a moment, like we was all frozen. Even the clock on the mantle held its breath. I swear it felt that if I'd given the wrong answer just then, everything would have shattered and fallen around us.

Joey knelt down beside me. His skirts whispered and breathed out gently as the material folded itself to a new position.

'You needn't worry about papers. I've already had something drawn up.' He grinned when he saw the look on my face. 'I know you, Kitty. I was certain you would help . . . well, almost certain. It needn't be for long . . .' He glanced at David, who was still holding my hands. I could feel a gentle pressure as he squeezed my fingers.

'There are things we need to settle here in Paris to make it right. I'll send word when it's time. Then we'll both come to Limehouse to take him back. If there are still . . . difficulties here, you might go on to America with him – that's right, isn't it?'

David nodded. 'If we can afford the passage. It's a vast country, they'll never trace us there.'

'If it comes to it, I'll buy your passage when we are in London, David.' Joey placed his hand over mine. 'Thank you, Kitty. I'll be relying on your hospitality when we next meet. It will be . . . interesting to see Paradise again.'

'No! You can't.' I blurted out the words.

A look of raw pain flashed across my brother's painted face – I saw it clear. But he mastered it and then he smiled. 'Don't worry, little sister, I'll come as Joseph Peck, if that's what worries you?'

'No! I mean you can't come to London at all.' I remembered the peculiar phrase in Lady Ginger's letter. The pair of them looked at me like I was a bedlam.

'She told me to tell you that you can't – ever.'

'I don't understand. Who told you . . . what?' Joey's plucked brows shot into question marks.

'The Lady. When she knew I was set on coming here to find you she sent me a letter. Tell him '*Bartholomew waits*' – that's what she said.

My brother's face went grey as ashes left after a fire. I could see it plain, even through the pearl powder and the dabs of rouge.

'What does it mean, then, Joey? You told me she never makes mistakes.'

Chapter Eight

Lady Ginger never made mistakes, but I was beginning to think that perhaps I had.

It had been so easy, hadn't it? Those two had it all neat and prepared like a patter act. They'd caught me off guard and bounced me into taking the kid home. I was sure I'd have been more sceptic if I'd been on clean gin all evening and not that yellow stuff.

Don't take me wrong. I wanted to help David, he seemed a decent type – more than that, tell truth – and Joey was so certain of me that I didn't want to disappoint him. I was flattered that he asked – like he knew I would be. But now, standing here on the platform waiting for them, it was a different matter.

I hadn't told Lucca about the baby. There hadn't been a moment when it seemed right, and anyway, since we'd met up early in the hotel lobby he'd had a mood on him as black as Mrs Conway's best hairpiece. I suspected he was nursing a head, which was unlike him. Mind you, if them Russian boys he was fraternising with had been anything like Old Peter, it was likely his belly was boiling over with firewater and his head was ringing out like Stepney belfry.

I glanced at his face. Even his good side was rough this morning.

He looked up at the station clock again. 'We have to board now, Kitty.'

'Just another minute, please. I know he'll come.'

Lucca twisted his lip and made a sound under his breath that could have been a curse. He pulled the collar of his coat higher, folded the brim of his hat so that it sat lower to cover the scars and went a little further out to get a clearer view of the platform. He seemed almost as reluctant as me to climb aboard.

Scores of people jostled around us. Some were passengers – you could tell them from their sober grey travelling gear – but mostly they were families and friends seeing off visitors. Just down the platform a row of neat dressed, solemn-eyed children stood waving at a generously upholstered gent already safely ensconced on board. I noted that he didn't look up from his newspaper.

Three windows along, a thin young man with a prominent nose and a hunted look leaned out to clasp the hand of a pretty girl who was still standing on the platform. The girl was crying. He didn't say nothing, he just kept patting her fingers and squinting furtively at the clock. I didn't need to be an oracle in the way of Swami Jonah to tell that tempus wasn't fugiting fast enough as far as he was concerned.

Porters raced past, pushing trolleys stacked high with trunks and parcels. An over-officious guard, whose prodigiously buttoned navy blue uniform served as a lovely backdrop to his dander, kept tutting and sniffing as Lucca and me refused to go up the slatted brass steps and along to our compartment.

The engine whistle went off again and a cloud of gritty steam rolled down the platform. I covered my mouth and nose. Where were they?

When the maid had come to my room at six she seemed most surprised to find me sitting in my evening gown. I hadn't been there for long, mind, just an hour or so. She helped me out of the dress, unpinned my hair – which was unravelling nicely by itself – brought me up a basin of hot water and, after I washed, she packed away the last of my things and helped me get ready for the journey home.

The evening had ended abrupt. Joey wouldn't tell me what Lady Ginger's message meant. He said it was unfinished business and that he was grateful to hear it from me, but I could tell he was rattled. When I pressed him he clammed up, went to the door and called for the Monseigneur. It was clear I was being dismissed. I didn't know much French, but I'd picked up enough to recognise what '*elle quitte maintenant*' meant.

While I waited the three of us talked briefly about what would happen the next morning. It all sounded so simple. I think I was even excited. Looking back, I reckon the champagne fizzled up my judgement. The whole evening had the quality of a performance and now I was one of the players.

After we'd gone over it a couple of times, David stood up to leave. He thanked me again and reached out to take my hand in a formal farewell, but then something came over him. He stepped over and suddenly crushed me against his chest. I just came up level with his shoulders. I could feel his arms around me and I could smell the leather of his cologne and the tang of smoke on his gear. I tried to fix the sensations in my head so I could bring him back at any time.

That was when I knew I'd agreed to take David Lennox's boy back to London not for the sake of the child, but because

I wanted to please his father. I was ashamed of myself.

Ten minutes later a Paris hack was waiting for me out on the shabby street beyond the courtyard of 17 rue des Carmélites. The Monseigneur, who never seemed to sleep so far as I could make out, came with me all the way to the hotel. He didn't say a word the whole time we was alone together, he just watched me, his watery eyes glistening in the dim light of the lamp inside the carriage.

By the time I got back to Le Meurice there didn't seem much point in going to sleep, and I knew I wouldn't anyway. I threw some more coals onto the little fire waiting for me – they never let the rooms get cold in a high-class establishment – drew up a chair and I sat there thinking about what I'd agreed to. That was when I realised I'd made a mistake, but by then it was too late.

According to the station clock it was now six minutes to eight.

'Hold this, Fannella. I'll go to the entrance.' Lucca handed me his crumpled leather holdall and turned back to the gate. I heard him mutter something in Italian, and caught a couple of words, *'Mi ha promesso.'*

Joey had promised all right, I thought, wondering about the kid. I shouted after him, 'Where are you going?'

'Just to the gate. We are lost here. He'll never find us in time.'

'Then I'll come with you—'

'No. One of us must wait here in case. Joey knows the carriage, *si?*'

I nodded. 'But don't be long.' I looked anxiously at the clock again – less than six minutes, now. 'The boat train is always punctual on account of the connections. It won't wait for you, Lucca Fratelli.'

There was a great shriek from the engine up front as if to confirm what I'd just said. The last of the platform stragglers started to climb aboard now. Along the carriage, blinds were being thrown up and windows wound down as passengers said their farewells.

Behind me I heard the guard rattle the door to carriage B in annoyance as Lucca loped back to the entrance gate. In a second or so he was swallowed into the crowd and then the crowd itself disappeared in another rolling cloud of dirty grey smoke. I coughed as the stuff fugged up my eyes and lungs. I could feel smuts landing across my cheeks and my nose so I rubbed hard, wondering if I was doing more harm than good.

I couldn't believe they wouldn't come – they had every detail planned right down to the compartment number. Thinking about it now, I was certain they had the bones of it all mapped out long before we had that little chat last night.

I buried my chin in the stiff material of my travel coat collar and took a deep breath. The steam billowing around was thicker than a London fog, I couldn't make out a thing. Perhaps if I moved down a bit away from the engine I'd get a clearer view?

I gathered Lucca's bag in my arms and stepped blindly into the smoke. The platform was broad, maybe twenty foot across. If I could just get to a place where I was a bit more visible then Joey and David still had time to find me.

I couldn't see the clock overhead, but I reckoned there were five minutes to go. I moved across the platform and walked back a little way in the direction Lucca had gone. The steam cleared for a moment leaving me standing alone in a little window of fresh air.

There wasn't a train waiting over on this side and there were no people clogging up the view neither. I hugged the bag close to my chest – Lucca had travelled light – and swayed from left to right, craning my neck to see if anyone came through the steam. There was a rumbling noise, and then a bulky shadow in the smoke ahead gathered itself into a porter's trolley stacked so high I couldn't see the man behind pushing it. It was coming towards me and coming fast.

I stepped aside to let it pass, only it didn't. It swerved and came straight at me, the metal rollers gnawing at the platform as it gathered speed. I dodged to the right, but the trolley swung towards me again. The teetering packing cases strapped together in a pyramid taller than a man juddered and slipped to one side at the sharp change of direction.

I still couldn't see the porter, but I called out to warn him I was there. The words became a yelp of pain as the metal-bound corner of one of the trunks stacked aboard clipped the edge of my left leg, sending me and Lucca's bag toppling over the platform edge and down onto the track below. I lay there, stunned I think, for a second. The bag had fallen into the middle of the track just ahead of me. It had broken open and was lying on its side. Bits and pieces had spilled out and something white, a shirt perhaps, was flapping about almost indecently over the cinders. Lucca wouldn't be happy.

I blinked hard as I lay there and thought I should go and pick it all up. My ears were ringing from the fall, but then I realised that the noise was coming from somewhere outside my head.

The metal rail below my cheek was singing. Something was coming.

I snatched myself up onto all fours in the cinders and twisted my neck to look back down the track. Two golden eyes blinked in the steam and a whistle fit to wake the dead ripped through the air. I tried to stand, but the coarse hem of my coat was caught up in the bolts holding the rail. I yanked hard but it wouldn't come free.

I could feel my heart going off like a steam hammer. The rail beneath my left boot was shuddering now as the approaching engine grumbled into the platform. I screamed for help but my voice was lost in the rumble and metal of the oncoming train.

Where was old dander and buttons when I needed him, I thought?

Buttons?

I ripped at the horn buttons on my travel coat, there wasn't time to undo them – I just tore like a wild cat. Mostly they popped off, but two at the bottom were stubborn buggers. It didn't matter. I'd freed myself enough to shrug my way out of the straitjacket.

Still holding the shape of my arms and body, it crumpled like the rough grey case of a new-minted butterfly, as I sprinted off down the track past Lucca's broken bag, holding up the skirts of my good blue dress for fear of tripping over them. If I could just get enough speed up to hurl myself over the platform edge, I stood a chance.

The engine was less than six foot behind when I jumped. I could feel its lick on the back of my neck as I cleared the brick-lined edge and rolled aside.

'*Mon Dieu, c'est une fille!*' A gentleman with a fine pair of mutton chop whiskers living around his ears stared down at me in alarm. He didn't even try to help me up, just rolled his eyes as he took in the grease stains on my skirt and the hair falling loose from the roll on my head.

The train juddered to a halt. Immediately, shiny black carriage doors clattered open along the side like toppling dominoes. The gent was blocked from view by a woman in a vast hooped skirt thirty years past its prime, like its owner. I caught the sour breath of old moth and fresh piss as she stepped down over me and billowed between us.

I struggled, unaided, to my feet. The platform was almost solid now with the heaving mass of passengers alighting from the train that nearly killed me. What time was it? I pushed against the flow and within seconds I was lost in the scrum. My head was throbbing and lights were going off like fire crackers in front of my eyes. Had I missed them?

I shoved through the crowd until I was level with carriage B.

'Fannella! What on earth?' Lucca caught hold of my arm and span me around.

'Your coat—' He stopped when he saw my face. 'What has happened to you?' He reached out to wipe something from my brow and I saw red on his fingers. The engine – our engine – whistled again and another bank of steam roiled up.

'Did you find them?' My head was whirling. I felt like I'd taken in a skinful of Old Peter's noxious stuff myself.

'Kitty!'

I heard Joey before I saw him. Seconds later two young men, one tall and dark, one slight and fair, emerged from the smoke and hurried towards us. They were dressed in dull workwear the colour of French gravy, and both of them wore mufflers and caps.

Between them they carried a trunk strung on looped leather handles set on either side. They came to a halt just in front of us and set the trunk down carefully. I felt, rather than saw, Lucca stiffen in surprise.

'You're bleeding.' Joey reached out to touch my forehead just as Lucca had done. I saw him dart a look at David, who was reaching into the pocket of his jacket.

'Here. Take it.' David handed me a white square. 'What happened to you, lass?' He bent to examine my face, brushing the tips of his fingers gently across my forehead and down the right side of my face.

The whistle shrieked again and the guard clapped his hands. '*S'il vous plaît, monter à bord.*'

I took the 'kerchief and gripped it tight. 'There's no time to explain. We have to go aboard.'

'First class, number 24?' David took up the strap again.

'It's that one.' I pointed at a blank train window several foot away. The blind was pulled down. I bit my lip as I looked down at the trunk. My ears were ringing again.

'Joey, take it up, quickly, man.' Without looking at me, David and Joey lifted the trunk. I made to follow them aboard, but Lucca pulled at my sleeve. 'Fannella?'

He glanced up at the two men who were just disappearing from view into the train corridor running alongside the compartments. He frowned and jerked his head in question.

'No time.' I gripped the brass rail and hauled myself up the steps. My head felt like a cracked egg.

I was surprised that Lucca didn't follow straight behind.

'*Monsieur! Le train quitte maintenant.*'

The guard barked again as Lucca dithered on the platform. He scanned the crowd one last time and then, finally, he climbed the steps to follow me along the narrow corridor to our compartment.

The trunk was now in the middle of the floor between the seats. David and Joey stood in the dim passage outside. I could feel the throb of the engine through the polished boards beneath my feet.

'I must thank you, bonny Kitty, from the bottom of my heart. I won't forget this.' David swallowed the words, took off his cap and twisted it about in his hands. He looked wretched. There were great bags beneath his eyes.

'Until we meet again.' He leaned forward to kiss my cheek and my skin burned.

'Robbie loves his poppet, don't lose it.' He whispered the words and then, before I could ask what he meant, he pushed roughly past. I knew it was because he didn't want me to see him crying.

Joey caught my hand and stared at me. I couldn't read his expression at that moment – there was such a stew of confusion, pain, fear and relief simmering through me I wasn't exactly sure what was happening. I thought he looked sad, but looking back now it was fear I saw in his eyes, I'd stake Paradise on it.

'Thank you.' He mouthed the words and hugged me tightly.

'Joey. I . . . I wish. Yesterday . . . I wanted to say—'

He put a finger to my lips. 'There's nothing to say. We've

found each other again and I must thank you, *for everything.'*
He kissed my forehead, wrapped his arms around me and
glanced at Lucca, who was staring at the trunk.

'Keep her safe, my friend. She's the only family I have.'

'Of course!' Lucca raised his hat as a sort of salute and
threw it down onto a seat. 'She is a sister to me too. Always
remember that.'

Joey nodded. He released me and reached across to clasp
Lucca's arm. The hollow sound of doors slamming echoed
down the corridor.

'You have to go, Joey. It's time.'

'It's never time, Kitty.' He winked and suddenly he was
the man – the bold, brazen, cocksure brother I adored. Truly,
Joseph Peck was the best actor I ever knew. Almost.

He blew a kiss, turned and sauntered away down the corridor. Old brass buttons and dander fluff was standing at the
end, twitching to slam the door.

I watched my handsome brother disappear from view and
then I heard the dismal, final thud.

'Quick, Lucca, open the blind and roll down the window.'
I needn't have asked. He was already working the brass
handle in the panelling, winding it furiously to make the glass
slide.

I stepped past the trunk, without giving a thought to what
was inside it, and leaned out. David had gone but Joey was
still there, wreathed in smoke. Lucca stood just behind me,
one hand gripping the rim of the glass. I could sense him
craning over my shoulder.

The train jerked forward and Joey started to walk alongside us.

'Joey, I've got these. They're yours. I meant to give them back to you.' I scrabbled at the high collar of the blue dress and freed the gold chain with the ring and the Christopher. I tried to pull it over my head, but the links caught up in my hair.

'Keep them.' Joey was running now as the train gathered speed. 'Or return them to me next time we meet. It can be a sort of promise between us?' He reached up to seize my hand. 'I . . . I'm sorry for everything, Kitty.'

I nodded. I couldn't speak. I felt like I was trying to swallow down a goose egg whole and my eyes were watering. It wasn't the smoke.

The train was rocking now. I had to drop Joey's hand, but I leaned out further to keep him in view. Lucca was no longer beside me. I heard a padded seat wheeze as he sat down heavily.

Joey stopped running. He waved and called something out but I couldn't hear him. There was an ear-splitting whistle and a tremendous whoosh as a torrent of steam rolled back from the engine ahead. My brother disappeared from view.

I covered my mouth and nose and stood on tiptoe desperate to catch a last glimpse of him. As the train veered to the left, the smoke cleared and I saw that there was someone standing watching at the very end of the platform, only it wasn't Joey. It was a man with snow-white hair.

A couple of seconds later he disappeared too as the train pulled round and a jagged outcrop of smoke-blackened buildings obscured my last view of the Gare du Nord.

I wiped my cheeks, drew back from the window and plonked down in the seat next to Lucca. I wanted to close my eyes and sleep for a hundred years, but my head felt as if it was about to burst. I couldn't tell if it was the drink from the night before or the tumble I'd taken. Both, most like. A little shower of lights went off in my head and a pain knifed through my right temple. I leaned forward, pressing the heel of my hand into my eye. At the same moment there was a wailing noise from the trunk. Lucca looked down at the lid, which quite clearly had holes punched across it at one end. The noise came again – the unmistakable sound of a baby crying.

Lucca stared at me and I stared at the trunk. He pushed his hair back behind his ears and bent to release the three clasps along one side. As the last one clicked open he spoke.

'Do you have something to tell me, Fannella?'

Chapter Nine

If I held my head to one side it was a bird, maybe two of them twined round each other. I narrowed my eyes. No, that weren't right, there was just one black body. It had two heads, though, which struck me as unnatural.

I swept Lady Ginger's dice up into my hand and scattered them across the desk again. They fell in a splayed triangle and I stared at the markings on their upper faces until the lines started to blur and shift for themselves. The same thing came to mind.

Whatever it was, it wasn't the answer I was looking for.

There was a knock. Before I had a chance to tumble the dice back into their rough green case, Peggy walked into the room that had, until the day before yesterday, been Fitzy's parlour at The Gaudy. Robbie was planted on her hip.

'We've been charming the ladies this morning, haven't we?' She jiggled him about and he squealed with pleasure. I noted that his big brown eyes never left her face as she settled in the chair across from me.

'He's got quite an eye, Kitty. He likes the pretty ones, don't you?' She shifted him onto her lap and bounced him about a bit, producing another gurgle of excitement.

Now, I knew Peggy would know what to do with a baby, but I have to admit that the way Robbie Lennox had taken to her was quite surprising. Looking back, I'd even say I was green of her, did I but know it.

'Do you want to hold him?'

I shook my head. 'He looks very happy where he is.'

Tell truth, every time I held him I felt like I might break him. He wriggled and fretted in my arms and his brown skin bruised up easy, even though I didn't cling tight. Not having much experience of handling anything more domestic than a mop I thought I was doing it wrong.

Lucca had been a wonder on that journey home. Once we'd got Robbie out of the trunk he was a natural with him. Then again, there was a time back in his village in Italy when he'd had four younger brothers and two sisters to look out for, so he knew what he was doing.

He'd had plenty to say to me about it all – and none of it was too comforting – but every time that baby made a sound he gathered him up in his arms, sang to him in Italian and was soft and sweet as mother Mary herself. Anyone passing our compartment would have taken us for a proper little family.

Peggy dabbed at some dribble on Robbie's chin. 'You've got his poppet, haven't you, Kit?'

I nodded and opened the drawer to my left. The small soft rabbit made from squares of brightly patterned cloth sat on top of the letter David had left in the trunk for me. I'd found it at the bottom after taking out a few bits of clothing, a blanket, glass feeding bottles and several large squares of cotton for Robbie's necessaries.

I handed the rabbit to Peggy and scooped up the dice.

'I don't know how you can touch them bleedin' things, they're evil, just like she was.' Peggy shuddered. 'There he goes . . .' She started to bounce the rabbit about on the edge of the desk.

I poured the dice back into the case and put it in the drawer on top of David's letter. If I'd hoped that it was a message of a personal nature, I'd've been very much disappointed. The envelope contained travel papers, good forgeries they was too, and a loving description of Robbie's likes and dislikes, accompanied by some advice on the best ways to handle him – feeding and that. He didn't take to cold so he was to be kept well wrapped. Apparently he had a tooth coming.

I realised then that David Lennox didn't have me down as the maternal type, not like Peggy. I closed the drawer and smiled as she hopped the rabbit back and forth. Peggy still had black rings under her eyes and I knew there was a rough bald patch at her crown where her thick dark hair wasn't growing. A few days before I went to Paris, I'd helped her find a mouse in Mrs Conway's wig store to cover it.

I'd told her pretty much everything about Joey and Paris, excepting going into personal detail about Robbie's father, and she was happy as a sparrow in springtime to take care of the little one for me. I had so much on my plate that I couldn't handle him, but I wanted to make sure he was cared for right, and Peggy was just the girl.

As far as she knew, I was looking after Robbie as a temporary favour to one of my brother's friends – none of them being the maternal type neither . . . which wasn't far off. When I told her about it, she didn't roll her eyes and she didn't mouth a mealy judgement, she just took the little lad in her arms.

Now, I didn't want any more acid talk about me in the halls than was already scraping the paint off the walls, so I asked her to put it round that she was sitting the baby for her cousin up Archway who had a misfortune to attend to – and everyone seemed happy with that.

Anyway, Robbie was good for Peggy.

Since that time at the warehouse she'd been low. Of course she had – anyone who knew the half of what those girls had been through would understand it. We'd sworn – all of us – never to talk about it to anyone. Thing is, Polly and Anna, they didn't want to be seen as damaged goods and I could see the justification of that.

They were damaged all the same, mind, damaged somewhere inside their heads. Polly had moved up north with her boy, Michael, and pretty red-haired Anna worked at The Gaudy where I could keep an eye on her.

I shut it all away in a place light never fell. I made sure of that. But Peggy wasn't like me, and worse had happened to her. I don't know what exactly, we never touched on the detail. All I knew is that she felt unclean, worthless somehow – and it made me sick to the stomach to think that someone as good and decent as my friend Peggy Worrow should ever think that of herself. If the man responsible was in hell – and I was sure he was – I hoped Old Nick was making him comfortable.

I locked the drawer and slipped the key into my pocket. 'They're just dice, Peg. The parrot's worse. It stinks, it doesn't like being alone and it curses like a docker's nancy, only in her voice. It's a good thing Robbie's with you most of the time, or he'd pick up a filthy mouth. I swear it's like she's in the room at The Palace with me sometimes.'

'Watching you! Did Joey know where she's gone?' Peggy huddled Robbie closer.

'No. He knows nothing more than I do, except that she has another place somewhere. Not here in Limehouse.'

'Well, let's hope she stays there.' Peggy looked at me narrow. 'You still all right about this, Kit?'

I nodded. 'Look at him. He couldn't be happier.'

'Not Robbie.' She smiled as a fat brown fist flailed against her arm to reach the rabbit. 'I mean what's happening to you. What's happening here. It's all so . . .'

She paused and shrugged. 'You're still the same Kitty, that's what I've been telling everyone.'

'What are they saying about me, Peg?'

She looked down to the floorboards where Robbie had dropped the rabbit. I could tell she didn't want to catch my eye.

'Well?'

'You know how they all go on – the girls in particular. It's just spite and flouncing mainly. But then there's Fitzy.'

I snorted. 'I thought he'd be happy to get his feet under Mr Leonard's desk at last. He's always wanted The Comet.'

It was true enough. The Comet was the finest of Lady Ginger's halls. It was no secret that Fitzpatrick had been itching to squeeze his wide chequered buttocks into the leather seat formerly occupied by Mr Leonard, the previous manager. The poor man had gone missing around the time Lady Ginger held her last gathering – sitting like a queen up on The Comet's curved stage while two of his fancy chorus girls had their heads shorn in public by her Chinamen. She was putting on a show for us all, making an example of Frances Taylor and Sukie Warren who had talked a little too freely about her affairs.

That was the same day The Comet's plaster ceiling came

down, taking me and my cage with it. Lady Ginger weren't too happy about that neither. I hoped dapper Solly Leonard had retired to his sister's place in Kent, but something told me that these days he was more likely to be pushing up daisies than pruning roses.

I was sorry – I liked him, which was more than I could say for old Fitzy with his tooth-rot breath and wandering hands. Trouble was, I needed him. No one kept order and no one knew the business of running the halls like he did. I didn't want him near me, but I didn't want to lose him – not yet, anyway. That's why I sent him over to The Comet.

'What's Fitzy been saying?' I leaned forward, drumming my fingers on the wood. 'You might as well tell me, Peg. I'd sooner hear it from you than anyone else.'

She hefted Robbie about in her lap. David Lennox was right, he was a bonny bairn.

'He's been stirring it with the hands. Putting it into their heads that you're not up to it – that they'll be out on their ears looking for dock work come summer because the business will fail.' She took a breath and looked at me direct. 'He says it's not natural them taking orders from a "chit of a girl".' She mimicked his heavy Irish.

'Well, that's rich – he was happy to take orders from Lady Ginger for long enough!'

'But she wasn't a girl, she was a . . .' Peggy trailed off. She was one of the few people who knew Lady Ginger was my grandmother and now she was uncertain what to say.

'She was a vicious old bitch,' I finished off for her. 'But she was a woman and Fitzy worked for her – they all did. What does your Danny think?'

'After what happened he'd do anything for you – you know that, Kit.' She shook her head. 'But he's confused as well. One minute you're a slop girl in the gallery, next you're an act and now you're running the place. They all want to know what's going on.'

I circled the pad of an index finger over a knot in the wood of the desk. She was right.

Apart from Peggy, Lucca and the Beetle, no one else knew exactly why Lady Ginger had left The Gaudy, The Comet and The Carnival in my hands, but I wasn't ready to explain it to them yet. And what's more, I wasn't ready to explain – to anyone other than Lucca – that I'd inherited a lot more than three flea-ridden halls on the City's skirts. I wasn't even ready to face that myself – or the meeting with the Barons. Every time I thought about it my mouth went dry. In a couple of weeks' time at the beginning of May I'd be dandled like a kitten in front of the most deadly company in London. It was a thousand times more dangerous than being hoisted up in that cage every night.

Just bringing it to mind now made my back prickle with sweat under the cotton blouse. I was beginning to wonder about the decision I'd made that day. I still had the words of the letter my grandmother left for me in her room at The Palace in my head.

The choice is yours, Katharine. You can walk from this room today and live a small, narrow life or you can build your own empire. Perhaps a better one. You have proved yourself capable in more ways than you know.

Capable of what? Everyone knew how the Barons ruled London.

'You need to make them respect you, Kit.'

'Respect?' My head shot up in surprise – but, of course, Peggy meant the hands.

I smiled. 'Now that's a funny word to use. Don't you mean fear? If you think I'm going to call a gathering to lay down the law like The Lady used to, you're mistaken. I'm not her and I'm not going to run the halls like she did. *I'm not.*' I thumped my hand down hard on the table and Robbie stopped wriggling and gurgling. He looked across at me and his lower lip trembled.

I stared at the bare walls of The Gaudy's office. Fitzy had carted his cheap patterned china, the fringed shawls and embroidered cushions over to The Comet. For such a big raw bruiser, his taste in furnishings was surprisingly dainty. I had no doubt that Mr Leonard's pristine office now looked like a trollop's parlour. And knowing Fitzy's keen appetite for gin it most likely smelt like one too.

Looking back it was odd, but the only items in the way of decoration I'd brought in so far had belonged to Nanny Peck. I'd tied her old plaid shawl over the back of the chair – I wrapped it round my shoulders for comfort when I was going over the books of an evening – and I'd placed a chipped blue and white jug that had come over from Ireland with her on the mantle over the fire. Every spring Ma filled that jug with daffodils and set it on the table in the front room at Church Row. That seemed like a hundred years ago now.

After Ma had died, The Gaudy had become a sort of second home for me – Joey had seen to that. I think it was why I wanted to set up my office here because it was a familiar place in an uncertain land. It was comforting to be with my 'family'.

I laughed out loud. I'd just parroted Lady Ginger at her most 'maternal'.

'You all right?' Peggy frowned. 'You still got a scar from that accident in Paris. Knocks on the head like that can be dangerous. I've heard you can go weeks before the effects show up and by then it's too late.'

I touched the crusted scab on my temple. I thought I'd pulled my hair forward enough to cover it. 'Is it obvious?' I asked. 'Do I need to dip into Mrs Conway's paint box?'

Peggy shook her head. 'No, but it don't matter about the size. It's where you were hit that makes the difference.'

I thought about that trolley again. Tell truth, I'd thought about it quite often since we come back. I couldn't shake the thought that the porter who'd knocked me over the platform and into the path of an oncoming train had known exactly what he was doing. Lucca was furious with the man, but when I finally told him what had happened – there being the question of a mysterious wailing baby in a trunk to deal with first – we were steaming through the countryside somewhere between Paris and Calais so it was too late to do anything about it.

When he'd calmed down a bit he said he was sure it was accidental, on account of the smoke and the crowd at the station, and he reckoned my recollection was likely muddled by the blow I'd taken. But I wasn't so sure.

Robbie started to cry now. He squirmed in Peggy's arms and plucked at the cotton of her dress with his fat little fingers. She began to rock him back and forth.

'He's tired, I'd best get him home. Danny's built him a crib, one that rocks. Your Lucca's going to come over and paint it.'

I let that pass.

'That working out all right then?' I nodded at Robbie. 'Danny doesn't mind you looking after him for me?'

She grinned broadly. For a moment there was a real flash of the old Peggy. 'Course not. Sometimes I think he's more fond of him than I am. He can tell Robbie's good for me, and besides, the money's handy, Kit. I'm grateful for that – we both are.'

'He still playing with the flat boys? I thought he'd given up on all that.' I tried to make the question sound casual.

Peggy shrugged. 'He swears on his mother's Bible he's not, but then half the pages are missing.'

'Surely he knows by now you can't throw good coins after bad? They never come back.'

'He's promised me, Kit, and . . . and I want to believe him. What's this, young man?' She dabbed the corner of her neat white cuff at something dribbling from Robbie's mouth.

I smiled. 'Well, if anyone can knock some sense into Danny Tewson you can, Peg, and you can keep an eye on him too. I'm glad you two are together now. You couldn't go back into lodgings on your own, not after . . .' I didn't finish, but Peggy knew what I meant. She stood and hoisted Robbie onto her left hip.

'Come on then, handsome. Mustn't forget poppet, must we?'

She scooped the patchwork rabbit from the floor. I watched as she knotted the ears securely around her belt, all the while swaying from foot to foot to soothe the kid. Like I said, she was a natural.

I could afford to pay Peggy well to look after Robbie

Lennox. The Beetle griped about it, but I was happy to set up a regular arrangement. I knew Danny was relieved too. According to Lucca he still hadn't got his gambling under control, although he talked often enough about paying his dues and swearing off the cards.

'He couldn't be in better hands, Peg. Thank you.' I stood and went round the desk to hold the door open for her. Outside in The Gaudy's main hall the murmur of work and conversation stopped for a fraction of a second as the hands and a group of the girls who were practising a new routine looked round. I could feel their eyes sliding over me, but then they all fluffed themselves up and carried on from where they'd left off.

Peggy leaned across to kiss me on the cheek, careful to let everyone see it. I was grateful to her.

'Thank you,' I mouthed.

She smiled. 'No need to thank me. I'm glad to look after him, especially when you think about that business in Mordant Street.'

She saw that I was confused. 'You haven't heard?'

I shook my head. 'Heard what?'

'There was a fire last night. Mrs Cudlipp's place – you know, the baby farmer – that's what people said of her anyway, God rest her soul.'

'You mean she's dead?'

Peggy nodded. 'Her and the four little ones she was boarding. Danny heard it was a fallen candle. Whole place went up in less than half an hour. They were all asleep on the top floor.' She cuddled Robbie close to her chest. 'Doesn't bear thinking about, does it?'

I watched as she walked to the back of the hall, picking her way round the tables set up for the night. She was thinner now too, I noted. She'd lost the plushy bloom that made Fitzpatrick watch her like a dog at a butcher's window.

She stopped for a chat with a couple of the girls. When I heard them laughing, it cut. No one was easy like that with me these days. Tell truth, since that very first night up in the cage I'd felt like someone held apart – just as Lady Ginger intended.

'Why the sad face, Mistress Kitty?' I turned. Old Peter was leaning against the curved apron. He was wearing a cape and a flat cap, his beard waxed into two points. Behind him one of the hands was testing the limelight flares. As The Gaudy's stage flooded with sudden brilliance, it threw half of Old Peter's face into shadow, giving him the look of a pantomime devil.

I say old, but he was probably a decade younger than Fitzy. He always looked sad – that was the thing, it was why he seemed ancient. The Gaudy's cornet player had the drooping donkey eyes of someone who'd seen a lot and suffered for it.

I went over to stand next to him and watched the lad, Eddie I think it was, fiddle with the cylinders along the edge of the stage. 'Careful – you don't want to lose a hand.' Eddie jumped like a roach on a skillet and scuttled off into the wings. Another one wary of me, I thought. I looked up at Old Peter. 'Kitty'll do fine. You're early, aren't you? Doors don't open for another hour and a half tonight.'

He raised the cornet and it shone in the limelight. That instrument was his pride and joy, he never went anywhere without it. He even called it Zhena, which means 'wife' back where he came from.

'They need music to rehearse.' He nodded at the girls who had been talking to Peggy – she'd gone off with Robbie now. 'It's a new song and a new dance. I said I'd play for them . . . as I played for you.'

I tried to smile. 'Those days are over now. I won't be going back up again, if that's what you're harking after.'

'But you were good, Kitty, very good – a born performer. You belong there,' he waved Zhena at the stage, 'not behind the doors of an office. Don't hide away.'

'I'm not hiding from anyone!' I was sharp, mainly because I knew he was right. 'I'm busy. This doesn't all happen by magic, you know.' I gestured at the hall, but he narrowed his eyes and tilted his head to one side.

'So, tell me about the new song. What do you think of it?'

I hadn't seen it and he knew. Something about a sailor coming home and finding *all* his wives waiting for him. Lucca, who'd painted up a bit of scenery to look like The Angel Tavern on West Ferry Road, said it was likely to be a coiner and I took his word on it.

When I didn't answer, Old Peter started to unfasten his cape and growled something in Russian.

'And what's that then in London?'

He draped the cape over a chair. 'A proverb from my home – the cat craves fresh fish, but she will not wet her feet. I think she is like you, Kitty. You want to be part of all this again.' He stared at the huddle of giggling dancing girls. 'Netta, are you ready?' He called the name of the chorus leader. She looked over and I saw her face harden when she caught sight of me with him.

'But you are . . . afraid. They won't bite, not if you speak to them. Take an interest, show them you care.' He sounded just like Peggy. I fiddled with the ivory buttons on my cuffs as he went on. 'Listen, I've known you a long time, Kitty Peck – you have a good soul. You need to let them see that the girl they knew hasn't changed.'

'Hasn't she?' I chewed my lip. Mrs Conway had just sailed in through the back, black hair piled higher than Swami Jonah's best turban and all painted up like a china doll – only one a child wouldn't care to find sitting at the end of the bed come midnight. She bloused over and waved a sheet under Old Peter's nose.

'I've got a new song I'd like to try here. "The Rani by the Fountain" – it's fresh and rather gay. Been very popular in Manchester. Bessie Ladely's done well with it.'

Bessie Ladely was a couple of years older than me, at the most.

Mrs Conway tried to bat her eyelashes like the ingénue she'd been forty years ago. One set detached itself and rested on her cheek like a dead spider.

It was time for that chat I'd been avoiding.

Chapter Ten

Tan Seng held my coat open and bowed. I pushed my arms into the sleeves, turned and bowed back to him.

'Is Mr Fratelli here?' He nodded and pointed downward.

The first fingers on both of Tan Seng's hands had long yellow nails which curled inward at the tips. Mostly he kept them tucked away in the loose grey sleeves of the tunics he wore, but every time they came out I couldn't help staring. Lucca said he used the nails to clear his opium pipe, but I wasn't so sure. They weren't black like the old cow's fingers.

He must have seen me looking, because he bowed his head again and deftly folded his hands back into his sleeves.

'He came early, Lady.'

I was almost getting used to that now. The first time I felt a twist in my gut and asked him to call me by my name, but he shook his head so violent that his silk cap came askew.

'You are The Lady.' He'd kept repeating the words, his mouse-black eyes never leaving my face. Over in the corner Jacobin woke up and went off, squawking the word 'lady' over and over like the parrot was agreeing with him.

I'd inherited Tan Seng along with the rest of The Lady's lascars and Chinamen. Mostly they worked in the dens and warehouses across Paradise, but Tan Seng ran The Palace in the way the Monseigneur ran Joey's establishment.

I swear the old man was a better mind-reader than Swami Jonah.

Sometimes I'd turn round to call for him and he'd be there already, standing in a corner silent and watchful. It would have been unnerving if it wasn't for the fact that he also had the knack of making himself invisible when he wasn't required.

He and his brother Lok, who was even older than he was with skin as rumpled as a bedsheet in a doss-house (which was unnerving seeing as how from behind he looked like a child), had a set of rooms in the basement. I never went down there. It seemed like an intrusion.

Now, I'll be straight about it – at first I thought Tan Seng and his brother were Lady Ginger's spies and I wanted rid of them. I said as much to Telferman at our second meeting.

The Beetle looked up at me from behind those half-moon specs and said very slow and serious, like he was talking to a child, 'You are mistaken. They are the most honourable men in Paradise. They are yours entirely and would give their lives for you. You will do well to remember this, always.'

That didn't alter the fact that they put me in mind of bits of old furniture she'd left behind.

For the first week Tan Seng and me circled each other like a couple of blinded fighting cocks waiting for the hoods to be drawn, but, tell truth, I began to warm towards him. It didn't matter what time I came in, he'd be there in the hallway waiting for me with sweet tea or a mug of hot spiced gin if it was late. And Lok was almost as keen as I was to clean and air the rooms that were coated with a sticky brown layer of Lady Ginger's opium smoke.

At first the old man tried to stop me working with him, but I wasn't having it. I needed to clean my grandmother's shadow out of The Palace before I could live there. I needed to make sure that every trace of her was gone. Looking back, I reckon I also needed to be doing something hard and physical to stop my mind. All those nights I spent on the end of a mop swilling out the gallery at The Gaudy hadn't been wasted.

Lok might have been ancient as the Bloody Tower and tiny as a child, but he was wiry as a stevedore on Timber Dock. Together we washed the walls and swept away the cobwebs that hung in dirty garlands from the moulded cornices of the chamber where The Lady had held court.

In better houses they hang chains of dainty paper loops across the ceiling at Christmas, but if Lady Ginger had ever celebrated the birth of the lamb, the only decorations she looked up at were stiff with dust and dead flies.

After we'd done the walls, we got down on our knees and scrubbed the floorboards. Although I couldn't make out a word Lok said – not that he said much, mind – I sensed that he approved.

I moved in after a week and that first night, when I found a jug of small blue flowers beside my bed, I knew he liked me.

I fastened the buttons at my neck and pushed the fancy shell comb deeper into my hair to keep it back. 'There's no need to wait up this evening. I'll be late.'

Tan Seng shook his head. 'Always ready for you, Lady, whatever the hour.' He shuffled across the boards to open the door for me, pushed his hands back into his grey sleeves and bowed again. 'Mr Fratelli waits in the hall.'

I bowed. As I walked out onto the landing the smell of beeswax polish filled my nose. Lok had been buffing up the oak stairs. I took a deep breath and nodded to myself. The Palace was changing – I was making it mine, but it wouldn't be so easy to put everything to rights outside, would it?

I adjusted the lid on a big china pot set next to the door so it sat right and went down. In the marble tiled hallway Lucca was admiring a painting. I went to stand next to him.

'I found it in one of the closed-up rooms at the top of the house. It seemed a crime to hide it away in the dark. What do you think?'

He brushed the canvas lightly with the tips of his fingers. 'I can't see it clearly in this light, but it is good, I think. The fabric of the coat has a quality – and the lace here at his sleeve is very finely executed. These are the clothes of a young man of fortune fifty, perhaps sixty years ago?' He took a step back and stared up. 'He is handsome and the expression in his face is . . .' he looked back at me and grinned, 'determined, a little like yours.'

I glanced up at the overdressed, pink-cheeked toff in the painting. He had a heart-shaped face and his large dark eyes were locked onto something over my shoulder. His left hand emerged from a spatter of froth at his cuff to gesture at a grand stone house fronted with columns and set among trees painted a distance behind.

I stretched my gloves and snaked my fingers into the leather. 'He's got a chin like mine, if that's what you mean, but nothing else. You can't even see his hair under the wig. As for handsome – I'll let you be the judge of that. He's not my taste. If you must know, I brought him down because I liked the colour of his coat. It brightens up the hall. You ready?'

Lucca's smile faded. 'Everyone has been summoned to The Gaudy. The call went out yesterday.'

'And what are they saying about it?'

When he didn't answer I nudged his arm. 'Well?'

'They wonder why you are calling a gathering.'

'It's not a gathering – it's a meeting!' I could hear the tightness in my voice.

'They see it as the same thing and they are . . .' He stared up at the ceiling as if he might unravel an answer from the scrolling loops of ornate plasterwork crawling about over our heads.

'Go on, they are what exactly?'

Lucca sighed. 'You know this already, Fannella. Some of them are angry. They wonder why you are now in this position. Some are scared that you have bad news, they believe you will sell because you cannot run the halls. Some of them – the girls mainly – are plainly jealous, and some of them are angry because . . .' He paused and picked at some paint caught under his thumbnail.

'Because?' I stared at him and waited.

'Because you are just a girl.' Lucca shrugged sadly. 'It is the way they think.'

'All of them? Danny too?'

He shook his head. 'Not everyone. Danny, Peggy and Anna – they have spoken for you. They will always support you after . . .'

I nodded, grateful to hear they took my part, even if they couldn't tell anyone why.

'And some others say you should at least be given a chance to prove yourself.'

'Well, that's generous of them, isn't it?' I reached for my bonnet from the hall table, planted it on my head and tied the ribbons so tight beneath my chin that it hurt. Lucca's words didn't come as a surprise, I'd heard as much from Peggy and Old Peter, but it didn't make what I was about to do any easier.

I span round, reached for the handles and threw the double doors wide open. It was raining and the cobbles of Salmon Lane outside glistened in the slick of light puddling from the hallway.

Lucca's voice came from behind. 'Remember what we said on the boat, Fannella, about family.'

'Family!' I snorted and started off down the steps, my boots tapping furiously on the stones.

'I'm not their bleedin' mother, Lucca, I'm their employer.'

⚓

I stood behind my desk and listened.

Out in the hall people were talking. I could hear the clomping of feet on the boards, the clinking of glass and just occasionally a short burst of laughter. The taint of cheap cigarettes and rough gin leached into my office through the gap beneath the door.

I looked down at my hands splayed on the desk top. The little finger and ring finger of my right hand were twitching. I tried to stop the movement but it didn't work. I raised my hand and twisted Joey's ring and Christopher between my fingers like all the times when I went up in that cage.

Get a grip, girl, I told myself. If you can dandle seventy

foot up without a net to catch you, then surely to God you can do this? The door swung open and I must have pulled tight of a sudden because the gold ring and the medal clattered to the floor, leaving me clutching a bit of broken chain.

The ring went under the desk, but I watched the Christopher roll like a penny towards the open door where Fitzy stood. His bloodshot eyes narrowed as he took in the changes I'd made and the faded bristles of his tache rippled beneath his broad red snout.

'If you're going to keep us waiting much longer, Mistress Kitty . . .' he coated my name with a greasy slick of insolence, 'then you're going to have to get the lads to shift another barrel up from the cellar. People are dying of thirst out there, so they are. And it's their night off. We've all got things to be seeing to, so if you don't mind, ma'am.'

There it came again, an insult barely concealed. I shoved the broken chain into my pocket and straightened up. 'Do you think I don't know that, Mr Fitzpatrick?' I gave his name the treatment and was surprised to hear my voice come out much stronger than I felt. 'Get them to bring the house lights up. I'm not going up on the stage to waste limelight.'

He didn't move. He just stood there in his chequered suit blocking my view of the hall beyond. I could still hear the sound of them all talking out there.

'I said bring—'

'Oh, I heard what you said, missy.' Fitzy took a step toward me and pulled at the door behind him so it was almost shut again.

He grinned and pulled on one side of his straggly tache.

'You've come a long way, haven't you, Kitty? The proprietor of three halls now, is it? I just wanted to remind you how important it is for a *girl* in your shoes to know who her friends are. You treat me right and I'll make sure no one bothers you.'

'Like you used to bother Peggy?'

He fiddled with one of the brass buttons on his waistcoat and then he took a fob from a pocket in the lining of his jacket. 'I haven't got time for that sort of dirty talk.' He flipped open the case and squinted at the dial. 'It's getting late, so it is. These good folk . . .' he jerked his head back at the hall, 'will be wanting their beds soon enough. I just wanted to be certain that we understood one another.'

I planted my hands on the desk and leaned forward. 'Is that a threat, Mr Fitzpatrick?'

He shrugged. 'With The Lady gone there'll be changes in Paradise. A new Baron moving in. They've been circling for years, waiting for her to give up the reins and now it's time. It's a . . .' he paused, searching for the right word, '. . . *nasty* world out there, so it is. I'll be well placed to help you with that – ease your way as it were. Fact is, I know some people who could work to our mutual benefit. Let's call it . . . a proposal, shall we?'

Now it was my turn to smile. 'Well, thank you very much, but I'm not in the market for a husband at the moment.'

He frowned. 'I don't think you quite understood what I meant—'

'Oh, I think I understood very well what you was driving at.' I came out from behind the desk and walked slowly towards him. 'But what I don't think you've quite grasped yet is that the very last thing *a girl in my shoes* needs is assistance, least of all from you.'

I stopped just in front of him and looked up into his pock-marked face. I folded my arms. 'Things to be seeing to, you said? And don't I know it! It's Thursday evening, so by my reckoning you must have an appointment at the pit in the cellar under The Old Queen's Head. Got to see a man about a dog, have you?'

Fitzy's eyebrows knitted together.

'No? Maybe it's Mr Tonkin tonight then? You got a nice little trade concern going on there with the Marine brew house. And then there's customs officer Legge over at Shadwell New Basin. That's a good reciprocal, I'd say. Dutch gin, is it, slipping over the back doorstep? Must be worth five or six guineas a month to the both of you.'

'I . . . I don't rightly . . .' Fitzy's little eyes darted about of an instant like he was a rat cornered by a tabby. I reached up to flick a little speck of imaginary dust from his sleeve as if I really cared for him. I rested my hand on his arm and smiled.

'And what about the cut you get from Mrs Dainty for supplying her trade with gut rot? According to the books I don't see much of that, do I? She keeps a very neat whorehouse, I'll give her that, but she can't keep a ledger. I've been through them all most careful with Mr Telferman and there appear to be some . . . gaps. Even he was surprised when I brought them to his notice.'

Fitzy looked down at my hand as I went on. I noticed the ginger bristles on his top lip quiver as his breathing came heavy. 'Do you know what I think?' I had to stop myself from laughing out loud at the look on his face now. The penny had dropped from a great height and it hurt.

'I think you and me are going to have to sit down together soon and go through some figures. You see, Patrick Fitzpatrick, I haven't just inherited The Lady's theatres. I've inherited Paradise itself and everything and everyone in it – the dens off Butchers Row, the warehouses, the wharves, the trades, the crews, the customs, the lascars, the knuckle boys and even you and all of them waiting out there. You do understand what I'm telling you, don't you?'

His eyes bulged and his lower lip dropped revealing the three stained, uneven teeth that still had a purchase in his gums. For a moment I was reminded of one of them fish the Billingsgate mongers sell cheap on account of their looks.

'As it happens, I haven't got all night neither. Do you understand me?' I repeated the question slowly.

He nodded, 'You . . . you are a Baron? But—'

'There are no buts about it. She chose me. It will be official in May.' I paused and swallowed. It was less than two weeks away now. I couldn't afford to let Fitzy know what I really felt about that. I clenched my hidden right fist and smiled up at him, sweet as a shepherdess. 'And if you breathe a word of what I've just told you to anyone – most 'specially to any of them out there – without my say so, you'll find out what a Baron, even one who's *just a girl*, can do. Now – get them to bring up the lights.'

I saw a vein twitching in Fitzy's right temple as he digested what I'd just told him. It was a risk on my part, but for all his bark and bluster I knew him to be a coward. The Lady – the real one – had practically made him a gelding, and God forgive me, on Peggy's behalf I enjoyed seeing him squirm. Soon enough they'd all find out, but in the meantime I was certain it wouldn't be from him.

'The lights, Fitzpatrick?'

'I'll get to it, ma'am.' As he turned and flung open the door I realised there hadn't been a dash of sauce in his reply. I glanced at myself in the spotted mirror over the fireplace. It was the only reminder of Fitzy's incumbrance still in the office on account of it being bolted to the wall.

The girl who looked back at me wore a dark, high-necked gown in a good plain crêpe and her hair was drawn back into a tight knot at the back of her head. I pinched my cheek and bit down hard on my lips to make them flush up dark. Then I pulled the pins from my hair and shook the ringlets loose.

The people waiting for me out there knew Kitty Peck, The Limehouse Linnet, not a bleedin' nun.

Chapter Eleven

'And finally there's the question of pay.' I paused and looked around at them all.

Most of the girls were lined up against the twisted columns at the back. Early on they'd been fluffing about and talking behind their hands. I'd heard more than a couple of hisses too, but I noted they were all paying attention now.

For some reason Professor Ruben and the rest of the orchestra had taken it upon themselves to crowd into one of the lower boxes at the side of the hall. Swami Jonah was leaning against the painted side and occasionally he turned back to them to make a remark. I didn't need to be a mind-reader to work out that not everything he said – in broad Liverpool – was flattering. I'll have a little chat with you later, I thought, and then we'll see who can really tell fortunes.

Mrs Conway was hovering near the side door. The thing on her head, I couldn't rightly call it a hat, put me in mind of something in one of the glass cases in Telferman's office. She waved and, God help me, I smiled back.

That little chat hadn't gone exactly to plan. When it came to it I couldn't seem to find the words to tell her she was stale as a Bow widow's bun. Instead I suggested that perhaps it was time for her to perform less often but at a higher rate – 'like they do up the Garden,' I said. She liked that.

The brothers Cherubimo, a tumbling duo, were over to

the left leaning against the red lacquered wall staring at the girls. The brothers liked the punters to think they came from Italy and they peppered their act with the lingo – *Pronto! Saltare! Cattura!* Ladies liked their compact, muscular frames and their fine black whiskers. I liked their Birmingham accent.

The scenery boys were sitting around the tables. Some of them had been playing broads. I could see the interrupted hands laid out in a fan in front of them. Danny was smoking and flicking the edges of the deck stacked next to his glass. There was a pile of coins between him and his two companions. I frowned. He'd never learn. I scanned the hall for Peggy, but I guessed she was back at their lodgings in Risbies with Robbie.

Lucca was at the back with deaf Bertie from the workshops. They were standing to the left of the serving board. Fitzy was there too. He faced the mirror set behind the narrow bar, and as I watched, his reflection knocked back another glass. Mr Jesmond from The Carnival was just along from him. They always let a respectful distance stand between them, but they liked to keep each other in sight. With thin black hair slicked down on either side of a parting wide as an alley and currant eyes that seemed to burrow deeper into his head during the hours of daylight, Aubrey Jesmond put me in mind of a mole. He was a good manager, though, I'll give him that. The Carnival was lousy as a fox with the mange, but from my reckoning of the books he made it pay, just.

'What about it then – the pay?' A Scottish voice from the hall brought me up. It was Dismal Jimmy, the Glasgow droll. Trust him to get to the meat.

I jerked my head to the stage just behind me. 'Listen. We all know this is an uncertain trade, even in the best of times. I've been up there on the boards, I've worked behind on the costumes, I've taken bucket and mop to the gallery . . .' I glanced up and paused. Something pale shifted up there.

I squinted. No – it was a trick of the light. Maybe the house lights bouncing off the polished brass rail?

I continued. 'I've hung seventy foot above where you're sitting and standing now, twirling and singing even though my heart was in my mouth' – actually, it wasn't, mostly, but it did no harm to let them think I'd suffered for my art – 'so I think I have a good idea of what working the halls – here, at The Carnival and at The Comet – really means.'

Another voice went off now. 'And what about The Comet? That ceiling you broke won't mend itself, Kitty.' People began to laugh and I let them, I was glad to hear it.

After a moment I raised my hands for some hush and I'll admit I was surprised they stoppered up. I placed my hands on my hips and tossed my hair so that a couple of ringlets fell over my face.

'I'll happily admit that the weight of my talent put enormous strain on the ceiling at The Comet. But it was the shoddy workmanship of them French plasterers that brought it tumbling down and me with it.' There were whistles from the hands and the rumble of approval.

'And now I'm going to get some local lads in to put it right again.' The rumble turned into stomping, clapping and even cheers as I continued. 'I've been looking at the books and there's enough *in the kitty* . . .' I paused for dramatic effect and it worked a treat '. . . to pay them a fair rate and to make sure that you, every last one of you, get a decent, regular wage, whether you're working that week or not.'

The hall went completely silent.

I moved away from the edge of the stage and climbed onto a table so that everyone could see me clear. 'Yes – you heard me right. I know what it's like scratching a living here. I know what it's like when you haven't got a stick to light and only a finger of bunter's tea to keep out the chill. I know what it's like to suck on dust for a week in order to pay the shylo.' I glanced at Danny, but he was still flicking at the boards. 'So I propose that we enter into a contract. You keep faith with me and serve the halls proper and I'll look after you, come what may.'

'That a promise, Kit?' The voice came from the shadows at the back behind the columns. I turned about in a slow half circle trying to make out the faces, then I spat into my right palm and held it forward.

'You have my word. Now, all of you, come and shake on it.'

There was low muttering. I looked at my outstretched hand and watched the smoke curl around my fingers. I was glad to see they were straight, not trembling now. One of the girls spoke up. 'What about Ada Rix? You going to help her too, then?'

There was a murmur of agreement from the gaggle at the back of the hall.

I shielded my eyes with my left hand, trying to make out the speaker. 'What about Ada?'

The voice came again.

'Terrible it is.'

I craned to see who was speaking. 'What's happened?'

'Accident. Two days back she was knocked into the Commercial in front of a brewery cart, with the babby tucked up in her arms. His head was stoved in by one of the horses. He died on the instant. I reckon he was the lucky one. Ada went under the wheels. They say she ain't got long. She's all alone, she can't work and she can't pay the crow. What you going to do for the likes of her?'

The last time I'd seen Ada she hadn't even known that she was carrying. She was glowing like an oil lamp that day in the workshops, telling me how her Tommy was thinking about setting up a coster stall. I didn't say much. Thing was, we all knew her Tommy was rotten to the pips and now he was in Pentonville thinking about five years treading the mill for stealing onions.

I dipped my head lower, peering to the back. 'That you, Mary O'Brien? Listen, I didn't know until just now about Ada, but I tell you this straight. I'll make sure she's got enough to pay for her lodgings, and for medicine too. I'll deal with it.' I paused, catching myself out for sounding just like the old bitch. But all the same, I'd make sure Ada was comfortable for as long as she needed. Then another thought occurred to me – not a comfortable one – something about Ada's little one and something Lucca had just told me on the way over to The Gaudy. I hadn't taken it in on account of thinking about what I was going to say tonight, but it was a peculiar coincidence.

Of a sudden I realised they were all quiet and looking at me expectant now. I pushed the thought out of the way.

'Now, here's my hand on it. Who's first?'

I held my breath for a long moment. I reckoned my heart was bouncing about so loud under the crêpe they could all hear it rattle.

'I'll shake your hand, Kitty.' Old Peter climbed over the side of the booth where the orchestra were packed in together like a crate of wet fish. He walked towards me, turned to take in the hall and then, gently, he bowed, turned my hand over and kissed it, like I was a queen.

'Thank you,' I whispered.

He looked up at me and grinned. 'The cat is no longer afraid.'

'I'll take it too.' Danny was on his feet now. He took a last drag on his Woodbine and ground the glowing tip into the bottom of a glass, then he swiped the boards into his pocket and came through the tables towards me. 'That's the best offer I'll get all year, Kit.' He winked and shook my hand.

I stood on tiptoe and narrowed my eyes to take in Lucca at the back of the hall. He raised his hands above his head, clapped and shouted out one word, 'Bravo.' Old Peter took it up too, and suddenly they was all standing – clapping and stamping and hollering. And then they started to come forward crowding around me and reaching up. I turned about on the table top and leaned down to catch as many hands as I could in mine. And when they'd had their fill of me I straightened up and called for a bit of peace.

'I'll tell you something now for free,' I began. 'These theatres of mine – the theatres Lady Ginger left in my care because she liked what she saw in me – well, they're nothing more than bricks, mortar, plaster dust and a little bit of make-believe. What I think is this – *you* are the real riches, *you* are the assets she left me. I'm going to invest in you and together we'll make these three halls the talk of London.'

Lucca pushed the shutters together and slotted the lock bar into place. The window in The Gaudy's office was high, narrow and barred across the outside. It looked over an alley running down the side of the theatre and round to the workshops out back. Even if a jemmy crew forced the bars, then broke the glass and the boards, they wouldn't find much to take in here, not unless they knew about the safe hidden in the little room beneath the trap under the desk.

I say room, but it was barely larger than a coffin. I had to breathe in to turn round down there. The trap opened to a narrow flight of stone steps that turned sharp right into a low brick-lined chamber barely four foot square. I didn't like it down there. It put me in mind of being buried alive.

Fitzy knew about it, naturally. He'd shown me it on the day he grudgingly handed over the keys. 'The hidey hole' he called it, pointing out the edges of the trap in the boards. 'Didn't have much call for it myself, but you might as well know it's there.'

Me and Lucca were the only ones now who knew where the takings went at the end of a working night. I glanced down at the rug to make sure the trap was covered. I shunted my chair forward so it was standing on top of it and then I checked the desk drawers were locked. It was a little routine I went through before leaving. I slipped the desk key into my pocket and felt the bit of broken chain.

Joey's ring had gone under the desk earlier, but his Christopher had rolled over to the door. I moved the oil lamp to the edge of the desk and bent down, scraping my fingers over the rug, hoping the ring hadn't slipped down between the trap boards.

'Have you lost something?' Lucca reached for his muffler and coat. They were folded neatly over the back of the chair on the other side of the desk.

'Joey's things – the ring and the Christopher. The chain broke when I was talking to Fitzy before going out there tonight. I was fiddling with them for luck like I used to when I went up in the cage.'

'You didn't need luck tonight, Kitty. *Eri magnifica!*'

I smiled. I didn't need him to translate that one. 'I remembered what you said on the boat about treating people fair and decent. It's what they wanted to hear. That and a bit of show – Old Peter was right there.'

'Does Telferman know what you have proposed?' Lucca arranged the muffler so it sat high round the lower part of his face.

I shook my head. 'Not yet. I didn't quite know what I was going to say myself until I was standing out there and it . . . came to me. I know one thing already, though: the Beetle won't like it. Can you look under the desk for the ring while I go back into the hall? I reckon the Christopher must have rolled out through the door. It can't have gone far.'

I turned the lamp up higher and took it across to the door, setting it down on the boards just before the door. 'You got enough light to see by there?'

Lucca nodded and knelt beside the desk. I pushed the

door open and moved the lamp forward a little so that a pool of light fell into the hall. The Christopher must have rolled to the right so in all likelihood it was just in front of the stage a few foot away.

I got down on my knees and shuffled forward scanning the floor and sweeping the flats of my hands over the sticky wood. I'd have a little chat with whoever was supposed to be mopping out down here, I thought. I caught the gleam of something round and gold stuck between a crack in the boards a couple of foot out and straightened up. At the same moment the door to the office swung shut.

'Lucca?' I shouted. 'Open up. I can't see out here now.'

I felt a hand on my shoulder. 'That you, Lucca?'

There was no answer as a hand moved softly to my cheek. I took a breath of leather, tobacco, wood and spice. It was like the smell that comes off the warehouses at St Katharine's when the wind's in the right direction. The muscles in my back went rigid and the hairs rose on the back of my neck.

'If this is a joke, Lucca Fratelli, it's not bleedin' funny.' My voice came out thin as watered milk.

The gloved hand moved to my ear, stroking the curve of the lobe and the vulnerable spirals of flesh above. I tried to stand but the fingers tightened. I stifled a cry. I wasn't going to give whoever it was bending over me in the dark the satisfaction. And then another hand crept round the other side of my face, leather fingers clamping over my mouth.

'Where is he, Josette?' The whisper came from behind, lingering over the name so it came out like a hiss. I could feel the man's breath on my cheek and taste the smoke in it at the back of my throat.

'Where?' The fingers twisted sharp and now I would have cried out if I could.

Of an instant the door behind opened and he let go. Framed in a slice of light Lucca fiddled about to push the door back to the point where it stayed put and then he held his hand up. Something glinted between his fingers.

'I have it – the ring. I heard you call. Can you see now?'

I leapt to my feet and narrowed my eyes trying to see into the furthest corners of the unlit hall. My heart swung like a pendulum on a tight-wound clock. It struck me then that if you're looking for a hiding place, a theatre with its curtains, columns, tiers, booths and secret trysting places was just the ticket. He was still here, I could feel him watching from the shadows.

'Bring up the house lights.' When Lucca didn't answer I span round. He was holding the lamp up now. He pushed his hair back. 'You are—'

I cut him off quick. 'Didn't you hear? The lights.'

He frowned.

'Now, Lucca!'

I watched him pick his way through the chairs and tables to the far side of the stage. He left the lamp on the edge and went up the steps disappearing behind the curtain. I kept my back to the stage and flattened my hands against the painted panel that separated the orchestra boys from the punters. I could feel the sweat on my palms as I stared into the hall.

After a moment I heard the familiar tick of the burners and then a gentle hiss as the gas came through. One by one the lamps set along the walls sputtered into life. The flickering light made The Gaudy seem alive, bringing some of it up sharp and sending parts into deeper clots of dark.

I dug my nails into the panel. 'Come on then, show us your face.'

Nothing.

'Oh, you were very bold when we were out there in the dark, weren't you? Well, you're not so brave now.'

Lucca jumped from the steps and came to stand next to me. 'What is it, Fannella – what's happened?'

I didn't look at him but I muttered from the side of my mouth, 'There's someone here with us.'

From the corner of my eye I caught the shake of his head.

'There is! If you don't believe me—'

I broke off as Lucca thrust something into my hand. 'I believe you, Kitty, take this.' We both started as a door slammed at the far end of the hall somewhere beyond the serving board and the red velvet drapes.

Without a word we were off, pelting between tables and chairs until we were through the curtain and standing in the wide panelled lobby leading out into the street. One of The Gaudy's three main doors swung open.

I went out onto the top step. Rain was hammering down on the metal canopy above, the wind caught at my skirts puffing them out around me like a bell. The only sign of life in the narrow street was a ripe pile of horse shit – mist coming off it like steam rising from a mug of hot cocoa. The last of the night hacks would be clattering home now.

It was only then I felt something trickling down into the material at my neck. I raised my hand and pushed through the sticky strands of hair that clung to my cheek. I looked at the black stain on Lucca's 'kerchief and then I reached up again to touch the stinging ragged flesh.

The man had twisted my earring and ripped it from my ear, tearing the lobe in two.

Chapter Twelve

We stood side by side in the rain on the cobbled street outside The Gaudy, but nothing moved in the shadows. After a minute, Lucca hustled me back inside, locked and barred the doors and led me to the office to clean me up. I was surprised at the amount of blood. The rip in my ear would heal soon enough, but for the moment it stung like hell.

'Did you see him?' Lucca rolled the spotted 'kerchief into a ball and thrust it into his pocket.

'No. It was black as Newgate's out there when the door closed. First off I thought it was you playing a trick, but . . .' I winced as he moved a strand of blood-matted hair away from my ear. 'I didn't see him at all, but I heard him. He called me Josette.'

Lucca's eyebrow shot up.

'And that's not all – "Where is he, Josette?" – that's what he said. Do you think . . . is it possible he mistook me for Joey? Remember how people remarked how alike we were when he was . . .'

When he was dressed as a woman, as Josette, was what I meant. Even now I couldn't quite say it. But why would anyone think Joey was here in London? As far as most of them in Paradise knew he was most likely sewn into a stone-packed oilcloth and resting at the bottom of the Thames. I pushed Lucca's hand away from my face, leaned forward on the chair and cradled my head in my hands.

What if it wasn't Joey he was after?

I couldn't help thinking that I'd brought trouble back with me from Paris when I agreed to help David. God help me, every time I said that name to myself – I didn't bother with Lennox now – I felt my neck flush and my cheeks bloom. It was true what they said about distance. That 'kerchief he'd given me at the station was in my pocket now. I'd washed it out, pressed it and of occasion in private I took it out to run my fingers over the 'D' embroidered at the corner.

Thing was, I was so happy to help that man, so flattered to be singled out by him and so keen to impress him that I never, for a moment, thought to ask him why he was frightened.

Him and my brother, too.

I sat up, fastened the top three buttons of my dress and unwound Nanny Peck's shawl from the back of the chair. 'It's getting cold in here. Let's get a fire going.'

'It is late, Fannella, better surely to go back to The Palace?' Lucca took my hat from the desk and held it out to me, but I pulled the shawl around my shoulders, stood up and went over to the little grate. I looked at myself in the mirror. 'The blood's stopped now – at least that's something.'

I knelt and started to heap the coals together, poking some bits of kindling and scraps of old newspaper beneath them. I paused as I ripped up a sheet from the pile. It was from *The London Pictorial News* – I recognised it from the picture. Sam Collins's over-lively account of the cage plummeting from the ceiling of The Comet with me clinging on inside had included a drawing of the sort that gentleman readers might find invigorating. The girl on the page looked like a canary crossed with a ripe dollymop. I screwed it up and forced it into the coals.

'Lucca, tell me again about Frank Seton's girl. I didn't take it all in when you were talking on the way over – I was too wound up.'

He reached into his coat pocket for a packet of Lucifers and came over to sit cross-legged next to me in front of the grate. It felt like the old days when I used to go to his lodgings with a paper wrap of cold cuts and a bottle to share. He'd got himself some better rooms now, I'd seen to that, but as he settled down beside me I realised I missed the closeness.

'Poor man – to lose wife and child in the same year. She was his world.' He struck a light and set it to a curl of newspaper. 'I think he will lose his mind.'

'But what actually happened? Little Rosa, how did she die?'

Lucca held the Lucifer to the edge of another ball of paper and ripped a couple of sheets from the pile of newspapers next to the scuttle. He scrunched them up and fed them to the flames. 'It was an accident. Frank was working on the gantry ropes. Rosa was in a basket at the back of the stage when the glass fell. Danny says she was asleep, which is a small comfort. She would have died instantly.'

'Danny was there when it happened?'

'*Sì*. He had taken some scenery from The Comet over to The Carnival. While The Comet is closed for the repairs we have been moving items between The Gaudy and The Carnival. Some of the acts say the atmosphere at The Carnival is better – more . . . *vivace*.'

I snorted. 'Rough, you mean?'

Lucca shook his head. 'No, they like it, truly. Jesmond is fair and the hall is smaller so the atmosphere is more intimate, more . . . *amichevole*, friendly.'

I held out my hands to the fire that was crackling in front of us now. 'Well, it might be friendly, but it's knackered. If it hadn't been for the ceiling coming down at The Comet I would have spent my grandmother's money on fixing The Carnival first. Peggy says when it rains you can see water dripping down the scenery at the back. The roof is full of holes and the skylight is shattered.'

'It's *your* money, not Lady Ginger's.' Lucca was quiet for a moment. 'The glass that killed Rosa must have slipped from the skylight. Danny said it pierced her chest like a knife.'

I felt the hairs rise on the back of my neck for the second time that night. I glanced at Lucca, the good half of his face was golden in the glow of the flames. He shook his head. 'Rosa's mother died giving birth to her. No wonder Frank is mad with grief. He took her everywhere with him, did you know that?'

I nodded. 'We – me and the Gaudy girls, that is – thought a lot of him for it. He sometimes helped Danny test the chains when I was in the cage and she was always with him, pretty little thing she was. He's a good man and a good worker. I'll see him all right.'

Lucca turned sharply. 'Money won't make him happy, Kitty.' His voice was oddly flat. 'I thought you of all people would understand that?'

I bit my lip and looked away. There was a hardness just then in Lucca's face I hadn't seen before. Of course I was sorry for Frank and Rosa, who wouldn't be? But I couldn't do a

Lazarus with her, could I? There was something I could do, mind.

I ripped another sheet of newspaper, scrunched it up and threw it into the flames. It caught in seconds, shrivelling into a blackened ball shot with orange veins. The fire didn't really need feeding, I just wanted to sort my thoughts for a moment.

I sat back. 'Them two little ones who've died, poor mites – it's a terrible coincidence, isn't it?'

Lucca nodded, but didn't answer my question. I went on. 'Paradise isn't the best place to raise a kid, I grant you, but two of them – Rosa and Ada's boy – in the past eight days, babes in arms the pair of them? That's not right.'

He sighed heavily. 'Bad things happen, Fannella. It is a hard world and a hard life for many. Those infants . . . *Dio benedica le loro anime . . .*' he whispered and crossed himself, before adding quietly, 'I think it is worse for those who are left – for Frank and for Ada.'

I was quiet too for a moment, wondering how to make Lucca see what I was driving at without sounding cold as a Billingsgate fish fag. A coal spat in the fire and I watched the page from *The London Pictorial* with the drawing of me spread across the top slowly unfurl before catching light at the edge. In seconds the doe-eyed, bow-fronted girl on the paper blackened and crumpled to cinders.

In the end I blurted it out.

'Don't you see? Them poor little sods were both dark skinned, Lucca.'

I looked again at him now. He was picking at the paint caught under his nails – Lucca Fratelli was the most fastidious soul I knew, but there was always paint under his nails. It was his habit to pick at it when he was thinking. I sat up straight.

'Since we brought Robbie Lennox back from Paris with us, two little ones with skin as dark as his have died. That's more than coincidence, I'd say?'

It was true enough. I'd realised it when Mary O'Brien called out to me in the hall earlier.

Rosa had had the gypsy skin of her mother and Ada's Tommy was dark as a lascar. His ma had come over from India with an English army family. Poor cow had worked as a nurse to the little rajlings until they were packed off to school and then the colonel and his good lady had thrown her out on the streets. A lot of them gentle souls uprooted from India and shipped back here with their starch-white families ended up in Limehouse – at least there were people here who spoke their patter.

Of an instant another thought came. I didn't know about the children who died with Mrs Cudlipp in Mordant Street, but it was like as not that at least one of them was the result of a late-night encounter down the docks between a local bob-tail and an outpost of Her Majesty's Empire.

'What do you think, Lucca?'

He stared into the fire, resting his elbows on his knees.

'It . . . it seems an odd coincidence, but . . .' He steepled his fingers. 'No – you are right – it seems more than coincidence. And what happened tonight . . .?'

'Exactly!' I pushed my hair back from my forehead. '"*Where is he?*" That's what the man said before he ripped out my ear-ring.' I felt for the scab of crusted blood. My ear was hot now and it was throbbing too. 'He meant Robbie Lennox, I'm sure of it. No wonder David and Joey were scared.'

'What?' Lucca's eye narrowed as he turned to stare at me.

I reached for an iron and poked the fire. Lucca took the iron from my hands and laid it down on the boards.

'You didn't mention anything about them being scared, Fannella, you said it was a favour to this, this . . . David.' He looked up at the ceiling. 'Let me see if I can remember correctly – you told me that Joey's friend had got a girl into the usual sort of trouble and that her family were angry. I think on the train your exact words to me were – "He has asked me to look after the kid until the trouble dies down."'

I nodded. 'That's right. He said it wouldn't be for long.'

'But there's something else, isn't there?'

When I didn't answer Lucca stood up abrupt. 'Well, if you are not going to tell me, I might as well go.'

'No, don't. You're right. There is more.' I pulled the edge of his jacket. 'Sit down again – please. I'll tell you as much as I know – and it's not much.' I kneeled up and caught his hand. 'Don't go. Please.'

When I'd finished, Lucca was silent. He shook his head and muttered something in Italian.

'I . . . I didn't know what I was getting into, exactly. It was late – I'd been drinking champagne and it doesn't sit well on me, unlike you . . .' As I spoke, Lucca tore another page from the paper and crumpled it viciously before hurling it into the fire. 'And that evening was all so . . . unreal. It was like being in a sort of dream. My head was full of a thousand things. I wasn't thinking straight, that's for sure. And by the next morning it was too late.'

Lucca brought his fist down hard on the boards and let out a stream of Italian.

I put my hand over his clenched fist. 'Don't – don't be angry with me. Please.'

He sighed heavily. 'I'm not angry with you, Fannella. I'm angry at Joseph and his friend. I saw him, briefly, at the station, remember? He's very dark, very handsome, very . . . persuasive, I'm sure.'

I didn't answer. Lucca was right. David Lennox had persuaded me all right. I felt my neck flush scarlet under the shawl and I was glad I'd buttoned up my dress. Something else came to me then.

'The station! That was no accident with the trolley. Someone tried to kill me before we'd even left Paris – and most likely they thought your bag was Robbie wrapped in a blanket or some such. I was clutching it to me when I fell.'

Lucca frowned. 'But why would anyone want to kill a child so badly? It makes no sense. His skin is dark, yes, and I can see that an old family would not be happy with such a situation. But surely they could pay this David Lennox simply to *disappear* with him? He is a performer, yes?'

I nodded. 'A ballad singer. He's half Scottish – he was born in Glasgow.'

Lucca picked at a thumbnail. 'Then he cannot be rich. Surely he would agree to come to an arrangement?'

Despite the fire, I shivered. 'I don't understand it neither. But I'm right, aren't I? It *is* more than coincidence. The little ones – and poor Ada. I reckon someone pushed her into the way of that cart.'

A burst of sparks shot up into the throat of the chimney

and a glowing coal shifted to the edge of the grate. Lucca took up the iron to prod it back. The firelight flickered across his damaged features as he turned to look at me.

'And what about Peggy? Is she in danger too, Fannella?'

Tell truth, the summons to Pearl Street had come two days later than I expected, but I was right about the Beetle not being happy.

'I cannot believe that you have made such a foolish promise.'

Telferman scratched the end of his nose with a thickened yellow nail. 'You are not a charity, Katharine.'

I noted that, as usual, he used my full first name when he wanted to emphasise my childish errors. 'You cannot buy popularity by the shilling.' He sighed and pushed his glasses further up his nose. 'You will, no doubt, learn this – in time.'

Right on cue, the clock on the mantle behind him struck the quarter. He took out his fob, flicked it open and nodded to himself. A new dead animal was set next to the clock today. The creature behind the glass looked like a masked cat with small ears and very short legs. The dermist had wired its mouth into a permanent snarl. The teeth were huge in its little flat head.

Telferman caught me giving it the eye.

'A polecat. Small, but utterly ferocious. They will take on animals four times their size and win. They do not make good pets.' He moved a glass paperweight and took up a sheet of paper, running a fingernail down a column of figures.

Without looking at me he continued, 'They are your employees, Katharine, not your pets.'

I leaned forward and tapped the paper under his nose. 'But I've got money – more of it than I could spend in a hundred lifetimes if my reading of the books is true. I don't see why paying a fair and regular wage is foolish. If it keeps them sweet and if that makes the halls a success, I call that good business.'

He looked up at me now. 'Do you? I know some who would call it weakness.'

There was a long silence.

I folded my arms. 'So, that's why I've been summoned to Pearl Street, is it? A lecture?'

Telferman shifted in his chair. 'Not entirely.' He reached for the key that hung on a long black silk ribbon around his neck and fitted it into the lock of the top drawer of his desk. I heard a click.

'I have something for you.'

Telferman laid two envelopes on the desk in front of him. He clasped his hands together and leaned forward so that his greasy black sleeves rested on top of the pages. I couldn't see the writing clear now, but from the briefest of views I thought I recognised the hand.

He didn't move, just stared at me. That roll of hair up top was so stiff with oil I could crack it with a spoon. 'This desire to be loved Kitty, Katharine . . .' he corrected himself. 'It is a flaw. The Barons will be looking for your weak spot. Remember this. You will have to account for yourself and show them you are worthy. When the summons comes you must be ready.'

'Summons?' It was an odd word to use. 'I thought it was all arranged. I was just waiting for you to give me the final details.' I glanced down at the edge of one of the envelopes poking out from under his cuff – perhaps it was all written there?

Telferman started to make a wheezing noise. At first I thought he was choking, but then I realised he was laughing. Considering he'd never done that before in front of me it was hardly surprising I didn't recognise the sound of it.

He wiped his mouth with the stained fingers of his left hand, but deftly pushed the letters to one side so that they remained hidden under the arm still resting on the desk.

'I am touched that you imagine the Barons would vouchsafe to me the workings of their innermost circle, but I am afraid that other than knowing that the Vernal Court will meet in the first week of May I can tell you nothing, not the place, not even the date or the time. It was always this way with your . . . with The Lady.'

I swallowed and pulled at a frayed loop of brocade parting company with the handle of the fancy cloth bag in my lap. I didn't want the Beetle to know how much the thought of this meeting scared me. I'm not a nervous type, I know that well enough. I push things down and lock them away when I don't want to dwell on them. I'd been doing this with regard to the Barons.

Lady Ginger, my grandmother as it turned out, had been one of them. For all that she was spare as a rake and likely a hundred years older than Queen Victoria, she was the most terrifying person I'd ever met (and I was grateful that hadn't occurred too often). Lady Ginger was brilliant and hard as diamond. Something like limelight came off her in waves shining a blinding light into the darkest corners, only it wasn't warming – that light was cold and it was cruel, like she was.

And if she was one of the Barons, what were the rest of them like?

I cleared my throat. 'Vernal Court, you say?'

'Spring, Katharine. The Barons hold court once each season. You will be . . . inducted to your place among them at their Vernal session and in good time I will furnish you with information sufficient to enable you to offer your first parable.'

He must have dialled the look on my face. 'The parables are reports, Katharine. You will be required to give an account of the quarter's business in Paradise. I will assist you in the compilation of this first submission, but soon, when you are fully conversant with the extent of your . . . holdings, you will assess for yourself, as The Lady did. There is little more to say – other than to be ready for the call. As you already know, it will come during the first week of May.'

Less than a fortnight then?

'So you aren't coming with me?' I don't know why – he certainly hadn't given me a reason to think it – but when I'd imagined the meeting, just occasionally you understand, I'd thought the Beetle would be there with me, standing just behind, all got up in shiny black and reeking of naphtha. In a way I found it comforting.

'What a ridiculous question.' He blinked slowly behind his spectacles and just for a second an odd expression crossed his face. Looking back I swear it was sympathy I saw there. Whatever it truly was I never found out because he looked down and pulled the letters out from under his sleeve with a flourish that put me in mind of a conjuror and a rabbit.

'I have been instructed to give you these. Read them when you are alone. I will make the necessary arrangements.' He flipped the letters over so I still couldn't see the writing.

'Here.' He pushed them across the desk top. When I didn't move he took off his spectacles and twiddled them about by one of the spindly gold arms. The glass caught the sunlight from the grimy window.

'Well, Katharine?'

'It's just . . .' I frowned. 'You said you didn't know where or when this meeting was going to take place so how are you going to make the arrangements?'

He sniffed. 'That will become apparent. Now please, I am a busy man – mainly on your account, I might add. Take them, read them and rely on my service.' He reached for the black ribbon round his neck and bent to lock the desk again, then he stood and went to open the door. The clock on the mantle clicked, drew breath and chimed eleven times.

'So late already?' As Telferman rubbed his hands together I heard the papery dryness of his skin. 'Good day, Katharine.'

I rose, took up the letters, pushed them into my bag and stepped past him into the narrow hallway. Just before he closed the door behind me he spoke again, quietly, through the crack.

'The most dangerous among them is Lord Kite – remember that, Kitty.'

It was almost a whisper. I turned round, confused and, I confess it, surprised to hear him call me that, but now the Beetle's door was shut.

Chapter Thirteen

When I got back to Salmon Lane I folded the letters together and pushed them back into my bag. One was easy enough to understand – a set of clipped instructions in a familiar looping hand. The other was . . . tell truth, I couldn't make head nor tail of it. Inside the second blank envelope was a fold of thick creamy paper with a pattern embossed at the top and a single word – a string of letters – written crisp in black ink underneath. The word began with a 'K'.

I looked down to fasten the strings of the bag and caught a movement in the gutter. A bird scuttled awkwardly away – a starling, it was, feathers all tatty and spare, one damaged wing held oddly to the side. I wondered what Nanny Peck would make of that.

As I climbed the steps to The Palace the doors swung open. Tan Seng bowed and moved aside to let me enter. I bowed back.

'Peggy!'

I threw my bonnet down on the hall table beneath the painting of the ham-faced lad from the attic and called again. A moment later she leaned over the banister rail a floor above and brought her fingers to her lips. 'He's asleep.' She mouthed the words, held her head to one side and brought her fingers together in a prayer steeple next to her ear in a theatrical proximation of sleep.

I smiled, Peggy was no actress. I allowed Tan Seng to help me with my coat and went up the stairs to the first landing.

'Robbie's in there.' Peggy nodded her head to the double doors leading through to the room I'd set up as a parlour. 'He's just gone off,' she whispered. 'Poor little lamb was tired out after our walk this morning, but I couldn't get him to settle.'

'You took him out! You know what I said about that – you're not to take him anywhere without telling me.' The words came out too loud.

'Shhh! You'll wake him up again. The bleedin' parrot's bad enough.' Peggy scowled. 'It seemed a crime to keep him inside on such a beautiful morning. Fresh air is good for him and besides he's used to coming around with me everywhere and seeing people. It's not natural being locked up in here all day, just the two of us, mainly. This is a dark house, Kitty.' She shook her head. 'And not just on account of the memories. Besides, even if his father came knocking for him we wouldn't have gone far, would we?'

I didn't know what to say.

⚓

Lucca was right about Peggy. After that encounter at The Gaudy, I didn't want to think that I'd put her in any sort of danger, or the baby come to that, but I didn't want to frighten her neither. So, next morning I went round to Risbies and told her that I'd had a message from Robbie's father. The gist of it, I lied, was that he was coming over soon to collect his kid. I explained that as David Lennox had given his son personally into my care, I felt bad about farming him out and thought I'd best take him back to Salmon Lane so that when he came for him he didn't know any different.

I saw the way Peggy's face fell as we sat there talking in her little room. I looked around at the dainty things she'd put together for her and Danny – good china, cushions and that – and at the little cot by the window, all fringed with lace, and smelling of soap. She was making a nest here, I thought.

'Look,' I said, 'if it's the money, I'll see you all right.'

'Money!' Peggy stood up and went to the window. She kept her back to me as she answered carefully. 'It's not the money, Kitty. Oh, it's helpful all right and I won't deny we need it what with Danny's . . .' She turned round and looked down into the cot. Robbie was babbling away and sucking on the edge of a blanket.

'I . . . I've grown fond of him. I know it hasn't been very long, but he's a dear little soul.' She knelt to pick his poppet off the rug and tucked it into the cot. 'You're . . . many fine things, Kitty, but you're not exactly, well, that's to say . . . you're not a natural with little ones, are you?'

I sighed. 'No. I'm not like you, Peg. But I won't have him for long. David will be coming for him soon.'

I wished that was true – for lots of reasons.

Then again, what was I supposed to say? There was every likelihood I'd put one of my closest friends in danger because I wanted to please a man I barely knew – even if he was a man I found myself thinking about more often than was decent. The only way to make sure Peggy was safe was to take Robbie away from her. I watched her tweak his fat brown fingers one by one and heard him gurgle with delight. That's when it came to me.

'Tell you what, Peg, why don't you come to The Palace each day to look after him for me and perhaps some nights too? Dan'll be all right about that, won't he?'

She grinned and nodded eagerly as I went on, 'Thing is, I don't want you letting on that you're still looking after a kid. If anyone asks, tell them your cousin's taken her boy home to Archway. You're to say you're coming to help me out at The Palace, nothing more. It'll be true enough.'

'But why can't I say anything about him?' Peggy's pretty brown eyes puzzled up.

Over in the cot, Robbie made a burbling noise as he chewed contentedly on the rabbit. I looked down at the rag rug. It was a good question.

'Because . . . because there's enough talk about me going round the halls as it is. If it was to get about that I suddenly had a baby in The Palace, then folk'd put their two-penneths together and make a bent sovereign quicker than Dismal Jimmy can down a pint of whisky. You see that, don't you?'

I was glad when she nodded.

'And you'll get Dan to button it too? I know what he's like for talk. You might as well stick a penny green on his forehead sometimes before you send him out the door to let people know he's got news.'

She grinned and nodded again.

'Listen, I'll pay you the same rate – more for nights – and when David Lennox comes for his son he'll find Robbie happy as a sandboy on Ramsgate beach.'

I wasn't too happy now.

'How did you get out?' I pulled Peggy across the landing and into a little room across the hall I used as an office. I closed the door and gestured for her to sit down on a wooden-ended couch pushed against the wall. It was a dark Chinese affair carved over with dragons and suchlike. It put me in mind of the chair Lady Ginger's men had carried her on to the side of Ma's grave. It was bleedin' uncomfortable, I knew that. I used it whenever Fitzy dropped by to keep our meetings short.

'Open the door, Kit.' Peggy perched on the edge of the red-padded seat. 'If he cries we won't hear him.' I reached for the handle and pulled the door open a little way.

'What do you mean "how did you get out?" I'm not a prisoner here, am I?' Peggy's large dark eyes were full of confusion. She shifted on the couch. 'This thing's worse than a park bench.'

'No, of course not.' I wondered what to say next.

Since I'd taken Robbie back to The Palace to live with me two days back I'd given orders to Tan Seng and Lok that no one was to come in or go out without my say so, and that meant Peggy too if Robbie was with her. Fact of the matter – she *was* a kind of prisoner, although I wouldn't want her to think it.

I pretended to arrange papers into a neat stack. 'I just . . . well, Tan Seng usually tells me about the comings and goings here – trade and that – and he didn't mention anything about you two taking a stroll, that's all.'

Peggy grinned. 'He was talking to a man at the door when we went. I was down in the kitchen—'

'You've been down there?' I was amazed. I always thought of going down to the basement as an incursion into the brothers' territory.

Peggy nodded. 'Lok lets me warm milk on the range. We'd gone down to do that, I had Robbie with me. I looked out into the yard and it was such a fine day that I just took it on me that we should go for a walk.'

'So you went out across the yard and through the gate at the back?'

'Yes. And then up Samuel Street into Catherine Street and along to the churchyard at St Dunstan's. We fed the sparrows.'

I flicked some imaginary dust off the book on the top of the desk. 'You . . . you must take care, Peggy, you can't . . .'

She stood up and covered my hand with hers. 'Don't worry about that, Kit. Robbie's been the best medicine possible to bring me back to myself again. Listen – he's awake.' She rustled out through the door and crossed the hall. I could hear Robbie crying for attention but he stopped almost as soon as Peggy got to him.

I followed and stood at the entrance to the parlour watching them. She scooped Robbie up from his basket into her arms and held him high over her head so that he squealed with pleasure. Then she swung him down and twirled around, holding him close – all the while humming a song from the halls. Despite myself I grinned and folded my arms.

'Good thing you're not teaching him the words to that, Peg. David Lennox will wonder what sort of company his little lad's been keeping if he comes out with the chorus one day.'

Peggy laughed and whirled around again. As I watched, I

knew that one day soon she'd likely be a mother herself to Danny's children and they'd be lucky to have her, like he was.

There was a sound from the landing behind me. Tan Seng bowed and I went out to join him.

'A man called today, Lady.'

I nodded. 'Peggy told me. What did he want?'

'You, Lady. He asked if you were here.'

I frowned. 'What did you tell him?'

'That you were not here. Then he asked if you were with Mr Fratelli.'

'Lucca?'

Tan Seng nodded. 'I said I did not know.'

'Did he leave a message or a card?'

He shook his head. 'The man was not from London, Lady. He was not from England. His voice was hard and his skin was pale, like milk. His hair almost white.'

'White?' Peggy had come out onto the landing to listen. Robbie was balanced on her hip now and chewing the ear of the cloth rabbit with a look of stern concentration.

'Now that's a coincidence.'

'What is?' I turned from Tan Seng to look at her.

'When we were in the churchyard a man spoke to us. He took quite a shine to you, didn't he?' She jiggled Robbie about. 'Didn't he?'

I straightened up. Something – maybe a sixth sense, if I believed in that kind of thing – made me suddenly very alert. 'Why was that a coincidence, Peg?'

'The white hair. The man who came to sit with us had long white hair and a foreign accent too. German he was, maybe? Or Polish. I reckon he was a sailor up from the docks. He had bright blue eyes. I thought he was odd-looking at first, but actually, after a bit I thought he was quite a charmer. Thing is, he was getting a bit . . . attentive and I knew Danny wouldn't like it, so we came back.'

Bells were going off in my head now like it was shift change at Grand Surrey. 'Did he follow you?'

Peggy shook her head. 'Why would he do that? I think he was just out for a bit of company. There were other people in the churchyard too – a young couple getting friendly. It made him feel lonely, I reckon. He said he knew a little lad back home – wherever that was – who looked just like Robbie here. He asked if he was mine.'

'What did you say?'

Peggy flushed. 'I . . . I told him he was. I didn't mean any harm by it. It's just that sometimes when I'm with him I like to imagine what it would be like if he really was mine. I'm that fond of him, Kit, it could almost be true.'

I felt for the letters in my pocket. 'Peggy – you all right to stay over tonight? If I send word to Danny? I've got to go out.'

'Of course. It'll be my pleasure.' She turned and swayed back into my parlour room. Robbie watched me over her shoulder, his large brown eyes solemn as a priest's at a death bed.

As she closed the door it came to me that her fancy might well have saved them both in that churchyard.

'I will prepare a room, Lady.' Tan Seng bowed and moved to the stairs.

'Tan Seng, wait please.' He paused and turned back at my call.

155

'Along with Danny, can you take a message to Lucca, Mr Fratelli, and ask him to come here?'

He blinked, folded his hands into his sleeves and inclined his head.

'After I go out tonight, lock the doors and shutter all the windows. No one – no one at all – is to leave or to be admitted until I return.'

'Lady.' Tan Seng bowed once more and headed to the stairs.

Chapter Fourteen

Katharine,
    I will speak to you. The churchyard. St George's in the East, nine o'clock this evening. Do not be late. Bring these papers.

Lady Ginger's sprawling signature curled across most of the bottom half of the sheet. If I brought the paper to my nose I could even smell her on it, her opium at least. The sour-sweet tang of incense laced with tar and vinegar made my hand tremble as I stood there at the end of Pearl Street holding the papers Telferman had given me.

Now they were in my bag. If I opened it the smell of the old cow coiled out like a genie from a bottle. I wasn't scared of her, at least I didn't think I was, but I'll admit it, I was frightened of what she'd been. Sometimes late at night before I put on my gown I moved a candle to the dresser and I stared at myself in the mirror. That was when I wondered about the future.

I thought about the past at those times too. There were questions I wanted the answers to.

Rain was splintering down. It fell so hard it sounded like someone was pelting the roof of my umbrella with tin tacks. The fine day had turned into a dismal, blustery evening. I kicked out – the bottom of my dress was heavy with water and catching round my boots. I could smell mutton rising from the damp wool of it.

The lamps were coming on along Commercial Road as we went west. It was just after eight, but I wanted to talk things over with Lucca so I suggested a walk.

I was beginning to regret that now. This was no April shower.

'You have written to Joseph?' Lucca ducked a little so I could hear him under the canopy.

I nodded. 'The letter went this afternoon. I wrote him everything that's happened – about the dark-skinned kids – Rosa and poor Ada's little one – and that business at the station and the man at The Gaudy. I said it was time for Da . . . his friend to make other arrangements.'

Point of fact I'd been sharp with Joey. He was still playing the old game, wasn't he? Palming off a load of trouble onto the one person he knew he could rely on. He must have thought it was his lucky day when I turned up on his doorstep.

My doorstep.

I tightened my grip on the ivory handle. 'I told him straight – said it wasn't right to put others in danger. I told him it had to end.'

'Good.' Lucca stepped sharply to the right as a shower of dirty water splattered from a broken gutter overhead, soaking into the sleeve of his coat. He brushed his shoulder and turned to look accusingly at the jagged pipe pumping out yellow fluid flecked with bits I didn't like to think about.

'*Merda!*' He turned to look again and his eyes narrowed. He shook his head. 'Then we must hope this David comes soon to take the trouble from our door.'

I didn't tell Lucca that I'd put a short note in for David Lennox too, telling him his son was well cared for here in London, but that it was best if he came over to fetch him as soon as possible. I wanted to say that if things were to change there would always be a place for a fine ballad singer in my halls. I wrote that three-line note a dozen times in a dozen different ways, but it didn't come out right so I left it simple.

I struggled to keep hold as the umbrella bucked in the wind. 'I've told Tan Seng not to open up for anyone. Not until I'm back.'

Lucca nodded. 'The man who called, did he give a name?'

'All I know for sure is that he was foreign and from Tan Seng's description he sounded like the man Peggy met in the churchyard later.'

Lucca clamped a hand to his crown as the wind caught the brim of his hat. 'What else did Peggy say?'

'Nothing. I didn't press it. I didn't want to frighten her.'

We walked on in silence for a moment or two before he spoke again. 'If this man was also looking for Robbie, why didn't he do anything in the churchyard?'

'Peggy said there were other people close by – a young couple. Anyway, she came over all maternal and told him Robbie was hers.' I paused, thinking about the question I needed to ask. I wasn't rightly sure how to put it. I wiped my dripping nose with the back of my glove.

'You heard from anyone in Paris, then?'

Lucca didn't answer so I piped up again. 'You were very friendly with ... with that dancer?'

'He is a musician, not a dancer. His name is Misha.' He

turned to look at me. 'And no, I have not heard from him yet.' Something guarded in his face made me choose my next words carefully.

'I . . . I'm sure it's nothing, just coincidence, but Peggy and Tan Seng said the man who called and the one later on in the churchyard had white hair. Peggy said he was a looker. Your Russian friend – he had—'

'*Capelli biondi.*' Lucca stopped in his tracks. 'As do half of the Baltic sailors who put in at the docks – the Swedes, the Danes, the Norwegians – and yes, the Russians too. Are you saying that the man I . . . met in Paris is a child killer, Fannella?'

Lucca's voice was low. Through the rain trickling off the brim of his hat I saw the muscles twitch under his good eye.

'The man who called knew you by name, so I just . . . Like I said, it's a coincidence—'

Lucca cut my blustering. 'Because I *know* Misha would be incapable of harming anyone. And for that matter, why Misha? Why not any of the others from The Moika? They all have pale hair and speak with an accent. Perhaps you suspect every man I spoke to in Paris?'

'But you have to see—' I began.

Lucca raised his hands. 'No more.' He didn't look direct at me, instead he stared over my shoulder. I guessed he didn't want me prying too deeply into his private thoughts.

'Come. We mustn't keep your grandmother waiting.' He buried his chin into the folds of the muffler and strode forward. I had to scurry to keep up with him. I glanced up at his face from under the umbrella. I was on his bad side. Raindrops glistened on the furrowed skin of his cheek.

No wonder he was angry, I thought. The first time he finds

someone who cares for him I sinuate he might be a monster. There was something there, though. Surely it was more than a coincidence that a white-haired Slav – I was sure that was the accent Peggy had described – had come calling at my house? If it wasn't Misha, then perhaps it was one of them others from the ballet – Ilya, Stefan or Akady – see, I remembered those names, despite the champagne.

And I remembered that Lucca's friend was a musician called Misha too, but I didn't like to let on.

We turned down into Lucas Street. From the corner of my eye I saw Lucca cross himself as we passed the big grey chapel to the right. It was one of his. He was always particular about Sundays, but since that business with the missing girls he'd become even more regular. Sometimes he took himself off to his Italian church up Covent Garden of a Friday.

He pulled his hat down lower as we passed a couple of lop-sided sailor lads. In the narrow street the stench of gin rolled off them like steam from a wash tub. It wasn't even late but they'd already taken a skinful on board. It was a wonder they could stand, let alone walk. One of them caught my arm and slurred out a sort of invitation, although I doubt the word 'fuck' appears in many manuals of etiquette. Lucca pulled me away and quickened his step. After a moment he turned to look back to make sure they'd got the message.

'Always the finest places for The Lady,' he muttered. Despite everything I smiled. Shadwell was the last place I'd expected to meet my grandmother again. She hadn't gone far, had she? All this time she'd been sitting on my step like a spindly black spider still spinning her web.

I stepped aside to avoid a puddle of stinking brown muck

spouting from a street drain. I had to hold my skirt up to stop it trailing in the foaming scum that bubbled across the cobbles. Lucca was right, this certainly wasn't the finest corner of Paradise.

Apart from that tart remark about The Lady he hadn't said a word since we talked about Misha. I needed to make peace with him.

'I . . . I'm glad you came with me this evening. I couldn't go alone.' I paused and tried again. 'She knew all about you. I think she liked you.' When he didn't answer I fought the wind to dip the umbrella to one side and looked up. He was scanning the dreary street behind us. There was only one gas lamp along here and that was thirty yards back.

'They've gone now, Lucca. Anyway, I've got you to protect my honour.'

He shook his head. 'It's not those two. There is someone behind us – someone who doesn't want to be seen. I wasn't sure at first, but now . . .' He folded back the brim of his hat and peered into the wall of rain. 'I think we were followed from Commercial Road. Look – there!'

He pointed. I turned and tipped back the umbrella to get a clearer view. 'What am I looking at?'

'*L'ombra* – the shadow there across the cobbles beyond the lamp. Someone is standing close to the entrance of an alleyway.'

'People live here. It doesn't mean there's someone on our tail.'

'Doesn't it? Let's go a little faster, Fannella.' He took my hand and began to walk very quickly, dragging me along with him. At the same moment I heard footsteps tapping behind.

Lucca picked up the pace and the steps came more rapid.

'Run!' He yanked my arm so hard I yelped. As the pair of us pelted towards the end of the street the heavy drumming sound of someone chasing us echoed off the narrow walls and I knew he was right. I scrabbled to hold my sodden skirt high and clear from my boots and dropped the umbrella. It clattered to the cobbles and blew away, the wind catching under the canopy. I heard it bumping across the stones behind us as we ran on.

At the corner we turned into Shadwell High Street.

It was lively here. People were dodging about trying to avoid the rain and there were others sheltering under the bulging striped shop awnings that had been left furled out. A timber cart rumbled past, splashing more mud up my skirt. A man carrying a tray of day's-end cabbages on his head pushed between us knocking me sideways into the gutter where a stream of water and God knows what else ran over my boots.

Lucca pulled me into the crowd and out across the road. We disappeared behind a hack pulled up outside a tavern. He tapped the side and the driver leaned down to speak to him.

I watched Lucca press some coins into the driver's hand and then he turned back to me and hustled me through the lamplit doorway of the tavern. The air inside was thick with the stench of liquor, smoke, wet clothes and sweat.

Keeping hold of my hand, Lucca forced a way to the frosted window letting out onto the street. 'We'll watch from here.' He bent to peer through the parts of the glass where the tavern's name, 'The Hop Pole', was picked out in gold letters set into small clear panes.

He rubbed a spy hole in the steamy glass and pulled me

closer. I hunched forward to see out to the street. The hack was still there, but of a sudden the driver cracked his whip and shouted, 'Right you are, sir, madam.' He called so loud I heard him quite distinct. The horse whinnied and the hack jerked forward, bouncing over the glistening cobbles.

I nudged Lucca. 'Well?'

He rubbed the glass and looked through the spy hole again.

'There – do you see him, Fannella?' I pressed my nose to the pane. A tall man in a long black coat stood just outside. He was wearing a wide-brimmed hat and a muffler that covered most of his face. In his left hand he carried a long cane. He watched the hack as it rumbled away up Shadwell High Street. There was a flash of silver as something arced into the air beside him. A moment later he smashed the gleaming head of his cane into the palm of his right hand. He stood and stared along the street for a moment and then he started to walk fast in the direction the hack had taken. I cleared a wider circle and saw him break into a run.

'Did you pay the cabbie to take off empty?'

Lucca nodded. 'I hoped it would put him off – whoever it was.'

I peered out through the misted pane again. 'Did you catch anything of his face?'

'Nothing – you?'

I shook my head. 'Do you think he's gone, then?'

Lucca glanced at the bar where a stout, red-faced woman with arms like joints of gammon was leaning across to talk to a punter. Cushioned in her low-cut gown plaited with dun-coloured ribbon, the barmaid's breasts looked like a couple of ostrich eggs jostling for space in a badly made nest.

His nose wrinkled. 'We'll wait here for ten minutes. We're in good time.' He nodded up at a fancy gold clock set in a wooden panel over the bar. It was twenty to nine.

Chapter Fifteen

As we turned off the Ratcliff into Cannon Street Road a bell went off in the tower. I'm no expert when it comes to buildings, not like Lucca anyway, but there was always something about St George's that struck me as sinister. It didn't look like a church, more like someone had been playing a game with a full-size version of one of them sets of building blocks you give to a child – Joey had one, I recall. Nanny Peck only let us break it out of its wooden box and over the rug in front of the fire on Sunday afternoons.

I looked up. All I could make out in the dark was the great black shape of the church over to the right, a jumble of sharp points and turrets – no lights in any of the windows. I wasn't surprised at that. Who'd want to be shut in there for the night?

Mind you, it was typical of my grandmother, I thought, to choose somewhere so grimly theatrical for a meeting. No doubt she'd arranged it to appear like Old Nick himself in a sudden flare of torchlight on the steps. She was going to give a pantomime performance, was she? Well, I was ready for her.

It was still pelting down. I bent forward to keep the rain out my eyes and saw the poor sodden ghost of a feather from my bonnet dangle limp in front of my face. I clutched my bag to my chest as we followed the line of the wall towards the entrance to the churchyard.

We turned at the gate and Lucca's hand tightened on my arm. I looked up.

There was a carriage drawn up ahead alongside the double set of curved steps leading into the church. It was lacquer black – neat with glowing lamps, two horses in the traces and a hunched figure up top. One of the horses turned to look at us. It tossed its head and skittered about on the stones.

The huddled driver leaned down to rap on the side.

Immediately the door opened. A narrow set of steps clattered down and a figure in a long dark gown stepped out. The old Chinaman bowed and motioned to the carriage. Of an instant I was minded of the time just before my first night up in the cage when The Lady had taken the trouble to visit me and remind me of my duties. Fitzy had to carry me across the yard at the back of The Gaudy because my slippers wouldn't take the snow, and then he'd delivered me through the door of this same carriage, practically into her lap.

I took a sharp breath. 'Lady Ginger might well want to speak to me, but I've got a few things I want to ask her as well. Come on then, Lucca.'

We walked towards the carriage, but as we came close the Chinaman stepped forward to bar our way. He drew a hand from a baggy sleeve, pointed at Lucca and shook his head.

I gripped Lucca's hand. 'Surely she can't mean to leave you out here in this! She knows I wouldn't have come here without you.' I raised my voice to be sure she'd hear.

He turned the brim of his hat lower against the rain.

'Of course, but it's you The Lady wants to speak to, Fannella, not me.' Lucca glanced up at the brooding bulk of the church. 'I will wait under the porch. At least it's dry there.'

He squeezed my hand, released it and loped up the steps. At the top he saluted before dipping into the shadow.

The old Chinaman watched him go and then he bowed again. Now he shuffled aside to let me climb into the carriage. I couldn't see inside, the curtains were drawn at the narrow windows and the door was only half open. But I could smell her.

I held the bag close to my chest and reached for the gilt handle beside the door. The carriage rocked about as I climbed the steps and dipped my head. The opium came strongly now as I pushed the door.

Firm hands gripped my shoulders and pulled me roughly inside. Something cold was clapped across my face. I struggled and tried to shout, but the cloth smothered my nose and mouth. I could feel bony fingers pressing it tight. There was another scent now – a sickly sweetness with an undertow of the cleaning stuff I'd used with Lok.

I tried not to breathe, but the hand clamped down harder. At the same moment I was hauled deeper and pushed down into the seat. It was black as a cassock inside the carriage. I twisted round trying to make some sense of what was happening, but I couldn't see anything clear – just shapes and shadows. Someone pinned my arms to my sides and another person forced me forward so that my forehead would have touched my knees if it hadn't been for the hand in between. Through the soaked rag, the fingers felt like a mask stiffened across my face.

My tongue began to burn and my nostrils stung. The last thing I heard before I went was the rattle of my bag as it tumbled to the carriage floor.

When I opened my eyes it was almost light. An arch of palest purple showed where a thin curtain had been drawn across a window a few yards away. My head was throbbing as if someone was standing over me twisting a fork into my right temple.

I screwed my eyes down tight and opened them again. The room was square with a large brick fireplace over to the right. The remains of a log still glowed in the hearth, filling the air with the rich scent of burning cherry wood. It would almost have been a comfort if I had the first idea where I was.

I was stretched out on my left side, my right hand resting on some thick, rough material. I could feel the embroidered pattern of it under my fingertips. I followed the line of the looped flower with the pad of my index finger and stared at the window.

I couldn't remember how I got here. The last thing I could bring clear to mind was Lucca standing at the top of St George's steps. He raised his hand, waved and then . . .

And then what?

I shifted about to see more clearly. I was fully clothed and lying on top of a narrow bed with a sort of canopy overhead. The folds of material above me were pleated into a tent-like affair fringed with tassels. Beyond the canopy I could see a ceiling supported by three broad wooden beams.

The bed creaked as I pulled myself into a sitting position and the tassels up top began to sway. Immediately my stomach turned itself inside out. I tried to swallow the bitterness that bubbled up into my throat, but it was no good. Someone had set a china bowl on the nightstand next to the bed. I took it quickly into my lap and bent forward, spattering clear liquid across the delicate painted flowers.

A minute later it came again, but after that second bout the cramping settled. I set the bowl back on the nightstand, pulled up my knees and stared at the panelled room around me, taking more of it in now in the thin light. There was a padded chair next to the fire and my bag and bonnet were on it, the ribbons of the bonnet had been laid flat over the arm so that the fire could dry them. My feet were bare – someone had removed my stockings and they were now hanging from the mantle. I saw that my boots had also been set neatly next to the hearth.

Something like this had happened before. I thought of that time I woke in my bed at Mother Maxwell's to find James Verdin curled up next to me. He was naked, point of fact we both were – my clothes were flung around the room like a bomb had gone off in a laundry. It wasn't a thought I liked to dwell on. I pulled at the stiff hem of my skirt, rifling through the cotton petticoats to check my unders. I was wearing my drawers. Apart from the stockings and boots I was still buttoned up tight.

Over to the left there was a door. I slipped from the bed, freezing up like one of them museum statues Lucca likes to draw as the old boards beneath my feet betrayed me. It didn't seem to matter where I stood, they groaned as if an elephant was tramping about on them. I made my way over quiet as I could and tried the handle, turning it gently so as not to make any more of a racket, but it was locked.

My hair had come loose somewhere along the way. I

pushed it back and knotted it tight at my neck. My head was still bad, but it was more of an ache now rather than the stabbing pain I'd woken to. A memory swam into my mind and I tried to net it before it vanished into the depths again.

Darkness – a carriage?

I frowned, leaned back on the door and stared at the unfamiliar room. And then, of a sudden, it all came back. The Chinaman, the hand over my face, the drug-soaked cloth.

Where the bleedin' hell was I?

I walked over to pull back the curtain. A dew-soaked garden several floors below was silver green in the early light. Rows of hedges romped off across a well-tended lawn towards a bank of trees. Some of the hedges had been clipped into shapes. There were balls, pyramids and great lumpen things that put me in mind of a herd of animals standing guard.

I could hear gulls making a racket, but that didn't mean much. You get them on the river and they follow the carts round Billingsgate, yowling and diving on the boxes like cats with wings.

I pressed my forehead against the glass, my breath misting the latticed pane. I rubbed it clear and caught sight of a lead pipe running down beside the window. I could climb down and sprint across the grass and into the trees and then keep going.

I listened for a moment. Except for the ticking of a clock set on a chest against the wall there wasn't a sign of life. I tested the window, quietly at first so as not to draw attention, but after a moment I was scrabbling at the lattice work and rattling the curled iron handles.

It was no good. Like the door, it was locked. I was a prisoner.

I went over to the fireplace and took my bag from the chair. I snapped it open. The letters were still inside along with my purse – and David Lennox's broidered 'kerchief.

None of this was making sense. Was this where The Lady was waiting for me or had I been drugged and taken to someone else? I thought about that night at The Gaudy and brought my hand up to my ear. There was still a crust of blood where the dangling jewel, a ball of faceted green glass, had been ripped away.

I glanced up at a painting over the hearth as if I might find an answer there. A young couple sat together on a bench in a landscape full of sheep. The man looked very pleased with himself and his livestock. His hat was set at a jaunty angle and his hand rested in a lazy, proprietorial manner on the shoulder of the girl with him.

If I was the fanciful type I might have said that she had the look of Ma about her. She was dainty and fair with large dark eyes that seemed almost too large for her small pointed face. Her stockinged feet, encased in prettily ribboned shoes, poked out from under a bell-shaped skirt. They weren't the kind of shoes a girl could walk far in.

I moved my bonnet, reached for my own stockings and sat down heavily in the chair to put them on. If I was going to make a run for it at some point I would need my boots.

The clock on the chest cleared its throat and began to chime.

On the sixth and final stroke there was a jangling sound as someone unlocked the door. It swung open and the old

Chinaman who'd come with the carriage last night shuffled into the room. He bowed once and gestured to the door. He coughed and dabbed his mouth on his sleeve, before speaking.

'The Lady will see you now.'

Chapter Sixteen

By the time we'd got to the second flight of stairs I'd given up trying to get anything out of him. Lady Ginger's Chinaman had turned his back and waited at the door while I pulled on my stockings and buttoned my boots, but when I stood up and asked him to tell me where we were he just shook his head and bowed. It didn't matter what question I put to him, the answer was always the same.

Now I was following the old boy down a long, dark corridor two floors higher than the room I'd woken up in. Like the bedroom below it was panelled and gloomy. Wide wooden floorboards creaked beneath our feet as we made our way along. The old man was brisk. I couldn't see his feet under the hem of his gown but I could hear the shuffling slap of his slippers as he led the way.

There were paintings along the wall to the right, but I couldn't see them clear because the tall, square windows all down the left side were shuttered or curtained. I could tell a fine day was blooming outside because the light creeping round the edges was tinged with gold. Just occasionally I could see dust dancing about in a brilliant sliver that dared to cut across the boards at our feet.

We walked on past the biggest fireplace I'd ever seen, propped up either side it was with life-size marble statues of men who had half a fish where their legs should have been, and into a part of the corridor where the curtains were pulled so close that the day couldn't come in. The only light here came from a couple of candles set in silver cups shaped like shells set either side of a massive door.

The Chinaman halted. He knocked once, bowed again and stood aside.

As the door swung open the smell of Lady Ginger – not just the opium, but the warm, sour smell of her old body – came rolling out to meet me.

And then it happened, just like all the other times. I suppose I shouldn't have been surprised, but it wasn't until that moment when the door opened and something of her leeched out that my body remembered the things my head was trying to bury.

My neck went cold like a frozen hand had clamped across the back of it. I tried to wrestle my breathing to a steady rise and fall, but of a sudden it came fast and shallow. I wasn't seventy foot up on a trapeze, but for some reason the impression of being dandled over something dangerous went through me. Of an instant the wooden floor beneath my feet felt less substantial than I knew it to be.

I brought Madame Celeste to mind. *Never look down; never let go; and never give up hope.* That's what the old girl told me time after time when she trained me for the heights and I was swaying under the beams in her attic. Tell truth, it all seemed like a game back then.

And that last is the most important rule of all. If you ever allow yourself to think you might fall, you will. It's as simple as that. I bit down hard on the inside of my bottom lip to bring myself up. I wasn't going to show weakness now. I wasn't going to fall. Out of habit I brought my hand up to my collar and felt for Joey's ring and the Christopher. For a moment I was surprised they weren't there and then I remembered they were lying together in a drawer at The Palace along with the broken chain.

I heard a scraping sound and a light flared in the room ahead before dying to a glowing red point.

'Tell me, Katharine, are you going to come in or are you intending to stand there gawping like a herring, girl?'

Oh, that voice – so sweet and girlish. Cultured too. When I heard it again, I realised that my grandmother's accent was very like the one I'd heard on Joey. Neither of them spoke Limehouse these days. Thinking about it, I wondered if Lady Ginger ever had.

'I am waiting.' The voice came again from the dark.

I know I said it was girlish, but don't for a moment think of it as soft. Lady Ginger's words were like something noxious coughed up by a pampered cat. One minute it's purring and curled up neat on your lap, next it's hawking out a half-digested rat head.

I tightened my grip on the handle of my bag and stepped into the room. Immediately the door swung shut behind me.

'Come closer, Katharine, I want to look at you.'

I paused, letting my eyes get used to the dark. At first all I could make out was a bulk of black shadow immediately ahead. Over to the right, but deeper into the room, a stubby candle stood on a low table set in a sort of alcove. As I stared I saw the pattern flicker on the curtains behind the candle and realised it was a covered window. The air was thick with opium smoke. The sweet tarry fug of it was so dense I could

almost feel it on my face. But there were other scents too –
something medicinal and tartly floral masking the smell of
disease.

'Bring the candle to me.' Her voice crackled like old paper.

I put down my bag, went across to the table in the window
and lifted the silver candle holder. The flame jittered about
as my fingers trembled. I counted to ten, willing my hand to
be still. When the candle steadied I turned and stared at the
shadowy mass that I now recognised as one of them great old
boxed-up beds with hangings up to the ceiling. I couldn't see
my grandmother through the thick folds of fabric.

'Set it beside the bed.'

I thought I saw the red drapery move. Beside the bed there
was a table with a glass and jug on the top. I walked over and
placed the candle next to the jug, pushing the glass back to
make a little more space. Just as I released the curved handle
of the candle tray a hand shot through the bed curtain, closing round my wrist so tight I yelped.

The hand was more bone than skin, yellow as parchment
in the dim light. I could feel the stone set into a great gold
ring on Lady Ginger's middle finger dig into the soft skin of
my arm and I heard the familiar clatter of the bracelets on her
arm. Sharp black nails gouged deep.

'You will adjust my pillows, Katharine.' The hand loosened
from my wrist and was drawn back into the curtains as she
began to cough. The rasping sound went on for several
seconds more than was comfortable. I was beginning to wonder if I'd been summoned to God knows where only to stand
by and hear the old cow choke up her last, when she spoke
again. 'Draw them back.'

I glanced up. The bed was at least seven foot high and Oriental in design. Black lacquer columns painted over with little gold figures and topped with gilded pagodas stood at each corner. On three sides the red hangings spilled down from curved pelmets of lacquered wood set high between the columns, giving the bed the look of a small theatre. It was very like a stage set Lucca might have painted up for Swami Jonah, only I got the impression it was a good deal older than any of The Lady's halls.

My halls.

'The curtain, if you please.'

I reached to the place where the hand had come from, catching the edge of the fabric to pull it aside.

I gasped and covered my nose. I couldn't stop myself – I had to take a sudden step back at the smell that came rolling out from the dark within. At the same moment my mind washed up a word Lucca had used once – catafalque. He was describing some painting he'd seen at one of the public galleries and I'd asked him to explain what it meant. I liked the sound of it, even if it was a box of death. I'd tucked that word away somewhere, but it came to me again now as I stood looking into what was most surely a fabric-lined tomb.

In just two months Lady Ginger had changed. In the flickering glow of the candle I hardly recognised the gristly knot of skin hunched in the midst of stained sheets and velvet bolsters.

She was dressed in a black embroidered gown that gaped wide at the neck revealing a throat that was strung like a broken violin. She still wore her grey hair in a plait, but it was a poor shabby thing. I noticed that the hair at the front of her head was so thin and spare I could see the moony gleam of her scalp through it. Her cheekbones jutted out so sharp now beneath the hollowed pits of her eyes that she put me in mind of a rook skull Joey kept on his windowsill when we were kids.

He'd found it in a park one day when Nanny Peck had taken us out and away from Ma. 'You keep that close, now, Joseph, and the King of the Birds will never harm you.' That's what the old girl had told him. It was another one of her superstitions from the old country. I always felt guilty about that little skull. I'd smashed it apart by accident one day when I opened that window, but I never told Joey what I'd done.

Lady Ginger smiled, her black lips pulling at the skin stretched tight across the bones of her face.

'Cat got your tongue, Katharine?'

I realised I was staring at her. I shook my head slowly and moved the candle to the edge of the table to give us more light. She blinked as the glow played across her sunken features, throwing valleys of flesh into shadow and bringing harsh illumination to the ranges of her chin, nose and cheekbones. She was a fearful sight, but I didn't want her to see I was scared.

And I'll tell you this for nothing: one thing about my grandmother was the same as ever. Her black eyes glittered like French glass beads sewn into her head. If the life I saw caught there was anything to go by, Lady Ginger would likely keep her body alive for another hundred years by will power alone.

As she looked up at me she began to laugh. Gobs of dark saliva dribbled onto her chin as she rocked in the bed, setting off the jingle of the little golden bells hanging off the roofs of the pagodas at each corner. She pushed the grey plait over her shoulder and scrabbled a claw-like hand into the nest of sheets beside her, the bangles clattering as they slid down her stick of an arm. She pushed a bolster aside and revealed a long carved opium pipe sitting on a small tray balanced across another cushion. She snatched the pipe up and brought it to her lips sucking greedily so that the bowl glowed red. It was what I'd seen through the bed hangings as I stood at the door.

She inhaled deeply and shuddered. Her eyes rolled back in the sockets as two thin trails of smoke wound from her nose, rising up into the canopy overhead. She nodded, opened her eyes and fixed her gaze on me again.

'It does not bring the dreams now, Katharine, not as it once did. Neither does it bring sleep. I do not sleep.'

She took another pull and sighed. 'It brings relief.' She placed the pipe back on the tray. 'I believe I asked you to straighten my pillows.' It wasn't a question.

She twisted about and indicated that she required me to pull up the pillows at her back so she could sit straighter in the bed. I hesitated for a moment and she saw it. Her lips twitched. 'You will soon become accustomed to the stench of corrupting flesh, Katharine, as I have. Now your assistance . . .'

I leaned forward and pulled the pillows into place behind her, then I moved a couple of the bolsters over too. I smoothed the sheets and helped her settle back. Through the black silk gown I could feel the knobbles of every bone in her back and the jagged edges of her shoulder blades. By accident I brushed the skin of her neck with my fingers and it was cold.

'Good. We may begin.'

She began to scratch the bed covers with the curved black nails of her left hand and it took a moment before I understood that she was inviting me to sit on the edge of the bed. I climbed up and sat there under the canopy. She was right about the smell, I was getting used to it now.

'I have received several reports on your activities. Some are not pleasing to me.'

I shook my head and raised my hand. 'I haven't come here for a lecture.'

Of an instant I realised she didn't frighten me so much as disgust me. This place, this room, wherever it was, it was all show. My grandmother was good at putting on a performance, I'll give her that, but I knew what she was up to. I found my voice again now.

'No. I've come here for some answers. After what I went through I think I deserve them.'

Lady Ginger coughed and wiped her lips with the back of her hand. 'Deserve?' There was a sharp, metallic edge to her little voice. 'That is an interesting word to use, Katharine, when I see very little evidence to convince me that you *deserve* anything.' She leaned forward. 'You have the letters?'

I held her gaze. 'I'm not here to talk about correspondence. Where am I? And why did your old China boy have to drug me to bring me here?'

She scratched the side of her nose and I could hear the scrape of her nails on paper-thin flesh. 'That is not your concern. I have summoned you here to answer some of *my* questions.'

I folded my arms and leaned back against the painted bed column. 'And I've come here to *ask* some. Let's start with our father, shall we – mine and Joey's, that is. Who was he, then? And where is he now?'

Lady Ginger closed her eyes. 'This is tiresome.'

'Maybe for you, but not for me. I reckon I have a good right to know about my own *family*.' I put an emphasis on that last word, echoing the way she used to mouth it about in the halls. 'And what about you and Ma? If she was your daughter you must have—'

Her eyes snapped open. 'I must have what?'

I wasn't rightly sure how to finish that. The thought of Lady Ginger indulging in any sort of romantic liaison seemed absurdly grotesque. When I didn't answer she reached into the bed sheets and produced a lace-edged 'kerchief. She spat something black into it and folded it carefully into a neat square. I noticed the rings hung loose below her knuckles now.

'I do not have time for this.' She pushed the square under a pillow again and flicked a desiccated hand at the room around us. 'This is my . . . retreat. It has been in my family – our family – for generations. At present you do not need to know more: not a name, not a town, not even a county. It is irrelevant.'

I shifted on the bed, so that I was sitting cross-legged facing her. The little bells up top went off again as I tucked my boots under my skirt. 'Irrelevant? That's an interesting word too. So all this . . .' I nodded at the room. 'It's another one of your secrets then, is it? Another one of your games?'

She blinked slowly, her hooded lids pleating themselves into the sockets of her eyes.

'Only if you regard dying as a pastime, Katharine. I do not

182

think it likely that I will ever leave this room again, let alone this house. That is why I left Paradise in your care. I thought you understood that?'

'Oh, I understand all right. Telferman's been going through it. You've made me a woman of property, a woman of means. You've made your own granddaughter a woman who's so deep in every filthy, stinking trade run between The Isle of Dogs in the east and The Tower in the west and from Bethnal in the north down to Deptford in the south that it's a wonder she's not coated in flies.'

Her lips twitched. 'Telferman tells me—'

'—That I'm good at it. I show promise. That's what your letter said. I've got all the details lodged right here.' I tapped my head. 'Every name, every penny. You don't need to fret about Paradise. My understanding of it is perfect and now I'm going to run it my own way. Like I said, I didn't come here for a sermon. I need—'

'You need my assistance.' Lady Ginger cut me off sharp. Her eyes narrowed. 'Tell me, it didn't take long before your charming brother brought trouble to you, did it?'

I didn't answer, but she must have read the look on my face because her eyes glinted with a sort of triumph.

'Oh yes, Katharine. Never underestimate me. I know what came back from Paris with you, even if you do not.'

All the questions I thought I was going to ask my grandmother when we finally met again went out of my head.

'You . . . you know about the boy – about Robbie?' I spoke too quick.

She smiled thinly. 'I know about his father too. I fear he is playing a very dangerous game.'

The thought of David Lennox made my cheeks burn. I saw him sitting in front of me again in Joey's room, his clear green eyes glassy with tears as he begged for my help. The thought of any harm coming to him made me catch my breath. Something lodged in my throat.

I swallowed hard. 'I've sent word to him, to Da . . . Mr Lennox, telling him to come and take back his boy, and I've told Joey too, told him to set things straight. Told him it wasn't right to put folk in danger.'

Lady Ginger reached up to pull her plait over her shoulder. She rolled the fraying end between her fingers. 'But it is too late.' She glanced up, the candlelight gleaming in her eyes. 'You do know, I trust, who you brought back from Paris with you?'

I shook my head.

'Death.'

The tip of her tongue appeared as she said it. I swear she savoured the taste of that word in her sticky, black mouth. She was enjoying herself. I could see that now and it made my belly boil.

'If you know so much already, why am I here? Why don't you *deal with it* yourself, like you used to?' I mimicked her voice and heard the shrill note rise in my own voice as I went on. 'Why don't you get one of your spies onto it? I know you've got plenty of them working for you still. Telferman, maybe Tan Seng and his brother Lok at The Palace. Then there's that dainty little man with the powder-white hair in Paris . . .'

'The Monseigneur?' Lady nodded. 'Indeed, he has been most helpful. You have his note with you as instructed?'

'*His* note?'

She sighed. 'I am losing patience, Katharine. Telferman gave you two items of correspondence yesterday. My summons and the note from Monsieur Chartrand, the Monseigneur. Where is it?'

So he *was* her spy. I rolled this nugget of information around in my mind and tried to make it fit into the right space. I picked at a thread on the coverlet in front of me, but jerked my head up with a yell as Lady Ginger clamped her hand down over the top of mine. She struck out quicker than an adder, twisting her nails into my skin. I was amazed to feel the strength in that wizened-up hand. Her fingers gouged like pincers.

'Where is it?'

I yanked my hand away, slipped from the bed and went to retrieve my bag. My eyes had adjusted to the dimness now. Apart from the bed and the tables, there was little else in the room. I snapped open the bag and reached for the letters.

'Here – is this what you mean?' I handed her the folded paper with the pattern embossed at the head and the peculiar script. Lady Ginger took it from me and flapped it open.

'And what do you make of it?'

I shrugged. 'There's not a lot to make anything out of, is there? Just a string of letters.'

She nodded and held the sheet near to the little candle flame. 'What do you see, Katharine?'

I leaned closer. The paper was quality, I'd known that from the feel of it. It was thick and silky to the touch. The creases where it was folded into three held their sharpness. Now, in the light, I could also see the finest trace of gold along the edges where it had been hand cut.

'Begin with the mark.'

Lady Ginger handed it back to me and gestured to the candle. I moved closer so that I could see more clearly. I hadn't really examined the mark pressed into the paper. Now I looked properly I saw it was a splayed-out bird, something like an eagle, pinned down at the breast by a sort of shield. I frowned as I ran my fingertips over the pattern. I'd seen this before or something very like it. I glanced up to find Lady Ginger staring at me.

'Unusual – is it not?'

I nodded. 'It's not like any bird I've seen. It's got two heads for a start, which isn't right. But the paper's the best money can buy. I doubt it's the sort of stuff the Monseigneur can afford on what you're paying him.'

Lady Ginger barked out a laugh, which turned into a cough. She reached under the pillow again and hawked out a ball of sticky black phlegm into the 'kerchief.

'And the word?' She pointed at the letters.

'Is it a word?' I asked, turning the paper around to try to make sense of the writing. 'I took it for a string of letters. I thought it might be a code.'

It was true enough. Joey and I used to play a game with letters. We'd each choose a familiar saying, or one of Nanny Peck's best-turned phrases, and try to get the other one to guess it by writing the first letter of each word, one by one, on a piece of paper. The winner was the one who guessed the most sayings in the least amount of letters.

This wasn't a saying I recognised.

'A code, you say? I suppose you could call it that. Look

again.' Lady Ginger shuffled to the side of the bed and tapped the paper with a long curved nail. I turned it around to see if it meant anything upside down and then I held it on its side.

'It begins with a "K". Is it a message for me?'

'In a way.' She smiled and leaned back into the pillows. 'It is a message for both of us.'

I'd had enough of this. I tossed the letter onto the bed. Lady Ginger was running the circus just as she always had. It was very clear to me of a sudden that the only reason she'd brought me here was to entertain herself.

I pushed my hair back from my eyes. 'You might as well tell me straight what you're driving at instead of talking in riddles. Start with Robbie. What do you know about him and Da . . . his father, and why is it dangerous?'

She plucked the paper from the coverlet and handed it to me again. 'The answer is here. If you cannot handle this simple matter then perhaps I have made a mistake. Protecting Paradise – and everyone and everything in it – is no easy matter. You will find enemies in the most surprising places, always remember that.'

She faltered, leaned to the right and took up the pipe again. I saw her hand shake as she fumbled for the silver strike box.

'You will light this.' I took the box from her hand and scraped a Lucifer along its side, setting the flame to the bowl. Lady Ginger sucked on the pipe and moments later another great tremor went through her as the opium did its work. Just as before, she sank back into the cushions and her eyes rolled up into her head, leaving flickering slits of white.

I looked at the paper again. If it was an answer, then the

question was clear as Thames mud at low tide. I ran my fingers over the embossed mark. I *had* seen something like it before when I rolled the I Ching dice – the ones Peggy didn't approve of. But what did that mean?

'Where is the girl I saw in you?'

The question made me start. Lady Ginger was staring at me again now. At the corner of her mouth there was a glistening trail of drool.

'I am prepared to guide you, Katharine, but you must make your own deductions. You must learn, as I did. It is the only way. This . . .' she nodded at the note in my hand, '. . . is just the beginning. Other threats will come to your door and you must be ready. I do not doubt your courage, girl, but I chose you for your intellect and your good sense. Use them.'

I scrunched the paper into a ball in my hands. 'I'm not Swami Jonah, am I? This doesn't tell me anything.'

'It is not Mr McCarthy you should be consulting, on this occasion. That is all I am prepared to say.'

I noted that Lady Ginger used Swami Jonah's real name. She hauled herself up from the pillows and sat up straight in the bed – a scrawny heap of flapping black silk and loose sallow skin. She started to cough again, a horrible rasping rattle of a noise, and reached for the glass.

Her hands were shaking quite noticeably now as she gulped down mouthfuls of water. I heard the gurgle of it in her stringy throat as she swallowed. When she'd drained the glass, she set it down again on the table beside her bed and scratched lower for the drawer handle.

'The thirst is an unavoidable effect of my . . . medicine. But it is a small price to pay for respite. I have something for you.

Here.' She offered me a roll of patterned Oriental material.

I backed away shaking my head. 'You're not taking me with that one again. The last gift I accepted from you was hacked from some poor bleeder's hand.'

She smiled and I heard the sticky smack of wetness as her lips parted. 'This is quite different. Take it – you may need it. One day.'

I reached for the roll from her hands and she nodded. 'Good. You will be leaving me shortly. Remember what I said, Katharine, trust no one. And remind your brother that he cannot come back to London, ever. Repeat to me the words of the message I sent to him.'

'But why can't he come back? I could tell them – the Barons – about the fire and what really happened.'

She snorted. 'They know already.'

I weighed the roll in my hands. There was something folded inside, I could feel it through the silk. I needed to know why Joey couldn't come home.

'In that case . . .?'

'Repeat the message, Katharine.'

'*Bartholomew waits*. I told him in Paris. What does it mean?'

Lady Ginger's face was a mask. 'You will understand soon enough. In the meantime you would do well to remind your brother of it. After all – he is your blood, he is your family.' She paused. 'Think on those words.'

I was about to answer, but someone caught me tight from behind, pinning my arms to my sides. Before I could cry out a hand clapped a cloth across my face. I struggled furiously, trying to stop my nose and mouth against the familiar burning sweetness, but it was no good.

The last thing I saw before I fell to the floor was Lady Ginger watching me as she rolled her rat-tail plait between the tips of her fingers.

She smiled and raised her hand in a sort of crooked farewell. 'Protect him, Katharine.'

Chapter Seventeen

Blood.

I could taste it in my mouth, and smell it too. I opened my eyes and stared at the ceiling above my bed in Salmon Lane. That wasn't right, was it? The last thing I saw was . . .

Of a moment I couldn't recall. I brought a hand to my face. My nose was crusted up with something, my lips were cracked and my dry mouth was full of metal.

'She's awake!' Peggy's voice came from somewhere over to the left. I tried to sit up but my stomach rolled and a hammer went off in my head.

'Lucca – a bowl, quick!' A hand thrust a china dish under my nose, and my throat stung as I retched over the blue and white pattern. I hunched forward and felt someone hold my hair away from my face.

'There – that's better.' Peggy rubbed my shoulders. 'Drink this, Kit – it's water.'

I took the glass she offered and leaned back to allow her to move the bowl away. It all came back to me now: the coach, the drugged cloth, the shuttered house and Lady Ginger in that bed. The only thing I couldn't work out was how I came to be here.

'What time is it?' My voice was hoarse. My throat burned like I'd swallowed a hot coal.

'Past ten. You've been gone for a night and a day.' Lucca

was sitting in a chair drawn up next to the bed. He reached for my hand and squeezed it. 'When the carriage moved off I ran down the steps, but the driver was like a . . . *un pazzo*, a madman. I chased you, but he used his whip and the horses ran like the Devil himself was on their backs.' He glanced at Peggy. 'I came here, but we didn't know what to do.'

She nodded and sat on the bed. 'Actually, Kit, Lucca *did* know what to do. He sent word to Telferman and the message came back that we was to wait. You came home just two hours ago. There was a great banging on the door, but Tan Seng wouldn't open up. Then Lucca looked out and recognised the carriage. By the time we went down it was gone, and you were curled up on the step. The brothers helped carry you up here and we've been sitting with you ever since. What happened, Kitty? Are you . . .?'

I took another gulp of water. 'I'm fine. This'll pass. It's just another of my grandmother's speciality acts. The old cow still puts on a fine show.'

In the lamplight I saw Peggy and Lucca exchange looks.

'One of her crew drugged me when I went up into the coach . . . last night, was it?'

Lucca nodded.

'And the same thing happened before she sent me packing. Lady Ginger likes her privacy – she didn't want me to know where she lives. Oh, she made that very clear. Even if everything else she said was a riddle.'

'Did she hurt you? Your nose, Fannella – it's been bleeding and your lips are cracked. Here.' Lucca filled my glass again with water from a jug on the floor beside him. I drank it down in one and wiped my sore nose and mouth with my hand.

'She didn't touch me . . .' I was beginning to remember our talk more clearly now, 'except when she dug her black claws into my hand. No, I think it's the effect of the drugs she used. When I woke up at her place it was the same – my head felt like there was a bare knuckle round going off inside and my stomach wasn't right. Ten o'clock, you say?'

'*Sí*, nearer to eleven maybe now.'

'Then I've been under the influence of God knows what for hours. It was barely light when we spoke. She must have used enough stuff that last time to down an elephant. It's no wonder I feel like a coopered Judy.'

'You need a bit of heat in your bones.' Peggy stood and went over to the fire. I watched her kneel, rip some sheets of newspaper from the pile, screw them into balls and feed them into the grate where a small mound of coals was already glowing.

'There – that's a bit better, but we'll need Lok to bring up some more if you're to warm through proper. The scuttle's empty.'

'Where's Robbie?' I sat up straight in the bed, pulling my knees to my chin. Just like last time, the clanging in my head was beginning to muffle and every word my grandmother said had come back clear. David was playing a dangerous game, that's what she told me, and whatever it was it involved the boy I'd brought back to London for him.

'Danny's with him now. He came over to find me, Kit. It was after midday and he was worried when I didn't come home this morning.'

'And he was let in?'

'Course he was. I made such a row down in the hall that

Lok couldn't stand it. Dan's been here all the time since. He helped Lucca and the brothers bring you up here. The noise woke the little one so I asked him to go and sit with him while we cleaned you up. There was blood all over your face and matted in your hair when you came back. We thought you'd cracked your head open at first.'

For some reason I wanted to reassure myself that Robbie was safe. 'Can you fetch him to me, Peg?'

'Danny?'

I tried to smile. 'Now, why would I want to see his ugly mug? I mean the little one.'

Peggy frowned. 'But that would wake him and it's so late he'd never go off again now. He's been very bad tempered all day, which isn't like him. I think he's teething. His gums are that sore. There was blood in his mouth this morning.'

'Please, Peggy. I'd like to see him – Danny too.'

She arched an eyebrow. 'Seeing your own flesh and blood has made you come over all maternal of a sudden, has it?'

'Something like that.' I nodded at the door. 'Bring them both. I won't keep Robbie long. I just want to make sure he's . . . well. For his father's sake – I promised David that I'd look after his son, remember.'

Peggy grinned and cocked her head to one side. '*David* is it now? I wondered if there was more to that story than you was letting on, Kitty Peck. If his lad's anything to go by I reckon he's . . .' She broke off and glanced warily at Lucca. I saw her cheeks redden as she looked quickly down and started to brush some imaginary bits of fluff off her skirt.

'That's to say. I wondered if he was . . .'

I rolled my eyes. Peggy Worrow still thought Lucca and I

might be a pair. She could be so blind sometimes. Then again, it wasn't so long ago when I couldn't see what was sitting in front of my nose, was it?

'Just go and fetch them, will you?'

Peggy nodded gratefully and bustled out of the room, imagining, no doubt, that she'd said the wrong thing. Lucca waited for a moment until we couldn't hear her tread on the stairs and then he leaned forward and spoke softly. 'So what did she want, Fannella? What did you find out?'

I shook my head. 'I didn't find out anything I wanted to know, that's for sure. It was all riddles and games just like before. Lady Ginger dandling tidbits of information under my nose and whipping them away again before I could make anything out of them.'

I rested my head on my knees. 'I found out one thing, though. That baby, Robbie, he's trouble. She knew all about what I'd done and she knew about his father too. She said he was playing a dangerous game.'

Lucca grunted. 'We both know that. Why else would a man send his son to London with a stranger? And since then . . .' He paused for a moment and rubbed at the scarred skin of his cheek. 'The man who followed us last night? Was he the man you saw at the theatre, Fannella?'

'I didn't see him in the dark. I couldn't tell you if the man with the cane was the same one who ripped my ear. But it can't be a coincidence, can it?'

Lucca shook his head. 'No – no coincidence. You are right about the children. I made enquiries – one of the infants who perished in the fire at Mordant Street was dark skinned, like Robbie. I believe the child *is* in danger – as it seems are you.

But how did your grandmother know of this? How could she know about Robbie and his father?'

'She's still got spies working for her, Lucca. The Monseigneur is one of them. He wrote to her from Paris, but he's not much of a wordsmith.' I scanned the room. The lamplight made the shadows in the corners look like the tarry stains that once covered the walls in Lady Ginger's receiving room. For a moment I could believe she was still sitting there wreathed in smoke, listening.

'Where's my bag?'

'It's here.' Lucca stood and went over to the dresser. 'We couldn't loosen your fingers from the handle at first. Even in your drugged state you wouldn't let go.' He handed it to me. Both letters were inside, along with the fabric-wrapped package Lady Ginger had given me. I handed Lucca the heavy cream sheet. 'This is what he sent – the Monseigneur. What do you make of it?'

Lucca took the paper, unfolded it and stared at the word. His good brown eye widened.

'Do you recognise it?' I shifted across the bed to kneel close to him. 'And there's a mark at the top, impressed into the page. If you hold it up to the lamp you'll see it.'

Lucca raised the paper so the pattern showed clear. He ran a fingertip over the two-headed bird. 'This means nothing to me, but this . . .' he pointed at the writing – as usual I noted there was paint under his nails, 'is like something I've seen before.'

I took the paper and flattened it out on the bed. 'I thought it might be a code. "K" could be for Kitty – and the rest of the letters might stand for words. Lady Ginger said it was a message to both of us. So if that's Kitty, what do the rest of the letters stand for? There's a "P" then an "O" and two "B"s.'

Lucca shook his head. 'No – I do not think it is a code. It is one word. I cannot read it but I think I know someone—'

'Here he is.'

The door swung open and Peggy walked into the room with Robbie cradled in her arms. Danny was just behind. I folded the letter and tucked it under the sheet.

Robbie's big eyes were glassy with sleep. He wriggled in the blanket Peggy had wrapped him in and his lower lip started to tremble. She rocked him from side to side, but it didn't help. Seconds later he screwed his face into a crimson knot of anger and began to bawl. Peggy scowled at me and dabbed a finger into his mouth.

'See! I knew we shouldn't have disturbed him. And he hadn't been asleep long, had he?' She glanced back at Danny who was leaning against the wall watching her. He came forward now and dangled the poppet in front of Robbie's face.

'He wouldn't go off after you came back tonight, but this helped.' He turned to me. 'You all right, Kit? Only you looked like you'd done a couple of rounds when we carried you up here.'

'It looked worse than it really was – a nosebleed, that's all.' I paused. I didn't want to tell him where I'd been. 'Thank you for watching over Robbie.'

'He's no trouble.' Danny tossed the poppet across to the bed and I caught it. 'Once he had this tight in his hands he was happy enough sucking on an ear until he couldn't keep his eyes open. You might want to put a couple of stitches in the side there. He loves it so much it's coming apart.'

I smiled. 'I'll get my old workbox from The Gaudy out for him. Won't do any harm to keep my hand in, eh?'

'You always had the neatest stitches, Kitty, before . . .' Peggy shrugged, 'before you came to live here.'

Just for a moment I caught an odd look pass between her and Danny and I wondered what they said about me when they were alone together. There was an awkward pause while Peggy went back to fussing over Robbie, and Danny stared at the rug.

I cleared my throat. 'Well. Thank you both for this evening. I appreciate it.'

Danny grinned. 'Like I said – the little one's no trouble. And anyway . . .' He glanced at Peggy who was humming to Robbie and turning in a slow circle in front of the little fire. 'I reckon it's good practice for our own, when he or she arrives.'

Peggy turned to face me again now. She nodded and smiled. 'Due around Christmas, I think.'

Chapter Eighteen

Sam Collins was the last person I wanted to see, but a promise was a promise.

After that business with the missing girls I owed him. He didn't know the half of it, I was careful on that score, but me and Lucca had given him enough to make a 'proper scoop', as he called it. Now he was sitting in front of me, twitching and drumming his ink-stained fingers on Fitzy's desk – my desk, I corrected the thought.

He took another sip of tea. 'This is better than the filth Peters serves up at the office. I swear he's got worse, Kitty. Or perhaps he's buying an inferior blend these days – although it's difficult to imagine anything more disagreeable.'

He grinned and stared around. Apart from Ma's jug on the mantle the room was still bare, I hadn't moved anything in yet. 'This is all something of a . . . surprise?'

'Is it, Sam?'

I smiled blandly across the desk and thought about what to say next. Tell truth, I was always careful around Sam Collins. I liked him, and I suppose you could say I trusted him, but under all that twitching and bumbling there was a mind sharp as broken glass. It was an act. I knew that now. Like they say, it takes one to know one.

Now, some girls might have thought him handsome, but Sam was too spindly for my liking. He put me in mind of a weed that's outgrown its strength in straining for the sun. His hair still needed a good trim, I noted, as he flicked that long brown fringe out of his eyes. He was wearing a shabby suit and the stained ends of his frayed shirt cuffs poked out from the sleeves of his jacket.

'News business good?'

'You know how it goes, Kitty, one day you're riding high, the next you fall to earth.' He placed the cup and saucer on the desk and leaned forward. 'Between you and me, *The London Pictorial* isn't exactly riding high at the moment. There's a lot of competition on the streets. That's why I'm here.'

He smiled, folded his arms and leaned back, tipping the chair on its rickety legs. It made a cracking sound and rocked to an alarming angle, forcing Sam to grip the edge of the desk to right himself again.

Despite myself, I laughed. 'I should have warned you about that chair – it's on its last legs, like a lot of other things round here.' I glanced up at the ceiling. There was a stain just overhead where the smoke from Fitzy's stubby cigars had spread across the ceiling. 'It's time for a change.'

Sam narrowed his sharp brown eyes. 'Exactly, Kitty! That's what our readers want to know. What does the future hold for The Limehouse Linnet? You are greatly missed, do you know that?'

'Missed by your block boys in the basement and them that want to see a lot more of a girl than's decent, don't you mean? You made me look like a penny bangtail in them pictures, Sam Collins. No woman with a shape like that could swing on a trapeze, let alone catch the ropes round those . . . impediments.'

He shrugged. 'Artistic licence. It sells newspapers – and that's something *The London Pictorial* needs at the moment. Our investors are nervous.' He delved into a pocket and brought out a notebook, flicking it open to a blot-marked page covered in fingerprints and scribbles. I couldn't make sense of them – it wasn't English. And nor, according to Lucca, was the single word written on the paper in my bag.

I wondered if he was right. We'd find out one way or another later today. I glanced down to the side of the desk. I could see the crisp creamy paper poking out through the metal clasp of the fabric pouch. Just before Sam's unexpected arrival I'd flattened the thick page out on the desk and stared at the odd letters.

'What's that then?' I pointed at the squiggles in the notebook.

'Pitman. I taught myself.' Sam turned the notebook round and pushed it across the leather work top so I could see it clear.

'It's the fastest way to write with accuracy. It's phonetic.'

I looked up.

'It means sound, Kitty – these symbols reduce whole words to dashes that represent distinct sounds. I can note conversations at speed without missing a word.'

I stared doubtfully at the marks on the paper. 'You might be able to get it all down, but can you read it back afterwards? It's just scribble – and your grubby thumb marks cover half of it.'

'Is that a challenge?' Sam clapped his hands and rubbed them together. 'O, ye of little faith. Here, I'll show you. Choose any page you like and I'll read it aloud to you.'

I folded my arms. 'And who's to say you're not just making it up?'

He smiled. 'Because I will read the same page back to you a dozen times and each time it will be word perfect. If I had the talent to remember so many lines I rather think I'd be performing on one of your stages, Kitty, instead of scratching a living as a scribe, don't you?'

There! He dropped it in, casual as a tom cat sunning itself on a yard roof, all the while keeping watch for a sparrow.

One of your stages.

I sat back. 'What have you heard, Sam?'

He twitched back his brown fringe and spread his hands wide. 'This and that. Gossip mainly – I have my contacts, as you know. I'd rather hear it from you, though. Our readers will be most intrigued to hear that their favourite songbird has slipped from the confines of her gilded cage to take up a new . . . perch.'

I raised an eyebrow. 'You've written that bit already, haven't you? I recognise your style.'

'Do you?' He grinned broadly. 'That's very flattering. I never thought of myself as a stylist, but now you mention it—'

'Stop it, Sam!' I was angry now. 'You haven't come here to make chit-chat, you've come here for a story. You've heard about me taking on the halls and it's true – The Gaudy, The Carnival and The Comet – what's left of it – are mine now. I'm in charge.'

I paused, wondering how much more he knew.

'But don't you see, this is excellent news!' He reached across the desk for his notebook, brushing the handle of the tea cup with his jacket sleeve. It skittered across the wood and fell to the India rug leaking a pool of gritty tea leaves to form a new pattern among the threads.

'No harm done.' He snatched it up and replaced it on the saucer.

Flicking to a clear page in the notebook, he produced a pencil from his pocket. The words came rattling out. 'Now, what I need from you, Kitty, is some background detail. Perhaps you might have some ideas for the future you'd like to share with our readers. Are you, perhaps, working in secret on a thrilling new act? Will you ever perform again? Remember this is all good publicity. It will bring in the punters, I promise. The ceiling over at The Comet won't mend itself.'

He licked the end of the pencil and stared across the desk, his eyes alert and suddenly quite hard. 'Let's start with *how* it came about, shall we? Why are *you* in charge?'

⚰

I thought about what readers of *The London Pictorial News* would like to hear and I gave it to them.

The previous proprietor, I told Sam, had been impressed by my courage up there in the cage night after night. When circumstances of health meant they could no longer play a part in the running of the three halls, their thoughts turned to a successor.

'There was no family to pass it on to,' I lied. 'But they liked what they'd seen and thought I was just the girl who could take on a challenge. So now, here I am.'

Sam nodded. 'It's almost like something from a fairy tale, wouldn't you say, Kitty?'

'Is that what you want me to say, Sam?'

He looked up and grinned. 'That would be a very good line to add. The readers will lap it up.'

I raised my eyes to the smoke stain on the ceiling and sighed. 'Scribble it down then.'

He was right in a way, but it wasn't the sort of story you'd read to a child at night. I'd found Joey again, just like the girl who followed a trail of breadcrumbs through that wood, but it looked like I'd found something else there too.

'And Mr Fitzpatrick who used to be here, I understand he's moved on?' Sam licked the end of his pencil again. I heard the squeak of lead as his hand flew across the page.

'He's still working for me. He's got an office at The Comet. When we fix it up I've a mind to install him there on a permanent footing as chairman. For all his faults he knows his way round the halls. And the punters respect him. You need a bit of beef to keep order in this line of work.'

'And how does he feel about the, ah . . . new arrangement?'

'Let's just say . . . it's nothing I can't deal with. But I don't want you writing that – it's just between you and me, right?'

Sam nodded, turned the page and paused. 'Tell me honestly – and this also is just between us not for public consumption – your predecessor must have been very . . . impressed by you, Kitty. Did you have to . . . That is to say, was part of the . . . deal something more . . . ?'

I was sharp. 'There were no personal favours involved if that's what you're driving at, Sam Collins. What do you take me for?'

He put the notebook and pencil down on the desk. 'No, please . . . I don't . . . I didn't think. I just . . .'

He flicked back his hair and stared at me. 'Forgive me. It was a crass question. I happen to know that your benefactor was a woman . . .'

Of an instant it slotted into place. I didn't know whether to laugh or throw him out.

'So you took me for a Tom? You wondered if I'd bought my place here through a woman's bed. Is that it?'

Sam flicked at the edges of his notebook. I could tell he was embarrassed so I let him stew.

When he finally spoke he didn't look at me. 'I know that in the theatres such things are common. People turn a blind eye. Lucca and you – it's a front, isn't it? You appear to be a couple, but I know he is . . . his interests lie elsewhere.' He looked up from his notebook now and stared across the desk. He'd taken on the look of a whipped puppy.

'Look, I know it's none of my business, but I am right, aren't I?'

I laughed, I couldn't help myself. On the one hand Peggy thought me and Lucca were a regular pairing, and on the other Sam Collins thought us a most irregular couple.

'You're right about one thing at least – it's none of your business. But as you're a *gentleman* of the press you might as well hear it straight to stop any rumours flying about. No, I'm not a Tom – and you can take that down in your Pitman and shove it.'

I was surprised at what happened next. Sam reached across the table and caught my hand in his.

'I'm so very glad to hear that, Kitty. You have no idea how

. . .' He stopped himself and released me. Taking up his book again he opened it at the notes he'd been taking during our conversation. I recognised the thumb mark at the top of the page.

'No idea what, Sam?'

He smoothed the paper and took up the pencil. 'I merely meant to say . . . you have no idea how these rumours can spread and the effect they can have on a business.' He swallowed. 'I will endeavour to make the situation very clear whenever I hear gossip about you.'

Something became very clear to me just then. He was sweet on me, I was certain of it.

Now, here's a thing. It wasn't Sam's feelings I thought about just then, it was mine. Of an instant David Lennox's dark face sidled into my mind. How would it be, I wondered, if he was sitting there in front of me now making a sort of declaration? Would the skin of my hand prickle where he'd just touched it? Would he look at me with his fine green eyes and lean across the table to stroke my face with his long fingers?

Of a rule, I'm not one to daydream, but it would have been sorely easy to carry that one along.

I dug my nails into my palms. It was ridiculous. Get a grip on yourself, girl, I thought.

I looked at Sam's straggly fringe as he bent over his notebook and I thought about fetching my workbox, taking out my scissors and giving it a neat trim by way of a peace offering.

We sat there in uncomfortable silence. From the hall outside I heard the sound of voices and a couple of seconds later there was singing. I nodded at the door and started to speak, but the words came tumbling out too fast.

'It's the new routine. "The Sailor in Peril", you should go out and see it – give it a write up for us in *The London Pictorial*. I've been running through it with them this morning and we've made a couple of changes to sharpen it up. It's fresh. The punters will go mad for it – all them girls dancing barefoot. And it's funny too – it's not the sea he's got to contend with, it's his wives. All of them furious and all of them waiting for him to come ashore.'

Sam grinned. 'Poor chap. I wouldn't want to do battle with an angry fish wife. I'll mention it in my article about you. Do you want me to read it all back to prove I can read my scrawl?'

I shook my head and snatched the notebook from his hands.

'That's too easy! Anyone could remember what I've just told you word for word. I'll choose and you can read it to me *twice*. I'll know if there are any changes.' I flicked through pages dense with curling symbols searching for a particularly complicated section of Sam's coded scrawl. They all looked the same, except just occasionally a proper word, written in English, stood out.

Of a sudden I stopped. I recognised a single word printed neatly (for Sam) halfway down.

'What's this?' I pointed at the letters. Sam took the notebook from my hands and scanned the page.

'Sometimes I write a word in full if it's unfamiliar or foreign. Pitman isn't foolproof, you know.'

'You're not a fool, Sam, whatever else you might be.'

He glanced up. 'Do I detect a compliment?' He frowned. 'You're very pale, Kitty, and thinner than last time we met. I noticed that when I came in. Is everything . . . all right?'

I fiddled with the ball of hair at the back of my head, pressing the pins deeper to hold it in place. 'I'm fine. Why wouldn't I be? Now, are you going to show me your party piece or not? Read that page.' I pointed at the notebook.

Sam looked down. 'Ah – this was at the end of last week. I talked to a representative of The Ballet Moika. Apparently Moscow and Paris are too small for them now, they wish to conquer new worlds. Have you heard of them?'

I nodded. It was the word Moika that caught my eye.

'Go on then.'

Sam ran his finger down the page. 'I was talking to a man called Misha Raskalov. He's come over to look at possible venues. They are very particular about the places where they perform.'

Misha?

Sam looked up and smiled. 'I'm afraid The Gaudy, The Carnival and not even The Comet, before you brought the house down, would be considered good enough for the illustrious Ballet Moika.'

I shifted forward. 'This Misha – you spoke to him here in London?'

'Of course. We arranged to meet outside The Opera House, Covent Garden. He had a parlez there with the management. Then I took him to The Nell Gwynne, but he didn't seem to like it a great deal. He asked for champagne, Kitty. Can you imagine the cheek of it? Of course I paid up. It will be something for *The London Pictorial* to have the news first. They were said to be a sensation in Paris. All the same it was very expensive.'

'Did he speak English, only I don't reckon your Russian—'

'He told me he speaks six languages fluently – Russian, obviously, French, German, English, Spanish and Italian.'

I tapped the page. 'So what did he say, then?'

Sam looked down and started to trace the pencil marks with his index finger. He cleared his throat. 'Mr Raskalov said, in quite impeccable English: "Only the finest dancers and musicians are admitted to our ranks. We enjoy the patronage of the Imperial Family and are fortunate to consider ourselves to be the most favoured of all the great Russian companies. Paris has been good to us, but now it is time to perform to new audiences. We wish to bring the brilliance of The Ballet Moika to London in the summer so that its citizens may be dazzled by our artistry. I assure you, it will be like a new dawn for your capital. When your people see us, they will shield their eyes and then they will faint with pleasure and amazement. Even the jewels of your queen will seem dull in comparison. Truly the English have never seen such majesty, we are extraordinary. Your city will be blessed by our presence."'

Sam paused and winked at me. 'He wasn't exactly modest, I must say. I'm going to have to tone a lot of this down for the readers or they'll turn up armed with rotten fruit and worse. Do you want me to continue?'

I cocked my head and tried to make out where he was on the page. 'Is there much more?'

'No – a couple more paragraphs in very much the same vein, then a bit about someone called Ilya Vershinin, who, according to Misha just here,' Sam pointed at a couple of squiggles, '"is the most remarkable performer of our age. He

209

inhabits the spirit of any character he plays. His mastery of physical transition has been compared to a kind of magic. Ilya Vershinin dances like a god, leaping so high he could pluck down the stars."'

I thought of Joey – he'd said much the same thing about Ilya, hadn't he?

Sam flicked over the page. 'Lovely bit of hyperbole there. I can't use it. And then there's some detail about dates and possible venues. Between you and me, I don't think the meeting at the opera went that well. Humility is a virtue in London, but not, it seems, in Moscow or Paris.'

He leaned back and the chair cracked again. 'So, do you want me to read that back to you to prove I can do it?'

I shook my head. 'No, I couldn't sit through it again. Misha Raskalov – what did he look like?'

Sam raised an eyebrow. 'Ah – intrigued by the thought of a wild Russian, are we?'

I pursed my lips. 'And not two minutes ago, Sam Collins, you reckoned I was a Tom. No, I'm professionally interested, that's all. It doesn't do any harm to hear about the competition out there. You saw him last week?'

'On Friday, but he told me he'd been in London researching for almost two weeks now.'

Two weeks? I clasped my hands together under the desk out of Sam's view. Lucca's Misha – it had to be him, didn't it? – must have arrived in London only a few days after we came back from Paris.

If I had any doubts on the matter, Sam's next words wiped them clear.

'He's quite a striking fellow – tall, piercing blue eyes, very blond. Most particular about his dress. And the smell of him – he was soused in something. All very continental no doubt. When we cut along to The Nelly together I noticed several ladies turn their heads. But to be perfectly frank, Kitty . . .' he leaned forward conspiratorially, 'I think Lucca would be more to his tastes, if you follow me.'

You don't know the half of it, Sam Collins, I thought.

There was a light rap on the door. Right on cue Lucca stepped into the office.

Sam jerked back like he'd been caught dipping a pocket. He sprang up and offered his hand.

'Mr Fratelli, Lucca, good to see you.' He shot a guilty look at me as he pumped Lucca's arm a little too enthusiastically. 'Actually, we've just been talking about you, haven't we, Kitty?'

I stood up. 'I was saying that it was time for Mr Collins here to go because you and I have an appointment. You ready then, Lucca?'

He nodded. '*Sì*, but it is raining again. We will need an umbrella even if we take a hack. The streets outside are like rivers. It's the drains again. You might need to take a look at the cellars here.'

'I'll get Fitzy on it. He likes to wallow in filth.' I reached for my bag and pushed the letter down inside before snapping the clasp shut. Lucca took my coat from the hook on the back of the office door and passed it to me. As I pushed my arms into the sleeves I wondered how to tell him about Misha.

I glanced over – he was looking at the open notebook on the desk.

'Another story for *The London Pictorial*, Fannella?'

Sam swiped up the notebook and shoved it back into his jacket pocket. He grinned awkwardly and jerked his fringe back from his eyes. 'I'll make sure you and your halls get a good showing, Kitty. It's a fine story – rags to riches and all that. A just reward for a plucky young woman. "Songbird Spreads Her Wings!" There – that's my title! The readers will like it.'

I smiled. 'You wrote that too before you came, didn't you?'

'Smoked again!' Sam held out his hands, the palms and fingers were smudged with ink. He looked like a naughty schoolboy.

I buttoned my coat. 'We'll walk out to the street with you. Normally I'd offer you a ride, Sam, but on this occasion I don't think I'm going your way.'

Chapter Nineteen

The cab swayed to a halt and the driver opened the little trap above my head.

'Can't take you any further, Miss. It's a warren through there.'

Lucca pushed some coins up to him and shifted to open the door. He helped me down to the cobbles and sheltered me under his umbrella. He looked up at the driver. 'Where is Pearmans Yard from here, please?'

The driver pointed to a narrow passage with his whip. 'Look for Providence Buildings a hundred yards or so along there. You won't miss it – great black block it is, with half the windows shuttered over. Take a sharp left when you've passed by and then you'd best ask someone. Little Jewry is a maze.'

He tipped his sodden hat, clicked his tongue and the horse trotted off.

It was as if the rain had washed the colour from Brick Lane. Everything around us was a shade of grey, and that included the grim-set faces of the men and women who jostled past. Across the street a score of dripping wicker baskets hung at angles from a tattered awning. The shopkeeper hadn't bothered to bring them in. Just above the entrance, there was a wooden cage with a dull brown bird huddled in the corner. There was nothing for it to sing about today.

I dodged back against the boarded shop front behind us

as a cart splashed mud up my skirt.

'Little Jewry? Is Old Peter Jewish then?'

Lucca nodded. 'Of course, half the orchestra are sons of Abraham. Did you not know that? Music is their gift to the world, just as art – painting, I mean – is the gift of my own people.'

'I know, The Trinity – Old Mickey, Leonardo and Raphael.' I tapped the side of my head. 'See, I do listen to you sometimes. So, it's Hebrew, is it – that word on the paper?'

Lucca shook his head. 'I think it to be Russian. I . . . I asked Peter to help me write a letter and I recognised the script. In Russia they use the Cyrillic alphabet. It's quite different.' He paused and then continued softly, 'It was a gesture. Even though he speaks and reads many languages I wanted to show him how important our time together was . . . to me.'

I knew immediately that Lucca wasn't talking about Old Peter just then.

I hadn't told him what Sam had said about Misha Raskalov being here in London. I'd thought about it during the cab ride over to Tenterground, gone over it in my head trying to find the words, but they didn't come, and anyway, I couldn't find the moment.

I bit my lip as I stared up at Lucca's face. Raindrops were sliding down the crimpled scars on his cheek. *How could anyone love a ruin?* That's what he'd said once. He thought he'd found someone in Paris, but now . . .

I dropped my eyes to my boots and watched as a half-rotten cabbage head bobbed past in the gutter, its passage blocked by a pile of greasy black muck wedged between some broken stones. At best, Misha had decided to ignore Lucca, not even bothering to look him up in London. At worst . . .

I thought about Peggy and Robbie and that meeting in the churchyard. Had that been Misha Raskalov? I brought my fingers up to the ragged tear in my ear. It was healing now, but the wound still smarted if I rubbed it too hard or caught it with the brush when I was pinning up my hair. Was it Misha who was there in the shadows at The Gaudy that night? According to Sam he would have been in London then.

I huddled closer to Lucca, pushing my arm round his waist. 'You got room for me under here?'

He dipped the canopy to shield us both and we stepped into the passage, following the cabman's directions. After Providence Buildings, which certainly didn't warrant the name, we turned left through a brick arch and into a scruffy circular courtyard with dark alleyways fanning out around us in the way of a dial.

'Which one, Lucca?'

There was a scuffling sound from behind. We turned to see a scrap of a lad watching us from one of the gloomy entrances. I say lad – he can't have been more than ten years old, but the black eyes in his hollowed face belonged to a man three times his age.

Lucca tipped the umbrella and peered out. 'Do you know Mr Ash? Peter? We are looking for him.'

The boy's eyes widened with horror as he took in Lucca's scars. He backed into the shadows. I felt Lucca stiffen beside me and thought again how hard it must be to negotiate your way through a world that takes everything at face value.

'Wait!' I called. 'There's a penny in it for you.' I ducked out from under the umbrella and reached into my coat pocket. I always kept some change there. I stepped forward. 'Here. Mr Ash. He's a musician – he plays a cornet. Do you know where he lives?'

The boy grinned and reached for the coin, but I snatched it away.

'Oi! Not so fast, young man. Which one of these passages is Pearmans Yard? It's where he lives.'

The dark eyes became wary. 'He done somefink wrong?'

I shook my head. 'I need him to help me with something, that's all. He's a . . . a sort of friend, you might say.'

The boy looked doubtful and glanced at Lucca.

'Listen – it's nothing bad. Do you want this penny or not?'

He nodded sullenly, wiped a ripe bulb of snot from his nose and pointed at an alleyway behind us over to the right.

'Fifth entrance down there. Four floors up. He's got the room at the top.' The boy held out his hand and I dropped the penny into his palm.

'Thank you.' I winked at him. 'Nothing bad. I promise.'

⚓

Old Peter raised the mug and slurped a mouthful of steaming tea.

'Good, yes?' He slammed a fist down hard on the wood and beamed across the table at me. I tried to nod and smile. It was filthy stuff. I'd lay a bet it was worse than anything Sam Collins had ever encountered in the offices of *The London Pictorial News*.

I'd watched Peter dissolve a knob of butter in the black tea he'd poured from a gleaming kettle on the hearth. The sour taste of that was bad enough, but there was something else in there too. Something that stung the back of my throat and made my belly boil over like a wash-day copper.

'The butter was my mother's secret – she had it from a servant from the Eastern provinces. In the winter or on days such as this it warms.' He took another swig and dabbed his bearded lips quite daintily with a napkin.

'It's not just the butter, is it?' I set the painted tin mug on the table and watched the floating yellow blobs disintegrate into the blackness. There was a thin film now on the surface of the tea.

Peter laughed. 'Of course – wodkya, firewater. It is life!'

He raised his mug and indicated that me and Lucca should do the same.

'*Zda-róv-ye!* Health!'

He clinked his mug against ours and turned to me. 'Now, Mistress Kitty. You do my home great honour. Are you comfortable?'

Tell truth, apart from the tea, I was. Despite the fact Peter lived down a mud-dark passage, four floors up in a narrow black building that looked like a broken tooth in the middle of a row of rotten stumps, he had managed to make quite a nest for himself and for Zhena. I noted that his beloved cornet sat on its own chair in the corner.

His room at the top of forty-four dingy twisting stairs was small, but comfortable. Colourful squares of patterned material were pinned to the walls, every chair had a fat cushion, good china and polished brass glinted on shelves above the little fireplace and a couple of small paintings hung on the wall over the box bed.

I nodded. 'Thank you, you've made us very welcome.'

'It is the way – a guest must be honoured. Drink first and then you can tell me the reason for your visit.' His smile faltered as he stared across the square table at me and then he looked mournfully at Zhena. 'You are planning to make changes. Is this why you have come, Mistress?'

'It's Kitty, remember? And no, that's not why we've come. You and all the orchestra boys – you got nothing to fret about on that score. You're bleedin' good, all of you.'

I felt, rather than saw, Lucca wince as I continued. 'I've come about a letter.'

Peter turned to Lucca. 'Ah, she knows. The lover – has he replied yet?'

Lucca stared at the greasy specks swirling in his tea. He shook his head, but didn't say anything. Peter shrugged and leaned over to pat his hand. 'Maybe soon, eh? It was a good letter – strong, honest. How could he not reply? It was an honour to translate it for you.'

Lucca raised the mug to his lips and took a swig. I reckoned it was firewater he needed right then. I cleared my throat. 'Actually, that's why we came. Not about the letter you helped Lucca with, but about a translation. It's very simple. I think – well, that's to say, Lucca thinks, it's Russian. Just the one word.'

I reached for my bag under the table and brought it to my lap.

'Here.' I handed Peter the folded letter and watched him open it out. He looked down at the word and frowned. Then he ran the tips of his fingers over the pattern pressed into the paper at the top of the page.

Immediately he dropped the paper on the table and wiped his hands. He hissed something through his teeth. I didn't catch the word, but I caught the meaning all right. He looked at me and his sad brown eyes hardened.

'Where did you get this?'

'Is it Russian?'

He just repeated the question. 'Where, Kitty?'

'It was sent to me. I can't make head nor tail of it, but Lucca thought you might be able to read it. And he was right, wasn't he?'

Peter nodded. He looked down at the sheet, but he didn't touch it. He folded his arms, hands tucked beneath his shirt sleeves and sat back from the table.

I tried again. 'What is it then, please? That word there?' I pointed at the neat letters written in the middle of the page.

кровь

Peter reached for his tin mug. 'It is pronounced "krov".'

He swirled the tea around and gulped back a mouthful. 'Blood – the word is blood.'

The fine hairs at the back of my neck stood guard as I looked at the letter. Of an instant I heard my grandmother's voice again – almost the last thing she'd said to me:

He is your blood, he is your family. Think on those words.

I thought on them now but it still didn't make no sense despite being set down there in black ink. I turned the sheet round and stared at the letters. She'd said it was a message, hadn't she? What's more she said it was a message for both of us, me and her.

Blood?

Peter slammed the mug down hard on the table.

'Do you know whose crest that is?' He pointed at the marks embossed into the paper.

I shook my head. Lucca reached for the page and held it against the fire so the unnatural bird showed up clear.

'The two-headed eagle is the symbol of the House of Romanov – the Imperial Family of Russia.' Peter nodded at the paper between Lucca's hands. 'Do you see the three crowns above the heads? And in the claws a sceptre and orb. The signs of majesty.'

He grunted, leaned back and spat past the paper into the little fire.

'*Ublyudki!*'

Whatever that meant, I was sure it wasn't a compliment.

'How did you come by this, Kitty?'

'I . . . I was sent it. I don't know anything about the . . . Romanov, you say?'

Peter stared into the fire. 'Then you are lucky. If it wasn't for them and their need for an army I wouldn't have been taken from my family at the age of eleven, and sent four hundred miles from my home to a frozen, stinking canton.'

I glanced uncertainly at Lucca. He placed the letter on the table, raised his eyebrow and shook his head just once. We waited for Peter to continue, but he pushed his chair back, rose and went over to the alcove at the back of the room. He pulled at the curtain that half-screened the bed so the little pictures showed more clearly. I could see now that they were portraits – a man and a woman, painted to face each other as they hung on a wall. Peter stood with his back to us. After a moment he started to talk again, very quietly.

'Twenty young male conscripts from every thousand head of the Jewish population were sent to the military colleges. It was not an honour – they were the harshest place you can imagine. We stole food from each other to stay alive. We fought in the snow-crusted yards over scraps of stale, worm-riddled bread. At night we picked our pallets open and filled our mouths with straw.

'Everyone knew how cruel the conditions were. The wealthy families – the merchants, the factory owners – paid to keep their boys at home. My parents were comfortable too, but the *qahal* chose me to punish them. We were *haskalah* – enlightened.' He paused and laughed bitterly.

'My mother would have gone barefoot to the synagogue every day, even in winter, if it meant they would have spared me. Here they are, my mother and father. I never saw either of them alive again after the day I was taken.'

He reached over the bed, murmured and touched his mother's forehead. 'So, the orchestra is my family now – and Zhena.' He turned, walked over to the chair and lifted the cornet from its cushion.

'She saved my life. If it hadn't been for the fact that I was musical and was chosen for the military band, I would be gone like the boys who starved in the schools and died out on the battlefield fighting for the glory of our Romanov masters.'

He spat into the fire again as if the words were poison in his mouth.

'But . . . how did you end up here in London, Peter?' I watched as he stroked the red cords hanging from the instrument, gently untangling the knots with long tapering fingers.

'Simple. I ran away at the age of fifteen. It was winter and I nearly died on the road, but people were kind. I played for them in return for their hospitality. When, finally, I reached my town, my parents and Lifsha, my little sister, were dead. I was told I was the lucky one.' He grunted. 'If I had stayed, the elders said, the influenza would have killed me too. I'd be with my family beneath the snow in the cemetery.'

He took a deep breath. 'I wasn't safe – too many spies eager to make friends in high places, besides there was nothing to stay for. Everything was different by then – even my name. Peter is what they called me at the canton – a good Russian name, but it has served me well. My real name is Pesach. All my family's possessions had been sold except the pictures over there. A friend of my mother's saved them as mementoes, but she gave them to me. So, Zhena and I travelled through Europe, but when we came here more than twenty years ago now, we stayed.'

He stroked the golden bell of the cornet. I pulled the letter over and smoothed it out on the table. The gold at the edges of the paper glinted in the firelight. I wasn't sure what to say.

'Have . . . have you ever wanted to go home again, Peter?'

He shook his head. 'London is my home. I fit, there are people like me here – and anyway in Russia I am still considered to be a traitor. I ran away from the Czar's army, remember? Even here, sometimes I wonder if I am truly safe. The Romanovs are a powerful family.'

I ran my fingertips over the double-headed bird on the page. No wonder he hated them.

'Now, I have a question for you, Kitty.'

I looked across at Peter. He was sitting in Zhena's chair, his bushy black eyebrows tangled together above troubled eyes.

'In Russia it would be a crime for anyone except a member of the Imperial Family to possess paper embossed with such a crest. Why would someone send you a letter from the desk of a Romanov with that word written on it?'

I couldn't answer him.

Chapter Twenty

At least it had stopped raining – or I thought it had. It was difficult to tell in the narrow confines of Pearmans Yard. I looked up at the crack of dirty yellow overhead and wondered if the sun ever shone down here. Nanny Peck would have called it a 'cat's piss sky' – the sort that threatens to scratch up a storm.

'I need a walk to clear my head, Lucca.'

He nodded. 'The tea was strong.'

'And not just the bleedin' tea. What does it all mean – '*blood*', that Russian crest, Romanov? Why would the Monseigneur send it to Lady Ginger? And why would she say it was a warning? Tell you something for nothing, it's times like this I wish Swami Jonah was the real thing instead of a scouser with a ringer in one of the boxes. I don't feel any clearer on this now than I did before.'

Lucca buried his chin in his collar and flattened up against the wall as a tiny, skull-faced woman with a half-naked baby in her arms splashed past. Her soiled skirt was sodden with rainwater up to the knees. I watched her disappear into an open entrance a dozen yards down.

I shook my head. How did a family keep the meat on their bones here? Robbie might be separated from his father – and his mother, whoever she was – but at least he was warm and fed. And loved.

I stepped down into the alley. 'I promised Peggy I'd be back before six. She's been at The Palace all day again with Robbie and I don't want to take another liberty with her time. We better get moving. Perhaps we should take a cab after all?'

Lucca nodded. 'And I think it will rain again.' He took my arm and we started back to the courtyard with all the passages running off. One thing I was sure of at least: the single thread running through all of this linking everything up was Russian. Once we were in that cab together I was going to have to tell Lucca about Misha Raskalov.

'*Che idiota!*' Lucca snapped his fingers and stopped. 'The umbrella! I left it in Peter's room.'

I wiped a splot from my nose and saw the scummy surface on the puddles around the yard begin to dance. 'We'll go back then. But I'll wait at the bottom for you. I'm not climbing all those stairs again – and I certainly don't want another mug of that tea.'

I stood on the step just inside the entrance to Peter's building and watched the brown water gushing past down the narrow alley. It frothed and whirled around the mouth of an open drain just a few foot away, sucking everything – sticks, leaves, little bones and clotted lumps of pallid gristle – down into the sewers under the City. From there I guessed it spat out into the Thames and then on to the sea.

I felt for Joey's ring and Christopher at my neck. I'd hung them on another, thicker chain now. I rubbed the medal, wondering about the letters I'd sent to Paris. Had Joey got them yet? David too? Perhaps David was bobbing about on the sea right now coming over to London to fetch his boy away?

I tucked the chain back into the ruffles of my collar. My brother attracted bad luck like a magnet.

Bartholomew waits.

What did that mean? What else had he done in the past to make him an exile? And what had he got me into now? The more I learned about Joseph Peck the less I knew him. I watched a scrap of soiled rag wind itself around the grille of the drain, catching more filth in its folds.

At the sound of Lucca's footsteps on the stairs I turned from the alley.

'*Where is he?*' The soft familiar voice was in my ear and the smell of leather and spice filled my nose. A hand crept over my shoulder.

But I was ready this time. I grabbed the fingers, yanked them up to my mouth and bit down hard. My teeth cut through the leather to the skin beneath. I was gratified to hear a yelp. I brought my left arm up and swung the point of my elbow back, catching something soft with a vicious blow.

I didn't turn. Instead I jumped up to catch a metal bar that ran across the top of the low doorway. My bag caught in the crook of my elbow as I lunged forward. Adjusting my weight, I arched my back, bent my legs, pointed my feet and kicked out behind as hard and fast as I could as I swung back. My boots connected with a solid mass. I heard a grunt of pain and a clatter as someone fell back onto the cobbles.

Lucca appeared at the foot of the staircase as I swung forward again and dropped to the stone floor. I whipped round to see a hooded man crouched in the alley. I'd knocked him against the wall opposite. He was winded, but he jerked the hood forward to cover his face, pulled himself together and reached behind to produce a black walking cane tipped with a heavy silver hawk head from the folds of his cloak. The cruel, curved beak was sharpened to a point. The man started to haul himself up against the wet black bricks.

He was tall. Under the black material his shoulders were nearly as broad as Fitzy's.

'Oh bravo, Miss Peck!' The harsh voice was almost a whisper. 'Now let me show you what I can do.'

'*Non la penso cosi!*'

Lucca stepped swift from behind and poked the metal tip of the umbrella into the man's face. There was another howl of pain. At the same moment he released the catch so the stiff black canopy opened with a flourish. It wedged itself across the passage cutting the man from view.

'Run, Fannella!' Lucca grabbed my hand and we leapt from the entrance of Old Peter's building and splashed along Pearmans Yard, moving in the opposite direction from the clock-dial courtyard.

I could hear scraping behind as the man pushed the umbrella aside and then the pounding of feet as he followed. The passage veered left. As we rounded the corner Lucca dropped my hand so we could keep pace. The space between the buildings narrowed again and the bricks closed around us. The cabman was right, this was a maze.

I sprinted forward, hitching up my skirts to free my boots. Lucca was just behind. My bonnet skewed to one side, and the ribbons came loose. I felt it bump down onto my back but I didn't catch at it. I couldn't keep hold of the bag and my skirt and deal with the hat. After a moment it fell off.

'K . . . keep going.' Lucca's voice was hoarse. 'I heard him slip in the water back there, but he's coming again.'

I didn't even turn to see where the bonnet had gone. Ahead, the passage branched into two. The dark alleyways topped by a pair of brick arches looked like unblinking eyes.

'Wh . . . which way now?' Lucca didn't answer so I jagged right. It was black along there. I could hardly see a hand in front of my face. The alley was low, the arched ceiling pressing just above my head. I supposed there was houses built above us – I could sense the weight of them. Since that time under the warehouse, I hadn't much liked being underground. It smacked of being buried alive.

I tightened my grip on the bag, the handle slippery with the wet, and ran on. After twenty yards or so, the alley opened out overhead. Thin yellow-grey light showed the way again. That's to say it would have done, if I hadn't led us into a dead end.

A great black wall reared up in front. I span round, rain streaming down my face and over my shoulders. Strands of hair were caught across my mouth and nose. We were standing in a rectangular space the size of the trap under the stage of The Comet, only no one was going to pull a lever to spring us out in a shower of sparks. We were like cornered rats.

I tried to catch my breath. My chest felt as if it was going to burst open.

The sound of footsteps echoed from the alleyway. Lucca turned.

'This way!' I caught his arm and dragged him into one of the two entrances set either side of the tiny yard. Inside it was like Old Peter's building. A couple of doors at ground level and a narrow staircase rising up at the back.

'We'll . . . we'll go up!' I ran across to the steps and started to climb. Lucca followed.

The steep stairs twisted back on themselves at the first landing and then turned again at the next so they ran up through the centre of the building, taking as little space as possible from the rooms on each floor. The doors were shut, some of them barred over. If anyone heard us clattering up them stairs they didn't think to poke their noses out to take a look.

'Wh . . . where are we going, Fannella?' Lucca's voice was frayed. He stopped for moment, gasping for air, and kicked out at a pile of empty wooden crates stacked against the wall of the fourth landing. I glanced back to see them tumble down the stairs creating an obstacle of sorts.

'I d . . . don't know. There was . . . wasn't nowhere else to go, was there?' I rounded the fifth flight and came to a boxy landing, the corners crusted with cobwebs and pigeon shit. We had reached the top. Patches of sky showed through ragged holes in a low ceiling that slanted down on three sides. There was a thumping noise on the stairs below, but from the muffled sound I couldn't make out how far down he was.

A pigeon muttered and strutted across the boards between us as I scanned the doors off the landing. Two were crisscrossed with wooden planks. They'd been nailed across by the landlord, I guessed, to keep out those who couldn't pay for such luxury. The third door was shut. Just above it a small window was set into the angled roof about six foot up. Most of the glass was missing.

'Look!' Lucca nodded at a spindly metal ladder propped in a corner. He pointed up at the window. 'It's the only way from here?'

Without bothering to answer I grabbed the ladder and set it against the wall under the window. I climbed up and pressed my hand against one of the remaining glass panes. The catch was broken like everything else here. It swung open easily. I pushed my bag out onto the flat bit of roof visible in front of me and scrambled through after it.

'Come on then. Quick as you like.' I knelt beside the window as Lucca clambered up.

'P . . . pull up the ladder too. Then he can't . . .'

The words died on my lips as the head of a cloaked figure appeared on the shadowed stairs below. I heard the scrape of his cane against the wall. Lucca leaned down and yanked hard on the ladder, dragging it up, hand over hand, until it was out through the broken window. We rested it against the sooty parapet.

'What now?'

I gulped down a lungful and patted the ladder. 'Well, he can't follow us up here, can he?'

Lucca shook his head doubtfully and leaned back against the sloping roof. I could hear the rattle in his chest. 'But wh . . . where are we to go?'

There was a huge thud from below and the sound of splintering wood. I sprang up and stared about. The flat part of the roof was about nine foot square. Over to the left it slanted sharply upward. A cluster of blackened chimney pots sprouted from a stack in the centre of the lead-tiled slope. I wiped the rain from my eyes and peered over the parapet on the right. A chasm yawned down to another alley running far below. And beyond that I could see a warren of passages running off in all directions separating the scores of buildings clustered around Pearmans Yard.

I straightened up. Across the alley, around six foot distant by my reckoning, there was another roof. Pointed it was, not flat like this one, but hemmed round again with a smoke-smudged parapet. I knotted my hair back. It had come loose with the bonnet and was flying all round my face up here. The sound of something heavy being dragged across wooden boards came from below.

'I think he's found a way to reach us.' Lucca was peering down through the broken window. 'That noise just now? He . . . he broke into the room across the landing and now he's piling things up against the wall.' He looked up at me, his good eye wide with fear.

'I . . . I don't think I could protect you from him again. He's . . .'

'Built like a brick shit house?'

Lucca nodded. 'I wouldn't put it qu . . . quite like that, but on this occasion you are right. And the cane?'

'You saw the hawk head?'

'*Si.* It is a vicious weapon.'

There was another grating sound from below. I stared at the roof of the building opposite. If I jumped I could clear the gap, but I'd need to take a run at it to be sure and I couldn't do that on account of the parapet. I scanned the bare roof for an alternative. There was nothing here except jittering puddles, a couple of dead birds, me, Lucca and the ladder.

The ladder!

I dragged it to the edge of the parapet, swinging it out so that it rested on the ledge of the building opposite. It reached easily.

'You got a head for heights, Lucca?'

He left the window and came to stand next to me. 'I don't have much choice, do I, Fannella?'

I knelt to pull off my boots, not bothering with the laces, and I hurled them over to the roof across the alley. They rattled across the tiles and came to a rest behind a chimney stack. I threw the bag over after them.

'Shall I go first?'

Lucca nodded and turned at an ominous thump from behind.

As I saw it there was two ways of tackling the ladder. I could swing from bar to bar underneath and roll myself up onto the ledge, using the strength of my arms and the curl of my stomach – just as Madame Celeste had taught me on the trapeze in her attic all them months ago – or I could go across on the top.

I took a breath. 'Don't even think about what you're doing. Choose one rung to step on – you won't need more to get across, trust me – fix where it is in your mind and go. Keep your eyes on the stack straight ahead and don't look down.'

I ripped off my stockings and without another word I took off. My bare foot made contact with a metal rung halfway along the ladder and then I sprang for the roof on the far side, throwing my weight forward to give me some heft. I landed safely in the gulley just beyond the ledge.

I turned back. 'Now you.'

Lucca just stood there. He was staring down into the alleyway some fifty foot below.

I swiped the rain off my cheeks. 'Take off your shoes and throw them over. It will be easier that way.' He shook his head slowly, but didn't make a sound. The window behind him crashed open and a dark hunched shape appeared. I saw something silver gleam in the thin light.

Lucca jerked his head up.

'You have to come *now*!' I stood and held my arms forward. God knows I wouldn't have been able to catch him if he fell, but it was something.

'Now, Lucca!' He crossed himself, cried out and lunged forward. I couldn't bear it. I closed my eyes . . .

Chapter Twenty-one

I heard the metal sing as Lucca's boot made contact with the rung, and a grating, clanging noise as the ladder slid to one side on the rain-lashed roof, plummeting to the stones far below. It scraped the walls of the buildings as it fell, the iron ringing out like a bell.

Lucca collapsed in a heap on top of me and I hugged him tight. I could feel his body tremble through the thick material of his coat.

'You're safe. You did it!' I stroked his hair – his hat had fallen away.

I remembered the time he had talked me down from the cage when the ceiling of The Comet had fallen in and I pulled him closer. It came to me again then most forcible that Lucca Fratelli was more of a brother to me than Joey ever was.

There was a movement over his shoulder. On the roof opposite a dark figure stood outlined against the leaden sky. The man stepped up onto the parapet and paused for a moment, considering whether or not to jump.

I saw him measure the distance and weigh up the likely outcome.

I glanced behind. The jumbled roof on this side ran along the top of a row of connected buildings. The man standing opposite couldn't see that because of the wide chimney stack blocking his view, but I could. Every so often there was a window set into the tiles, just like the one Lucca and I had climbed out from. I knew then that we were likely safe. We could choose any window in any building to make our exit and disappear into the labyrinth of passages below. I loosened my grip on Lucca and called across the gap.

'If you're thinking about coming after us I wouldn't recommend it.'

The man lowered his head so that the hood covered his face completely.

'I just want to talk to you, Kitty.' The voice was low, silky and heavily accented. I watched as he twirled the hawk-headed cane about on the parapet. 'I need some information, that's all.'

'If that's true why don't you just make an appointment at The Gaudy?'

He raised a gloved hand, spread his fingers wide and then he pressed his thumb down hard on the tip of the hawk's beak. Even at this distance I could see something dark well up to stain the leather.

'Because, when we talk, I want to be sure that you'll give me what I want.'

I felt cold rain trickle down the neck of my dress and trace a path under my bodice between my breasts as he stepped down. He turned his back on us, the cloak flapping about like the wings of a great black bird, and retraced his steps towards the open window.

Lucca twisted round and moved a little way back along the parapet. He watched the other roof for a moment, his hand pulling at the scarred flesh of his right cheek.

'He is gone.'

I stared at Lucca and I thought again about Misha Raskalov. He'd been here in London all the time.

'Who is he, Fannella? What does he want?' Lucca bent to retrieve one of my boots from the gulley. I gathered up its pair and didn't answer straight off. I loosened the laces and pushed my wet bare feet down into the leather.

Where is he?

'I don't know. Truly I don't.' I bit the inside of my lower lip. 'There's something I need to tell you, Lucca. You're not going to like it.'

Lucca didn't say a word after I told him about Misha. He just stared out of the little steamed-up window of the cab. I tried to catch his hand, only he moved it away.

The streets were running like rivers now. It was the sort of rain that comes at you from all sides. Even if we hadn't abandoned the umbrella back in Pearmans Yard we would have been soaked to the skin underneath it. There was a low rumble and the cab rocked about as the horse spooked. A second or so later the dim interior flashed up lightning sharp so I could see the scribbles of mud on the floor from our boots and the buttons missing from the leather seats.

Nanny Peck had been right about that cat's piss sky.

We jerked to a halt at the end of Salmon Lane. I paid the driver and Lucca helped me down to the street. It was past seven.

'You coming with me, Lucca?'

'I'll walk you to the door. It's not safe.'

We started along the narrow cobbled way together. I caught his sleeve.

'Listen. I . . . that is, I wish . . .'

'Don't. I wish a lot of things, but it doesn't make them happen.'

We stopped at the foot of the steps. I looked up at the black brick walls of The Palace. It was still hard to think of this place as a home – as my home. The double doors swung open. Tan Seng shuffled out on the step, stood to one side and bowed.

'Lady.'

I nodded up at him and pulled on Lucca's arm.

'At least come in for a while. You can't go home alone to-night, not after . . .'

'I need to think, Fannella. If he – Misha – is here in London, as Sam Collins says, that is . . .' Lucca shrugged and stared down at the rain-slicked stones, '. . . understandable. At least I know why he didn't reply to my letter.'

'But if he's here, why didn't he tell you? Why didn't he come and find you?' The words came out too quick and of an instant I regretted them when I caught the look on Lucca's face. He stepped away from me and flicked up the collar of his coat, burrowing his chin into the folds of the muffler. He didn't answer my questions. Instead he shrugged, hunched his shoulders against the rain and turned away, walking quickly up the passage towards the street.

'Kitty!' Peggy's voice echoed from the stones.

I looked up to see her hovering behind Tan Seng, Robbie in her arms.

'Go in!' I hissed. 'I told you about bringing him outside.'

'I thought you were the crow.' She huddled Robbie against her and scanned the street. 'Why isn't he here?'

'Crow!' I ran up the steps and pulled the doors to a close behind me. 'What do you mean? Why do you need a doctor, Peg?'

'It's not me, it's Robbie. That fucking parrot bit him.' She moved Robbie in her arms so I could see him properly. I brought my hand to my mouth. The pale blanket she'd wrapped him in was covered in blood, great vivid streaks of it glistening in the lamplight.

'Jesus! What happened?'

'He wouldn't go down a couple of hours ago. I fed him the pap, but he kept crying and thrashing around in his basket. You wouldn't know this, Kitty, but when he gets like that he likes to be on the move. So I took him up and we went for a little stroll about the house. I carried him through to that room you've set up as a parlour. Then the parrot went off in the corner, but Robbie started to calm down. He actually likes it.

'I took him over for a closer look and then on account of nothing, the vicious thing lashes out. It happened so fast. One second I was holding him up to see the bird, next thing it's clinging to the cage digging its beak into his hand. It wouldn't let go.'

Peggy pulled at the material wrapped round Robbie's body and gently freed his hand. It was bound up with a soaked crêpe bandage.

'Lok helped me with that. The blood's stopped now, thank God, but you should see this.' She loosened the bandage and Robbie started to make a little mewing sound.

'He's too tired to cry, poor lamb. Here . . .' She held up his left fist very gently. The brown was mottled purple and his hand and wrist were swollen to twice their normal size. From his elbow to the tips of his fingers, Robbie's skin looked ripe to burst.

'It's not normal. Here's the bite.' She smoothed the tips of her fingers over a crusted v-shaped gash across the back of his hand. 'It wasn't even that deep. At first the blood wouldn't stop, but when it did his arm bruised up so badly. I didn't know what to do.' She glanced at Tan Seng. 'None of us did.'

Robbie began to cry properly now. Peggy rocked him back and forth. 'It hurts – he's in pain, Kit. That's why I called the crow. Lok's gone to fetch him.'

Dr Pardieu didn't ask too many questions and I was grateful for that. From what little he did say, I guessed he was already something of a regular at The Palace. While he was packing away his bandages and his bottles he glanced warily at me and cleared his throat.

'The Lady . . . I gather from Mr Lok that she has . . . uh . . . moved on?'

'That's right.' I nodded and watched as he deftly rolled up a skein of fresh white crêpe. He'd tied the rest round Robbie's arm.

'And you are . . . Miss Peck, is it?'

I nodded again, but I didn't give him what he wanted. He took his jacket from the back of the chair and brushed something from the shoulders before putting it on. As he swung the jacket round the smell of naphtha came to me. I realised then who it was Dr Pardieu reminded me of – Telferman. Not to look at, mind, but in his manner. He was careful with me – superior, but servile at the same time. It was an odd combination.

It was difficult to put an age to Dr Pardieu. He had the sort of face that could have seen anywhere between fifty and seventy summers . . . if he ever took it out in daylight, which I doubted. Limp grey hair, cut to one length all the way round in the old style, brushed his dusty collar and two front teeth jutted out over his bottom lip.

Along with Telferman, he also put me in mind of a hare.

'Change can be a good thing, Miss Peck. I was often called to attend your . . . predecessor. She did not find me wanting. I trust she is in . . . er . . .'

I swear he was about to say 'good health' or something similar, but, as we both knew, that would have been a lie.

'She's in the country, Dr Pardieu.'

'Excellent. Fresh air . . . I am sure that will be . . .' He faltered again. The thought of Lady Ginger taking a country rest cure was as ridiculous as Florence Nightingale taking a box at The Carnival. I nodded at Robbie on Peggy's lap. His good thumb was stuck in his mouth now and his round brown face glowed in the lamplight.

'Is he going to be all right, then?'

Dr Pardieu frowned. 'I've done what I can this evening. The tincture of laudanum will ease the pain. Ice should be applied regularly to cool the swelling and the bandage should be kept firm, but not constricting. I've applied a salve to the bite. It is not unusual for people to react after contact with such birds. I once treated a woman in Wapping, a captain's wife, who could not stay in the same room as her husband's prized companion. She was forced to move him out in the end.'

'The parrot?'

'The captain.' Dr Pardieu didn't smile. He looked at Robbie who was sound asleep now. 'This was a very severe case. I would almost describe it as unique. I've not seen engorgement quite like it before. I recommend that you keep the bird and the boy apart.'

Peggy stood up, Robbie cradled in her arms. 'Can I put him to bed now?'

He nodded. 'That would be the best place for him. Do not hesitate to call on my services again, if there is anything you need.' I got the distinctive impression he wasn't talking to Peggy.

I went to the door and found Tan Seng waiting outside.

'The doctor is leaving now.' He stood to one side as Peggy walked to the stairs with Robbie. I turned to Dr Pardieu. 'Thank you. If I need you again I'll call.'

He bowed his head. 'The Lady would not be seen by anyone else. I am always most discreet. I can assure you, Miss Peck, that nothing I ever see here will be spoken of beyond these walls.'

When I heard the doors slam below I went over to the window. I watched the rain slide off the top of Dr Pardieu's umbrella, the drops twinkling in the gaslight as he scurried back towards Salmon Lane. I wondered what those last words meant. What exactly *had* he seen here in the past that called for such discretion?

I rested my head against the glass. The cool eased the throbbing at my temples.

It was all going round and round like the water gushing down the drain in Pearmans Yard, only I felt like the rag caught in the grille. Misha, the letter, Romanov, the man with the cane on the roof, and now Robbie? I wished David Lennox was here right now to take his son away. Tell truth – I wished he was here to take me away too.

'He's sleeping sound.' Peggy pushed open the door and walked over to the fire. 'That must mean something at least?'

'It means he's been given enough laudanum to lay out a chorus line.' I turned from the window. 'Thank you for calling the doctor. You did the right thing.'

'I couldn't see him suffer, besides it was frightening. I've never seen anything like it before. It happened so fast – his hand swelling and that. You can't be too careful with a little one.'

I nodded. 'Can you stay here tonight, Peg? I'd count it as a favour if you did.'

She poked at the coals to make the fire burn more brightly and straightened up. 'I'm happy to. In fact, I've already sent a message to Dan. I hope you don't mind. It's fine by him. Anyway he's got a regular appointment on Thursdays.'

'Is that in the back room at The Lamb, Peggy?' I noted that she turned away and pretended to busy herself again with the fire.

'It's just . . . I don't think he's cut out for it. I've seen enough in my own family to know what happens when the cards don't run in your favour. Look at Joey.'

She didn't answer, so I tried again.

'Let me help with some of the debt and you can pay me back when you can. It's got to be better than digging yourself deeper every time you're dealt a duff hand.'

'You don't understand, Kit. It's his pride. And now – with the baby coming – he's more determined than ever. I can't tell him what to do and he won't take your money, so let's just leave it, shall we?'

'*Pretty girl. Pretty girl. Tits like ripe apples.*' I looked over at the covered cage in the corner, grateful, for once, for Jacobin's profanity.

'I don't think he's talking about the feeding habits of little garden birds, do you?'

Peggy scowled. 'It's got a filthy beak on it. You ought to get rid of that damn parrot. Take it back to your grandmother next time you see her.'

I shrugged. 'I don't know when that'll be. She does the calling, remember?'

'Maybe you should get Marcus Telferman to parcel it up and send it to her.' She paused and ran a hand through her dark curls. 'I forgot – something came for you today. A package. I was down in the hall with Lok when it arrived. It's on the table.'

I smiled. 'You and Lok are quite the best of friends, aren't you?'

'He's a kind man, Kit – matter of fact they both are, him and his brother, and Lok loves little Robbie as much as I do. You heard from his father, this David, then?'

I shook my head. 'Nothing. Unless that package downstairs is from Paris?'

Chapter Twenty-two

I pushed at the wide door to the workshop behind The Gaudy and it juddered open. I paused for a moment, surprised at how the familiar scent of paint and sawdust made me feel. It smelt like the past and it smelt . . . clean. I know that's an odd word to use, but I can't put it another way. It made me think of the time when I was just a seamstress and a slop girl and everything was straight.

I stepped inside. The sound of sawing came from behind a wide flat board painted up to look like the outside of a tavern. I'd know Lucca's hand anywhere. The tavern looked so real you'd think you could step through the half-open door, slap your coins on the board and order yourself a jug of eyewater. Just above the door he'd painted a square wooden cage with a little yellow bird inside.

I took a step closer and stared up. I could even see the feathers.

'Anyone at home? You there, Lucca?'

The sawing stopped. 'Who's that?'

I stepped round the scenery to find Danny working at a plank stretched between a couple of chairs. He laid down the saw and rubbed a hand over his forehead.

'Hello, stranger. We haven't seen you here for a month or so.'

That was true enough. It was the first time I'd visited out

back since I'd took over. I'm not entirely sure why. If I took it out and examined it there was something about not wanting to lord it over people who'd been my friends, not wanting to make them feel uncomfortable around me. But looking closer, it was most likely the other way round. *I* didn't want to feel uncomfortable. Tell truth, I didn't go to the workshop across the yard at the back of The Gaudy because I was frightened to find I no longer belonged there.

I tried to smile. 'I reckon you don't need me poking about in your business. I trust you all to get on with the job. What you doing there?'

'I'm making up the flats ready for Lucca.' Danny pointed at the tavern scene behind me. 'It's the other half of that. This side needs a window that opens out.'

'It's for the sailor song?'

He nodded. 'First proper performance on Monday. We need to be able to take it all over to The Carnival too, so it's made portable – you can see the joins on this side, but not from out front.'

I looked back and realised that Lucca's tavern scene was painted across four panels. Even up close I hadn't noticed.

'It's a lovely job, Dan.'

'And it's a ripper of a song. It'll bring in the punters. Jesmond's hot as Colman's for it to move over to The Carnival. Netta Swift's got a decent pair of lungs on her.'

I raised an eyebrow. 'I wouldn't let Peggy hear you say that.'

He grinned. 'She's got nothing to worry about on that score. But she is good, Netta I mean. Almost as good as you were, Kit.'

Danny glanced over his shoulder and then I saw it – my

cage. It stood in the shadows at the back of the workshop, half-covered in sacking. Planks of wood were propped up against it. I walked over and put a hand on one of the bars. Strands of glittering ribbon studded with paste jewels were still threaded through the metal.

'It seems like a long time since I was dandling in here.'

'Would you do it again, Kit? Go up, I mean?' Danny came to stand next to me. 'I reckon we could make it safe for you. Put a net up underneath. I couldn't make out why you never had one.'

I shook my head. 'It was part of the thrill, wasn't it? Will she, won't she? The punters came to see me perform, but they also came to see me fall. It gave them a little bit extra. It excited them – the men 'specially. You wouldn't believe what I saw them doing with their hands from up there sometimes.'

'It was good for takings, though. Fitzy says . . .' He trailed off.

I swung round. Danny was scuffing at some wood shavings with his foot. He didn't look at me. 'Go on, what does he say?'

'Something and nothing. The books and that. With The Comet closed for the duration, he reckons there's not enough coming in to pay out.'

I planted my hands on my hips. 'Well, he's wrong. The books are good. I've been through them all a hundred times over. Fact is, once we get The Comet open again we'll treble our takings. I'm thinking of taking out the tables and putting seats in. We'll pack more in that way and we can attract a better class of trade. I've got the carpenters booked in now and

246

Fitzy's supposed to be dealing with the plaster boys and the gilders. It won't be dark for long.'

Danny didn't answer.

'Listen to me. Patrick Fitzpatrick's fat boxer's nose has been knocked so far out of joint by me taking over the halls that he's practically sniffing out of his arse. He'd say anything to undermine me. I'll have it out with him and make it very clear that I don't want him spreading lies. And that goes for you too, Dan.'

Danny shook his head. 'It's just . . . well . . . me and Peggy we need all the money we can get right now and if the halls aren't going to pay—'

'But they are! This is just rumour and rot.' I stared up at him.

Big Danny Tewson was a handsome lad with broad shoulders, thick black hair and fine brown eyes. There were pouchy grey bags under his fine eyes today. I reckoned he'd been spending more than Thursday nights at the card table. There was something else too now I looked – a purple bruise stretched around his throat like he'd been gripped too tight. He must have seen me mark it because he pulled at his shirt collar to cover up.

'What's that, Dan?'

He fiddled with a button and mumbled. 'Nothing – an accident, that's all.'

'Accident with someone's fist, was it?' I took a deep breath. 'If you're worried about money, you only have to ask. I've said as much to Peggy.'

'She had no business—'

'She's my friend. Course she had a right to tell me. And if

247

we're talking business, then you need to get it straight in your head that the halls – all three of them – are in good order.' I poked him in the chest and he stepped back. 'If you want you can come over to my office right now and I'll show you the books.'

He raised his hands. 'I believe you. Peggy always said you had a temper, Kit.' He grinned. 'Anyway, it's not me you came to see here, is it?'

I shook my head. 'I was looking for Lucca.'

'He's not been in yet. We're expecting him later. When the lads get back with more wood I'll need to cut it to shape before he can get to work on it. It'll be a late-night job I reckon.'

'Well, when he comes in, whenever that is, can you ask him to come over to the office? I'll be there until after tonight's house. It's important.'

Dan nodded. I rapped the cage once and a long low note rang out around the workshop.

'Lovely tone.'

I remembered how Fitzy had said that the first time he'd shown it to me. Now I was going to use a 'lovely tone' on him.

The lascar stood up when I opened the door to the office. He seemed to fill the room. He towered over me and most other people in the street, I noticed, as we'd walked to The Gaudy earlier.

He'd been waiting for me in the hallway at The Palace when I went down that morning and I'd been expecting him. Tan Seng held out my coat and nodded at the dark-faced man perching on the hall chair under the painting of the young toff in blue. The lascar sprang to his feet.

'Amit will walk with you and stay close to you, Lady.' Tan Seng bowed. I shot a look at the lascar and then at Tan Seng. How much did he know?

Tan Sen cleared his throat. 'The streets are dangerous for a lady alone. It is better this way. Amit is mute, he will not disturb you. I have taken the liberty to employ him here, for you, Lady. He is known to us.' He bowed and held the coat open.

I already knew the giant wasn't here to protect *me*.

I sidled a glance at the lascar. The man's face was long and deeply lined. The jutting bones of his forehead were so heavily pronounced that I couldn't clearly see his eyes. His hair was black except for a single streak of grey that sprang from the crown. He clenched and unclenched his huge fists as he stood there staring at me.

'It's Amit Das, isn't it?' The lascar nodded and I was pleased to see Tan Seng's eyes flicker in surprise. 'You and your brother Ram have lodgings near Bell Wharf Stairs?' He nodded again. I turned to allow Tan Seng to help me push my arms into the sleeves. 'I know him from the books. I pay their rent. They worked for my . . . for Lady Ginger, didn't they?'

Tan Seng bowed. 'The Lady knows all.'

I wished that was true.

I went over to the desk in The Gaudy's office and sat down.

'You can take off for a bit, Amit. I won't be leaving until after we close up tonight. Here . . .' I handed him a couple of pennies. 'Get yourself off to a cookshop.' He looked doubtfully at the coins. 'It's all quite safe. Come back this evening, please.'

I pushed the pennies across the table and after a moment he reached down. His fingers were so big I was minded of one of them wind-up mechanical grab machines at the travelling fairs, the ones where the claws are deliberately made too big to pick up the sugar sticks. I lost a purseful on one of them once when Joey took me out to London Fields. Nanny Peck gave me what for when she found out. I learned a lesson that day and I didn't chance it ever again.

Amit couldn't seem to catch hold of the pennies, so after a couple of tries he just swiped them off the desk into his paw. As I watched him lower his head to dip out through the door I thought about that cage again. I was still trapped, wasn't I?

I emptied the contents of my bag over the desk top. The letters tumbled out and I spread them over the leather. I'd gone through them all – the ones I could read – over and over last night and the story they told made a sort of sense. Now I wanted to show them to Lucca to see if he agreed.

My grandmother had included a note with the package. Her old-style, looping hand fluttered across the page.

Katharine,

I have reflected on our last conversation and I feel that I may have been unreasonable.

While it is vital that you learn to navigate your own way in the affairs of Paradise, I concede that, in the current instance, a little more information will be of value. It is unfortunate that you have allowed yourself to become embroiled in a side show when so much is at stake. Your brother has always found it difficult to separate his own needs from that of the wider good. This episode will, perhaps, serve as a valuable lesson.

I trust that you have now ascertained the meaning of the word on the paper and, more pertinently perhaps, that you know the significance of the family crest embossed into the page.

With these details in mind, I have instructed Telferman to extract the documents enclosed with this note from my vault at Persimmons Bank in the Strand. You will, no doubt, be aware of the existence of this holding.

Over the years I have made it my business to obtain many items of valuable correspondence. These examples are among the jewels of my collection. Their worth is incalculable.

I trust that you will find them enlightening. Telferman will collect them from you tomorrow at nine sharp. While they are in your hands, I have made arrangements for their protection.

Read them well, Katharine, and think on the story they tell.

The story?

I reached for a yellowing sheet and followed down the slanting lines of close-packed writing again with my finger. It wasn't complete. The first page, at least, was missing and it wasn't in English. Across the top there were two names and a date scrawled in capitals in my grandmother's hand.

1 – FROM GRAND DUCHESS ANNA FEODOROVNA TO MARIE L.V. DUCHESS OF KENT MARCH 1821

A word was repeated several times in the text and each time it began with a capital letter. I wondered if it might be a name.

The second time the writer had underlined it and the words in front – *ihre kleine Tochter, Drina*

The letter was signed with a flourish.

Juli – Ihre liebevolle Schwester

I stared at the sheet for a moment and reached for another. There were a dozen like it, all written in words I couldn't read. At least three of them appeared to be in the Russian script Old Peter had translated for me. Every one of them was carefully numbered, dated and noted with my grandmother's capitals. By my reckoning I had correspondence in front of me from half the nobility of Europe – duchess this, grand duke that, a couple of princes, a bishop and a patriarch . . . whatever that was.

I leafed through the pages again and took out the one I could read – number seven. The bold scrawl across the top told me the writer was: *SIR WILLIAM JENNER, SEPTEMBER 1864.*

Like before, the first page was missing. I don't know who Sir William was writing to – and presumably neither did my grandmother seeing as how nearly every other letter was itemised most careful. I knew one thing, though. He had a ripe story to tell. I followed the meandering lines. His writing was terrible.

. . . can at best be described as unfortunate, at worst a disease of the most gross and incurable nature. In confidence – writing to a brother physician – I cannot imagine the young Prince will make old bones and that may be for the best. Indeed, to imagine

him passing such a defect to any children, for I believe that to be the hidden legacy of this cruel malady, would be unthinkable.

I bound his lower limbs in hope that the swelling will dissipate, but I fear internal bleeding at the joints will continue for some time. The Prince is in great pain. I was able to give him something for that at least. I have also given strict instructions as to his future recreation. He is to be supervised at all times. If he were to fall from a horse again or even take a knock from a bat or a ball, I cannot guarantee a good outcome.

I asked Her Majesty if she recalls any member of her family having been struck by a similar condition, but she is still so mired in mourning that she cares little if she herself lives or dies. The welfare of young Leopold is so far from her mind that, truly, I pity the boy. He is a clever and amenable child. I believe he understands the gravity of his situation.

I looked at the date again. Whoever this William was, seventeen years back he was writing to someone about Prince Leopold, Queen Victoria's second youngest. But he was still alive, wasn't he? As far as I knew – and that wasn't much seeing as how the nearest I'd come to Her Majesty in the bosom of her family was on the lid of a biscuit tin – there was nothing wrong with him.

I read on.

The sad matter would have limped to its foregone conclusion – this year, perhaps in a decade or so if the Prince is fortunate and lives quietly – and I would not have thought deeply upon its cause, had it not been for an encounter with George Denman at the club three nights ago.

Denman was in his cups, as is usual I believe, calling for brandy and generally making the most extraordinary nuisance in the dining room. His voice has a tone that is difficult to ignore – one would think he imagined himself to be in court – and members in the library across the hall complained. It was clear he wanted to pick a fight and didn't care two figs who his opponent might be. Chilvers, the night man, took me aside and asked if I could give the honourable gentleman something to 'calm his nerves'. This I did most gladly. I had come direct from the hospital and my bag was lodged with the porter.

And now we come to the meat of it.

With gravy, cabbage and a steaming pile of boiled potatoes, I thought. Old William couldn't wait to pass on some highly titillating information. I flipped the page, noting that the handwriting sloped more violent to the right as he scribbled out his tattle.

While we sat privately in the smoking den waiting for the light sedative I had administered to take effect, Denman gripped my arm and started to babble about physicians. He has little liking for our breed, that much was clear, but that is always the way with lawyers, is it not, brother? I listened – at first out of the desire to steady the man, but then out of interest.

I'll lay a bet it was something more than interest. If my understanding of the letter was right, Old William's ears must have been on fire.

I was dimly aware that Denman's family were in medicine as

well as the law. His aunt, it transpired – and I have since veri-
fied the truth of this part of his story at least – was married to
the late Sir Richard Croft. A terrible business, suicide, but of
course, the death of the Princess Charlotte in childbirth must
have weighed terribly on the man's conscience. There cannot be
many royal physicians who have presided over the death of the
future monarch and his mother.

That was true enough. If it hadn't been for the fact that
fat George's daughter – Princess Charlotte in the letter –
had died giving birth to a son, we wouldn't have the benefit
of Her Majesty on the throne. I knew all that from Nanny
Peck who had an interest in the doings of the royalty, despite
cordially hating them all for ruling over Ireland. In Church
Street she used to read aloud stories about them from the
newspapers lingering most particularly over descriptions of
what they'd eaten.

But I stray too far. The point I wish to bring to your attention is that
before he slept, Denman talked incessantly about 'Aunt Margaret's
great secret'. 'Dangerous knowledge' he called it, known only to
those who served the royal household and their intimates.

I turned to the next page. At some point someone had spilled
something, water perhaps, over the top part of the paper
so the first two paragraphs were obscured. William's story
picked up clearly again halfway down.

. . . most interesting, but perhaps also the gossip of a woman in
great anguish?

As there is no suggestion of the malady in Her Majesty's paternal or maternal line – I have made discreet enquiries into the latter – then it is either a spontaneous anomaly, which may be possible, or perhaps Denman's aunt has the key. If it was true that the Duke of Kent was by then incapable of fathering a child, then the root of the terrible disease currently afflicting the little Prince could, indeed, lie <u>elsewhere</u>?

He'd underlined that last word twice.

Of course, to speculate upon the parentage of our great lady is the grossest and most disloyal act of treachery. I shall say no more on the matter except to draw your attention to some medical details which may serve to illuminate.

In the library at the college I have found an account of 'a haemorrhagic disposition' existing in certain families. In 1828 a Dr Otto recognised that the condition was hereditary and, in the main, affected males. He traced the disease back through three generations to a woman who had settled near Plymouth, New Hampshire, in 1720. And again in 1828 Hopff uses the word 'haemophilia' in a report of a very similar case in Zurich. If you are interested, and I feel most certain that as a brother you will be, you can find it in a tract housed at the library. It is a copy of Hopff's original, lodged, unaccountably, under Z.

I know I do not need to tell you how delicate this matter is. Not only with regard to our great lady, but also to her poor child and any others among her offspring, and so on, who might carry the condition. The Crown Princess of Prussia has already given birth to four children, two have been born to the Grand Duchess of Hesse. Only time will give us the answer.

Meantimes, discretion must be our touchstone and we must pray that it is the spontaneous anomaly I mentioned. My only reason for writing to you on this matter is, of course, founded upon our mutual interest in the furtherance of medical science.

I hope to visit Hampshire soon, old friend – it will be good to breathe something sweet and clean. The air in London is as foul as ever. Adela sends her good wishes to Julia and to the children and hopes that . . .

After dropping his incendiary remarks, the old chaunter put in another two pages' worth about his wife, his children, his medical colleagues at the college – he didn't think much of them – and his gardener, Fossett, who had a lovely way with plums, but I knew that wasn't the point of it.

Sir William called Denman's Aunt Margaret a gossip? The man should have been ashamed of himself. I've heard herring girls with tighter tongues in their heads. No wonder my grandmother kept his letter in a bank vault.

As far as I could make out, William Jenner was sinuating – no, it was more than a sinuation, after all it was there in blue and white – that Queen Victoria's father wasn't actually related to her at all and that the condition affecting her son, Prince Leopold, might well have been passed down from someone who was.

Tell truth, I didn't understand all of it, but I knew it was dangerous. I looked at the other papers strewn across the desk – all them names, all them titles. I guessed they all told the same story, or parts of it.

Poor little Leopold, Sir William didn't hold out much

hope for him, did he? And yet Queen Victoria's eighth child and fourth son was still alive and . . . Well, he was alive. That was something.

I flicked the page back and re-read a couple of lines of Jenner's scrawl, the bit about binding the boy's limbs, the swelling and the blood in the joints. Dr Pardieu was wrong. Robbie hadn't reacted to the parrot – there was something already wrong inside him, something he shared with the little boy in the letter.

My grandmother's voice sounded clear in my head: *He is your blood, he is your family. Think on those words.*

Blood and family – she hadn't been talking about me and Joey, had she?

There was a rap on the door and Lucca walked into the office. If it had been anyone else I would have gathered up the letters and locked them away, but I wanted to show them to him.

'Sit down.' I nodded at the spindly chair. He shook his head.

'You must come with me, Fannella. Come now.'

I held out Jenner's letter and flicked through the pages on the desk searching for the one that might have been Italian. 'I haven't got time for a walkabout, Lucca. I need you to look at—'

'No!' His voice was harsh. I looked up. His face was grey. There were lines stretched around his mouth and eye on the good side.

'It's Peter, Fannella, Old Peter. He is dead. It was not an accident.'

Chapter Twenty-three

I almost had to run to keep pace with him.

'Why are we going to your place, Lucca? Surely we should be going west?'

He didn't answer. He paused at the corner of White Horse Street. The traffic on the Commercial was tight as cod in a Billingsgate box. There was a roaring sound overhead. The bolts in the viaduct rattled as a train veered off towards the Blackwall Extension. The street disappeared from view for a moment as the steam rolled down and folded over the bus and the dray cart blocking our way over.

I rubbed my left eye with the back of my glove as a smut lodged in the lashes. As we stood there Lucca's hand tightened round my wrist. I felt the bag with the letters stuffed inside bump against my leg through the cotton of my skirt.

'You said it wasn't an accident – what do you mean?'

We stepped into the street and dodged round the back of the dray.

'The way he was found. It was very clear.'

'Clear in what way?'

On the other side of the Commercial we headed left and pushed along to the Caroline Street turn.

'In a way I cannot bear to imagine, Fannella. His body was . . . *mutilare*. His stomach had been ripped open, the organs

. . . placed.' Lucca pushed his hand through his hair. 'It is enough for you to know he had been tortured in his room.'

I stopped. Something squirmed about in the pit of my stomach. I tried to swallow the lump in my throat. I thought of Old Peter in his bright, comfortable lodgings. I saw the yellow knobs of butter dissolving in the fiery tea he'd served up and I thought of the story he told us about his life in Russia. He was happy in London. He fitted – that's what he told us.

'Who . . . who found him?'

'Tommy and Isaac. They went to Pearmans Yard this morning. They were concerned that Peter hadn't joined them at The Lamb last evening as was usual.'

'They went together? I thought those two hated each other?'

Lucca shook his head. 'It is a game, a front. The orchestra is like this.' He loosened his grip and clasped his hands together, '*La famiglia*. Professor Ruben is talking to the police now.'

'The rozzers!'

Lucca stared at me, his expression unreadable. '*Sì* – it is a crime, a murder.'

'But I can't . . . they can't . . .' I faltered as he turned away. I could read his face now – he was angry.

'Don't worry, Fannella. They won't come to you. I am certain. Pearmans is a . . . *nido di corvi* – you would say a rookery? Such things are not unknown there. Death is commonplace.'

I gripped the handle of the bag. 'I'm sorry. I didn't mean—'

'I think it was clear what you meant.' Lucca pushed forward and I ran to catch him. I pulled his sleeve.

'It was our fault, wasn't it?' When he didn't answer I carried on. 'We brought that man straight to his door. I'm right, aren't I? You think it too? He went back there after that business on the roof to find out what we'd said. Peter didn't stand a chance.'

Lucca nodded curtly. I blinked as tears started to glaze up my eyes. Peter had always been kind to me. A fortnight back it was him who had made me see straight.

I've known you a long time, Kitty Peck – you have a good soul. You need to let them see that the girl they knew hasn't changed.

But he was wrong, wasn't he? The first thought of the girl he knew would have been for her friend, not her own skin.

'What should we do now, Lucca? I can't let this go any further. What if he comes for Peggy . . .'

'She is safe at The Palace with Robbie.' He turned to look at me now and the hard lines of his face softened as he saw the tears. He reached forward and brushed my cheek.

'It was not your fault. You weren't to know.'

'All the same, it was me who brought him to Pearmans. We need some answers, Lucca. Robbie and Peggy are safe behind the doors and shutters at The Palace – God knows my grandmother had it set up like a fortress. But that baby is . . .' I trailed off. Who exactly was Robbie Lennox? More precisely, who was his mother? What was it David said that night he and Joey jumped me into taking the kid? I dipped for the exact words.

I didn't realise until just before Robbie was born who his grandparents were. They are an old family – a . . . powerful family.

'All I know is . . . this is something big, Lucca, something very big. And it's deadly.'

He took my hand and glanced along the street behind me. I realised then that he'd been keeping a watch out all along to make sure we weren't being tailed.

'I know. And that is why there is someone I want you to meet, Fannella.'

Lucca's new lodgings were in a good house with tall, wide windows overlooking the river. It had been built for an old-time merchant who liked to keep a watch on his ships. Lucca said the light was good for painting. I'd been there just once before, when he moved his gear in.

We rounded the stairs and came out onto a broad landing. Lucca tapped three times on his door. We stood there for a moment in silence and he knocked again. There was a sound from inside and a voice fired off something in rapid Italian.

'*Sì!*' Lucca followed that up with something else that included my name. I heard the sound of a bolt being drawn back. When the door opened I froze. The man standing just inside was the last person I expected to see.

'Kitty, let me introduce you properly to my friend, Misha Raskalov.'

Lucca stepped back to let me go inside, but I just stood there. Misha bowed and came forward. Taking my hands in his, he lowered his silver-white head to kiss my fingers. He straightened up and smiled.

'The honour is entirely mine, mademoiselle.' His voice was clipped, but his English was perfect.

I looked over at Lucca.

'I . . . I don't understand, he's . . .'

'He is not a child murderer, Fannella. Go in, please.'

Lucca and Misha gabbled together in Italian.

I stood and went over to the window. Today the river was green as David Lennox's eyes, ripples of silver flitted over the water as weak sunlight caught at the waves. The rain had stopped at last, but a wind was blowing from the east. Over to the left the masts of ships moored in rows four deep across the Thames swayed like a forest. They towered over the rooftops at the bend. Even from here I could hear the wailing as the wind cut through the cat's cradle of ropes.

I turned to watch the pair of them. Lucca nodded energetically as Misha pointed at the pages laid out on the table in between them. The large square room was furnished simple. The grandest thing in it was a marble fire surround clustered with carved fruits and flowers. It put me in mind of the one I'd seen in the long hallway at my grandmother's house.

Apart from the table, a tall cupboard and a bed over in the corner, there wasn't much in the way of furnishings. The room smelt of paint and turpentine. There were drawings – fine ones – pinned to the walls and half-finished canvases stacked in the corners. It was like the little space he'd made for himself over the workshop at The Gaudy. Them days seemed very long ago and far away now.

A large black book bound with ribbon was propped against the window next to my foot. I recognised it immediately. Last time I'd opened it out to look inside I'd found my naked brother staring back at me from a page. That was when I first began to get an inkling about Joey, even though I shut it away as soon as it had come. He'd brought trouble again now.

I turned away from the window. 'You've been here in London for two weeks?'

The pair of them looked up from the letters. Misha nodded. 'We took rooms at The Langham and made appointments.'

'We?'

He smoothed out the page in front of him. 'Ilya insisted on accompanying me. He said it was important for the performer to understand the stage – to feel the spirit of the place. But then . . .' Misha clicked his fingers. 'He went. It was as if he had never been there. His clothes were gone, his room was cleared. There was nothing, not even a message.'

I glanced at Lucca. He was watching me to see that I understood. He raised his eyebrow. I nodded.

'And you didn't think that was unusual, Misha?'

'Yes and no. Ilya Vershinin is well known for his capricious nature.'

'His what?' I joined them at the table.

Misha smiled, his clever blue eyes slanting up over his carved cheekbones. I could understand why Lucca thought so highly of him. He wasn't slight like the ballet boys I'd seen at rue des Carmélites. Misha was tall and masculine and his full lips had something of the generous curve to them that brought to mind the angels in Lucca's painting books. Although, on the quiet, I reckoned a celestial being would probably wear more in the way of clothes.

He smelt of lemon cut with incense – like the stuff them Romans use in their churches. He was beautifully dressed too – his shirt was whiter than his collar-length hair and his coat flung over the unmade bed was finished with sleek black fur at the collar.

'Ilya is an artist, a performer of great power and passion, but his temperament runs like the water out there.' Misha nodded at the river through the window. 'He follows his own rules. When I found he was gone it was not, at first, so surprising. I simply thought he had tired of the meetings with petty bureaucrats at the theatres and gone back to Paris. It is his way, always.'

He paused and stared at me. His lips parted as if he was forming a question in his mind and trying it out for size.

'Besides, Miss Peck, in Paris . . . he and your brother—'

'I know – and call me Kitty, please.' I cut him off. 'How long had you been here when he took off?'

'Two days.'

'But you've been here a fortnight, Misha. Why didn't you . . . I mean, you could have . . .'

I sidled a look at Lucca who was now engrossed in the faded script of one of the letters my grandmother had sent over – it was written in Italian from a marchesa. Misha cottoned on immediately. He reached across the table and caught Lucca's hand. Lucca looked up and I saw the good side of his face flush. I noted that around Misha he didn't try to hide the scars.

'I didn't know how to contact him. At the hotel there was a mistake – at least I thought it was a mistake – with the bags. Ilya took one of mine. It contained a wallet of documents and addresses. Lucca's was among them. I was furious when I found the error. There were important names there – people I needed to approach, venues and, of course, my . . . friend.' I saw him tighten his grip on Lucca's hand.

'I went to Sam last night, Kitty.' Lucca put the letter back on the table. 'I knew he'd be able to tell me where Misha was staying. After I left you I went to Holborn, to the offices of *The London Pictorial*.'

Misha grinned. 'Your journalist friend was very full of his talents, Kitty. He thinks most highly of himself.

Hadn't Sam said much the same of Misha Raskalov? They were two clever street cats, fluffing out their fur and arching their backs at each other. Sam Collins was right about Misha's talents, mind. He'd identified the origin of all but three of the letters from the bank vault, recognising the languages at a single glance.

'So, what do you make of them?' I nodded at the pages strewn across the table.

'You are right, the answer is here, Fannella.' Lucca took up Sir William Jenner's letter and handed it to Misha. 'This one is the key, but the others tell much the same story. What do you say?'

Misha rubbed his chin. In the sunlight the stubble grazing his angular cheeks had a red-gold tinge. 'I always wondered why your queen did not use her given name. Perhaps now I begin to understand?'

'Her given name?' I frowned. 'She's Victoria – always has been.'

He shook his head. 'To you, but not to us. She was baptised Alexandrina Victoria. Her godfather in absentia was the Czar. In Russia there was offence when the name was so quickly forgotten.'

Of an instant, it bumped into place. That was a name in the letter – Alexan*drina*.

I watched Misha sort through the pages on the table until he found it.

He pulled it free from the pile and nodded to himself. 'But now it seems there are many things left forgotten. Her true parentage, for example? According to this letter sent from her aunt to her mother . . .' He pointed at the yellowing page dated 1821 and signed '*Juli – Ihre liebevolle Schwester*'. 'Your queen's father is not the Duke of Kent, but someone . . . else. It's not clear who, that part is missing, but my guess is that the man is a Russian of noble birth – a sick Russian.'

'How would she know that?' I stared at my grandmother's note at the top of the page:

SENT FROM GRAND DUCHESS ANNA FEODOROVNA TO MARIE L.V. DUCHESS OF KENT MARCH 1821

Something else fell into place. 'So, she . . . married a Russian – Queen Victoria's aunt is the duchess?'

Misha nodded. 'But Russian was not her first language – it would be natural for sisters to communicate in their mother tongue. He turned the page round and pointed at some words near the bottom, reading them aloud '"*Diese schreckliche Krankheit*". It means, "this terrible disease". She is warning her sister to be alert for the condition in her little daughter, here: "*ihre kleine Tochter, Drina*" – I believe it is a pet name, from Alexan*drina*? See here, she goes on to call her "*meine liebste Nichte*" – "my dearest niece".'

I scanned the letters. 'And the rest of them – all these others?'

Misha sat back. 'There is a canker at the heart of the great houses of Europe. A sickness. They are all related by marriage – dynasty linked to dynasty. Look at the names here at the top of each page. From Russia in the east to Portugal in the west they are joined. It is like a dance – the partners change but the music goes on. It has been like this for centuries. The same blood flows in all their veins.'

'And that blood is corrupted!' Lucca took up the marchesa's letter again. 'Here – this one is more than a hundred years old, but it is the same thing. A sickness passed from mother to child, swelling, pain, bleeding. She calls it "*maledizione del sangue*", the "blood curse".'

'But surely they can't all have it? They would have been wiped out by now and we'd be like America.' I took the marchesa's letter from Lucca's hands and felt the fragility of the old paper between my fingers. I ran my eyes over the beautiful slanting script and saw it: *maledizione del sangue* – the words themselves looked sinister.

'You're right.' Misha rifled through the papers. 'It doesn't always appear. Generations seem to pass without occurrence and they write of their relief and their gratitude. This one . . .' he produced a page covered over in the script Old Peter had translated for me, 'is from the Czarevna herself to the Patriarch of Moscow, giving thanks that her children are free from what she calls "the stain". She sends him a great deal of money.'

'And what exactly is a patriarch when it's at home?'

Lucca shrugged. 'He is like the Pope in Rome or your Archbishop of Canterbury, a holy man.' He stood and went to the window. It was bright outside now. He moved the curtains to allow more light into the room.

I leaned forward and rested my head in my hands. Thoughts were flitting about in my mind like silvery fish darting in the river, if I managed to catch one, another wriggled free and disappeared from view.

'So, if Robbie really does have the . . . *stain* or whatever you want to call it, it's likely that his mother comes from one of these families?' I stared at the letters. 'But why would they want to hunt him down and kill him? Queen Victoria didn't kill Prince Leopold, did she? And all these others – they all seemed to get on with it.'

'That's not entirely true, Kitty.' Misha reached for another of the pages covered in Russian script. 'This is from a physician at the court of Czar Nicholas the First. He has been ordered, under pain of death, never to speak of the condition afflicting the family. No one, *no one* is to know that the Romanovs carry the disease.' He pointed at a word repeated several times – Романов.

'This is their family name, Romanov. As far as the world is concerned, they must be thought clean, perfect.'

'Why?' I folded my arms.

'Because the Romanovs rule by the grace of God. Their kingship is sanctified. Russia is an old land and her people are devoutly superstitious. They must continue to believe in this divinity or there will be revolution.' Misha leaned forward. 'God would not choose a family riddled with disease to be His representatives on earth.'

A sudden gust of wind along the river rattled the window pane. From outside the whistling from the rigging rose to a banshee howl.

We sat there listening for a moment and then Lucca spoke.

'When we walked here earlier today, Fannella, you said we had become involved with something big, something dangerous.' He shot a look at Misha. 'I . . . *We*, agree with you. It's why I could not bring my friend here to The Palace or to the theatre. I could not take the risk if you are being watched. I did not want Ilya to know that we have made contact.'

'Because he's still here in London?'

Misha nodded. 'And because I believe he is Okhrana. Ilya Vershinin is an agent of the Czar.'

Chapter Twenty-four

We were wary as we hurried back to Salmon Lane. Lucca made certain the narrow street outside his lodging house was clear before he allowed me to step out, and then he kept close. We made our way up to the Commercial where there was safety in the bustle. But every time someone came too close or bumped against me I whipped around, expecting to see Ilya's sly face in the crowd.

It was a fine afternoon now. The blue sky was flicked across with mare's tails and the damp cobbles had shined up like brass buttons on a military, but as far as I was concerned it was dark. I kept thinking about Old Peter. In my mind the door to his room opened wide and I saw blood spattered across the walls, soaked into the bright fabric hangings and smeared across the painted face of his mother.

I tightened my fingers around the bag handle.

'Lucca, how long has Misha suspected Ilya of being . . . what was it? Okhrana? Only he didn't give the impression back then that it was something new to him.'

I paused as a tall gent ahead stopped dead to peer into a shop window. His dark coat flapped open and he reached inside to take out something . . . silver. A woman with a basket of flowers blocked him from view for a second. I gripped Lucca's arm tight, but breathed easy as the woman hefted the basket round to her other hip and I saw the old man flick open the lid of his snuff box.

Lucca huddled me closer and spoke quietly. 'He told me last night that he has thought it for some time. When The Moika first visited Paris last year some of the company became *infatuati* – obsessed with the ideas of the young people they met in the bars, in the cafés, in the dance halls. When they returned to Moscow they spoke too openly about their desire for change. Their views were radical, dangerous. Misha thinks Ilya was . . . approached to report on them – keep a watch on who they met. Vershinin does not come from a rich family and even though he is a great dancer The Moika does not shower its performers with wealth. They dance for the glory of its reputation. But this past season in Paris he has spent money like water. Misha wondered where that money came from. Now he is certain.'

'Money?' I bit my lip. 'I bet Joey liked that, all right.'

'*Sì.*' Lucca sighed. 'Your brother does not always choose his . . . companions wisely.'

'Not like you?' I squeezed his hand and felt him return the gesture. 'I'm sorry I doubted him, Lucca. He's a good man. A clever one too.'

We stood to one side to let a woman with a black-covered perambulator the size of a costermonger's trolley cart get by. From somewhere deep inside I heard the baby babbling to itself.

I watched her bump down the street.

'Well, we know one thing now: Ilya's been looking for Robbie and I reckon Joey gave the game away, not deliberate, though. That's why the Monseigneur sent that note to my grandmother.' I thought about the economy of that paper and the single word scrawled across it. She knew what it meant immediately. It wasn't only Sam Collins who knew how to use shorthand.

I hugged the bag to my chest. 'Joey truly seemed to care for David. He helped him smuggle Robbie onto the train, remember? He's not part of this, I'm sure of it.'

'But your brother has been unwise.' Lucca picked at the leather stitching on his gloves. 'That poor child. It would be best if his father took him away, as soon as possible. They must vanish together, it's the only way. Have you heard anything – a reply to your letter?'

I shook my head. 'Robbie's safe as possible at The Palace. And Peggy's there round the clock now with him, I've made sure of that. It can only be a matter of time. I hoped my answer came out more confident than I felt. I counted back. The letter (letters) had gone off, three, no, four days ago now. A thought struck me then.

'Does Misha know anything about David – Robbie's father?'

'I asked him that. He did not. It's not so surprising – your brother's world is full of people who come and go. Artists, performers from the dance halls, the theatres, the ballet – as you know. David is a singer, yes?'

'A ballad singer.' I thought about his soft low voice and remembered the way he'd cupped my hands in his as we talked. I felt my palms tingle.

Lucca shrugged. 'As Misha says, Joseph has many friends. He always did, Fannella.'

Bartholomew waits. I ran those words around in my head again. By the sound of them he had a share of enemies too.

I brought a hand to the neck of my coat and felt for the

chain with the ring and the Christopher under the collar of my dress. For some reason, as long as they were there, I knew my brother was safe. Some of Nanny Peck's superstitious old blarney must have rubbed off on me after all, I thought.

We'd be turning into Salmon Lane in a moment. Despite the letters, despite what Misha said about Ilya, there was still something that plucked at my brain like a crow turning over a bit of rotten meat in a gutter.

From my membrance of things – and I'd had a lot of champagne that evening so it wasn't all clear – Ilya Vershinin was tall, but he was also slender and graceful in the way of a dancer. The man with the cloak and the hawk-head cane was built like a navvy. There was something, though – something Sam had told me. I ran our conversation through my head again. I didn't need Pitman to bring it back. I saw Sam's inky finger trace down the page of squiggles and I heard his voice reading it to me.

Ilya Vershinin is the most remarkable performer of our age. He inhabits the spirit of any character he plays. His mastery of physical transition has been compared to a kind of magic.

There! He was an actor as well as a dancer.

It was him, I was suddenly sure of it. Ilya Vershinin was the man in the theatre that time and up on the roof at Pearmans Yard. And he'd murdered Old Peter and those two little ones. He was searching for Robbie – it was obvious now.

Lucca's voice cut my thoughts. 'We'll go to the alleyway at the back. I'll walk you to the yard gate, Fannella, but then I have to go to the workshop. I'm late already.'

I glanced up. 'The scenery? You won't be there alone, will you?'

Lucca shook his head. 'There will be many at work to-night. Monday night is important for The Gaudy – the sets must be right and the paint will need a day to dry.'

I nodded. 'Danny reckoned on a late night. What about your friend?'

Lucca grinned and the good side of his face burned. 'Misha will be waiting for me, Fannella, whatever time I return.'

We dipped off Salmon Lane and turned into the passages that connected the yards behind the houses. A little way along we paused in a bricked-up doorway, listening out to see if we were followed. There was nothing.

Lucca leaned out to check and then he took my hand.

'Come. There is no one.'

When we reached the gate at the back of The Palace I squeezed his hand. 'Look out for yourself, Lucca. Don't take risks. When you get to The Gaudy, you'll find someone called Amit hanging around near my office – you won't miss him. Can you give him a message, please? Tell him I'm fine and the letters are fine.'

He frowned as I rattled on. 'And tell him he's to stay close to you, no matter how late you work this evening. Then he's to escort you to your door, like you've just done for me. After that he's to come back here. You got that?'

'Sì, but—'

'No buts, Lucca. I want you safe. Amit Das is a mute so don't expect a reply.'

I watched until he rounded the corner at the end of the passage and then I pushed open the gate. A black cat out for a ramble flattened itself against the sooty wall for a moment so it was difficult to make out brick from fur. Then it gave itself away blinking up at me with fog-lamp eyes. It slipped round my ankles and darted out into the alleyway. Nanny Peck always reckoned it was lucky when a black cat crossed your path. As I headed across the yard to the rooms in the basement I hoped she was right.

I didn't come down here. It was the brothers' territory, although Peggy had clearly made herself at home.

As usual the door swung open. These days I wasn't even surprised.

Tan Seng bowed and moved aside as I walked into the kitchen. Copper pans sitting along a dresser against one wall gleamed in the glow from the black range on the other. The air smelt of spice and soap. I wondered if it had always been like this down here, even in my grandmother's days. I suspected it had – and for some reason the thought was comforting. For all the filth up top, it was good to think that there was always some order somewhere. I was glad I'd inherited the brothers along with The Palace.

I nodded at Tan Seng and walked to the stairs leading to the hallway above. From behind I caught the grating of bolts being drawn and then the soft slap of his slippers as he followed me up.

Crossing the black and white tiles to the hall table, I pulled off my gloves and tossed them into a painted Chinese bowl under the painting. I started to unbutton my coat and Tan Seng shuffled forward to help. He folded the coat over his arm, bowed again and cleared his throat.

He pointed at the stairs.

'The Lady has a visitor.'

Chapter Twenty-five

I was surprised, I'll admit it. But even with his back turned, a coil of plaited blonde hair piled on the top of his head and grey skirts sweeping the floorboards, I'd know my brother anywhere. The air was thick with that floral cologne he used.

He was standing in front of Jacobin's cage.

'Joey?'

He span about swiftly. Of an instant I caught a wary look in his eyes before he masked it.

'You inherited everything, I see, little sister?' He turned back to the cage, holding up a finger to taunt the bird. He scraped a nail along the bars, careful to avoid Jacobin's nutcracker beak.

'Don't! It gets him all het up and when he's like that he's vicious.'

It was too late anyway.

'*Pretty girl, pretty girl, pretty girl.*' The bleedin' parrot was off, plucking grey feathers from its chest and bobbing up and down on its perch.

'I wonder who he means?' Joey smiled at me now. He walked over to the couch between the parlour's two tall narrow windows and sat down heavily. I noted that his travel coat and a bonnet with a muslin veil were laid out on the bolsters next to him.

'Well? Is that it, Kitty? A warning about the parrot?

Anyone would have thought you weren't pleased to see me.'

I raced across the room and wrapped my arms around his shoulders, planting kisses on both his cheeks and his forehead. 'Of course I'm pleased. How could you think otherwise?'

Tell truth, when Tan Seng pointed at the stairs a little voice went off in my head suggesting that David Lennox might be up there waiting for me.

I pulled my brother tighter. 'How long you been here?'

'Not long.' He folded his arms around my shoulders. I could feel him taking in great draughts of me. His back moved under my fingers as he breathed deep. It was as if he didn't want to let go.

Eventually he released me and pointed at a china service laid out on a side table. 'I've been here long enough for Lok to bring some tea. I confess I was surprised to find the brothers still here. I see you've made some changes. Quite the dainty residence now, isn't it? Shall I be mother?'

'No!' I jumped up and went over to the table. 'I'll do it.' For some reason what he'd just said didn't seem decent. Joey grinned and I realised he was playing a game, teasing me like he did when we were small.

I'll tell you one thing, though, if I didn't know better I wouldn't have taken him for a man under all that gear. He looked like a proper bit of frock. It was only when he spoke that something didn't ring quite true, but even then you might have thought him to be a woman with a naturally low voice, or maybe an enlivened throat.

Joey looked down at his neat, French-cut dress and smoothed out the skirts.

'I . . . I don't, as a general rule, travel like this. I think you should know that.'

I wasn't sure what to say. I arranged the cups on the saucers and poured in the milk.

'It's not for me to say how you go about, is it, Joey? As long as you're comfortable.'

He snorted. 'That's not the word I'd use. Back in Paris, I'm among friends, but here on the streets . . .'

I quizzed at him.

'It's a disguise, Kitty, the best I could think of at short notice. It was a risk, but I had to take it. Come over here.'

He stood and went to the hearth. An old mirror crackled over and spotted with age leaned out from the wall. It was so heavy that the top two corners were suspended from hooks in the ceiling. It must have been there for years. I was of a mind to replace it.

I set down the jug and went to stand next to him. On account of the heat, the mercury under the glass had bloomed into a mass of twisted shapes. Joey's reflected face was half-covered by coral-like fingers that bubbled through the surface.

'Do you see, Kitty?'

I looked from his face to mine in the mirror, and despite the flaws in the glass I saw.

'In Paris so many of my friends remarked on it, especially after that night. You and I, Kitty, we can be very alike. I knew I could use that, if I needed to.'

'And you need to now?'

He nodded.

'You want people round here to think I'm you?'

He nodded again. 'It's safer that way. I . . . I'm not supposed to be here. The message you brought to Paris was clear enough.'

'*Bartholomew waits*? She, our grandmother, told me to tell you that. Only she didn't say what it meant.'

Joey moved away from the glass and went back to the couch. 'It's best that you don't, Kitty, believe me.'

'Well, this is just like old times, isn't it?' I whipped around and gave him the arrow. 'You don't know about half the things I've done on your account and all because of secrets and shadows. I think I deserve a proper answer. What have you got yourself into now, Joseph Peck?'

'It's not something I've *got myself into now*.'

I flinched as he mimicked my voice and I heard the difference between my coarse Limehouse and his smooth English. He glanced up and his cool blue eyes softened.

'Look, it's not something new, Kitty, it's an old . . . complication. You don't need to know any more and I'm certainly not going to tell you, so leave it. It's for the best.'

He pushed at some loose hairs, forcing the pins that kept the coil in place tighter into his scalp.

'Where's that tea, then? I'm dry as a nun's quim.'

Despite myself, I laughed. 'You better not let Lucca hear you talking like that.'

Joey grinned. 'He's an old woman and he's not here. So where is it?'

I knew my brother of old. It was clear I wasn't going to get any more out of him. I poured two cups and added three spoonfuls of sugar to one of them before handing it to him. Then I took mine and sat down cross-legged on the rug in front of the couch. The stiff folds of my skirts peaked and then collapsed gently about me as the fabric settled.

'You got my letter and the note?'

Joey nodded, stirring the tea around and around. 'That's why I'm here.' He didn't look at me direct as he spoke. The spoon went around again.

'Robbie's here with you at The Palace?'

'Peggy's upstairs with him. You remember her?'

'Fancy Worrow's girl? Pretty, dark – nice smile. About your age or thereabouts.'

'That's her. She's been good to me since you . . . She's been almost like a sister. Peggy's good with kids too, better than me. I got her to look after Robbie over at her place at first. I didn't think anything of it. Then, when . . . everything started up, I asked her to come here to care for him. It was safer. I told her it was because I felt bad about farming him out. She doesn't know the real reason.'

I paused and scanned Joey's face. 'Robbie's . . . special, isn't he?'

Joey put down his tea cup and saucer. 'I'm sorry, Kitty. I thought it would be safe, but I was wrong. When you arrived in Paris it seemed so obvious. We thought it was the best thing to do. It won't be for much longer. We'll take him from you and . . . they'll realise soon enough that he's gone. It will be over.'

We?

'Is David . . . David Lennox here too?'

Joey shook his head. 'Not until Monday. It wasn't wise to travel together and there are still . . . affairs in Paris that need attending to before they can take ship to America.'

'David's coming for Robbie?' God forgive me, I felt something flutter under my bodice as I said his name again. I felt in my pocket for his 'kerchief and caught the point embroidered with the 'D' between my finger and thumb as Joey continued.

'I came ahead. I arrived yesterday to make the arrangements. There's a ship leaving London for Hamburg on Tuesday morning. If all goes to plan they'll be on it.'

'But I thought you said they were going to America?'

'They are. I've also arranged for their onward passage from Hamburg to New York. They are booked on the *Frisia*, a steam ship. Don't you see? I'm covering their tracks. No one would think they'd go back to Europe.'

At last I felt on firmer ground. At least I understood why David wouldn't want to take his son back to a world where there was most likely an assassin waiting round every corner. I put my cup down carefully.

'I know all about Robbie's mother, Joey, so you needn't worry about keeping secrets there.'

'You know?' His eyebrows shot up.

'Thanks to our grandmother I know enough. She's got a spy in Paris keeping watch over you.'

'The Monseigneur?' I was surprised to see Joey shrug. 'I guessed as much. He came with the house, like Tan Seng and Lok. She's watching both of us, little sister.' He sighed. 'So, you already know—'

'—that Robbie Lennox is descended from most of the royal families in Europe and that his mother carries the sickness the Romanovs want to hide. Yes, I know all that.' I felt quite smart rattling it off. I raised my cup again, took a sip of tea and watched Joey's face. I was one up on him now.

'It's not because his father's a low-born, black singer from the halls that they want to kill him, is it?'

Joey stared at me and I saw his eyelid twitch. When he answered it was slow and careful. 'No. It's the disease. The Romanovs can't allow the people to know. Within the great families of Europe it is a closely guarded secret, but they are not murderers. In Russia it is a different matter. Those who carry the condition are forbidden to procreate, but the sickness still returns in almost every generation. It is a curse.'

'So Robbie's mother is . . .?'

'A brave woman, Kitty. She gave her baby away to save him. And now we must make sure that he lives. Robbie was an accident, but he is greatly loved. Almost from the day he was born his . . . family tried to wipe him from the face of the world. We've all tried to keep him safe, but it was becoming more and more dangerous. Just a week before you arrived one of our friends, a woman who cared for him during the evenings, was found murdered in her room.'

There was a rattling noise from the corner. Jacobin was clinging to the side of his cage, tearing at the bars with his claws and beak.

Joey glanced over and I saw him flinch. 'Her body had been ripped apart.'

I thought of Old Peter and that spattered painting of his mother.

'Do you know who did it?'

'No – they have people, spies, working for them everywhere. It's their way.' He leaned forward and cupped his forehead in the palms of his hands. 'I didn't think it through. Of course they'd follow him. They always find a way.'

I took a deep breath. It was time.

'Misha Raskalov reckons Ilya's a member of the Okhrana.' I didn't dress it fine.

Joey's head snapped up. 'What?'

'You know what that means?'

Joey nodded. 'Of course I do. They are the agents of the Czar. But how—'

'Misha's here in London. He told me.'

'I know. He has come here to arrange venues. Ilya has gone to Venice to do the same thing – they are The Moika's best representatives. They are always sent ahead to make contacts. They . . . they are ambassadors for the company.'

'I saw Misha today. Ilya lied. He didn't go to Venice. He came here with Misha and he went missing a day or so after they arrived a fortnight back. We think he's still here – and you've just confirmed that.'

I went to sit next to my brother on the couch.

'Ilya Vershinin didn't go back to Paris to see you last week, did he?'

Joey looked blank. 'No. He is meeting the owners of La Fenice. It will be a great spectacle if they can secure it next year. I've promised to travel to Venice to see him perform. It's as I told you . . .'

I took Joey's hand in mine and stared at a tuft of red wool coming loose from the rug at my feet. I wasn't sure how to put my next question.

'I . . . I think you've told Ilya some things too, haven't you? You're . . . close, you're bound to share secrets with each other.'

284

Joey pulled free and stood up. He walked over to the mantle and I heard the hem of his skirt rip a little as it caught on a nail poking up through one of the boards. Peggy was going to ask Lok to hammer it flat because of Robbie.

'No, Kitty, I don't believe it. He wouldn't . . .' I watched him move a little posy of china roses an inch to the left.

'Wouldn't he? Remember when you and David brought Robbie to the station and you asked about a cut on my head? It was still bleeding?'

Joey balled a fist and rested his head against the cool marble of the mantlepiece as I carried on. 'There wasn't time to tell you, the train was about to leave, but just before you arrived, someone, a porter I thought, knocked me onto the tracks in front of a train. Only it wasn't an accident.'

Joey stared at me in the mirror. 'I was carrying Lucca's bag at the time and it could, perhaps, have been taken for a baby. It was deliberate, I'm sure of it. At the station as we drew out I saw someone watching. Someone with white blond hair. It's very distinct.'

I faltered for a moment. 'You need to think, Joey. After I left you and David that night when you persuaded me to take Robbie to London, did you tell anyone else what was planned?'

He swallowed. I saw his Adam's apple move under the lace trim of his collar.

'And the children here in Paradise – the ones I wrote to you about. Those things all happened after we came back here with Robbie. There's been others too – you remember Old Peter?'

In the mirror Joey nodded.

'Did you know he was Russian? It don't matter whether you did or didn't, because he's dead. They found his body ripped apart in his room. And only because I involved him in all this. I've got blood on my hands too, Joey.

'Peggy met a man in St Dunstan's churchyard, a handsome man with snow-blond hair, slanting eyes and foreign talk. Robbie was with her at the time and he asked all about him – most particular he was.'

I paused. 'The only reason that boy is still alive is because Peggy said he was hers.'

Joey stared at himself in the mirror. From the couch I could see his expression in the glass – it was something between horror and disgust. He slammed his hand down hard on the mantle and the china posy leapt into the air, shattering to splinters across the stone hearth.

'Christ! How could I be so stupid? He knows it all. I told him because I . . . trusted him.'

I went to stand next to him. 'You told him because you loved him, Joey. We all make bad choices.'

He began to laugh, but it was a bitter sound. 'Not you, Kitty, you never make a bad choice. That's why she chose you.'

I put my hand on his arm. 'You and David chose me too. Robbie's safe here and David's coming for him. We can still make it right, make it stop.'

Joey didn't answer. I stared at the broken bits of china at my feet, a single red rose was the only part of the posy that was complete. I bent down to pick it up and turned it over in my palm, wincing when a jagged edge nicked a finger drawing blood.

'Do you have Robbie's toy, Kitty, the poppet?' I looked up, surprised at the oddness of Joey's question.

'Fetch it, please. It's time.'

Chapter Twenty-six

I met him on a Monday and I thought him quite the thing,
With his whiskers and his baccy pipe and glinting golden
  ring.
We married on a Tuesday and off he went to sea.
And then I waited patient for my Sam to hove to me.

Bella Cundle was a big girl with thick blonde hair and prominent talents, two of them. I knew if she went on first the
punters would sit up. I watched them shift about for a clear
view as she came to the front of The Gaudy's stage, dipping
low into a curtsey at the end of the verse.

'Bring it over here, girl. You could balance a jug on that!'

I stifled a laugh at the catcall, but standing next to me at
the back of the hall, Lucca clicked his tongue.

Jessie Rintoul went next. She was more delicate than Bella,
a fine-boned redhead with neat ankles and wrists. Jessie was a
dancer rather than a singer, I noted.

I met him on a Tuesday and he worked his sailor's charm,
With his blue eyes and his earring and his mermaid on his
  arm.
We married on a Wednesday and off he went to sea.

And then I waited patient for my Jack to hove to me.

The chorus that followed featured a good deal of flouncing skirts and plenty of leg. All the girls performed that together. They were good. I watched them whirl around in front of Lucca's painted tavern and then I turned to scan the hall.

It was going down like free beef and dripping. The punters were craning their heads for a glimpse of flesh, thumping the tables and swaying in time to the music.

I glanced back at the empty seat in the orchestra in front of the curved stage. Lucca said Old Peter was already in the ground according to the ways of his people. Professor Ruben and the boys had insisted on playing tonight and I was grateful to them. The girls too – they all had a soft spot for him and I reckoned it was hard for them.

Home, home, home from the sea,
I'm waiting for my man to sail back to me.
And when I next see him I'm sure he'll be gay
To meet the good friends I've found while he's away.

After the chorus Marnie Trinder stepped forward through the cigarette and cigar smoke that was beginning to thicken the air. The Gaudy reeked of hot tar, cheap gin and stale bodies – it was a ripe night.

Marnie was a bit older than the others, but her looks were holding up. She gave the lines just the right amount of twist to make the meaning clear.

I met him on a Wednesday and he wooed my maiden soul,
With his maps and charts and documents – he showed me
  the north pole.
We married on a Thursday and off he went to sea.
And then I waited patient for my Tom to hove to me.

Little Cissie Watkins looked like a golden angel. When she moved down to the front of the stage they all hushed up like they were sitting in rows at a Sunday school.

I met him on a Thursday and he showed me his tattoo
Of a little foreign gentleman out punting a canoe.
We married on a Friday and off he went to sea.
And then I waited patient for my Mick to hove to me.

Now, she didn't only look like a celestial, she sang and acted like one too, which made the punters roar even louder when her dainty gestures indicated exactly where that tattoo was.

And finally, Netta Swift twirled to the centre of the curved stage. I saw her pause to work out where the best light would catch her. Danny was right – she was a star in the making. Not only was she darkly handsome, but her voice carried right to the back of The Gaudy's upper gallery without any visible effort on her part.

I met him on a Friday and he showed me what he's worth.
He took me to his cabin, he's a man of noble berth.
We married on a Saturday, but as we left the vicar
I noticed that his footsteps hit the cobbles that bit quicker.

'Oh wait!' I called as Roger disappeared across the shore.
You haven't climbed the rigging yet or shown me any more
Of your special nautic talents or your wonders of the deep.
And you promised that you knew enough to make a maiden
weep.

But as I stood there calling loud I heard another girl
A shouting for her husband, by name of Samuel Pearl.
And by and by three others were stood by us on the prom
All calling out for their old men – a Jack, a Mick, a Tom.

And as we stood there bawling, it came upon us all
We was married to the self same man who had us in his thrall.
So now we sit here waiting, there's nowhere he can hide.
He'll never know what's hit him when we grapple his portside.

Netta was a good comic actress too. I reckoned I could do trade with her. In fact, I knew I could make a packet with this routine. Word had gone round and tonight The Gaudy was almost as full as it was on the occasions when I was up in the cage. We'd already taken another two barrels up from the cellar.

I watched the tray girls moving round the tables deftly avoiding slops spilt across the floor and the hands of the punters. I thought then of Jenny Pierce and Alice Halpern, those two little scraps. I wouldn't allow anything like that to happen again, not to my girls, not in my halls and not anywhere in Paradise – never.

As they sang the chorus a third time, Dismal Jimmy

dressed as a sailor staggered from the right. The punters jeered good-natured warnings as he clutched at a twisted column supporting one of the boxes nearest the stage, drunkenly rolling his eyes at the girls and working his wide-lipped mouth in a theatrical manner. He made a most convincing ar-farfan'arf. But then Lucca said he'd had enough practice.

Netta swung round, pointed at him and shrilled 'Roger!' And then they all called out a name and thundered across the stage. Dismal threw up his hands in surrender, windmilled and fell backwards into the wings.

The shouts, whistles, stamping and cheering made my ears ring. Lucca nudged me. 'Well, what do you think?'

'I think it's done The Gaudy no harm.'

A hundred grinning faces glowed in the flickering gaslight down here and as many more were packed like herrings in the tiers above. The booths were full tonight too.

'I want Fitzpatrick to see this tomorrow and I want to hear what he has to say about it. Jesmond's keen.' I nodded across the hall.

Aubrey Jesmond from The Carnival was leaning against the wall opposite. He was observing the punters with his little mole eyes in the way that a cat might watch over a particularly well-stocked mouse hole. He must have sensed me looking because he straightened up, lifted his bowler and tipped it at me.

'Tell the girls there'll be something more for them all in their packets at the end of the week, Lucca. The orchestra boys too.'

'Why don't you tell them yourself? You could go out back now, or go to The Lamb later. It's where they'll be.'

'I . . . I think they'll enjoy it all the more without me. I don't want them to think I'm spying on them.' I pushed my hand into my pocket and closed my fingers round the small, tight-wrapped package nestled under The Gaudy's keys. If the half of them out there knew what I was carrying around tonight, they'd climb over their dead mothers to take it from me. I scanned the doors at the back for the hundredth time that evening.

Lucca's eye narrowed. 'Surely you're not scared of them still?'

I shook my head. 'This is their moment. I'm not going to queen it over them. Besides, Amit doesn't take drink. It wouldn't be right.'

I looked over to the curtained door leading from the hall to the office. Amit Das was standing there in the shadows. He was so still you might have taken him for a plaster decoration.

Lucca followed my gaze. 'He is still with you?'

I nodded. 'Never far off. Telferman collected the letters yesterday and Amit went with him, but I asked him to come back to The Palace. It's safer having him near. And you should be careful too, Lucca. Ilya knows you're my friend. After what happened at Pearmans . . .' I trailed off.

'You shouldn't worry about me, Fannella. I am always . . . resourceful.' Lucca buried his chin into his collar and leaned back against the wall. He folded his arms and stared out over the punters. I was standing on his good side. I sidled a look and saw his expression harden as a couple of sleek young toffs, half cut on cheap brandy, tried to make free with two of the tray girls. They yapped and pawed like puppies, but the girls were sharp with them – just like I'd told them.

Lucca swore under his breath. I knew what he was thinking – I thought it too every time I saw a group of tot-hunting swells. Christ, there was a time when I was flattered by that sort of attention, but now I wanted to smack their hands away, spit into their slack ham faces and tell them to sling their hooks.

But I couldn't turn them out because of what happened in the past, could I? It wouldn't be good for trade. And it wasn't just the girls – poor boys were rich pickings for a certain type. We never spoke about revenge, but it occurred to me then that what he'd just said about being resourceful was true.

If it came to it, Lucca Fratelli could kill a man.

I craned my neck to take in the hall again. I wasn't only standing out here to see how the new act played, but Lucca didn't know that. I hadn't told him about Joey's visit. I wanted to, but Joey reckoned the safest and simplest thing was to keep everything close between us. He couldn't forgive himself for trusting Ilya and now he couldn't sift gold from dross or tell light from dark. I suspected Joey Peck wouldn't be able to trust anyone for a long time.

Betrayal is a terrible thing.

There was only one person who knew what was happening tonight – some of it – and she was sitting in The Gaudy's office looking after Robbie.

'Here.' I released the package and delved deeper into my pocket. 'Give Professor Ruben this.' I handed Lucca a sovereign. 'Tell him to buy some good stuff when they're at The Lamb tonight – not the usual turps. They're all to drink to Old Peter. Tell him to say "*zda-róv-ye!*" And then they can use the rest to celebrate.'

Lucca stared at the coin in amazement. 'They'll be there all night on this and most of tomorrow. Are you sure, Fannella?'

I smiled. 'Tell them to make the most of it. They'll be wearing the skin off the soles of their feet when we start moving the act between The Gaudy and The Carnival every night.'

I watched the tasselled red curtains close over Lucca's tavern on the stage. 'You'll have to paint another scene for The Carnival – we can't move this one, it's too much of a risk. Your Misha seen it yet?'

Lucca nodded and stared at his feet.

'Didn't he like it?'

He rolled a sticky discarded cork under the sole of his shoe and didn't answer. I was angry for him.

'Listen, your friend might come from the grandest company in Europe, but if he can't see that what you do here is as fine as anything The Moika prances around in front of, then he's a fool, for all his languages.'

Lucca picked at his nails as I warmed up.

'I'll tell him that myself next time I see him. You're an artist, Lucca. I've said it before and I'll say it again, you're wasted here.'

'That's what Misha says.' His voice was so low that even though he was standing right next to me I hardly heard it.

'What?'

'He . . . he has asked me to go back to Paris with him to paint for The Moika.'

'And what did you say?'

Lucca was silent.

'Well?'

'I . . . I haven't given him an answer yet.'

He was thinking about it! A shoal of fish flipped about in my belly. The thought of not having Lucca around was impossible. I stared at the stage. Mrs Conway was leaning down between the flares talking to Professor Ruben. Tonight the wig on her head put me in mind of a badger. She pointed at the sheet of music propped up on his piano and clapped her hands together rapidly to give him the time.

I'd planned the order so that Mrs C went on after the girls, thinking that the punters might be in a more amenable state of mind, but now I wasn't so sure. I didn't want to see this. And I didn't want to think about what Lucca had just said. I turned to speak to him again, but he'd gone.

Professor Ruben started to play. The jaunty tune made the punters turn expectantly towards the stage. Mrs Conway billowed in the limelight flares. The spots of rouge on her cheeks looked like an infection. She brought a fluttering hand to her breast and stepped forward.

I fled down the side to the office, slamming the door behind me just as the catcalls started up – not appreciative ones.

Peggy stood up abrupt.

'Shhhh! He's been sleeping like a lamb this evening. Even through the sailor act and the racket afterwards.'

I walked over to the desk and peered down at the open trunk behind it. Robbie Lennox was curled up inside, contentedly sucking on the corner of a blanket.

'Back in Paris he was likely used to being backstage when his father performed. Perhaps it's like a lullaby? Is the arm still bad?'

Peggy smiled and knelt beside the trunk. She moved the knitted blanket aside. Robbie stirred, but didn't wake.

'It's much better, see? The ice made the swelling go down and the bite is healing nicely. It's still bruised, though.'

I didn't want David Lennox to think I hadn't looked after his child. That was important. Any time now he and Joey would come through the door to take him away and I wanted to show him . . .

Well, I wasn't entirely sure what I wanted to show him, but I knew it was more than the fact I could look after his kid.

Joey reckoned on there being safety in a full house. The more happening around the hall, the less anyone would notice them, he said. The new act helped. It was the busiest The Gaudy had been since my last performance up in the cage.

It was getting on now, mind. If they didn't turn up within the next hour the crowd would be gone. I adjusted the neck of my blue satin, pulling it just a bit lower at the front where the lace met the dip of the collar. When I tricked out earlier that evening I told myself I was dressing to put on a good show for the punters, but that wasn't true.

Peggy straightened up and brushed her skirt down. 'I don't know why you've put him in this thing, Kit. It's not exactly comfortable. The perambulator we brought him over in is better. Why would his father, this David, want it?'

I moved some papers on my desk. The less she knew the better. Ominous noises were swelling beyond the door. Through the soles of my boots I could feel the floorboards of the office shifting in time with the stamping outside.

'I . . . I suppose it's because this is a good strong way to carry him. It's got leather straps.'

Peggy sighed. 'If he doesn't come soon I'm going to have to go. I promised Dan and I can't let him down. I haven't seen him for two days now. He sent word that he'd be at The Lamb with the others later and he's expecting me.'

I smiled. 'You go. You've done wonders enough, Peg.'

Tell truth, I was relieved at the thought she might not be there when Joey and David arrived. She bent to tuck the blanket round Robbie's arm again. When she straightened up her eyes were glassy.

'It's probably for the best. I reckon I might disgrace myself in front of his father.' She rubbed her cheeks roughly with the heels of her wrists. 'Look at me now! I'm soft as butter these days, but I'm going to miss him something terrible. I said as much to Lok when we were packing his things together before we came over to The Gaudy this evening. He's fond of Robbie too.' She nodded at the door. 'He doesn't say much, does he, the new fixture? He didn't open his mouth when we walked here.'

'Amit's a mute, Peggy. He doesn't say much to anyone.'

'He don't need to. He's the size of a bull. Have you seen his hands?'

I nodded. 'He used to work for my grandmother. I trust him.'

She looked down at Robbie again. 'If his father never turned up, me and Dan, we would have taken him in, Kit. Two can't be much more bother than one, can it?'

I almost laughed aloud at the thought of Robbie not being a bother, but the look on Peggy's face made me button it. She really cared for that boy and it was a wrench for her to see him go.

She bent low and brushed a kiss on Robbie's brown head. 'When we were packing his things up, we couldn't find his rabbit. I looked everywhere, but it was gone. You were mending it, weren't you? That's why you come up to get it.'

My hand strayed back to my pocket. 'I . . . I think it's still in my workbox.'

Tell truth, I didn't like to show Peggy what had happened to Robbie's toy. It was hidden in a drawer of the desk right next to her.

The office door opened and we both swung round.

Aubrey Jesmond stepped into the room. He pulled the door shut to muffle the sounds coming from the hall and raised an eyebrow. 'I think you'd better run the sailor routine again, Kit – the punters are tearing the place up out there. Lally Conway's hiding in the yard.'

It was late now. Too late.

The last of the punters had rolled down the steps of The Gaudy and into a rising fog an hour back. I went to the office door again and looked out into the hall. The lamps were still burning. Amit Das unfolded his arms and looked at me hopefully.

I shook my head.

'Not yet.'

I heard the clatter of someone cleaning high in the gallery. I walked a little way out between the tables and chairs and shielded my eyes against the gaslights.

'Who's up there tonight?'

A small voice came back. 'It's me, Edie Strong, Miss.' I squinted. Less than six months back it had been me up there with the bucket and mop, swilling out the unmentionables. I moved deeper into the hall trying to catch sight of her wiry little body.

'Tell you what, Edie – you can pack that up now. It's late and your mother will be worried. Get off home.'

'You sure, Miss? I'm happy to do a bit more. It's a right old state up here.'

'And it'll be a state tomorrow morning too, but you'll be fresh on the job. Go home, Edie. Use the side, the front will be locked.'

I turned and walked back to the office, the hem of my skirt catching in the sticky pools of spilled alcohol staining the boards. I paused when I was level with Amit, dug in my pocket and handed him my keys. 'When Edie's gone lock the side. If you hear a knock out front, don't open up. Come and get me.'

He took the keys in his paw, nodded and leaned back against The Gaudy's red varnished wall.

I closed the door gently behind me. Robbie was making little snuffling sounds in his sleep now. His hand clenched and unclenched on top of the blanket. He missed his poppet.

I pulled the package from my pocket and let it fall open on the desk in front of me. The big emerald, green as a new-hatched pea, glinted in the soft light of the lamp.

I was amazed when Joey slit that cloth rabbit open. I watched, puzzled, as he forced his fingers inside, pulled a small felt bundle from its stomach and rolled the contents into his palm.

Three emeralds had been sewn into the poppet. Joey had taken two and left the third with me as a precaution. After he left The Palace he was planning on going straight to a Dutch stone dealer in the rookery by Goodman's Fields. He reckoned he'd get a fair price on the smaller of the two and use part of it to pay the remaining portion of the passage on the *Frisia*. The rest, he said, was their future – David's and Robbie's.

But there was something else in that rabbit. Joey had been rough with it when he freed the emeralds and one of its ears had come loose. I reckoned it was the one Robbie had been chewing on. When Joey handed the poppet back to me I'd found a ragged strip of paper folded in two and rolled up tight inside the fraying ear.

I placed the emerald next to the lamp, smoothed the paper out over the desk top and looked at the Russian script. At the bottom there were three signatures – that, at least, was clear. I recognised one of the names now – Романов – it was Romanov in their writing. Misha had shown me.

When I asked Joey what the paper was he wouldn't say, but he told me it could never be parted from Robbie. That was why he left it with me. I folded it again and slipped it back into my pocket.

I closed my eyes and rested my forehead in my hands. Why weren't they here?

There was a soft click and a rustling sound. I looked up.

Joey was standing with his back to me staring out into the hall through the half-open door. He was wearing a woman's travel coat, cut in the French style, and the hat I'd seen before, the one with the muslin veil.

'Joey! At last.'

I stood as he turned from the door to face me. He drew

back the veil and my heart twisted in my chest.

It wasn't Joey standing there after all, but I knew who it was.

The tall, dark-skinned woman stepped forward and held out a gloved hand.

'Not Joey, Kitty. And it's not David either. I'm Della, Della Lennox. Robbie's mother.'

Chapter Twenty-seven

I didn't say a word. I couldn't. My mouth felt like the bottom of Jacobin's cage. I stared down at the long tapering fingers in fine leather. It was the hand I'd held in Paris thinking it to belong to David Lennox.

And it did, in a manner of speaking.

I dragged my eyes from the outstretched hand and looked direct into a pair of pale green eyes set in a long face, broad at the temple and narrow at the chin. It was David's face all right, but it wasn't him.

I glanced down at the woman's coat, taking in the ruffles and tucks that nipped the fabric into an unmistakable shape. David's clothes had hung loose on his tall, spare frame, but all the while underneath it all . . .

'No!' I don't know if I said the word aloud or just formed the shape of it. I stepped back abrupt, sending the chair behind me toppling to the floor.

Della moved closer. She wasn't exactly beautiful, but she was striking, in a hard and angular way. 'Where is he? Where's my boy?' Her voice was low and husky. The Scots accent gave it an edge, but now it was undeniably female. Even in his sleep Robbie must have recognised his mother. Little mewing noises came from the box behind my desk as he struggled to wake himself.

Della's eyes widened. She darted around the desk and froze

for a moment as she stared down at the trunk.

'Oh, thank God!' She brought a hand to her mouth and gulped down a shuddering lungful of air, before swooping to gather Robbie up into her arms. The blanket fell to the floor as she stood there with her back to me rocking from side to side, cradling his head against her neck. I watched her shoulders rise and fall as her fingers caressed the back of his downy head.

Then she loosened his white cotton gown and gently probed his skin. I knew what she was looking for. Della's back stiffened.

'What's this?' She didn't turn to show me, but I was certain she'd found the nick on his hand and the bruising.

'He . . . he had a little accident, that's all. We called a doctor out. It's healing. The doctor says he'll be fine.' Without thinking, I rattled off the explanation I'd prepared for David. A part of me couldn't take in the fact it wasn't him standing there.

She didn't say anything for a moment and then I heard her whisper, 'Thank God, thank God.' She nuzzled against Robbie's cheek. 'I'll never leave you again, never. I promise. Never again, my little prince.'

Although she spoke softly, the words were shot with a violent passion and I knew she was swearing an oath to him. Della brushed her lips over the top of his head and breathed deeply as if she was inhaling him, body and soul.

And then she began to sob.

The sound was muffled as she buried her face in his gown, but to my ears it was halfway between joy and a sort of despair. Robbie tightened his fat little fingers around the trailing ends of the veil hanging off her hat and he crooned with pleasure.

Of an instant the office disappeared. The world contracted to a point that was Della and Robbie Lennox, mother and son bound together so tight they were one person. It was as if I wasn't there. And it came to me then that love was a very different thing to the fancy glittering bauble I'd been rolling around in my head for the last few days.

There was a day, long ago, when Nanny Peck had taken me and Joey to see a circus set out on London Fields. I remember the tiger most particular. Beautiful he was, with his paint-sharp stripes and his great golden eyes. But he was terrifying too. As we watched him through the bars of the cage, his musky animal scent filled my nose and I could sense a power rolling off him. I remember how it made the hairs on my arms prickle.

I felt something like that now. Real love is a beast that can't be tamed or controlled. It's raw and fierce and savage, and it gives off a heat like a furnace so you can actually feel it on your skin.

Great waves of love were coming off Della and her boy. As I just stood there watching them, I found myself wondering how she felt that day at the Gare du Nord when she handed Robbie over to me. She must have been tearing herself in two inside at the thought of being parted from him, at passing him like a package to a virtual stranger, but she went through it without giving the game away.

Della Lennox was the best actress I've ever seen – and the bravest.

All the same, I was furious with her – Joey too.

I curled my fingers round the edge of the desk and cleared my throat.

'Where's Joey? He said you'd both come for him.' My voice sounded like chalk on a blackboard. I wanted to scream at her, swear at her, call her a hundred names not fit for a woman to hear – or use come to that – but I tried to swallow it down. I gripped that desk so hard I could feel my nails gouge into the wood. Two of us could put on an act.

Della looked up. She huddled Robbie close, just as Peggy had always done, and kissed his head again.

'He's not here?'

I shook my head, but didn't say anything. Something was roaring in my mind and I didn't want to let it out.

Della blinked slowly. 'Then I'm sorry, Kitty, I don't know. He was supposed to meet me earlier this evening, but he didn't come. It's why I left it so late before . . .' She broke off and allowed Robbie to bat her cheek. She closed her eyes and revelled in the pleasure of that touch. It was a moment before she even remembered I was there.

'He met me at Victoria Station this morning and gave me the travel bills. It was all planned. We didn't come over together because it was safer and besides there was someone in Paris I had to find. I've been searching for him for so long. It's why I had to send my boy on without me.' She smiled and kissed Robbie's head again. 'You know where we're going, the plan?'

'You . . . you're leaving tomorrow for Hamburg, all three of you.' My voice came brittle as fine bone china.

'Yes. Then Josette will go back to Paris and Robbie and I will sail to New York. But we'll need papers. We'll be travelling under new names. Your brother knows someone here in London who can help us.'

Della half sat on the edge of the desk, one arm folded around Robbie, the other lightly stroking his head.

'He left me at the station to collect the documents. He wouldn't let me come with him. Instead we arranged to meet again in the ladies' waiting room at five. I've been there all day – I can't remember how many cups of piss poor tea I've drunk, Kitty, how many polite conversations I've had about the weather, when all I could think about was my bairn.'

She shook her head. 'When he didn't come back for me—'

'You came on here to The Gaudy alone?'

Della nodded. 'I didn't know what else to do. Joey is . . .' She glanced at me. 'It's seems odd to call him that. Your brother is my friend and without him I don't know what I would have done, but he has secrets.' She shook her head. 'God knows, we all have enough of those, but Jose . . . Joey's secrets frighten him. The message you gave him that night, something about Bartholomew?'

I nodded. 'It was from our grandmother – *Bartholomew waits*. Did he tell you what it meant?'

'No. I asked after you'd gone. He wouldn't say anything. Besides there was so much else to arrange it didn't seem important. But this morning when we met at the station, he couldn't settle. We didn't speak for more than ten minutes and all the time he was in a fret – watching the door. His hands were shaking, even though he tried to hide it. Your brother is usually very good at . . . deception, Kitty, you must know that?'

I folded my arms. 'You're not so bad at it yourself, David.'

I let that hang there for a moment and was gratified to see her look down.

'You used me. Both of you!'

I couldn't help myself. Now I'd started, the words came spitting out like sparks off a Catherine Wheel.

'You played the gentleman with me, Della Lennox, stroking my hands, speaking soft, running your eyes over me, making me feel . . . making me think that you might . . .' I stopped, gripped the edge of the desk and carried on. 'Making me think that you might be a man, when all along you were playing me like a trout in a stream. And it was a dangerous game you got me into, wasn't it?'

She opened her mouth to say something, but I cut her off sharp.

'No! There's nothing you can say to make it right, so don't try. People have died here for the sake of your child: a little one pierced through the heart with a shard of glass, another crushed under a cart, the mother maimed for the rest of her life – which won't be long – and a good man . . .' I swallowed, '. . . a good friend torn apart in his lodgings.'

Della clutched Robbie tight to her side and unpinned her hat. She laid it on the edge of the desk, but the weight of the trailing veil made it slip to the boards. Her hair was cropped close to her head. Pearl earrings trembled from her ears. The lamplight made them glow like tiny moons against her skin. She shifted Robbie's weight and reached out to try to catch my hand.

'I'm sorry, so sorry. I didn't think – *we* didn't think. Truly, Kitty, I never meant for you or anyone here in London to be in danger. We thought we'd covered our tracks. We thought it was safe.'

'Well, you thought wrong.' I drew back. I was shaking with fury now, but the worst of it was that I was angry with myself. I couldn't tell whether I was blaming her for putting us all at risk, or – most shameful to admit – for not being David.

I forced a pin deep into the roll of hair at my neck and almost welcomed the sharp prick of pain as it nicked the skin.

'Anyway, it's too late for sorry. I reckon it's time for some answers.' I leaned forward, flattened my hands on the desk and nodded at Robbie who was playing contentedly with a button on her travel coat. 'Like who's his father?'

Della's eyes slid from mine. She folded her arms around Robbie again and began to rock him gently. 'Your brother and all his friends tried so hard to help us. The halls in Glasgow, Paris, London – they're not so different. They're full of outsiders, but that makes the bonds strong. We're a family. I don't know what we would have done without Joey. They would have killed Robbie by now.'

'*They* being the Russian royal family – the Romanovs?'

Della nodded, but didn't look up. When she answered it came as a whisper. 'Sergei, that's his father's name. And I was a fool to imagine that we could ever be together. They would never stand for it.'

She looked up now and I caught a flicker of guilt in her eyes. 'I know about Ilya, Kitty. Joey warned me about him this morning at the station. He blames himself, but he shouldn't.'

Della shifted about so she could hold Robbie in the crook of one arm as she placed her free hand over mine. My skin didn't fire up when she touched me now.

'Listen, you must know this, I didn't entirely lie to you. I am a singer and the night we met I'd come straight from The Chapeau Rouge where I perform *en travesti* – as a man. It was Joey's idea that I should meet you like that. He said it would be more . . . persuasive.'

'He said that, did he? Oh I was persuaded all right. And you knew it, didn't you?'

Those sea-green eyes slipped away again.

'I . . . I didn't want to deceive you, but I knew Joey was right. I'm a woman too, after all. When a man begs a woman for help it's . . .' She trailed off.

'Seductive? Is that what you're trying to say? You deliberately tried to seduce me that night!'

'No—'

I pulled my hand out from under hers and stared at her. If she didn't have Robbie huddled close I might well have gone for her.

'All right, yes, a little. I'm sorry, but it was for the sake of my bairn. They want to kill him, Kitty. You'd do the same for your own. Tell me you wouldn't?'

The question swung in the air.

I turned from her, righted the chair and sat down heavily. 'Go on then. If you're in a mood to confess, you might as well carry on.'

Della stared up at the ceiling. Just above her head the stain of Fitzy's cigar smoke spread across the plaster. She was quiet for a moment, but then she began to speak slowly and quietly.

'The winter before last Sergei came to see me perform at The Chapeau. It's the fashion for the Russian nobility to visit Paris and when they come they are great patrons of the arts. They and their women are seen at the ballet and the opera. But the men also like to muddy their boots. Sergei came to The Chapeau night after night. I didn't know who he was. He was just another man – and there were plenty of them at my door, the costume excites them. At first I wasn't interested, but he was clever, gentle and kind – not like the others. And he was handsome too. But there was something else – he was, he *is* . . . fragile. I wanted to protect him, can you understand that, Kitty?'

I was silent, but it didn't matter. Della carried on, swept along by her own story.

'We became . . . close. Then . . . then I found I was to have a child – his child. And when Robbie was born Sergei tried to protect us, but his family . . .' She looked across at me and shook her head. She made a handsome woman, I'll give her that, but there were hollows in her high dark cheeks and shadows beneath her eyes.

'You have no idea how ruthless people can be. His family will stop at nothing to make certain that Robbie does not exist. He was never supposed to happen, Sergei was never supposed to father a child.' She hugged the baby and rocked him back and forth.

'But he did, and no one can tell me that it was wrong.'

I stared at the bundle folded in her arms and the thought came to me of how much that child was loved. Peggy and Danny would have taken him for themselves, Lucca had painted him a cradle and even Lok had proved a better temporary mother than me. Whatever Della had done, little Robbie was an innocent in all of this. He deserved a life, or as much of one as he could manage.

We both started at a harsh rattle. It sounded as if someone was throwing stones at the narrow office window. Della slipped from the desk and bent to take up her hat.

'I'd forgotten the rain here in London, how it never stops. We have to go. The boat leaves on the tide at six. I have to be on board at least an hour before.' She glanced down at the trunk and bit her lip. 'Without Joey here I don't know how I can carry him.'

I reached for the chain at my neck and felt for the ring and the Christopher. They were warm to the touch. I rolled them between my fingers.

'Did Joey tell you where he was going, Della, who he was seeing?'

She shook her head. 'He said it was better if I didn't know.'

I rolled my eyes. 'That sounds like him. What about the travel papers? You'll need them.'

'I have this . . .' She hefted Robbie onto her hip and pulled a small tapestry purse from the folds of her coat. She loosened the drawstring at the neck and delved inside to take out one of the emeralds.

'Sergei gave them to me before Christmas when I last saw him. He told me they were our insurance and he begged me to leave Paris, but I couldn't, not then, for Robbie's sake. I sewed the stones into the poppet. It was the only place I could think of where no one would look.

'And I was right. Just after you left with Robbie my room was torn apart. It was an act of vengeance. We'd been there less than a week – we had to keep moving. They knew Robbie had gone and they wanted to punish me. If I hadn't sent the emeralds ahead with him and the . . .' Della took a deep breath.

'That's the past. We have a future to think about. Joey gave me this stone at the station this morning. He kept the smallest to pay for our papers and he told me you have the third?'

'It's here.'

I reached for the emerald sitting near the lamp on the desk's leather worktop and dropped it into her open palm. The two stones, one slightly larger than the other, chinked together and glinted in the light.

'Wherever we go next, it won't matter who we are if we can pay our way.'

There was a truth in that I couldn't argue with. As Della pushed the stones back into the pouch and slipped it into her coat Robbie stirred and made a soft sucking noise. He had fallen asleep.

'Is the poppet in the trunk with the rest of his things, Kitty?' I glanced up at something in her voice as she continued. 'He loves it so – he can't be parted from it. I told you that at the station, remember?'

I pulled the drawer open and handed her the cloth toy held together now with quick crude stitches. It wasn't my finest work.

'Here. It's been in the wars. I've sewn it up again, but you'll have to do a neater job yourself when you have the chance.'

Della snatched it from me and dropped it into the trunk on top of the blankets. I thought about the strip of paper in my pocket and some devil in me told me to keep quiet, for a while anyway. We can all play tricks, Della Lennox, I thought.

Robbie made a cooing sound and his perfect curved lips puckered for an invisible bottle.

She smiled and nestled him closer. 'When he wakes I'll

feed him, Kitty. He's always greedy.'

'There's some pap in a bottle here. Peggy . . . and me, we've been giving him that.' I stood and went to the trunk, but Della caught my arm. 'He won't be needing pap any more.'

Of course not. Stupid of me. She was his mother. I bent to take the bottle from the trunk and the Christopher slipped out from beneath my collar, dangling over the blankets.

'Does Joey know the boat you're taking tomorrow?'

'He arranged it. It's called the *Albertine*. It leaves from Steam Boat Dock near West India Dock. It's a regular timber carrier.'

'And he knows it leaves at six?'

Della nodded. 'Do you think he'll meet us there, Kitty?'

I hoped so. In the meantime, she and little Robbie needed help. I put the pap bottle on the desk and went to the door to take my coat.

'I'll come with you. You can't manage alone.'

There didn't seem to be much sense in waiting around at The Gaudy for Joey. If we could find a hack at this time we'd take one down to West India. I'd get Amit to come with us. As I pulled the coat from the hook a thought struck me. I whipped round.

'Della, when you came in here ten minutes ago, was there a man outside?'

She shook her head. 'I didn't see anyone except the girl who let me in at the front. She was emptying a bucket into the gutter. I asked for you and she took me back through the lobby into the hall and showed me your office.'

Edie hadn't gone home when I told her to, then? She was a good girl, but I wished she'd done as I said. There was a reason I'd locked the front. Something prickled at the back of my neck.

I opened the office door.

'Amit?'

Chapter Twenty-eight

The Gaudy glowed red and gold in the soft light of the gas jets ranged along the first tier. The light they gave off was generally enough to clean by. Edie must have left them on.

I scanned the hall. It wasn't like those grand jewel-box palaces Joey had taken me to in Paris. They were beautiful enough, for them that like that sort of thing, but they weren't big on comfort. The stiff-backed golden chairs in the tiny curtained boxes made you perch like a canary out on a pole, made you think that you were being scrutinised as much as the performers on stage. Which, I suppose, was the point.

My hall gave out a faded, threadbare welcome that didn't ask questions, didn't look too close and didn't care who came so long as they paid. I walked a little way forward.

'You there, Amit?'

I turned about. Tonight there was something almost edible about The Gaudy. I wondered that I hadn't seen it before. The plaster decorations – swags of fat-bellied fruit – on the booths and on the tiered horseshoe balconies ranged above looked so real I could almost reach up, pluck one free and take a bite.

The twisted columns put me in mind of the penny sugar canes set out in trays in the window of Geddlers on the Mile End Road. Once, when we was out for a stroll, Nanny Peck bought me and Joey a stick each and she let Joey carry them home in the brown paper. When we got back to Church Row he hid them away for himself. I never got a lick.

I loved my brother. I always looked up to him, worshipped him, you might say. When I'd thought him dead, in my mind he'd become like one of them painted statues in Lucca's churches. Standing up there on his plinth, hand on heart, lips pursed in prayer, his wide blue eyes locked onto something celestial – in death Joseph Peck had become someone perfect, flawless, almost holy. Just recently, now he was very much alive again, I'd been turning up things that cracked the feet of that statue.

Why wasn't he here now?

I took a deep breath. The air was thick and warm. Despite Edie's best efforts with a mop and a bucket, the smell of spilled gin, rough tobacco and soap-shy bodies lingered. I savoured the familiar taste. This was my real home.

I stepped forward and something hard snapped underfoot. I bent to gather the bits of broken oyster shell from the floor. Edie had missed it. As I straightened up I caught a movement at the far end of the hall beyond the stacks of tables and chairs.

I dropped the shell into my pocket. 'Amit?'

Something moved again – my reflection in the big French mirror behind the serving board. Of an instant there was a ticking sound and a soft familiar hiss as the lamps lined up along the wall beneath the first balcony tier flared. The flat, stale smell of gas came strong as The Gaudy's lights burned up bright.

I blinked. The magic was gone. The sudden, unnatural brilliance showed the hall for what it was. There was nothing comfortable about the stains on the boards, the holes in the curtains, the smears on the rails, the great grey lump crumpled against the wall.

For the longest moment I didn't entirely understand what I was looking at, my mind couldn't make sense of it. It was bulky and formless, a jumbled heap of something covered with a bolt of cloth.

Only this something had a hand – a big one – and it was resting flat in a pool of black.

'Amit!'

I ran over and knelt beside the slumped form. His square jaw rested on his chest and his legs were splayed out beneath him at an awkward angle. I touched his arm and he toppled forward. A slim knife was embedded in the centre of his back. The curved silver handle was patterned with a swirling enamelled design and the wall behind him was patterned black with his blood. Amit Das was dead.

The hissing came on stronger. I turned from the body to see the gas jets along the walls at ground level spurt anew with a vicious energy – the flames dancing unnaturally high above the crimped rims of their moulded glass cups. This wasn't right. I ran a hand over my damp forehead. It was hot in here.

Over to the left another black stain began to spread across the red varnished wall beneath the balcony. I watched, mesmerised for a second, as the paper above the gas flame detached itself.

It peeled gracefully away, the darkening edges fringed with a filigree of intense gold that blossomed into a bouquet of fiery curling petals when it reached the wooden boards. I sprang up and darted across to stamp on the burning paper, grinding my boots into the crisp scorched embers until they were powder beneath my feet.

I span round to take in the rest of the hall, only it was too late.

The flames from the gas jets were climbing the walls now, flattening themselves out under the overhanging balcony. Pools of yellow fire fanned out overhead – lapping greedily for tassels and the trailing ends of curtains from above. The plaster fruits draped in swags along the first tier were black with smoke, popping and shrivelling in the heat.

I covered my nose and mouth with my hands and ran out to the centre of the hall. The same thing was happening on every tier. Overhead a cloud of billowing grey obscured The Gaudy's painted ceiling.

I felt a hand on my arm and jerked round.

Della was standing behind me, Robbie clutched tight to her side. He was completely silent, his brown eyes huge as he took in the flames spreading above and around us.

'We've got to get out, Kitty.' She started to wheeze. 'C . . . come on, girl. What are you waiting for?' She pulled the veil of her hat down and tucked Robbie's head beneath it. 'The front doors will be open. It's where I came in.'

'You and who else?'

Della ignored me. I caught her arm as she pressed forward. 'The Gaudy, it . . . it's my theatre. I can't just leave it.'

'We can't stay here. I have to take him away.'

I tightened my grip. 'And I . . . I have to do something. I have to call the brigade. The sand buckets are over there, help me.'

She shook me off roughly. 'The only thing you can do is

leave with us, now! Look at the place, Kitty – it's going off like a tinderbox. Open your eyes – don't be a blind fool.'

A blind fool!

That's what I was all right. I couldn't bear to look at her. My eyes locked on Amit's body propped against the wall. I was a fool to have been taken in by her and Joey. A spurt of anger hotter than anything scorching around us blistered my tongue.

'You selfish bitch, Della Lennox! I see things very clear now. This is all on account of you. All of it! Them murdered kids, Old Peter and now—'

I broke off as my mouth and nose filled with smoke. It forced its way down my throat blocking my lungs with hot tar. I bent double as I started to choke. At the same moment there was a whiplash crack as the old mirror glass behind the board bar exploded into a thousand fragments. A hail of deadly glittering splinters burst across the hall.

I gasped as something cut into my scalp and into the top of my arm. I straightened up. Della's head was bent low, the baby cradled close in her arms. On her left shoulder and down her back small red marks bloomed through the coarse grey material of her travel coat. Robbie started to cry. I moved closer to shield him in case it went off again. Of an instant, I couldn't bear to think of the mirror glass tearing into his smooth brown skin.

'Is he . . .?'

Della grimaced. 'He's fine – I caught it.'

We both span around at a roar from behind. All along the apron the limelight flares were spitting and burning like columns. I'd never seen them fire up so bright or so high. The blinding, white-hot light they threw off was cruel.

She pointed. 'Did you see that?'

I couldn't look straight at the stage. I had to shield my eyes, but when I looked again, I saw it too.

Between the pulsing, crackling columns of flame something moved on the boards. A huge shadow reared across Lucca's beautiful painted scenery boards. It darted to the left and was gone. Moments later the long velvet curtain to the left of the apron burst into a brilliant sheet of rippling golden flame. Anyone hiding there would have been roasted alive.

As we stood there, the banner curtain along the top of the stage caught. A delicate ribbon of golden fire began to spread like embroidery through the red velvet cloth. It would almost have been beautiful if it hadn't shown that The Gaudy was beyond my help.

It was beyond anyone's help now.

I grabbed Della's arm. Together we ran under the burning balconies towards the lobby leading out to the street. Broken glass crunched under foot as we hurtled to the double doors.

I reached to pull one side open and cried aloud as the metal handle seared into my palm. I couldn't see the lobby beyond, but I could hear the growling of the flames and the groan of burning wood. Even if I managed to yank open the door I knew it was hopeless.

I spat into my stinging palm. Edie's bucket was lying on its side at my feet. The foul mop water had puddled on the boards and was turning to vapour.

Oh, Christ – not Edie too? I span round trying to see if she was lying nearby, but the air was filling with smoke.

'Edie!'

I choked out her name over and over, but it was lost in the sound of splintering wood and cracking plaster.

Robbie's muffled sobs were coming between bouts of wracking coughs.

'It's no good.' Della held him close. 'We . . . we can't get out this way, can we?'

'No.' I covered my nose and mouth again as a billow of smoke from the lobby crept under the door and coiled upwards. We both turned at a screeching, ripping sound from the hall behind us. A flaming curtain rolled down from somewhere high above, hooking on the balcony overhead and draping over the serving board, blocking half The Gaudy from view. Once the gin caught, the whole place would go up in a minute.

'Is . . . is . . . there any . . . oth . . . other way, Kitty?' Della could hardly get the words out for coughing.

When I didn't answer she began to cry and Robbie, catching his mother's desperate misery, wailed loudly with her. She held him close and stroked his head through the muslin veil. I bent double again and retched. Black smoke was everywhere – in my eyes, my nose, my lungs, and now my stomach. My hair came loose, falling forward to brush the boards.

I found I could breathe deeper near the floor, the smoke was thinner here. I gulped deep, coughed again and tried to clear my head.

There was another way out.

The door from the back of my office, the one Fitzy had always draped over with a fancy curtain, led into the passages behind the stage and out to the workshops. I hacked again as another plume of smoke wound around us. The air was foul with gas now too.

Forty foot away on the right I could just make out the shape of the door to my office through the smoke.

I reached for Della's arm.

'This way.'

We huddled low and picked our way back across the hall. The flames had taken hold on the left-hand side and now they were spreading to the right. Overhead they were licking round the curtains of the balconies and leaping from tier to tier. We had to dodge as gobs of flaming stuff started to rain down on our backs.

I glanced over at Amit's body as we neared the office. He had my keys, didn't he? I shrugged Della off and scuttled towards him, trying not to breath. His huge right hand was lying flat in a pool of blood, but I could see a metal loop poking out beneath it. I mouthed a silent apology as I knelt and lifted Amit's hand from the sticky mess to fish the keys from the boards.

If I managed to get out of this alive, I'd make it up to his brother Ram. I swore it to myself on Joey's Christopher. As I caught hold of Della's arm again I thought about that knife in his back. The man I'd seen on the stage – the flaming curtain? Surely it was Ilya?

And surely he was dead?

I kicked open the office door and bundled Della and Robbie through first. The room seemed to be filled with mist. The air was tainted here, but not as bad yet as the hall outside. I slammed the door behind us and ran to the passage door on the far side of the room.

My hands shook as I lifted the bloodied ring and sorted through the keys until I found the right one. I fitted the key to the lock and pulled back the door. The wood-panelled passage beyond was lit up like the mouth of hell. As I swung the door back, the fire gathered itself together, forming itself into a ball that rolled towards me. I swear it was like a living, knowing thing seeking us out.

I slammed the door, but I felt the heat flatten itself against the other side, roaring with hungry disappointment. It wouldn't be long before it ate its way in. We'd die here, basted in our juice like fatty joints in a cookshop oven . . . that's if the smoke didn't suffocate us first.

Della coughed and the muslin flattened itself against her face like a winding sheet. She pushed it back. Beneath the veil her face was grey with ash and rigid with terror. Robbie squirmed and wailed like a banshee in her arms.

'There . . . there's nowhere else, is there, Kitty? This is our c . . . coffin.' She started to choke.

Something leapt in my mind.

Coffin. That was it!

The secret room under the office, I always thought it was like a coffin. If we could cram ourselves down there with the stone walls to protect us, then perhaps, if there truly was a God and He was in the mood for a miracle, perhaps we could still come through?

'Lay him down in the trunk for a moment and t . . . take this.'

I pulled off my boot and offered it to her.

'Smash the window glass.'

She stared at the boot. A tear brimmed over and slipped down her right cheek, marking a dark trail in the ash.

'It's no g . . . good. We can't get out that way, there are b . . . bars.' She could hardly get the words out for the smoke filling her lungs.

'We're not going out that way. We need the air. Put him down and use this.'

I heard the sound of breaking glass as I turned from her to take Nanny Peck's blue and white jug from the mantle. I threw the fading daffodils I'd filled it with into the hearth. I looked at the jug and then at the shawl tied to the back of the chair. For some reason I needed the old girl with me. I took up the fraying plaid and wrapped it round my shoulders.

'Give me a hand with the desk, will you?'

Della shook her head. 'I don't understand.'

'Just do as you're bleedin' told. I'll push, you pull. Now!'

We shoved the desk against the wall and I knelt to fold back the rug to reveal the square trap in the boards. I rolled the rug tight and packed it hard against the gap beneath the door leading out to the theatre. A jolt went through me as a tremendous crashing sound came from beyond the door, followed by the gut-wrenching sound of falling brick and timber.

But I couldn't think about The Gaudy now. I forced my stockinged foot back into the boot. It was almost comic that I'd worn my best pair with the highest heels to impress David.

'Give me your hat, Della.'

'Kitty, I don't . . .'

'And I don't have time to explain. The hat!'

She pulled it from her head and handed it to me. I ripped the trailing veil into three long pieces, then I took up the jug and poured the stinking water over the muslin strips. I handed two of them to Della and wound the third around my nose and mouth.

'This will help us breathe if the smoke gets to us.'
I took up the oil lamp and moved towards the trap.
'We're not going out, Della, we're going under.'

Chapter Twenty-nine

'At the bottom it turns right – go on.'

I set the oil lamp on the stone just below me and turned to pull the trap shut above us. The steps were so narrow my hips scraped against the wall as I shuffled about. No wonder Fitzy didn't have much call for the 'hidey hole'. If he'd ever managed to cram his corporation down here then I reckoned he had a future as a contortionist.

I called down. 'You'll have to bend your head, Della, the ceiling's low.'

Her coughing echoed from the walls as she reached the bottom and I heard the material of her coat rustle as she turned the tight corner. I took up the lamp and followed.

Della leaned awkwardly against the stone, her head bowed forward under the low bricks arching above. The damp muslin hung like a scarf at her collar. She brushed her lips over the top of Robbie's head and he blinked at the light as I paused at the curved entrance to the little chamber. He'd stopped crying now.

I loosened the muslin and breathed in. The air was foul down here too, but it was the foulness of a street sewer, not smoke. That was something at least. It was cold, too. I could see my breath, not smoke, fug up in front of me. I was glad of Nanny Peck's shawl.

'Budge up then, Della. There's just enough space. If we

can sit it out down here then maybe—'

We both flinched as a thundering crash rolled overhead. The ominous sound echoed from the stones. Brick dust pattered from the arches, falling across my eyes, my nose. I wiped it away, tasting the earthy metallic powder on my lips.

Then maybe what, I wondered? Even if we didn't suffocate, would anyone find us buried down here?

I pushed the thought away.

'Sit, Della. It's easier than leaning.' I dipped my head to go through the arch and I shrugged Nanny Peck's shawl to keep it over my shoulders.

'We can't sit, Kitty – there's water everywhere.'

I heard a soft splash as I stepped down. There was a rush of wetness in my boot. I held the lamp forward. Della was right. A shimmering black pool covered the four square flagstones I was expecting to see.

'But that's never been here before. I don't understand . . .'

Of course! It was rain – Lucca had said as much when I was entertaining Sam. The cellars at The Gaudy always took on water when the drains couldn't cope. Mostly it didn't matter – the bottle stacks were sound – but the barrels, 'specially the older ones, could soak through corrupting the liquor inside.

I should have listened to him and got Fitzy on it, like I said I would. Not that it mattered now.

'What next?' Della stared at me. Her pale eyes were like pebbles in the lamplight. They were dead, like every last bit of hope had been rubbed away. The light carved out great dark hollows beneath her cheeks. Her strong-boned face didn't have the usual curves or cushions of a woman. Of an instant I could see how I'd fallen for the lie and, for some reason, that made me feel better.

I raised the lamp and the flame jittered in the glass.

'We'll wait it out. The water won't rise above here.' I made a chopping motion with my free hand below my knees. 'It never does.'

Another rumbling sound came from above. The wall at my back juddered and more dust fell over my head and shoulders. I coughed as it caught at the back of my throat.

'And then what, Kitty? Even if we live, no one will find us down here. They won't think to look for us under the rubble. No one even knows we're here.' Della nodded at the lamp. 'When that goes out it will be dark as a tomb. It's hopeless. One way or another we're dead.'

My heart began to rattle about in my chest like it was trying to find a way out. Thing is, I didn't much care for small spaces. When I was around five or six, Joey had locked me in a tea chest when we were playing in the old goods yard up Shadwell. He'd gone off and I'd cried and screamed and beat on the sides thinking he wouldn't come back. I scraped so hard on the lid that my fingers bled. It seemed like a day, but half an hour later when he finally slipped the wooden peg to free me I'd disgraced myself.

I didn't mind heights, but there was something about crouching here while a hundred tons of bricks and rubble collapsed overhead that put me in mind of that tea chest.

Wedged up against her, I felt Della tremble. Then she began to cry, not loudly – which, curiously, made it worse. No, these were dry, heaving sobs she tried to swallow down. Robbie stared up at his mother's twisted face and then he began to bawl. His thin reedy wails bounced off the stones so they cut straight through you.

Christ! That was all I needed. I couldn't stay here.

I gathered up my skirts, gripped the lamp, ducked my head through the arch and went up the first two steps. I held up the light and saw tendrils of black smoke creeping around the corners of the trap. The air smelt of gas and burning wood.

My heart was beating so hard now it was knocking against my ribs. I could hardly breathe. I tried to gulp down some air and heard the ragged sound in my throat as my chest tightened up to block the way.

Della was right. It was hopeless. I rested my head against the cool damp wall for a moment.

Think, girl, think. My head was spinning. I breathed deep again, trying to force the air down into my lungs.

Think.

I turned back and squeezed through the arch again, the water reached above my ankles now. It was rising faster than I expected, but where was it coming from? I scraped my eyes across the walls. The safe was lodged halfway up in the bricks at the end of the chamber. The wall to the left seemed to be blocks of stone. Over to the right, behind Della and Robbie, there was more stone and a band of bricks curving up to fan across the low ceiling.

'Della, shift forward.'

When she didn't move I shouted at her. She stopped sobbing and stared at me blankly, her hand softly caressing the furred brown ball of Robbie's head.

'Why? What's the point?'

'Because the water's coming in from somewhere, and I

want to see it. Now, move.' I softened my tone. 'Please.'

She shrugged and shuffled away from the wall. We danced around each other until I could take a better look. At the bottom, just above the water line, there were a couple of missing bricks, and a thin trickle of water spilled through the hole. I bent lower and blocked my nose at the evil smell. That was where the sewer stink was coming from. I pushed my hand into the gap, expecting to make contact with more brick. When it didn't I forced it in further. It went straight through to the elbow and I groped into nothingness beyond.

I pulled my arm back. As my hand came free it dislodged another of the bricks, dragging it partially from the wall so it jagged out at an angle. I ran my fingers over the wall. The mortar at this level was soft and crumbling to the touch. Years of water had softened the bonds.

I straightened up as far as I could.

'Della, can you take the lamp for a moment and still keep hold of Robbie?'

She balanced him on one hip and reached for the lamp. She didn't say anything as I knelt in the water and scrabbled at the brickwork, gouging the mortar out from the bricks with clawed fingers.

First one, then two, then three, four bricks came loose. I pulled them free and piled them carelessly beside me. There was a hole the size of a man's head low down in the wall now.

'Pass me the lamp.'

I held it to the gap and peered through. At first I couldn't make anything out, but as the flame flickered it cast light on what seemed to be an arched tunnel of a man's height filled with water. I glanced up. Della was leaning back against the wall with her eyes closed. Robbie freed an arm from his blanket wrapping and reached down to the light, his fat little fingers opening and closing on nothing.

'There's a way out. If we can make a hole big enough we can get through. It must go somewhere. Well?'

When Della didn't move I snapped at her. 'For God's sake, and if not His, for Robbie's, help me!'

That did the trick. I didn't have Della Lennox down as a Bible type, but I knew enough now to realise that baby was her religion. She nodded sharp, folded herself over to lay Robbie on the step leading into the chamber and turned back to kneel beside me.

Gathering some of the discarded bricks together she took the oil lamp from me and balanced it on them above the level of the water.

'Here.' I fumbled in my pocket and took out the shards of oyster shell I'd found on The Gaudy's floor. 'Use these to dig at the mortar. It comes out easily enough, but some bits are more solid than others. These are sharp and hard as stone.'

We knelt there side by side, hacking at the wall with our fingers and the bits of shell.

Within five minutes we'd trebled the size of the hole in the brickwork. At first Della worked slowly as if she couldn't believe it would make a difference, but as the gap widened and the bricks came free she took in the empty blackness beyond and she began to believe.

Once she began to believe she began to work.

'That's enough.' I sat back. 'We can get through now. It's easily big enough.'

We glanced at Robbie on the step as another booming

sound reverberated above, loosening dust from the ceiling and more bricks in the gap we'd made. One of them fell back into the blackness beyond and we heard it splash into the water.

Della rubbed a hand across her face. She'd taken off her gloves to scrabble at the wall and her dark skin was criss-crossed with cuts where she'd misjudged her frantic gouges with the shell.

'How deep is it?'

'I've no idea. The only thing I know is that it's a way out. I'll go first.'

Della caught my arm as I pulled up my sodden skirts and made to scramble through the gap. 'I . . . I can't swim, Kitty.'

'Neither can I – least I've never tried. But there's not much else we can do, is there? Once I'm through try to pass me the lamp, then Robbie, then you follow him. Is that clear?'

She looked doubtfully at the hole.

'It can't be any worse than this, can it?' We both ducked as something heavier than brick dust rattled from above. It came to me then, that for all her *en travesti,* or however she liked to dress it up, I was the one with what Lucca called coglionis.

I was about to say something of the sort, when I caught the expression on her dust-smeared face. She was staring over at Robbie, her face tight with a terrible aching determination that set the raw bones even sharper in her cheeks. She was gathering herself together for his sake.

I felt a whip smart of shame and buttoned it. Della must have gone through so much already to protect her kid, things I couldn't imagine. I took her wet hand in mine and squeezed it.

'Listen – this is a way out. We have to try it. I'll go first.'

I ruffled up my skirts, leaned forward and squeezed through the hole into the darkness. When I was halfway through I plunged my hand down into the water and my palm scraped against something solid. The water in the tunnel was less than a foot deep, but it wasn't clear. I was glad I couldn't see the things bobbing against my skin. Beneath my hand I could feel something like a mat of slime-coated hair floating up to knot itself between my fingers. The stench was something chronic.

I hauled myself through, flopped down into the muck and tried to block my nose as I splashed to my feet. I bent level with the glowing gap.

'It's not deep, Della. I can stand. Your turn now.'

'Which way?'

I held the lamp higher and tried not to notice that the flame was burning perilously low. The dim light splashed up the walls around us, lighting an area no wider than Nanny Peck's Sunday crinoline.

Della hugged Robbie against her dripping coat and stared at the fork in the tunnel. She shook her head. 'Either – it's all the same down here. It must go on for miles.'

I splashed forward, my foot skidding on something hidden beneath the surface. It was shallow here at the sides of the passage. A deeper gulley carried a torrent of foaming, lump-flecked water out along the centre, but just ahead it split in two – the rank water tumbling and gushing either side into twin arched black mouths.

I wiped the back of my hand across my face and instantly regretted it.

Five minutes back we'd narrowly avoided a waterfall that came crashing down without warning from an overhead grille. We were lucky; any earlier and we'd have been drenched, but that wouldn't have been the worst of it.

From the foul stink – and it was a thousand times more noxious than the general air down here – I'd say it came direct from the tannery pits off Spread Eagle Street. As the deluge slammed down into the sewer, the raw, ripe smell of shit, piss, blood and rotting flesh made us retch. Our eyes burned and the insides of our mouths scorched like we'd been sucking on cinders. The skin on my face and hands where the tannery water had spattered up stung like an open wound now.

I looked at the passages. The one on the right sloped downwards. If I was right and we had gone under the tannery pits off Spread Eagle Street back there, then the river wasn't far off. Surely the drain discharged itself into the Thames?

I blinked hard, my eyes were streaming from the fumes and whatever it was that had spattered up into them. I resisted the urge to rub them again. I rested my hand against the damp black bricks to steady myself and tried to imagine what might be above our heads, trying to picture the likely layout of the streets.

It was no good, the passage turned and twisted about so much I had as much idea of what direction we were taking as a mole at midday. I felt something brush against my ankle and looked down.

Della yelped as a pink-eyed rat the size of a well-fed cat skirted round me and disappeared into the passage on the right. We heard the scratching of its claws on the stones as it skittered away.

'That's it, then – we go that way.' I splashed forward, but Della clutched my elbow.

'You're not following that . . . that thing, are you?'

'It has to go out into the world somewhere. You got any better ideas?'

She didn't have time to answer. A metallic grating noise rang down the passage. It sounded like a bell had fallen through the floor of The Whitechapel Foundry and was rolling down the passage towards us. The scraping and clanging set every tooth in my head against its neighbour.

Then there came a deep rumbling sound. Moments later a torrent of water hurtled round the turn of the passage twenty foot back, slapping up against the wall in a great foaming wave.

I grabbed Della and pulled her up onto a ledge skirting the passage wall. We watched as the stinking scum-laced water gushed past us, tumbling like a river in spate down into the mouth of the right-hand tunnel. It kept on coming. I guessed that somewhere a sluice had been opened.

I pushed a matt of sodden hair back from my eyes. 'Looks like we'll be going left, then.'

I didn't give her time to answer. I raised the lamp and waded into the entrance of the left-hand tunnel. Moments later I heard Della splash after me.

We walked in silence for a couple of minutes and I was glad to see the way the passage began to slope more keenly. The yellow water running down the centre seemed to take on a tumbling urgency that suggested it might know where it was going.

I turned to Della to remark on it, but she had stopped to look back the way we'd come. Robbie watched me over her shoulder. I heard the skittering noise again and thought of those pallid bony feet scratching their way through the muck.

'There are rats everywhere down here. I'm not going back if that's what you're thinking, Della Lennox. This is the right way. I can feel it.'

I swung the lamp round and splashed on, my skirt weighed like plaster around my legs. The passage veered left. I put one hand on the wall to steady myself as I took the turn and slipped again on something greasy underfoot. I stopped dead.

The lamp showed up a circular space ahead with three passages running off it. But we couldn't get to them. A wide ribbon of shadow cut across the chamber floor. The sound of water falling from a height echoed from the bricks. I kicked forward to the lip of the ribbon and raised the lamp. The drain discharged over the edge of a brick precipice and fell thirty, perhaps forty, foot down to a frothing channel. The lamp showed up the jagged water-slicked edges of old masonry work and glinting black water below.

'Shit!' I closed my eyes and took a deep breath. I swallowed down another lungful before turning back to Della. That was when I noticed the air tasted different here – cleaner, almost fresh. I opened my eyes and looked again. The chamber was washed over in a thin grey light that had nothing to do with the lamp. The light came from above.

I tipped my head back and there it was – another grille twenty foot up, only I could see stars and a tatty rag of cloud caught between the broken bars. The grille sat at the top of a brick-lined cone like a brewery chimney built underground.

It was old, I could see patches where the masonry had crumbled away and where loose bricks jutted out from the wall, but there was a sort of ladder up there too, the rungs curved out from the wall and climbed up to that dish of faint grey light. I took another gulp of good air.

'I reckon we can get out here, Della. We made the right choice back there after all.'

'I would say you have made the wrong choice, Kitty. And not only tonight.'

The soft, sibilant words seemed to slice through the air. It wasn't Della's voice.

I span around and felt the damp, freezing material of my dress press hard against my flesh.

It was like I'd been drawn across a whetstone and opened out. Every sense was keen and raw as a January wind off the Thames. From the oyster cuts on my hands, to the tannery splashes that burned on my cheeks I was suddenly aware of every shrieking part of my body. I heard the smallest drop of water sliding off the walls, I saw the rainbow iridescence in the oily film of the tiniest bubbles of scum that tumbled past me in the drainage channel, and above the stench of sewer filth I smelt lemon cut with incense.

The cloaked figure threw back a hood. White blond hair caught the lamplight and shone like the moon against the slick black bricks of the passage.

'You?' My tongue was like a lead weight in my mouth.

Chapter Thirty

Misha Raskalov's clever, fox muzzle split into a smile so broad that it looked like a wound running across his face. He held the bundle in his arms a little higher so that I could see it clear. Robbie fretted and wriggled. One hand flailed free from the blanket, clenching uselessly at the air. He screwed up his nutshell face and began to cry, although the sound came as feeble ragged gulps.

Behind them in the tunnel a mound of grey lay motionless in the water huddled against the blackened bricks. Della.

Misha stepped into the circle of light cast by the lamp. His cloak was ripped and covered in dust. He nodded at the precipice.

'You cannot go any further, Kitty. It is . . . *Schicksal, suerte, sort, destino.* I can say it in many languages. In my own tongue it is *sud'ba.* I believe you would say fate?' He paused. 'The other word you will learn today is *smert* – death.'

The skin of his hand was blotched and livid. The cloak seemed to be welded to his flesh. He saw my eyes flick to the burns and he shrugged. 'It is nothing – it will heal.' He licked his wide pink lips. I tried to force the thought of him and Lucca together from my mind.

Lucca? My heart shrivelled beneath my bodice as Misha's eyes narrowed.

'In the Okhrana we are trained not to feel pain.'

He took a step towards me and held Robbie in front of him at arm's length. I knew without a doubt that he intended to drop him over the precipice and into the drain forty foot below. Robbie wailed louder and twisted his head about, trying to catch sight of his mother.

As Misha came closer his broad shoulders and trailing cloak blocked my view of the passage where Della lay. He was over six foot tall. I brandished the lamp between us. It was all I had.

He started to laugh. 'You are well named, Kitty Peck. Lucca told me you spit like a little cat.'

I felt something spit all right, something like a limelight flare spurted deep inside. I clenched my free hand into a ball so tight the nails dug crescents into the palm. I had to keep control of my fury. I had to use it.

I needed time to think.

'Where's Joey? What have you done with him?' My voice could have scraped the slime off the walls.

Misha shrugged again.

Blood pounded in my temples. If he hadn't been holding on to Robbie I would have swung the lamp at him. 'If you're going to kill me I might as well know what you've done with my brother. You won't have anything to lose. Where is he – and Lucca?'

Misha snorted. 'I have no idea where Josette is, Kitty. My only interest in your brother is that he told his beloved Ilya about this child and its mother. That's why Ilya Vershinin has to die, as will your brother in good time. I'll deal with them both when I return to Paris.'

'Paris? You mean, he, Ilya, went back?'

'Of course not.' Misha's over-ripe mouth twisted into a sneer. 'I mean he was never here. As to your friend Lucca – he is waiting for me in his daubing room by the river. I've no doubt he is wondering where I am, aching for me to return. He was so eager to believe, so useful. He made everything so very much easier. London is a great capital but it is still a small world – your friend Mr Collins? What a fortunate coincidence that was.'

I nodded slowly, it was falling into place. Sam had got the measure of Misha Raskalov, hadn't he? He didn't think him a murderer, but he didn't trust him. And Joey hadn't given Della and Robbie away neither – he'd been beating himself up for nothing. But Lucca, my poor Lucca. He was so sure that Misha cared for him.

A blind fool! Della's words trickled through my mind again.

I swallowed. 'I still don't understand. Why didn't you go to Lucca as soon as you came to London?'

Misha raised a brow so pale that it was almost invisible against his milky skin.

'Because it would have been too obvious. *Chem dal'she, tem dorozhe.* I think you have a similar saying – absence makes the heart grow fonder? I wanted to be sure that Mr Fratelli would be . . . receptive when we finally met again. I was waiting to meet him seemingly by accident, but your journalist friend did the work for me.'

'What . . . what will you do to Lucca?'

'Kill him. What else?' There wasn't a trace of emotion in Misha's perfect English. His heart was as cold as his eyes.

'From the moment Lucca found me everything slotted

341

into place. It all became so easy. I knew your brother and Della had concocted something. When I saw her leave Josette's house on the night of the gathering in Paris I knew they were making plans and I suspected they involved you.

'I . . . entertained your friend that evening to gain his trust. But it was you I was watching, Kitty. I moved too fast at the station, that was a mistake, but when I saw them with the trunk I knew I was right.'

And I knew right then it was Misha Raskalov I'd seen watching the train from the end of the platform as we left Paris.

'You followed us to Limehouse?'

'As soon as I could without arousing suspicion. There had to be a reason for my visit – but the trail was cold when I arrived. I knew you had him here somewhere, but I had to be sure.' His nostrils flared. 'There are so many . . . *chernomazy* in London.'

I wasn't sure what he meant by that, but I had an idea.

'You came here to kill him – you were searching for little ones like Robbie?'

'Of course – and I found some, but I had to be certain. I confess I was confused when your friend – Peggy, is it? – told me in the churchyard the black child was hers. But once Lucca came to me, I knew exactly where to find Robbie Lennox and what to do. It was simply a matter of watching. The woman would come for him sooner or later.'

He grinned. 'And she came tonight to the theatre where you were waiting with the child. It is a matter of some importance that this . . . *obez'yana*,' he spat out the word and shook the bundle in his hands, 'and its mother do not trouble my masters further. Now stand aside.'

I shook my head. One thing was clear, Misha Raskalov liked to talk about himself. *Humility is a virtue in London, but not, it seems, in Moscow.* Wasn't that what Sam had said? I could use his vanity to buy myself time.

Think, girl, think.

'That was you on the stage – you started the fire?'

He shrugged. 'I know how to control the gaslights in a theatre. Your system, however, is primitive. I did not expect—'

'To die with us? Is that it? You thought you'd bring the building down on our heads and get away.'

'Something of that nature. I was overcome briefly by the smoke and by this . . .' Misha swung Robbie around abruptly and I thought he was going to drop him, but instead he brought his burned arm level with my eyes. 'I saw you go to the office and I knew you must be trying to escape. So I followed.

'In your . . . *theatres*,' he made the word sound like a sneer, 'you have magicians who make people disappear, do you not?' I didn't answer as he carried on. 'Phwoof! And the girl is gone in a shower of sparks. I wondered where you had gone, Kitty, until I found the door in the boards.'

He took another step forward, forcing me back with his bent arm. I knew the drop was less than two foot behind me now. I could hear the water rushing far below.

'You have to disappear tonight, Kitty Peck, along with the child and his mother. I must thank you for everything you have done. Those letters! My masters will be fascinated by their existence. They will find a way to obtain them . . . after your death.'

'Bastard!' I hissed the word through gritted teeth.

Misha shook his head. 'I think we both know that this is the bastard.' He raised the cloth bundle to eye level. I saw Robbie's feet kick under the blanket. Now, at last, he began to cry out loud. The desperate mewling echoed from the walls of the chamber. It was a sound to wake the dead.

I stood my ground, willing myself not to turn away as Misha lowered his moon-pale head. He brought his fleshy lips to my ear. 'You first, I think, and then the bastard.' He jostled my shoulder, forcing me to take a single step back.

I stared up at his pointed face. The guttering light from the oil lamp smudged deep shadows beneath his brows and under his jutting cheekbones. For a moment I was minded of Mr Punch hanging out over the edge of his little striped tent. He was a murderer too, wasn't he?

Beyond Misha's shoulder something grey moved in the dim light of the lamp. My heart started up so violent I thought he could catch the drumming of it. I kept my eyes latched on his. Keep him talking, girl, I thought, keep his attention fixed on you.

He shifted Robbie higher.

'It squeals like a piglet. My masters will be pleased to know this episode is concluded.'

I needed to make him concentrate on me now, me and nothing else. I lifted the lamp trying not to notice the way it shook in my hands.

'Episode! Is that all it is to you? You've been paid to murder children and that's a natural day's work, is it? I don't know how you can live with yourself. You disgust me, Misha Raskalov. Look at him. He's just a baby, a sick little boy who's not likely to live much beyond a decade. And it's not just him – those little ones here in Limehouse. And Della and what you did to Old Peter just because I showed him the Monseigneur's note . . .'

I faltered, confused by the sudden light of genuine interest that sparked in those cool slanting eyes.

'Useful to the end, Kitty. I thank you again. I suspected the Monseigneur knew about my . . . responsibilities for some time and you have just confirmed it, but this other – Peter, you say? If he too knows something of this matter . . . Tell me, where can I find him?'

The smell of lemon and incense made my stomach clench up tight as a limpet. To my mind it was a hundred times worse than the stench of the shit, piss and God knows what else we was standing in. But as I breathed in the stink of Misha Raskalov's putrid soul, something came to me, something important.

I tried to net it before it slipped away, but he swung Robbie above his head, shaking him so hard the blanket slipped down to the gulley, racing past me in the foaming water and over the lip of the precipice.

'I am willing to dash the piglet's brains out on the wall here and smear your face with its blood. Must I repeat myself? Where can I find this Peter?'

'Mile End – in the Bancroft Road Jewish cemetery where you put him!'

The moment I said it, I knew it was wrong. It wasn't Misha who killed Old Peter, but I didn't have time to unravel it in my head because at the same moment I caught the flash of something silver in the air beside Misha's ear.

Della plunged the steel hatpin swiftly and viciously into the side of his neck.

His eyes widened in surprise. He hunched forward, but she pulled the long pin free and drove it again into the soft white skin just beneath his lobe, pushing it deep and grinding it about with her fist. Blood spurted up from the first incision spattering her hand and her sleeve. The little fountain stained Misha's trailing hair a pink that quickly turned to crimson. He tried to say something, but a gurgling sound came from his throat like something was catching his words in a strainer.

Dark glistening liquid bubbled over his lips. He turned to look at her – disbelief spreading across his pointed features as she wound a black hand into the overlong hair that fell over his shoulders. She pulled tight, yanking his head back to expose more of his throat. His back arched and he pulled Robbie down to his breast like a shield.

Misha's lips moved but his drowning voice couldn't sound the words.

Della tightened her grip on the back of his head. Her green eyes burned with hate as she raised the pin again. I said she put me in mind of a wild creature, but the strength in her now was something more than savage.

That was when I moved. I dropped the lamp into the water at our feet, hearing the glass shatter against the stones beneath the slime. As the light died on the instant, I wrenched Robbie from Misha's arms and darted past them both.

I held Robbie close and nestled his head into my damp bodice. Five foot away, two figures were silhouetted in the dim light spilling down from the grille. Misha's empty arms flailed at his sides now, clenching and unclenching like he was trying to catch hold of his life.

I cupped the crown of Robbie's head, folding my hand over his soft curled ear. For all that he was not yet eight months, he shouldn't see any of this nor hear it, neither. No matter how long he had left, Robbie Lennox should never know what his mother had done for him.

I watched as Della swung back her arm and hacked again, forcing the pin into the cleft beneath Misha's Adam's apple. He tried to scrabble the weapon from her hand, a feeble gesture that turned to a desperate effort to fend her off as the steel plunged – in out, in out. The terrible rhythm of it was almost mechanical.

Misha sank to his knees, his bloody hands pulling at the folds of Della's sodden coat. A sound somewhere between a choke and a wail came rattling from him as a gush of thick black stuff vomited from his mouth into the water. He crouched forward, gaping and rasping for air that would never reach his lungs.

Della took a step back like she didn't want him staining her gear. And then she kicked him over the edge.

Chapter Thirty-one

I tugged at the knot round my neck and loosened the shawl, careful that Robbie didn't tumble out. I pulled the loop of plaid over my head and laid him gently on the stones next to the grille, tucking the old fabric under his chin against the cold.

There was a fingernail of moon overhead now and the clouds were scurrying eastward. It wasn't raining, but the chill sliced through my stinking dripping clothes like a Smithfield skinner's knife. I tried to tie my wet hair into a knot to keep the wind from slapping strands of it across my face.

The broken grille led out to a yard bounded on three sides by a jumble of buildings. It smelt of straw and the sweetness of horse. I could hear them stabled over to the right. When I scrambled out from the drain with Robbie slung across my back in Nanny Peck's shawl, a couple of them whickered and kicked out at their stalls, thinking I was the stable lad come with a bucket of oats.

From my reckoning it looked like a brewery yard and it was near the river. I could smell the foulness of the earthy, briny water. The unmistakable stink of the Thames had never been cleaner to me.

I could hear it too – the shrieking whistle of wind through ropes meant tall-masted ships were riding nearby. My teeth chattered as I crouched over the broken bars. Looking back, I don't reckon it was entirely on account of the cold.

'Your turn now, Della. It's easier than it looks. See the bricks to the right – the broken ones? You can use them to pull yourself up to the lowest rung. It's easy from there, except the fourth one up. That's come loose. Don't try it.'

Of an instant Madame Celeste came to mind. I wanted to add something about not looking down and not thinking about the fact that there was a gulley with Misha Raskalov's body wedged across it fifty, maybe sixty foot below, but if I put it in Della's mind now it was a thought that would be difficult to shift.

I needn't have worried.

The sound of boots on brick echoed up the shaft of the drain. There was a rattle of stones too as patches of the wall came loose. I leaned over again. I could see movement down there, but nothing clear.

I thought I should encourage her.

'The rungs are firm. They'll take your weight, all of them except the fourth. I'll reach down to pull you through when you get to the top.'

Della's voice echoed up the shaft. 'Robbie. Is he . . .?'

'He's fine, he's all wrapped up and waiting for you to come and take him.' I glanced over. He was staring up at the moon and sucking on the edge of Nanny Peck's plaid.

A bell started up from somewhere. I rocked back on my heels and counted. One. Two. Three. Four . . . There was a scuffling sound from the grille. Dark fingers appeared around one of the broken bars. I leaned over again and hauled Della up off the last two rungs and through to the flat stones of the yard. She knelt for a moment, her breathing fast and shallow.

Then she stood. Without a nod to me she scooped Robbie up and flattened him to her breast.

'I heard the bell. We have to go – there's still time.'

I nodded. 'It's five o'clock. You should be boarding now. But if Misha's dead then you don't need—'

Della began to laugh. 'We'll always need to run. I don't know how long my bairn has, but as long as he draws breath he's a danger to them. He's living proof of their flaw. We have to go to the boat.'

She held Robbie close and ran a hand over the back of her close-cropped head where Misha had landed the blow that felled her. She looked down into her palm.

'Is it bleeding, Della?'

She shook her head. 'It hurts like hell, but it will pass. Where are we?'

'Near the river, I reckon. It's in the air.' I scrambled to my feet and pointed to the open arch at the end of the yard. 'If we go through I'll be able to get my bearings.'

Della turned and walked swiftly towards the arch. I followed. The sky was lightening from the east now. Out on the road I knew immediately where we were. It was Emmett Street, down by West India. The main Dock Office was over to the left and Steam Boat Dock was less than ten minutes' walk away. Over the rooftops I could see a cat's cradle of ropes strung across a forest of masts. Lights were burning in some of the windows as workers roused themselves for the six o clock queues. You weren't always guaranteed a job at the docks. There were plenty of men, and women too, who had to get up early and beg for it.

I caught Della's arm. 'This way. It's not far.'

Della shook her head.

'He's not on board, Kitty. I'm sorry.'

I stood at the bottom of the swaying gangway leading up to the deck of the *Albertine*. It was a neat little working boat, smaller than the *Leopold* that had carried me and Lucca over to France, and a good deal less fancy. Timber was strapped in piles along the centre of the deck. The smell of it put me in mind of the workshop at The Gaudy.

Something trickled down my cheek and I swiped it away with the back of my hand. Tell truth, I didn't rightly know if I was crying for my brother, for Lucca or for my theatre. Maybe it was all three?

Della tucked Robbie against her hip and reached across to cup my face in her free hand. It was the nearest she'd come to a sign of gratitude.

'Josette . . . *Joey*,' she tried to smile, 'is always clever, always resourceful. He'll turn up soon. I know it.'

'Do you?' In the light things were falling into place, little bits of puzzle that didn't have a home up to now were locking into their corners. Misha's cologne had dripped something into my mind. I didn't think I could ever catch the scent of lemon now without feeling soiled.

I wiped my face again, rubbing my fingers roughly across my stinging cheeks.

'The captain all right with you . . . like that?' I nodded at Della's stained, sodden dress. You couldn't tell it was blood in this light. Not yet.

She snorted. 'The amount I've offered, he'd take me on

board if I had the typhus. Anyway, I've asked for a change of clothes. When we get to Hamburg we'll be travelling as father and son.'

I stared at her. 'And I'm sure you'll be very convincing, David.'

She shook her head and smiled tight. 'And I . . . I'm sorry about that too.'

She offered me her hand.

'Tell me you wouldn't do the same?'

I looked down at her long fingers.

'I wouldn't lie.'

'Kitty, it . . . it didn't seem wrong, but now . . .'

'Now it's too late, Della.'

A bell went off up top and the *Albertine*'s horn blew twice. Della glanced back over her shoulder at the deck above where crewmen were loosening ropes. A man on the quay beside us pointed up to the top of the gangway and made a swimming motion with his hand.

'*Sie müssen an bord zu gehen. Wir segeln.*' He pushed past and tramped up the boards making them bounce and swing perilously over the river. The tide was high now, I could hear waves slamming and sucking against the creaking wooden hull. We both ducked as something belched deep in the *Albertine*'s belly and a cloud of black steam hiccupped from the squat funnel in the middle of the deck.

Della clutched the guide rope to steady herself and then she gently brushed smuts of smoke and God knows what else from Robbie's face. He was pulling at her coat and pursing his lips together, making little smacking, sucking noises. He knew he was with his real mother again.

'We have to go. If Josette . . . Joey is already waiting in Hamburg, I'll make sure he contacts you, Kitty. I promise.'

She turned to make her way up to the deck, but stopped. She held Robbie away from her and started to unwrap Nanny Peck's shawl from his body.

'I can't take this, it's yours. I think it means something to you?'

I nodded. 'It belonged to my . . . my grandmother.' Lady Ginger's black bead eyes bored into my mind, despite the fact she wasn't the grandmother I was thinking of just then.

He is your blood, he is your family. Think on those words. That's what the old bitch said about Joey, didn't she? Only it wasn't just about him. Blood and family – she was talking about Robbie as well.

She said something else too: *Protect him.* That was for Joey. But what did she mean? *Protect him* from what?

I swear Della must have read my mind.

'Family is important. Take it.' She handed me the shawl and turned away again. I pulled it round my shoulders and watched her tall, straight figure move away from me up the swaying boards. I thrust my hands into my pockets against the chill and my fingers closed over the paper hidden in the poppet along with the emeralds.

'Wait!' I called out and Della turned.

I ran a little way up the springing planks. She came back to meet me halfway.

I bit my lip. 'I . . . I think this is something else you need, something important.' I held the scrap of paper forward and Della frowned. Then, shifting Robbie to her hip, she reached into the folds of her coat and pulled out the cloth rabbit. She'd had it with her all along.

I watched as she brought the poppet to her mouth and ripped at the right ear with her teeth. My crude stitches tore instantly apart to reveal the strips of rag and knots of wool stuffed inside, nothing else.

She threw the toy down. It rolled over the planks into the river.

'No! He loves it.' I gripped the rope and knelt to see where it had gone, but the dark waters had already carried it away.

I straightened up. 'Why did you do that?'

'Because the poppet was nothing. This is the prize.' She snatched the paper from my hand and it flapped about in the wind.

'It's worth more than emeralds, Kitty. Without this we . . .'

She shook her head. 'You took it. Why?'

I couldn't look at her direct. 'It . . . it was the day Joey showed me where the stones were. The ear came free and I found the paper rolled inside. He knew what it was, but he wouldn't say anything other than that it should never be parted from Robbie. When you came tonight I was angry. I just wanted to . . . to . . .'

To punish her for not being David.

I trailed off and stared into the water. Of an instant I felt like a child, a stupid, stupid child. Della was a grown woman with a little one to look out for and I'd been playing a game.

I took a deep breath. 'I'm sorry. I would have given it to you, truly I would, but with everything else—'

Up on deck someone called out to us again.

'What is it, Della – why would a strip of paper be worth more than emeralds?'

She stared at me for a long moment and then she smiled.

'Do you remember I said there was someone I needed to find in Paris before I came to London?'

I nodded.

'It was a priest – a Russian Orthodox priest. He was in hiding. It took so long to find a way to reach him. Hold this.'

Della handed the paper back to me, reached into her coat and took out the tapestry purse where she'd stowed the emeralds. It hung on a cord from her waist. She pulled the strings to open it and fished another small roll of paper from inside. She hoisted Robbie into a more secure position and deftly rolled open the scrap of paper from the purse. It was covered in Russian script, just like the one I'd found in the poppet.

I shook my head. 'I don't see—'

'Wait.'

She reached forward and held it against the torn paper in my hands. They fitted together exactly– two halves of one page.

'Our marriage certificate, Kitty. I was married to Grand Duke Sergei Alexandrovich Romanov in Paris on the first day of June 1880. The ceremony was conducted by Father Pavel Suvorin, a priest of the Russian Orthodox Church. There were witnesses – it is a legal and binding match and this document is proof. Father Pavel kept half of it for safety. They knew that – it's why he went into hiding. I finally found out where he was last week and I went to take the burden from him.'

Robbie watched with fascination as Della eased the paper from my fingers, folded it with the other half and pushed them both back into the purse. She looked at me. In her dark skin, those beautiful glass-green eyes shone in the first rays of the morning sun.

'Misha was wrong. Robbie is a not a bastard. He never was. I am a Russian princess – by marriage – and our son is a prince of the blood.'

I didn't need to knock again. Lucca's door swung open into the darkness of the hallway. Disappointment washed his face before he could mask it, but he stepped aside to let me in. I gave a curt nod and went over to the fireplace. Despite the hour a little pile of coals glowed in the over-sized hearth. I glanced at the table. A fancy four-armed brass candle piece holding a couple of low-burning wax stubs sat in the middle. Next to it a bottle and two glasses stood ready.

He'd been waiting up for Misha all through the night.

I knelt and stretched my hands out to the coals. I couldn't feel the heat. Tell truth, I couldn't feel a thing, not the bruises, not the burns, not the scratches, not the cuts. I was numb to the core. Back there on the quay I was so certain that this was the right place to come, but now . . .

Lucca closed the door and I heard him sigh heavily.

'I don't know whether to say it's too early or too late for a visit.' He crossed the room and his knees cracked as he knelt down beside me. Instantly he covered his nose and mouth.

'*Dio! L'odore!* Where have you been?'

He stared over the hand clamped across the lower half of his face. I must have looked like a bedlam crouching there in my sodden, ripped dress, my filthy hair matted to my head and my face covered in scratches and spatters of sewer. Lucca muttered in Italian and reached out to push sticky strands away from my forehead. I winced as they pulled at something dried on my skin, opening a wound that began to sting. My teeth chattered now.

'You are frozen.' Lucca scattered another handful of coals into the hearth. 'You must change, immediately.' He stood up. 'I have some things, I'll get—'

'No!' I caught his arm. I couldn't have him bustling around, fussing over me like a mother hen, not now. It didn't seem right.

'Take this at least.' He went to the bed and pulled a blanket free. Returning to the fire he bent to drape it round my shoulders.

'And your face!' Lucca's eye widened in alarm as I stared up at him.

'You are injured, your clothes are scorched and yet they are wet through and you reek of smoke and sewer. What has happened?'

I opened my mouth, but nothing came out. Lucca's scars were hidden by the shadows cast from the fire and by the thick dark curls that fell to cover the burned side of his face.

How could anyone love a ruin? His question ran through my mind again, but the young man I saw was beautiful. How was I going to tell him about Misha?

My eyes flicked to the glasses and the bottle. Lucca saw it.

'He . . . he didn't come, Fannella. I waited and he didn't come.'

I swallowed hard as he continued. 'I think he knew I wouldn't go with him. But I thought at least that he would . . .'

'You weren't going to leave?' I found a voice at last, but it was thin as the pap in Robbie's bottle.

Lucca shook his head. 'I was . . . tempted, but no. There is more for me here. Everything I know, everyone I . . . love.' He tried to smile. 'Besides, Russia is cold and I was not born for snow.'

He leaned down to kiss my forehead, but then he straightened up, brought his hand to his lips and wiped the foul taste of me away. He frowned. 'And you need me by your side. What has happened tonight, Fannella?'

I didn't know where to begin. I tried to find the right place – maybe with Joey and Della or perhaps the fire at The Gaudy? But as I looked up at Lucca I knew it kept coming back to Misha Raskalov. That was what I had to tell him and I dreaded it.

We were a pair of blind fools, me and Lucca, weren't we?

I reached under the blanket and shawl and felt beneath the scratchy damp collar of my dress for the chain. I needed to hold Joey's Christopher and his ring tight between my fingers. I pushed deeper under the fabric, trying to catch the links of the chain. I loosened the knot of the shawl and then I pulled at the buttons forcing my hand down into the ruffled neck of my dress. I caught at something and pulled it free. The chain had broken somewhere along the way tonight.

It was an omen. Frosted lips kissed the back of my neck.

I felt my nails scrabble across the skin of my throat and then lower across my breasts nestled up in the bodice as I delved frantically under the fabric. Perhaps the ring and the Christopher were lodged somewhere?

When, truly, I knew they were gone I began to cry.

Lucca stroked my head and rocked me from side to side as heaving sobs tore me apart. I could hardly breathe for the tightness in my chest, but all the while my lungs kept pumping away like a pair of knackered foundry bellows. Eventually I was able to snatch down enough air to make a voice.

'He . . . he's gone.'

'Who? Who's gone?' Lucca sat back and took my hands in his. His eye was huge in the firelight. 'You must tell me, tell me everything.'

Something hardened in my throat, blocking the words. 'B . . . but you won't want to hear it. I can't—'

'You can, Fannella and you must.' Lucca stood and went to the table. Collecting the bottle and glasses, he came back to the fire. 'Here.' He unstoppered the bottle and poured clear liquid into one of the glasses.

'This will help. Take it.'

As I reached out my hands were shaking so violent that the liquor splashed over the rim and onto the boards. Lucca placed his own hands over mine to steady me and helped bring it to my lips. My throat and stomach burned as I sipped down a mouthful, but the feeling kicked something to life inside. I swallowed again and then again and again, greedily revelling in the churning, burning sensation.

In less than a minute I'd drained the glass. Lucca took it from my hands and filled it to the brim again.

'Take this one more slowly, Kitty. Now, tell me.'

At first I could hardly make the words form on my lips, but the liquor helped. Once I started they came tumbling over themselves like the filthy water running through that drain. Lucca listened in silence. He didn't look at me as I spoke. Instead he stared down at the boards in front of the great marble fireplace in his room, circling the tip of a finger around a knot in the boards. When I'd told him everything he stopped. His hand hovered just above the wood like he'd been turned to stone.

His hair had fallen forward to cover his face. I could see the place on his head where the burns crept up across his scalp. Pink furrows of skin were visible through the dark curls. He was usually careful to cover them.

I looked away. Pinned to the wall just behind him was a sheet of paper. The sweeping charcoal lines dashed confidently across the page to form a man's face. It was Misha, his slanting eyes and curved lips taunted us both.

I folded my hand over Lucca's. 'I . . . I don't know what to say.'

He didn't answer for a long time. When he finally looked up both sides of his face were wet.

'There's nothing you can say, Fannella.'

I gripped tight. 'He's not worth your tears, Lucca.'

'I am not crying for him, Fannella. Amit, The Gaudy, the fire, Della, the child . . .' He faltered. 'These are tears of shame. I should have been there with you, but instead I was so caught up with . . .' He shook his head and something hot splashed onto the back of my hand. 'I'll never forgive myself. I should have listened to you – all along you felt—'

'You didn't know! He lied – he tricked us both. Misha was clever, I'll give him that.'

'And I was a fool.' Lucca reached for the bottle between

us. 'A stupid, selfish, lovesick fool.'

His hand faltered. Instead of taking the bottle he span round and stared at the drawing behind him. I saw him hesitate for a moment and then he lashed out, ripping the paper from the wall. He flattened it out on the boards between us, dug into the pocket of his breeches and produced a fat black stub of charcoal.

I watched in silence as Lucca slashed thick black lines across Misha Raskalov's grinning face, swiping down hard again and again until the features were cancelled by a jagged cross. He raised his hand above the paper, clutching the charcoal like a blade, and then he slammed it down again, circling wildly until there was nothing but a storm of scrawl.

When the stub tore through the paper and squealed on the boards below, I reached across and prised it gently from his fingers.

Chapter Thirty-two

The pounding came again. The violent blows hammered on the door with such a force behind them that the panes in the second-floor parlour window rattled. I turned the oil lamp down, went to the shutter and pulled it open to a crack.

Through the gap I watched Fitzy stagger down the steps and out onto the street. He stared up at the double doors to The Palace like he couldn't believe they were closed to him. He squinted and rolled his massive head on shoulders padded like a couch. It was evening and cold for the dying day of April. I could see steam fug the air around him as he breathed out his fury like a tethered bull.

He took a step back and scanned the windows. He was looking for me.

Shaking his head, he slammed a fist the size of a roofer's mallet into the palm of his hand. He was itching to strike out at something. His days as a bare knuckler on the streets were never far below the surface. The fancy suits in unlikely colours and the over-patterned waistcoats gave him the air of a genial, but I knew he was a brute. It was why Lady Ginger employed him and why I kept him on. I needed him.

'I see you watching me, girl. Don't think I don't know you're there.'

I flinched and narrowed the opening between the shutters as the bellow echoed off the stones. 'It's a fucking wreck – do you hear me? The Gaudy is a smoking pit in the ground, so it is.' He'd been drinking. His accent was thicker than treacle and his words were bound together in it.

'You're a cowardly bitch, so you are. Hiding behind your shutters with your cat-faced yellow men when people need to see you. All day they've been waiting for you – wanting to know what's going to happen. If you haven't got the balls on you to speak to me now, how are you going to face them? All the people who rely on you. Tell me that, eh?'

He put a foot on the lowest step and steadied himself on the rail. He swayed a little as he craned his head back.

'She's gone. My lovely girl is gone.' I heard something catch in his voice, something like a sob. Christ! He was talking about The Gaudy like he was married to it. He looked up again.

'What are you going to do now? How you going to pay them all a fair wage like you promised when the only hall you still got open is no more than a pimple on the City's arse? Call yourself a Baron, do you? You're no more a Baron than I'm a fucking prince of the realm.'

He swung back from the rail onto the cobbles and pulled at the shoulders of his jacket, like he was attempting to prove his sobriety. He twitched his head to one side and scanned the building once more, his little eyes sweeping the bricks from the top to the bottom. He wiped a hand across his mouth and called up again.

'But I'll tell you what I call you, Kitty Peck, and I'll tell you it for nothing. You're a Jonah, so you are. You've brought nothing but misfortune to us all.'

He spat on the step, turned and lumbered away towards

the end of the passage. I watched his bulky shadow trail along behind, moving against the greasy stones of the wall opposite.

I pressed my forehead against the shutter, feeling the ridge of the wooden panel dig into the cuts in my skin. Of an instant I was minded of that time when it was me standing out there bawling up at the closed doors. I knew she was there, my grandmother, watching me, listening to me spill my heart out on her steps. Like I'd just done with Fitzy.

But I couldn't face him now. I couldn't face any of them. I glanced at the note on the table beside the couch where Lucca sat staring blankly into the fire. A pain shot across my temples.

Not now, not today of all days.

The heavy fabric of my finest dress was tight around me. The high collar and long sleeves trapped me like a moth bound up in a silky purse on a web. The ruffles of the collar scratched into my neck. Beneath the stiff satin I felt the absence of Joey's ring and his Christopher like a dull ache in my chest.

Lok had filled the tin bath in my room with steaming water and I'd tried to scrub the night from my skin. It didn't work. No matter how hard I scraped and how much geranium I poured into the water I couldn't shift the stink of the sewer in my nostrils. I didn't think I'd be able to smell anything other than shit ever again. That and Misha's filthy lemon and church cologne.

After a while I threw the cloth aside and lay there, staring up at the ceiling. By rights it should have made me drowsy, but every part of me was crying out loud and not just at the thought of the evening ahead.

Della was wrong. Joey wasn't going to turn up in Hamburg. He was here in London somewhere – and he was in danger. Overhead a spider with a fat body and long match-like legs probed across the plaster. I knew there was another just like it, snug in a shroud of web in the corner above the linen press. I'd meant to take a dust stick to it.

I watched as the spider above reached the centre of the ceiling where a crack ran across the plaster. It stopped there, waving its front legs around like it was taking stock of its position, and then it turned and scuttled back to its own corner. There were two of them waiting to set their traps up there, both of them killers and both of them barely aware of the other's existence.

Two of them.

As I stood at the window I pulled the blue sleeves lower so the lace cuffs covered the burns and scratches on my hands. I wasn't going to let them think I was damaged goods.

I wrapped Nanny Peck's shawl around my shoulders, folded my arms beneath it and pulled the shutter open a little wider. I stared down at the rain-slicked cobbles again, but it wasn't Fitzy I was looking for.

A few minutes before the hammering started up there was a rattling sound on the panes of the parlour window. I'd thought it was raining again and I'd gone over to look out.

Down below someone was bent double in the passage outside. I watched as a hand stretched out, sweeping the cobbles to gather up another handful of stones to patter against the windows.

My heart leapt under the plaid. It was Joey. I was sure of it. He was trying to catch my attention. I threw back the shutters and stood in the lighted window as the man straightened up. When he saw me he paused and moved his cloak aside to hold out a hand. He opened his fist and let the pebbles fall to the ground. The movement revealed the cane held in his other hand – at the tip the vicious hawk head glinted in the soft light from the window. The hooded man bowed once, turned and walked slowly away.

My spine felt brittle as ice as I watched him melt like a huge black cat into the mouth of an alleyway off Salmon Lane.

It wasn't Misha – he was rat meat at the bottom of a sewer – so who was it? Who was the man who killed Old Peter? Who was the man who smelt of leather and spice when he tore the earring through my flesh in The Gaudy, the man who mistook me for Joey?

Where is he, Josette?

I brought my hand to my ear and touched the rip in the lobe. He hadn't mistaken me for Joey, and he wasn't asking about Robbie Lennox. He was asking me where my brother was. I should have known that all along.

'There were always two of them.' I turned to Lucca who was staring into the fire like he was watching a story there. I reckoned I knew what he was seeing – running it through again and again, punishing himself.

'Did you hear what I said?' I moved away from the window and went over to the couch. Since we'd come back to The Palace earlier that day he'd closed in on himself, folding up tight like a jack-in-a-box forced back into its painted home. But I knew he was going to burst out soon and when he did he'd bring all his fury and his sadness with him. That was why I asked him to come to stay at The Palace with me.

God knows I didn't need protection – not with all the locks and shutters and bolts Lady Ginger had installed about the place. No, Lucca needed protecting from himself.

The clock on the mantle chimed twice for the half. It was a delicate little thing, gold set with china panels painted with shepherds and shepherdesses frolicking among flowers. I couldn't imagine my grandmother choosing such a thing, but it was there in the parlour when I'd thrown back the shutters that first day, sitting on a mantle in a finger of dust, tented over with a loom of cobwebs.

Less than two hours to go. The pain shot through my head again, so sharp this time it made the skin around my left eye twitch. I sat down heavily next to Lucca and placed my hand over his.

'If you want to take any comfort from this, Lucca, you need to know that it wasn't Misha who killed Old Peter.'

When he didn't react I repeated myself. He dragged his eyes from the flames and turned to me. 'Who was it then?'

I bit my lip and felt a cut there from the exploding glass of the mirror open again. I could taste blood on the tip of my tongue.

'I . . . I don't know.'

'Then why is that a comfort?'

I couldn't answer. I rifled through the papers on the table.

'Will you stay here tonight? When I get back it would be good to know you're here.'

Lucca nodded. '*Sì* – of course, but I don't understand why I can't come with you. After what happened . . .'

'You can't – that's all I know.' I squeezed his hand and wished he could come with me, wherever it was I was going.

'I have to go alone. No one can come with me, not even the Beetle. It's the law.'

Lucca raised a brow. 'A strange word to use, under the circumstances, Fannella.'

I took up Telferman's note again. It had been waiting for me on the hall table when I returned with Lucca earlier that day. If Tan Seng noticed the state I was in when he opened up to us both he didn't show it. Instead, he bowed and gestured towards the package of papers.

'For The Lady, it came an hour ago.'

Telferman was brief and to the point.

Miss Peck,

The Barons meet this evening. The Vernal session will begin at one o'clock.

You will be summoned before midnight. I regret that we have not been able to prepare as thoroughly as I would have wished. I was not made aware until the latest moment that the session would take place so very early in the month.

I trust, however, that the information enclosed with this letter will enable you to offer your parable. I believe the financial résumé on the third page will be deemed sufficient for your first session.

You have a keen mind, Katharine, use it. Offer nothing, but pay close attention. Speak little, but listen well. Watch, but do not act.

Choose carefully.

His name crept across the bottom of the page. There were tiny spots of ink where the nib had leaked over the paper. I noted that my hand trembled as I held the paper closer to the lamp.

None of that, girl, I told myself. You master it now, or they'll master you.

I took up the pages enclosed with the letter and scanned them again.

Telferman was thorough, but there was nothing set down there I didn't already know. The dens off Glass House Street were turning a decent profit. The customs officers at West India, St Katharine's and London Shadwell were satisfied with their cut. The tail parlours off Narrow Street were clean – I'd had the girls checked by a crow and they were turning a tidy sum along with tricks. Three of the screwsman parties had done good trade with the brokers on the Commercial – and no one had made a provable link between their jemmy raids up west and the pawny shops in the east. One of my toolers had been taken by the law, but Telferman was paying to see it right.

I nodded to myself. I had it all clear. I'd gone through it all a hundred times over the last few weeks. If a vicar's wife farted in Paradise I'd know it. I turned the page. The accounts of The Gaudy, The Comet and The Carnival were listed in columns. Only one of them was making a fine profit

– and now it was a smouldering wreck. I flipped over the page and stared down at a list of every soul in my employ.

I ran down the page looking for a name. I found it, but it was crossed through – Peter Ash. I brushed the tip of my finger over the words. There was a pantomime where a China boy had a magic lamp. Every time he rubbed that lamp a genie came to life. I touched the letters, but the ink came off on my skin, blurring the writing.

I moved on, pausing at 'D'. Amit and his brother Ram were both there. I blinked and took up the next page. Near the end under 'S' little Edie Strong was listed with her mother. Jesus, I didn't even know if she was still alive.

Fitzy was right, I was a Jonah.

They were all here in my hands, not just the crews on the streets and the warehouses, but everyone who worked for me in the halls, scores of them. All the people I'd made a promise to. A fair wage – that's what I'd told them. Where were they going to work for that wage now?

I heard a cough and looked up. Tan Seng was standing in the doorway. He bowed.

'It is time, Lady.'

Chapter Thirty-three

The square black carriage stood at the end of Salmon Lane, its lamps unlit. Two dark horses nodded in the traces and up top I could see the stooped shape of the driver. He didn't even turn to nod at the sound of my heels tapping on the stones as we came alongside.

Tonight, for some reason, the lamp boy hadn't lit the gas in this part of the lane. The globes were blind, like the windows of the waiting carriage. Now I was up close, I could see the curtains were pulled across inside. The only light on the cobbles was cast from the lamp carried by Tan Seng. The golden glow bounced off the lacquered sides of the carriage and showed that the wheels were felted over. Even the horses' hooves were muffled with rolls of black cloth that reached up over their fetlocks like the woollen socks Nanny Peck used to knit in the winter.

Lucca's hand tightened on my arm.

'You cannot go alone, Fannella.'

Now the driver moved. He shifted about and the carriage creaked and bounced on its springs as he leaned over. He pointed down at me with his whip.

'No one else.' The rough voice was muffled by the scarf covering the lower part of his face.

Tan Seng raised the lamp. In the dim light he looked even older than usual.

'It is always this way, Lady. We will be ready to welcome you, when you return.' He bowed and gestured to the door. Lucca didn't release me.

'You can't—'

'I have to. It's not a matter of choice. When I agreed to take on Paradise I agreed to this. It's just a meeting.' The words sounded hollow as they echoed in the deserted street. I turned to Tan Seng. 'That's right, isn't it?'

The old boy bowed again, but he didn't catch my eye. 'We will be ready for you, Lady.'

Lucca muttered something in Italian. I pulled away and moved towards the carriage.

As I reached for the handle I paused. 'You don't . . . judge me, do you, Lucca?'

He glanced down. I saw him twist his fingers together and then he looked up.

'You must do what you believe to be right. It's all you can do. But I think,' he stared at me, his eye round as an owl's, 'I think you are not playing a game any more, Fannella. After tonight you truly will be a Baron, whatever that means. You will be changed, tell me you don't feel that?'

I didn't have time to answer. The driver cracked his whip and the horses bucked and pranced, their hooves bumping on the stones.

'It's late.' The muffled voice came down again. 'We've a way to go.'

I stood back from the carriage. 'And where, exactly, are we going? I think I've got a right to know that.'

I waited, but he didn't say another word. I took a breath, caught the handle of the door, pulled it open and clambered up inside. The carriage rocked and jolted forward. The door swung shut as the movement jerked me back into the leather seat. It was black as a tomb in there. I felt to the side to pull back the curtains to let some street light in and to see where I was being taken.

'Good evening, Katharine.'

My hand froze as the cracked, familiar voice sliced through the dark. A point of red glowed up opposite and of an instant my nose filled with the smell of her – disease and opium, foulness and sweetness coiled together.

I yelped as an invisible hand slammed suddenly and with a deadly accuracy across my right cheek. I felt the jewel from one of my grandmother's rings cut deep into the flesh.

'*That* is for The Gaudy.'

Of an instant another blow came from the dark, this time catching me on the left.

'And *that* is for your brother.'

I brought my gloved fingers to my stinging cheeks, amazed the old witch had so much strength in her. Part of me wanted to lash out blindly and give as good as I'd just got, but another part of me whispered that I should bide my time. Lady Ginger never did nothing without a reason, did she? The last time I'd seen her it looked likely that the next trip she took would be to a churchyard pit, so why was she here?

I heard her cough in the dark. Moments later the end of her opium stick glowed again. As I became used to the darkness I began to make out a shape opposite. The red point moved and I caught the wet glint of her eyes. I felt for the cords securing the curtains.

'I would appreciate it if you kept them drawn.'

'How am I supposed to know where I am?'

'You will know soon enough.'

Apart from the glowing tip of her stick and the occasional flash of a jewel, she was just a shadow. I dropped my hand into my lap.

'Y . . . you said it was for Joey. Where is he?'

There was a sticky smack as she took the stick from her lips.

'Where indeed?'

'But I thought you—'

The hand lashed again. Something hard caught the point of my chin and I cried aloud.

'You thought what, Katharine?'

'That you'd know where he was. You have spies working for you everywhere, don't you?'

The sucking noise came in the dark.

'He is not in Paris. I know that much, so I must conclude that he is here. I understand he came to London with the woman to collect the child?'

'You . . . you know? But you didn't say anything about her – Della. You said . . . you *told* me that Robbie's *father* was playing a dangerous game.'

'Naturally. A Romanov prince married to a black woman? A prince, moreover, who has been forbidden to bear fruit? How could that not be dangerous – and to so many? Repeat to me the message I gave you, I wish to hear it from your lips again so that I can be very sure your brother did not misunderstand.'

'*Bartholomew waits* – that's exactly what I told him.'

The stick flared brightly for a second.

'Then Joseph is the fool I suspected. Now listen to me and listen carefully. Tonight they will test you. No matter what happens do not react. Many people rely on you now, Katharine, and you must be strong. If the Barons do not find my choice to be worthy, they will move – and you and everyone you know will suffer. Do not mistake me.'

'There you go again, you and Telferman together. You both have a lot to say, but you don't tell me anything. You just crumble ideas into my head like you're hand-feeding a chick.'

She didn't answer. The opium stick glowed and dimmed a couple of times before she spoke. 'Mr Pope tells us that a little learning is a dangerous thing, but he is mistaken. The more you know about the Barons, Katharine . . .' she sighed. 'I have tried to protect you, but tonight . . .'

She tried to swallow a cough. When she continued her voice came out on three wheezing notes at one time, like it was broken. She put me in mind of a boy who'd just scraped the first layer of fluff from his chin.

'Have you never wondered how Paradise found its name? It is the land of plenty – a land of spices, silks, jewels, exotic creatures of bestial and human kind. We have fallen, but the wonders and riches of the world are crammed into the warehouses that huddle beside the Thames.'

'And what's that got to do with tonight?'

'Tonight you will meet the men who run the City and, by extension, the men who rule the Empire. Your holdings, Katharine, are the gateway to the Empire. It is your strength and your weakness. Remember that, always.'

I ran my hand over my bag. Telferman's notes were rolled inside. She was right about riches.

'What about Queen Victoria then – and Mr Gladstone? Don't they have a say in the order of things?'

Lady Ginger barked like a vixen. She laughed so loud I thought she might do herself a mischief.

'P . . . puppets!' She could hardly get the word out. It turned into another choking fit.

'You thought your bravura display in the cage was a trial, did you not?'

I nodded in the dark as her shattered glass voice came again. 'Did you not?'

'Yes – it was a test. That's what you said.'

'It was a mere game compared to what is to come. Tonight you must give the performance of your life. It is always the way when a new Baron is invested. I have seen—'

She broke off as a deep rasping cough stole the words from her lips. I waited for her to finish. When nothing more came I asked, 'What? What have you seen?'

'Enough . . .' The tip of the opium stick winked. We must have been passing down a well-lit street now. As the carriage bounced over a rut one of the curtains moved forward and I caught a sudden glimpse of her before the fabric shifted back. She was there for a moment and then she was gone – a tiny chalk-white face swaddled in a mound of furs.

My grandmother cleared her throat. 'Enough to convince me that what I have done for Paradise was justified. Tell me, Katharine, was there a time when you thought of me as the Devil herself?'

Now she'd put the thought in my mind, it was difficult to shift.

'We – we was terrified of you – all of us – if that's what you mean. Even Fitzy.' Tell truth, even now, she still put the fear in-to me. I couldn't see her proper in the dark, but I could feel her. I said I reckoned I could sense something savage rolling off Della Lennox when she fought for her boy and it was like that now, here in the carriage. Disease riddled my grandmother's body like colours through a ha'penny sugar stick at the fair, but the embers flickering in her soul could fire up a furnace.

'Good!' It was almost a whisper. Her sour opium breath filled the carriage as she exhaled. I began to feel a lightness in my head.

'Take me as your pattern, Katharine. You cannot be their friend. Paradise is more than three theatres. They are merely a painted facade. Surely you know that now? You have responsibilities that weigh far heavier. You might dream of running Paradise in a new way, I dare say you would call it a fair way, but that is not possible. Not now, not while the Barons are circling.'

Her words put me in mind of Telferman. I'd no doubt he'd been reporting everything back, right down to the brand of soap I used to wash my hands and face of a morning. Truly he was a beetle, scuttling around in the skirting, living off dust. What was the point of Lady Ginger handing Paradise and everything in it over to me if all she was going to do was sit on my shoulder? Besides, it was a cess pit – it needed cleaning up, just like The Palace. I was always good with a mop – and she knew it.

I folded my arms. 'What did you expect? That I'd just pick up where you left off?' I shook my head and heard the beads in the tiny blue bird sewn to the veil of my hat rattle.

'All that filth, all that corruption? It can't go on like that.

Don't think I haven't yet scraped the bottom of it, because I have – and what I found disgusted me. The little girls in Orchard Court? All of them under nine . . .?'

I waited for an answer that didn't come.

'That was well named, wasn't it? All them children ripe for the picking by dirty old goats who were five times their age. Well, I put a stop to it. Three of them are training up to work in my halls now and a dozen more are at school. And I pay their board.'

'Your halls?' Lady Ginger began to laugh. The broken sound bubbled in the dark. 'By my count you have just one left. Where will they all go now, Katharine? Where will they earn the fair wage you so foolishly promised? Where will those little girls you . . . emancipated work now?'

I clenched my fist. 'I'll see it all right, somehow. I'll find them something. You said you knew me. If that's true you knew how I'd go about it. Paradise is rotten as a tanner's pit, but I can make it a better place.'

'Can you? And do you think the Barons will accept that?' Her voice was tight, like she was rolling something tart around her mouth.

'They're going to have to.' I gripped the edge of the seat as the coach veered to the left. I flinched as a claw-like hand closed over mine. Even though she was less than a foot in front of me now, I still couldn't see her face, but I could smell the tomb stench of her breath.

'Do you never stop to consider for a moment that, once, I too might have wanted Paradise to be a finer place? That I might have tried—' She broke off as the driver thumped twice on the roof overhead.

'Already? We have wasted so much time. Listen to me, child . . .' I blinked in the dark. My grandmother had never called me that before. 'I chose carefully. Once I was chosen and now I have made my choice. The Barons always name their successor, it is the custom . . . but that person is tested as you will be tonight. They will be watching. You will be the only female in their number, Katharine, as I was. It is a dangerous path – walk carefully, traps will already be set. If you want to deal fairly for your friends and those you care for you must become cold and hard as a diamond.'

Her grip tightened.

'Do you understand me?'

'You mean I have to be like you?'

The clawed hand released mine and felt its way over my lap, climbing to my waist and up to my breast to rest over my heart.

'You already are like me, Katharine, like the girl I was, but you will have to be dead here . . .' her hand plucked at the ruffles of satin sewn down the bodice, 'if you truly want to protect Paradise.'

There was a soft rustle as she leaned back into the seat opposite. A moment later she began to cough. I caught the faintest glint of her jewelled rings as she moved her hands to her mouth. I wondered if I should go to sit beside her as the choking rattled from her lungs, but she quietened and spoke again.

'I fought so hard, for such a long time to keep the wolves from the gates. There are worse than me . . .'

We shuddered to a halt and I was thrown back into the padded leather. There was another rap on the roof and a click

379

as the door opened. The carriage was flooded with light. I screwed up my eyes and leaned forward.

Outside a dozen foot away I could see two figures standing either side of an arched entrance. They both carried a flaming torch. Just above them there was a tall narrow building, timbered over and plastered in the old style. The uneven panes of the wide windows set in two rows overhead reflected the torchlight.

I turned to my grandmother and stifled a gasp at the shrunken face huddled in the furs. Her head shook slightly. There were open sores across her nose and cheeks and the scraps of grey hair that still clung to her head were scraped up into a mangy knot at the crown. Clots of rubies shivered from her ears. I thought about her making herself ready to come to me and all at once the jewels seemed ridiculous and defiant.

She waved the opium stick in front of her face, so I caught the tang of it in my nose.

'It is a cruel death, but there are worse. Go now and remember what I have said.'

I never thought that sitting in a carriage with Lady Ginger would seem like an appealing way to spend an evening, but now it came to it, I didn't want to leave her. I stared at the men and the torches again and felt my heart racket off the cage of my ribs.

'You must go, Katharine. They will be waiting.'

I pulled my skirts together and moved to the edge of the seat. I reached for the leather strap hanging above the door to steady myself and turned back to my grandmother.

'Where are we? I'm here now, so I may as well know from you.'

Lady Ginger's black eyes slid to the flame-lit gateway visible through the open carriage door. She took a deep, shuddering breath.

'Smithfield has always been a place of blood. The Barons of London have gathered here for nearly seven hundred years. You are about to be inducted into one of the oldest guilds of the City at their ancient church. St Bartholomew the Great.'

Chapter Thirty-four

The door slammed shut behind me. I whipped about but the carriage was already moving away. I watched until it turned a corner, clutching the handle of my bag so tight my knuckles cracked aloud. I turned back to the archway. The men with the torches were watching. I walked slowly towards them and paused when I was level. They both dipped their heads and the one on the left nodded the way through.

A line of torches glowing beyond the arch marked the way. I went through, hearing my feet echo from the stones that fanned overhead. It was a gatehouse leading to a path through a churchyard. On the left torches set into a high bank made my shadow flicker over the wall on the right, like there were two of us walking towards the open door.

The flames threw the building into shadow. I was aware of the bulk of it looming over me, but I couldn't see it clear. I knew where I was – Smithfield Market and the hospital were close by – but I'd never been to the church before.

A single bell sounded the hour. It wasn't the bell at St Bartholomew's, the sound came from somewhere else. In a moment a dozen bells went off, all of them clanging just the once as the City marked the first hour of May Day in ragged time. Oranges and Lemons – that was their song, wasn't it? Joey and me sang it as kids. It was a pretty tune. I ran it through my head as I paused at the black doorway and then I wished I hadn't.

Here comes a candle to light you to bed.
Here comes a chopper to chop off your head,
Chip, chop, chip, chop,
The last man's . . .

'Late.'

The voice came from the darkness inside the doorway.

'You are late. The session begins on the stroke of one. You have already disappointed us. Follow.'

Footsteps sounded on stone, the crisp clipped rapping growing fainter as the man moved deeper into the church. I tried to steady my breathing as Madame Celeste had taught me. It was a cold night, but under my dress something trickled between my shoulder blades and snaked down my back. Beneath the buttoned leather my palms sweated round the handle of my bag.

I looked up at the stars glittering in the clear sky – thousands of brilliant-cut gemstones scattered across a jeweller's cloth.

Cold and hard as a diamond.

I stepped inside.

The smell came first. Mice, must and centuries of dust and damp. There was a bit of incense there too – a ghost of it anyways. It made me think of Misha – that sharp cologne of his. I pushed the thought away but the trace of him lingered.

Incense – at least it would have made Lucca feel homely. I wished he was here.

I was standing in a stone lobby. Ahead, a crack of light divided a pair of heavy curtains. I went forward and pushed them aside. I was at the right-hand side of the church. Five foot in front of me a dozen lighted candles sprouted from a metal tree, dripping wax and light into a pool on the stones. They lit up a ledgerstone set into the flags. The name and dates were unreadable. Centuries of butchers' boots, most likely, had worn them away, although I doubted many of them were regulars now. The Smithfield men I knew were more likely to worship at The Old Red Cow.

I moved to the right. I couldn't see the rest of the church from where I stood on account of the wide columns blocking the view. The sound of my heels catching on the stones came too loud. I tried to walk dainty, but of an instant the echo of my boots was drowned by voices – men's voices speaking together, almost like a chant, only not as musical.

As I rounded the pillar to stand at the far end of the aisle, a span of rounded black arches marched away from me on either side. Halfway down more candles burned in brackets set on the columns and on the arms of floor-standing metal trees set between the arches. The voices came again. One man called a question and others answered.

'Do you bring news, brothers?'

'Aye, we do.'

'Is your parable clothed in truth?'

'Aye, it is.'

I walked towards the sound. As I moved deeper into the church I began to make them out. Dark figures holding lighted tapers stood just inside the arches leading up to and circling round the altar. I couldn't see them all, but I counted the flames. Eleven – there were eleven of them.

As I came level with the first man I stopped. He was old and finely dressed. Sparse grey hair fell to the collar of his floor-length coat. He glanced over at me and his lips curved into a smile beneath his long nose. He inclined his head, but he didn't miss his place in the chant.

'Are you faithful to the brethren?'

'Aye, we are.'

'Would you lay down your life for a brother?'

'Aye, and our soul if called.'

'Will you walk in silence from this place?'

'Aye, and to the grave.'

'It is finished.'

The church was peaceful for a moment and then the voice that led the chanting came again.

'And so, at last, the newest of our number has come among us.' I felt nearly a dozen pairs of eyes turn upon me.

'Come forward. Your place is to the right – the darkened space. It will remain shadowed this evening until you are proven. Take your position.'

I paused for a moment not understanding where I should go. The man who'd dialled me first moved his taper a little, inclining it towards a dark archway just down from the altar. I nodded to him – at least he seemed friendly – and walked up the centre of the aisle.

They watched in silence.

I don't know what I expected the Barons to look like. I hadn't imagined any of them to be my age, that's for certain. Mostly they were ancient – bald heads, grey heads, hair in un-likely places. Shrivelled and bent, with eyes like jack stones held in string pouches – eyes that scraped my body from the top of my hat to the hem of my skirt.

But one of them, standing three arches along from the first man to notice me, was a good deal younger than the rest. He was tall, dark and not five years older than me, I'd say. He nodded as I passed and I felt his eyes on my back as I carried on.

Two men stood beneath the next arch on the left. I paused for a moment. We were to come alone, weren't we? Then why . . .

'Proceed to your place.' The voice echoed again.

I quickened my step, aware of a wheezing sound as I passed the final arch before my allotted space. The air was suddenly foul – thick with sweat and worse. I glanced to the right. The man sitting, rather than standing there, almost filled the gap.

I say man, but he was more like a mound of flesh. He was so vast he couldn't even wear normal gear. Instead, his body seemed to burst from a dark gown that pooled on the stones around him. His head looked ridiculous balanced on a roll of pallid flesh that had once been a neck. He was so wide that his arms stuck out at an odd angle, propped aside on obscene ridges of fat. Like his head, the arms looked absurdly small. A lighted taper was clutched in a child-like fist at the end of one of them. He smiled at me and his eyes almost disappeared into the folds of his face.

I looked away and took up my place. I stood in the shadow, trying to block my nose to the stench rolling off the walrus. I could still hear him breathing, though. It sounded wet, like he was slurping soup from a saucer. If I could hear him, I was sure he could hear me. My heart was beating so fast and so hard that I could feel it flutter in my throat.

'We will begin the parables.'

There was a movement behind the altar and a man backed into view.

I couldn't quite make him out because of the stone table in the way. He stretched his arms into the shadows and another man stepped out. Still with his back to me, the first man led the second round the altar table, guiding him down the steps, until they were both at the centre of the nave. The first man, tall he was and broad with it, bent to whisper something and ducked to the side. I watched him disappear behind the altar again and into the arched shadows.

Now I saw why the second man needed guiding. He was blind as a stone – his eyes glazed over with a milky film. He stood completely still for a moment and then he turned slowly towards me, like he knew exactly where I was. He seemed to stare at me, although I knew that couldn't be true. The angular face was carved like a marble statue on an old church monument. It was completely still, too – bland and expressionless like one of them plaster masks that still hung over the arch above the stage of The Comet.

The man's narrow nose was crooked and his high forehead was interrupted in the middle by a pointed widow's peak that carried his thick hair off to the right in a blunted wave that curled below his ear.

Excepting for his sleek black coat, there was no colour to him at all. His skin and his hair were like bleached cotton.

He nodded at me. 'Greetings, brother. We would not expect you to lead the parables tonight.'

I realised it was the man who led the chanting I'd heard at

the beginning. He turned back to the church and raised his hands, spreading them wide.

'I, Lord Kite . . .'

I started as the Beetle's words scuttled through my head – *The most dangerous among them is Lord Kite – remember that, Kitty.*

'. . . of Temple, first of the chapters of London, do offer my parable prepared in good faith for this day, the first of May, 1881, the Vernal session . . .'

Chapter Thirty-five

As I finished up, I knew I'd done well. My grandmother and the Beetle might even have been proud, I thought, as I scanned the faces turned towards me. I had the lingo now. I'd heard it over eleven times, enough to take in all the patter.

The bastards.

Truly, I never knew such evil was walking the streets of London until I heard the Barons listing their assets and running through their business like they were checking the stock in a smart haberdashery. Murder to order, children, violence, beatings, robberies, blackmail, arson, even treason – name a crime and at least one of them was happy to reel it off like he was offering his grandmother's recipe for elderflower cordial.

At the heart it was all about bodies – the quick and the dead – traded from London to Timbuktu. People bought and sold like apples on a market stall. If they had a mind to it, they'd turn Paradise and everyone in it inside out without a second thought. Jesus! And I'd thought my grandmother was a heartless bitch.

The Barons was toffs, most of them, their accents moulded at the finest schools. Even the walrus spoke like Queen Victoria herself – if she was gargling a ladle of dripping, that is.

I had a moment, I'll admit, when the two men I'd seen in the shadows shuffled forward to offer their parable. They were joined at the hip and the shoulder. Brothers in a single coat – two arms and three legs – so far as I could make out.

The Lords Janus came from the travelling people. They didn't speak like the others, but they didn't have to. I reckoned their brains worked faster than anyone's there. They quizzed a wizened old git on a point of finance – making him go through his figures over again in front of us all. They were right – he was wrong. Nearly two thousand times wrong, as it turned out. I saw his hands tremble as he offered his papers to Lord Kite, who deftly took a tinderbox from his pocket, flicked up a flame and burned them.

At the end of their parable each man (except the walrus) went forward, knelt and kissed the back of Lord Kite's hand. He was clearly the most notable among them. As they knelt he placed a hand on their head, and pronounced a figure to be prepared and collected within the week from our agents. I supposed that meant Telferman. I made a note to ask him about it.

From my reckoning, between them they had London stitched tight as a corpse in a shroud. Mostly I could work out their particular interests by their name. Lord Kite came from the law, Lord Oak and Lord Iron from the navy and the military respective, Lord Mitre stood for the church and Lord Silver for the money. But some were more difficult to reckon until they got going and even then I found it hard to smoke a couple of them, as Sam might have said.

As I listened, I wondered what he'd make of it all.

The tall younger man, Lord Vellum, gave the impression of being very well connected, but I couldn't catch on to some of the terms he used. And the walrus, Lord Fetch, might just as well have been speaking underwater for all the sense he made.

Most of them referred to papers, I noticed, but Lord Kite and Lord Vellum spoke free and they seemed the stronger for it. I knew I could do that. I had it all locked in my head to the last name and number, to the last brass farthing.

'... And so in good faith, I humbly request that the brothers accept my first parable, given on this day, the first of May, 1881 on behalf of the chapter of Paradise.' I bowed, and went to kneel at Lord Kite's feet.

I'd been good. I knew it. I'd mastered my nerves and spoken clear and accurate. They were terrifying, all of them. Every man there had a soul the Devil himself might think twice about welcoming with open arms, but I'd come through and stood my ground. A part of me wondered if perhaps I could do this after all. Give them a performance, that's what she'd told me. To my mind this wasn't anywhere near as bad as hanging up in that cage, seventy foot over the punters without a net to catch me.

Lord Kite extended his clenched hand. There was an ugly ring on the first finger. A silver bird's head with a cruel curved beak that stretched across the back of the middle finger, ruby studs in the place of the eyes.

I waited. I knew the words now: *We accept your parable in gratitude and instruct your agent to make ready the sum of . . .*

'You are wrong.'

I caught my breath. I hadn't made a mistake, I was certain of it.

As I stared at the back of Lord Kite's hand he turned it over and opened his fist. The green glass earring ripped from my flesh that night at The Gaudy was in the middle of his palm. I felt something move under my hat. I didn't realise until that moment that a scalp could actually crawl.

'Stand.'

I gathered my skirts together, straightened up and locked my hands in front of me to hide the sudden tremor. I heard the rattle of the beads sewn onto my bag. Lord Kite reached forward to run a hand over my face, probing the set of my eyes, my cheeks and my nose as if he was trying to get a sense of what I looked like. Then, swiftly, he moved to my chin and gripped hard.

'You are wrong to come here, and give such a . . . brazen display. Tell us how you intend to offer a fair wage in Paradise.' He turned to the others. 'It seems The Lady's choice has a limited grasp of the laws of equity.'

I heard laughter and glanced along the arched rows to the side of us. They were all staring at me like hunting dogs in a kennel waiting for the master to release them. The fingers tightened.

'Tell us how The Gaudy burned to the ground last evening.'

'I . . . It was delib—'

He cut across me.

'Tell us . . . about your brother.' A muscle beneath his blind right eye twitched and just for a second I saw the mask drop. He was barely holding on to a fury that could tear the place apart if he let it free.

'But I . . . I don't know where my brother—'

'Cease.' Lord Kite let me go and clicked his fingers. The cloaked man who had guided him down the steps appeared again. As he swept past I caught the scent of him – leather, tobacco and spice. My stomach folded over on itself as I recognised that cologne. This was the man who ripped the jewel from my ear in the theatre. The man with the hawk-head cane on the roof at Pearmans Yard. The man who had torn Old Peter apart and draped his insides around the room like bloody Christmas garlands.

'Have you prepared, Matthias?' Lord Kite stretched out a hand and the cloaked man took it.

'Everything is ready as you instructed.' That voice. I knew it now – heavily accented, almost guttural.

Lord Kite nodded. 'Come, brothers. The hour is late. Bartholomew waits.'

Chapter Thirty-six

At the centre of the narrow chapel that ran from the back of the church, a ledgerstone stood upright on its side. It looked as if it had been raised from the floor like the cover of a great old Bible. The blackness under the stone gaped wide. The smell of something putrid rose from deep beneath the chapel. Candles burned at each of the four corners of the hole.

Matthias and Lord Kite had led the way. I thought about running down the aisle and out of the church into the night, but the Barons closed ranks behind me, forcing me to follow the men at the head of our silent procession. They were excited, I could feel it. If I looked to the side or turned around, their eyes slid away from mine, but I knew they were all watching me.

At a gesture from Matthias, Lord Kite stopped and turned to face us as we gathered at the end of the chapel. Matthias shrugged back his hood and blinked. Even in the candlelight I could see the extraordinary blue of his eyes. His hair was a reddish gold blond that threw off a halo. You might almost have taken him for a well-built angel, if you didn't know what he was capable of.

Lord Kite stared direct at me. He seemed to know exactly where I was.

'Before we conclude our gathering this evening we must witness an execution.'

He paused and the muscle beneath his eye twitched again before he continued.

'We have not had cause to open the vault for at least a dozen years now. Our newest . . . brother has joined us on a significant occasion. Bring him.'

Matthias forced his way past me and through the knot of men gathered at the entrance to the chapel. I stared at the hole in the ground and then at Lord Kite. Why did he ask about Joey? Out of habit I reached to my bodice feeling for the comforting bump of the ring and the Christopher.

I dropped my hand.

There was a shuffling sound from behind. We all turned.

A hooded figure stumbled down the steps. Matthias forced the man forward until he stood just a couple of foot from the open vault. A ball tightened in my chest. I couldn't tell if it was my heart about to burst or the beginning of a scream loud enough to bring every stone tumbling down on our heads.

'Remove the hood, Matthias.'

I dropped my eyes to the floor. I didn't want to see him. I didn't want the last sight of my brother to be here, like this. I rifled through every part of my mind, desperate to find something, some way to make this stop.

'Kitty?'

My head snapped up.

Oh, thank God!

The moment the words went through my head I regretted them. To this day, I regret thinking them more than anything I've ever said aloud.

'Danny!' I reached out, but Matthias came between us.

'This man has sinned.' Lord Kite rubbed his hands. His palms rustled together like dry leaves. 'Tell us how you sinned, Daniel.'

Danny stared at me like he couldn't believe I was there. Bruises spread like mould across his face, his nose was crusted with blood and knocked out of line. Around his wrists and bare ankles bracelets of torn skin showed where he'd been bound. He opened his swollen lips and I saw the stumps of broken teeth in his bleeding gums. Christ! What had they done to him?

I saw a light flicker in his bloodshot eyes. He tried to twist his wreck of a mouth into a smile.

'Y . . . you've come for me, haven't you? Like you came for Peggy. She's right – you're a marvel, Kitty Peck.'

My mouth was suddenly dry as the sawdust floor of The Gaudy's workshop. This wasn't like that time under the warehouse.

'Tell us your sin, Daniel!'

At the command Matthias jerked him forward so that he fell in a heap at Lord Kite's feet and then he kicked him in the stomach. Danny cried out and folded into a ball at the edge of the yawning pit.

'Stop this. You can't . . .' The words came out before I could master them. It was what they wanted. I heard muttering. The air around us changed as if it was suddenly alive.

Lord Kite smiled. 'You know this man, I believe?'

I nodded once.

'He is part of your estate and yet you have not controlled him. Tell us how much you owe, Daniel. I have the exact figure. If you lie, I will know.'

Danny tried to pull himself to a kneeling position. He bent double clutching his stomach and I heard him mumble. As he swung his bloodied head and caught sight of the pit at his back he twisted his hand into the tattered cotton of his shirt. I saw his knuckles whiten.

'Again, Daniel. We cannot hear you.'

'T . . . twenty.' Danny coughed up something black and looked up at me. 'For pity's sake, Kit, make it stop.'

I whipped around to face them all. 'I'll pay it. Twenty stinking pounds is nothing to you. Paradise can shoulder that. This is ridiculous.' My voice came out shrill and the stones bounced back a thin echo of that last word.

Ridiculous ridiculous ridiculous.

It sounded weak.

Lord Kite grinned wider. 'You are right. To execute a man for twenty pounds would be . . . extreme. *Twenty thousand pounds*, however, is a different matter. I've no doubt that you could bear even that, but where would it end? What would it profit us? This is about making an example. That sum is correct, is it not, Daniel?'

Danny bowed his head. 'I . . . I can pay it b . . . back – all of it. Tell them, Kit – you'll make it right. You'll help me, won't you?'

I clasped my hands in front of me. I felt my bag bump against my thigh through the satin. Such a clumsy, pointless, female thing.

Danny croaked again, 'I . . . I just need t . . . time and a run of luck.'

Lord Kite steepled his fingers. 'I am afraid your time and your luck have just run out.'

'Kit, please. Make them listen.' Danny shuffled towards me. He reached out and clutched the hem of my dress. 'I was tricked. They said my credit was good. They encouraged me to play and to borrow and then to play and to borrow again and again until I didn't know where I was. And every time the debt got trebled. Please, Kit – make it stop. I will pay – somehow. I give you my word.'

I couldn't see straight for the tears glassing up my eyes.

'Now, Matthias.' Lord Kite's voice cracked like a whip.

'No!' I tried to snatch the man's cloak, but I was a fly on the rump of a dray horse. Matthias flicked me aside as he aimed a kick at Danny's midriff. There was a scuffle as Danny tried to fend off the blow. He caught hold of the swinging leg, but Matthias reached down and yanked up a handful of the thick dark hair Danny had always been so particular about. He dragged him by it to the brink of the pit, forcing him to look down.

'Oh Jesus – no, please.' Danny began to whimper. I knew then that he understood completely what was about to happen.

'You can't do this!' I tried to run across to him, but arms folded around me from behind, pinning me like a moth to the stones.

Matthias rocked Danny back and then with one vicious lunge, he sent him toppling forward into the darkness. After a long moment there was a sickening thud. Then from somewhere far below, I heard Danny wail. The hollow sound echoed from black depths, climbing to a howl of agony and terror that sang out from the arches around us.

The man holding me loosened his grip. Lord Kite wiped

his mouth with the tips of his fingers – a dainty, prissy gesture like a duchess who'd swallowed a fly.

'Let us depart in peace.'

Peace? I stared at him, couldn't he hear Danny down there? This wasn't the back end of a Sunday service.

'Our business is concluded.' He reached for Matthias's hand and paused.

'Except for one last thing. As we have a new brother among us, the right of sealing must go to him. Come forward.'

At first I didn't realise who he meant. I waited for someone else to step out of line, all the while hearing Danny screaming from under the stones. He was calling my name now, over and over.

Lord Kite held his head to one side. 'Ah, you do not have a title, but we have already agreed on one, have we not, brothers?'

There was a general mutter of assent.

'Step forward, Lady Linnet, and seal your bondsman into his tomb.'

I dragged my eyes from the open vault. I couldn't do that, not to Danny, not to Peggy. She was carrying their child. They were going to be a family. I shook my head and the tears brimmed over to streak down my face.

'Lady Ginger made a strong case for you, but perhaps, after all, you are not worthy?' Lord Kite gestured to the Barons gathered at my back. 'Perhaps we should look elsewhere for a successor? Perhaps Lady Linnet does not have the . . . heart for this work?'

My grandmother's voice rang through my head.

'You will have to be dead here . . . if you truly want to protect Paradise.'

Cold and hard as a diamond.

'What must I do?' The words came out as a whisper.

Lord Kite nodded.

'It is a simple mechanism. The stone is levered and weighted. All you need do is touch it and it will fall into place.'

I swallowed and walked forward, trying to block my ears to the desperate sounds coming from below. Perhaps there was a way to save him? I could come back with some of the lads and some tools from the workshop. He'd be down there in the black five, maybe six, hours at most, but he'd still be alive, wouldn't he?

It would be days before a man died down there.

Cold and hard as a diamond.

I stood behind the ledgerstone and brushed my hand against it, trying not to use any force or pressure. Instantly there was a grating, grinding sound and it began to move, slowly, gracefully, folding itself back into place like Swami Jonah's magic box.

Lord Kite clapped once and then again. As the sound echoed off the walls of the chapel, they all joined in. Gradually the applause built to a thunder of approval like the times when I swung high in the cage. I stared at the leering faces circled around me.

I wanted to spit at them.

'Bravo!' Lord Kite performed a mockery of a bow. He raised his hands and the clapping stopped.

'We have used Bartholomew's vault for hundreds of years, Lady Linnet. In the last century, one of our more practically minded brothers made some refinements. You will recall I said that it was mechanical?'

I looked at the moving ledgerstone behind him. Any moment now it would complete its journey.

'By closing it you have reset the device. It cannot be opened again for one hundred days.'

There was a soft thud as the slab settled into place and dust flew up around us in the candlelight.

Epilogue

'Lady?'

I shook my head and walked to the stairs. Tan Seng closed the doors behind me. He didn't say another word. I wondered if it had always been like this when she came back. I wondered if my grandmother's soul had been eaten away by the things she'd seen and the things she'd done.

A door opened somewhere above.

'Fannella!'

Lucca clattered down the stairs until we were level. He caught my hand, but I shrugged him away and carried on up. I'd let down the veil of my hat to cover my face. I didn't want anyone to look at me. Beneath the lace, my eyes burned in my head like coals in a fire.

In the carriage I'd waited for the tears to come, only they didn't. I wasn't surprised. I could weep every hour of every day for the rest of my life but nothing would wash it away. Nothing would clean my head of the sound of Danny sobbing in the dark.

Alone in the dark.

At the second landing I paused and looked over the rail. Lucca was staring up, folding his hands over and over. Lok patted his shoulder and tried to usher him gently back into the parlour.

'Kitty?' Lucca wound his fingers together like he was

praying. 'Why won't you speak? Tell us, tell me – what happened tonight.'

I turned away, crossed the landing and went into the little room I'd set up as an office. The remains of a fire were burning in the grate. It was the only light.

I locked the door behind me, threw my bag onto the couch and pulled off my hat, letting it fall to the rug. I went to the hearth and stared at my face in the mirror over the mantle. In the semi-dark my eyes glittered in the glass like beads of hard black jet. They were usually blue – if I was given to vanity, I might even have said that in the right light they had a violet tinge to them. But not tonight.

I unbuttoned my gloves at the wrists. It seemed such an ordinary, commonplace thing to do. As I eased my right hand from the leather I glanced down at the fingers that had brushed, so lightly, so gently, against the slab.

I let the glove fall onto the coals. In a moment the sickly smell of burning skin came up. I watched as the glove clenched up on itself before shrivelling to a blackened fist.

Over my shoulder in the glass I saw my desk, the wooden surface covered with a jumble of papers – names, addresses, numbers, accounts. On the top there was a bill listing the craftsmen about to fix up The Comet. They were lucky, there was enough work for them now to keep them occupied until 1884.

I turned. All of Paradise was laid out there before me.

Peggy was there somewhere. My kind, sweet Peggy who had Danny's child growing inside her. How could I face her knowing what I'd done? How could I ever look that poor kid in the eye when, every time, I'd see Danny reflected back? I could never tell her – some things are best not known. No, I'd have to keep it locked away, festering inside me like Lady Ginger's canker.

I closed my eyes and lashed out, sweeping everything from the desk. Papers scattered across the room. The brass ink-stand clanked to the boards and came to rest on its side, leaking a pool of black that seeped into the fringes of the rug. I heard, rather than saw, the oil lamp with the dainty patterned glass smash to pieces against the fire guard.

I sank into the chair and slumped forward, resting my forehead in my hands.

There are seven deadly sins, that's what Nanny Peck taught me and Joey. I ran through them – anger, lust, gluttony, avarice, envy, sloth and pride. That last was reckoned to be the worst. But the Bible was wrong. I knew now that there are eight deadly sins and the eighth is the worst of them.

Betrayal.

I looked down at the drawer to my left. After a moment I reached out and ran my fingers over the looped handle. I drew my hand away like it had been burned, but then I grabbed the metal and pulled the drawer open. There was only one thing there, a small cloth-covered bundle. I took it and went to the fire.

I weighed the bundle, passing the little package wrapped in bright Oriental silk from hand to hand and then I knelt and pulled the black string ties. A sweet familiar smell rose from the fabric as twenty thin black sticks rolled onto the rug. I took one, held it to the embers until the tip glowed red.

Then I brought it to my lips.

Acknowledgements

Weather is always said to be a peculiarly British preoccupation. I was never much of a linguist when I was at secondary school in the late 1970s, but even to this day I can comment, quite accurately, on the colour of the sky, the likelihood of precipitation and the quality of fog in both French and German. Back then, the ability to discuss meteorology in extreme detail was clearly thought to be a cultural passport for a girl about to be set loose on the world beyond Watford.

I was reminded of this when I read through the first draft of the book you've just finished.

Kitty Peck's first adventure was written during a winter of heavy snowfall and biting cold. I work in the basement of our house in St Albans and back in December 2012 and January 2013, every time I looked up from the table and squinted out through the half-window to the street, all I could see was a mound of snow or, occasionally, the slush-covered boots of people skidding by. There is a lot of snow in *Kitty Peck and the Music Hall Murders*.

Much of *The Child of Ill-fortune* was written in the winter of early 2014, but this time the world outside my window was wet and grey. I think the damp and the rain permeated my writing. Kitty Peck's 1881 London is a sodden and ultimately bleak place.

And more clouds are gathering . . .

I'm indebted to Hannah Griffiths, my brilliant editor at Faber & Faber for believing in Kitty and allowing me to take her to a dark place, to Katherine Armstrong (Faber & Faber Crime) for her warm pragmatic encouragement, to Sophie Portas (Faber & Faber publicity) who has held my hand at various events . . . and, in fact, to everyone at Bloomsbury House for their enthusiasm and support.

Beyond Bloomsbury I am so grateful to Tamsin Shelton for her sensitive, eagle-eyed handling of the text and for the fact that her language skills far outstrip my own! I'm pretty sure she can talk about the weather (and much more) in at least four languages.

Thanks also to Eugenie Furniss, my fantastic and energetic agent. Now there's a woman who loves a gothic tale almost as much as I do!

I must also mention my friends and family who 'lived' this book every step of the way, especially Lisa Aston my 'tester' whose desire to know more after I emailed her every chapter as I wrote gave me a huge boost of energy each time I turned on the computer. And also to lovely Daisy Coulam – she knows why!

Finally, last but not least, I must thank my completely ex-cellent husband Stephen who could not be more supportive and loyal (except about the heating in the basement).

He misses me when I'm writing – but I've promised to make it up to him.

The first in the Kitty Peck series

ff

KITTY PECK AND THE MUSIC HALL MURDERS

Shortlisted for the CWA Endeavour Historical Dagger

LONDON, 1880

In the opium-laced streets of Limehouse the ferocious Lady Ginger rules with ruthless efficiency. But The Lady is not happy. Somebody is stealing her most valuable assets – her dancing girls – and that someone has to be found and made to pay.

Bold, impetuous and with more brains than she cares to admit, seventeen-year-old seamstress Kitty Peck reluctantly performs the role of bait for the kidnappers. But as Kitty's scandalous and terrifying act becomes the talk of the city, she finds herself facing danger even more deadly and horrifying than The Lady.

This thrilling historical mystery takes us deep into the underworld of Victorian London. Take nothing at face value, for Kitty is about to go down a path of discovery that will have consequences not only for herself, but for those she holds most dear . . .